My Fake Rake

THE UNION OF THE RAKES

MY FAKE RAKE

EVA LEIGH

THORNDIKE PRESS
A part of Gale, a Cengage Company

Copyright © 2019 by Ami Silber.
Thorndike Press, a part of Gale, a Cengage Company.

ALL RIGHTS RESERVED
Thorndike Press® Large Print Romance.
The text of this Large Print edition is unabridged.
Other aspects of the book may vary from the original edition.
Set in 16 pt. Plantin.

LIBRARY OF CONGRESS CIP DATA ON FILE.
CATALOGUING IN PUBLICATION FOR THIS BOOK
IS AVAILABLE FROM THE LIBRARY OF CONGRESS

ISBN-13: 978-1-4328-7762-0 (hardcover alk. paper)

Published in 2020 by arrangement with Avon Books, an imprint of HarperCollins Publishers

Printed in Mexico
Print Number: 01   Print Year: 2020

For Zack, who believes in me, always

ACKNOWLEDGMENTS

Every book I write is the product of many hands' labor. Without the help, encouragement, and all-round badassedness of some incredible people, my work would be a pale shadow of what you hold in your hands now.

Thank you, firstly, to Nicole Fischer, who always puts smiley faces in her editorial notes, even when she and I both know that there will be major revisions ahead. Thank you to the Avon Books PR team for their incredibly hard work, and to the Avon Books Art Department, who has given me the covers I have dreamed about since I became a romance author.

Thank you to Kevan Lyon, my tireless agent, and Patricia Nelson, who is graciousness personified.

Much gratitude to Fran Strober Cassano for her willingness to do research deep dives. I am also grateful to Sally Jennings, Rachel Bond, Sarah Loch, and the invaluable input from my beta readers, Caroline Linden, Megan Frampton, and Victoria Dahl — who rightly reminded me that even heroes have to take baths.

I'm especially thankful for the input of Dr. Gregory Pauly, PhD, Curator, Herpetology and Co-Director of the Urban Nature Research Center, Natural History Museum of Los Angeles County. Thank you, as well, to Polly Lasker, Reference Librarian, Smithsonian Libraries. I tried hard to make my science factual, but any inaccuracies are entirely my own.

By the time this book comes out, I will most likely have said goodbye to my sweetest boy, my mischief maker, my jester and chirping bird of a cat, Whiskey. You filled my days with joy and laughter, and I will hold you in my heart forever.

My earliest days as a writer came from writing Duran Duran fan fiction back in the sixth grade, and now here I am, over three decades later, still writing while listening to *Seven and the Ragged Tiger* — and I owe it to you, dear reader. Thank you for making this '80s girl's dreams come true. You are, in the truest sense of the word, *awesome.*

A note from the author: Please be aware

this book contains depictions of social anxiety.

PROLOGUE

Eton College, 1797
It's just the library door, not the entrance to
Hell. Stop delaying.

Sebastian Holloway tugged on his jacket cuffs, but no matter how much he pulled, his bony wrists protruded, proclaiming him to be firmly in the awkward stage of adolescence.

Logically, he understood that this period in a young man's life was temporary. Countless volumes had been written about it and not one of those esteemed scholars ever mentioned that some boys remained permanently fourteen. So it stood to reason that eventually, he'd stop growing like a dandelion and his clothes might fit properly for longer than two weeks.

"You going in," a voice growled behind him, "or are we going to stand here all day like a couple of sap-skulls?"

Seb whirled around to face Theodore Cur-

11

tis, who glared at him from beneath a heavy fringe of dark hair.

"I . . . uh . . ." Seb swallowed. Those two syllables were the first he'd ever spoken to Curtis. Normally, Seb gave the other boy a wide berth, given Curtis's propensity for destroying school property and getting into fights.

"For fuck's sake." Curtis rolled his eyes. He reached past Seb, grunting when Seb flinched, and planted his hand on the door. "We're going to get extra punishment if we're late."

Doubtless, Curtis spoke from experience. He was always being called before the headmaster, always being placed On the Bill for infractions, always getting flogged, but no matter how much penance he was forced to endure, it didn't stop his unruly behavior.

"Sorry," Seb muttered. "First time here."

"I know." Curtis pushed open the door. "I'd say do as I do, but you had better not. Unless you want a cane across your arse."

Seb followed Curtis into the library, but the rows of books didn't calm his racing heart, and the neatly arranged tables didn't stop the film of chilled sweat slicking his back.

Three boys sat at tables scattered around the library, and they all turned toward him

12

as he shuffled into the room.

Paste seemed to fill his mouth as he looked at the boys he knew only by name. They were all in the same house, and were all of them in E block, but it didn't matter — Seb had almost no interaction with them. There was Noel Edwards, Lord Clair and heir to the Duke of Rotherby. Though Clair was the same year as Seb, the other boy practically ruled the entirety of Eton, but not by force. Everyone, from students to teachers, sought his good opinion. If Clair decided that mutton pie was his favorite supper, all the boys would insist on eating mutton pie. He once showed up to class without tying back his hair, and the next day everyone's hair was loose. Those boys who were part of Clair's inner circle were an elite and favored few.

Seb doubted Clair knew his name. Judging by the disinterested look in his eyes, it was a safe assumption.

Sitting nearby was Duncan McCameron, a Scottish earl's second son. McCameron sent a brief smile toward Seb. The football match they'd played together the other day had been a high point of the week, with their team trouncing the other boys. On the pitch, Seb didn't feel like a tongue-tied clod, and the match's win had gained him a measure of McCameron's respect.

The third boy gave Seb a tiny nod of recognition. Naturally. Seb and William Rowe weren't friends, but they both dwelt on the edges of school society. At least Seb had a few chums. No one talked to Rowe. He rarely spoke, and when he did, it came out in an unintelligible mutter. A few whispered that he was mad, and most of the boys found him to be too eccentric to warrant an attempt at friendship.

Seb took off his spectacles and rubbed them on the corner of his jacket. The gesture was so habitual, he barely noticed.

Curtis strode past him, then threw himself into a seat and propped his feet up on a table.

"Sit, Holloway," McCameron said, not unkindly. "Eddings is going to be here any minute."

Seb grabbed the nearest chair and dropped into it. A strained silence fell.

The door to the library opened again and Eddings, a senior boy, marched into the room. He went to stand in the middle of the chamber, planting his hands on his hips and gazing sourly at each of the boys. Seb sat up straighter.

"As you can well imagine," Eddings said without preamble, "I am decidedly unhappy that, rather than enjoying the half holiday, like everyone else at this sodding school, I am instead consigned to supervising you five miscreants."

Not once in his life had Seb been called a *miscreant*. *Bookworm*, perhaps. *Misfit* was favored by his brothers and cousins. But to be lumped into the same category as the lawbreaker Theodore Curtis? Appalling.

Clair must have also taken offense to the term, because he raised his hand. "Sir, I don't think I belong here."

"You most certainly do, Lord Clair." Eddings sighed. "Like the others in this library today, you have committed serious offenses, and like the others, you will accept your punishment with grace. Can you guess what that punishment might be, Holloway?"

Everyone looked at Seb, and a choking panic clutched him. Self-consciousness grabbed hold as he struggled to put words together. It was as though he was back at his family's dining table, with his father's sneering words ringing in his ears.

"You can't get respect in this world if you're scribbling in that notebook all the sodding time. Always watching. Never taking charge. What do you have to say for yourself? Speak up, boy, or you're hardly fit to call yourself my son."

Then, as now, Seb found himself struck mute. Each word was weighted, and he couldn't heft them to construct even the most basic sentence. He'd been thrown from all his prepared scripts, and he didn't know what to say.

"Gone dumb, Holloway?" Eddings jeered.

Clair glanced sharply at the senior boy. "Give him a chance to speak."

"It's all right, Holloway," McCameron said with surprising gentleness.

To Seb's utter surprise, Curtis added, "Take your time."

Rowe nodded encouragingly.

Heat prickled Seb's eyes, and he blinked back surprised tears. These four boys whom he barely knew offered him patience and acceptance — exactly what he could not find within his own blood family.

Finally, Seb managed to ask, "What *is* our punishment?"

"The house captain felt flogging was rather clichéd, so he decided that the five of you are to spend the next —" Eddings consulted his timepiece. "Eight hours and fifty-four minutes contemplating what brought you here today."

Clair and McCameron groaned, while Curtis snorted in derision. Both Rowe and Seb remained silent.

16

"In addition," the senior boy continued over the sounds of protest, "you will each pen an essay, the topic of which will be your thoughts on who you believe yourself to be. Said essay shall be no fewer than a thousand words."

Seb felt a little lighter. Essays were his forte. He could write an essay, and it wasn't uncommon for other boys to pay him to write papers for them. Such an endeavor helped to pay for books he ordered from the shop in the village, books his father would never buy him since they had nothing to do with the British iron industry — the only topic John Holloway considered worthwhile.

"I'll leave you to it, then," Eddings said. He walked briskly to the door.

"You're not staying?" McCameron asked.

Eddings paused on the threshold. "God, no. Like hell will I imprison myself in this library until nightfall. But I will check on you — at irregular intervals so you cannot predict if it's safe to leave. Anyone caught by myself or the ground staff will be subject to more severe punishment. Flogging will seem delightful by comparison." His lips curled into an acrid smile. "Enjoy your day, gentlemen."

The door closed, and Seb and the other

boys were alone.

Curtis surged to his feet and regarded each of them with his habitual smirk. "My, my. How droll. Trapped in the library with" — he looked at Clair, McCameron, Rowe, and Seb — "Lord Perfect, the Honorable Corinthian, Sir Bedlam, and Professor Lanky." He chuckled at his sobriquets.

"A poet as well as a criminal," Clair drawled. "Well done, Curtis. Or should I call you Mister Newgate, since that's where you're headed."

"Shut your goddamned mouth." Curtis stalked to the young nobleman, who jumped up with fists at the ready.

McCameron shoved himself between them. "Quiet, both of you, or Eddings will come back and cane us raw."

Five minutes hadn't passed, but already chaos had erupted. Seb looked over at Rowe, who hunched down in his seat and mumbled to himself.

Seb grimaced. Was the kindness the other boys had shown him an aberration? Or were they all simply too different to be cordial, let alone friendly?

It was going to be a very long day.

CHAPTER 1

London, 1817
Reptile or human, you were guaranteed to make a cake out of yourself when mating season arrived.

No, that wasn't fair — to reptiles.

Take the eastern fence lizard, *Stellio undulatus*. When it came time for the creature to attract a mate, a male performed a series of charming head bobs to show off its lovely bright blue stomach and throat, all of this done in complete silence.

But the human male — more specifically, aristocratic human males of London Society — sported garish clothing while striking poses in conspicuous places and making harsh, barking noises that guaranteed any female in the vicinity had no choice but to take notice.

As she approached the Benezra Library in Kensington, with her maid Katie in tow, Grace Wyatt's naturalist's eye couldn't help

19

but observe the trio of young bucks congregated on the corner of Knightsbridge and Sloane Street.

Dandium vulgaris. The Common Dandy.

Grace neared the three men who appeared to be between the ages of twenty-one and twenty-five years old, of average height and coloring, possessing no distinguishing facial features, and notable only for the expense of their coats and waistcoats, which let prospective mates know that at the least, their material comforts would be assured.

Their sexual and intellectual comforts, however . . . those were less certain.

"Did you clap peepers on the selection of beauties last night at the Haverfords'?" one of them bleated.

"A few rum morts, that's certain," another said. "Quite a bevy!"

"Jolly right," the third added.

As Grace drew closer, she realized she knew the men, having encountered them at numerous galas and fetes over the years. She couldn't recall their names — one overbred lordling was much the same as another — but was fairly positive she'd danced with two of them as they had considered her potential as a wife.

Earls' daughters were infrequent, their dowries substantial and bloodline impeccable. At twenty-six, she was somewhat old for an unwed woman, but she was healthy and all the women in her family lived long, fertile lives, bearing their husbands several sons. A few daughters, too. But the sons usually lived into adulthood, and there was no reason to assume she also couldn't bear healthy heirs to whomever she granted breeding privileges to. Having assessed her physical features as they'd developed over the years, she'd determined that she was, by most standards, reasonably attractive.

These factors alone made her a *good catch*. Any gentleman would be lucky indeed to marry her.

But did she want to marry *them*?

"Lady Grace," one of the men chirped as she neared. The three bucks all bowed.

"Gentlemen," she replied.

A second dandy added, "Looking charming — as usual. Are you out for a bit of shopping?"

"Headed to the library, in fact," she said.

A look of profound bafflement creased the men's faces.

"Er, with books?" the first dandy asked.

"Generally," she answered levelly, "the thing that qualifies something for being called a 'library' is the presence of books."

"Are you sure you wouldn't rather buy a

bonnet?" the third dandy said with a hint of desperation. "My mother and sisters love the things. Always getting new ones."

"Much as I enjoy new bonnets," she said, "they are not repositories of information about amphibians, nor reptiles."

"I suppose not," the second dandy said glumly.

After a long pause, Grace said, "Thank you for the charming conversation, but I'll be on my way now. To the library. With books. Not bonnets."

The trio of men bowed again, wishing her a good day, before she moved on.

A wry smile tilted the corners of her mouth. Evidently, she wasn't missing much by failing to land a husband from the ranks of Society.

Grace and Katie mounted the stairs leading up to the Benezra Library. Pleasure rushed through Grace's body as she climbed higher and her fingers itched with the knowledge that soon she'd be thumbing through the pages of the latest books in natural philosophy.

She reached the columned portico, then pushed open the heavy door and stepped into the marble-floored foyer. The smell of paper and leather and the faint musk of aged vellum filled her lungs.

Her smile widened with genuine happiness. Far more than any ballroom or parlor, *this* was her home.

Leonidas Benezra was an extraordinarily prosperous textile merchant with a fascination for the sciences, and his personal collection of natural philosophy texts was so substantial that he'd opened a private circulating library. Its members were vetted by Mr. Benezra himself. Once a person gained entrance, they had access to both ancient tomes and current volumes, covering topics as varied as botany, astronomy, anthropology, and zoology, with occasional forays into mechanics, mathematics, and folk dance, because Mr. Benezra proclaimed himself to be inordinately fond of dancing.

The best part about the library was its policy of admitting anyone, male or female, white or black, young or aged, impoverished or wealthy, provided that the person seeking entrance displayed a genuine love of the sciences.

Grace moved into the library itself, a former house that had been renovated to contain thousands of books. The walls between the rooms had been taken out, with columns added to bear the weight, so that the main chamber was the entire ground floor. Rows of bookshelves lined the perimeter, and stacks took up half of the room. Long tables where one could read undisturbed made up the rest of the chamber's furnishings.

Upstairs, the living quarters now held specialized subjects, which patrons could either peruse themselves or request a librarian to fetch particular volumes.

"Good afternoon, Lady Grace."

"Good afternoon, Mr. Pagett." She nodded as she passed the library assistant, wheeling a cart down the central aisle.

"Greetings, Lady Grace," Mrs. Sanford murmured from where she sat at one of the tables.

Grace paused and smiled at the older woman, whose freckles dotted her fair skin with little rosy constellations. In a lowered voice, Grace asked, "How fares your inquiry into orthogonal trajectories of curve families?"

"I'm beginning to believe that Bernoulli wasn't entirely correct." Mrs. Sanford patted the open book in front of her. "But I'm not concerned. I know I'll get to the bottom of it. Won't we, Khayyam?" She petted the library's orange tabby cat, curled up on a nearby stack of papers.

"I've every confidence in your abilities." With that, Grace moved on, eager to reach the circulation desk.

"Your parents want you home for supper with Lord and Lady Pugh," Katie said in a whisper. "Shall I fetch you at three?"

"If you must."

Following their usual routine, Katie veered off to find a place to read the novel she pulled from her reticule. Grace pressed her lips together to hide her smile when she saw that the author was the Lady of Dubious Quality. Grace herself owned four of the unknown author's works, but she kept them in her bedside table for late night — solitary — enjoyment. If Katie wanted to read erotic tales in public, well, that was her business.

"Lady Grace." Chima Okafor, the head librarian, smiled at her from behind his desk. His whispered words were lightly accented with the music of the Igbo language. He bowed. "What a pleasure."

"You always greet me as though I've been away for twelve months, not twelve hours." She set her reticule on the desk, pencils and the edge of a small notebook poking out from the top.

"Because I am always glad to see our most dedicated patron."

She laughed quietly. "Somehow I doubt that I hold that honor."

Mr. Okafor inclined his head. "Perhaps

there is a small cadre of individuals who vie for the title."

"*Biggest Bookworm.* That's what the trophy shall read."

"Don't mention bookworms here. Mr. Benezra is most particular about the health of his books and has a hatred of anything that feeds upon paper and bindings."

She held up her hands. "I shall speak of them no more. Has the copy of Cuvier's *Le Règne Animal* arrived yet?" Cuvier's views on different races were highly problematic, yet she had to see what the latest in zoological research contained so that she could position herself within the field.

"I would fetch it for you immediately. But . . ."

A voice behind her said, "I'm afraid that I reached it first."

The sound of that familiar voice made her heart pump faster. She took a steadying breath before turning around to face Mason Fredericks. He held a substantial book beneath his arm, but she barely noticed it.

"You're back," she said, and congratulated herself that she'd managed those two words without stammering.

"The wilds of the Orkney Islands were fascinating," Mason answered. His eyes sparkled with good humor. "But one's funds

26

have a tendency to run out when one is in the field."

"Rather than cozying up to deep pockets here in London." She smiled, hoping her face wasn't as red as it felt. All the cool presence of mind she'd summoned for her conversation with the three dandies sizzled away like droplets of water on a skillet.

At the least, her head was level enough for her to refrain from pointing out that, as a viscount's son, he likely didn't have to ask anyone for money to subsidize his research. Having met Mason's father at numerous social events, and hearing the viscount speak glowingly about his naturalist son, there would be no shortage of capital for Mason's work.

"I must continue cataloging our newest acquisitions, so please do excuse me." Mr. Okafor bowed before retreating.

Leaving Grace alone with Mason.

Her mouth dried and her pulse hammered as she looked at him. Damn, he was pleasant to look upon. She could study the shape of his curved lips for hours, and fill page upon page in her sketchbook with the angle of his jaw or the dimple in his left cheek. He wore his light brown hair neatly trimmed, revealing a high, intellectual forehead. His green eyes regarded her with fondness.

Only fondness.

Summoning her courage, she said with as much breeziness as she could muster, "Now that you've returned to London, perhaps you'll join my family for dinner tonight? We're having guests, so it wouldn't be any trouble to add another." Her pulse hammered — she'd never before asked Mason to dine.

"Alas, I cannot." He sounded genuinely regretful. "Within a day of my homecoming, my social calendar became appallingly overcrowded. Especially as I intend to leave for an expedition to Greenland in less than two months."

She ignored her plunge of disappointment. "Of course."

"Nothing would please me more than a tête-à-tête with you," he continued. "Every day brings new developments in the field, new texts with new theories —"

"Such as the Cuvier." She eyed the book he held.

"Indeed." He sighed. "But, unfortunately, I'm expected at no fewer than three dinners tonight."

"To be seated beside young, unmarried ladies," she said, before silently groaning at her gaucheness. Why did she have to bring

28

that up?

He chuckled. "Highly unlikely. Who would want their daughter to marry a naturalist? No one dreams that their beloved girl will spend her honeymoon tramping through the wastelands of the subarctic, tracking the migration patterns of the local fauna."

"That sounds ideal." Just her and Mason, out in the wilderness, devoted to their studies and the expansion of knowledge during the day. And at night . . .

Her cheeks grew warmer.

"Of course *you* would think so." He grinned and her insides went gelatinous. "Because you're a true scholar. But, unfortunately, no prospective bride offers such delights. No," he said, sobering, "when I do find the right woman to marry, I can only pray she tolerates my work. Ah, well. She's out there, somewhere. I merely need to be patient and hope to find her."

Grace made herself smile, but within, she shriveled. "I wish you luck in your search."

"My thanks." He regarded her warmly. "You're always so easy to talk to, Lady Grace. Will you also be at the Creasys' garden party? I believe it's next week, and they were adamant I stop by."

She'd never intended to go. "Wouldn't miss it."

"I'll see you there, then, and I'll finish with the Cuvier quickly." He bowed before strolling off with the book.

Dejected, she headed into the stacks, barely aware of the rows and rows of comforting books, or how their spines formed trees in a colorful, reassuring forest. She turned at random down an aisle, hardly noticing the little cards that proclaimed the section's subject matter.

She stopped and rested her hand on a book from the shelf. *System and Methodology for Creating Algebraic Taxonomies.* Despite knowing next to nothing about algebra, she pulled the volume down.

With the book absent from its place on the shelf, a small gap opened up, revealing the face of a man standing in the next aisle.

He glanced up absently from the tome he held. His gaze slid back down to the book, then moved up again before a smile bloomed.

"Lady Grace."

"Oh!" She lowered her voice when an unseen person shushed her. She pulled herself out of her gloomy haze enough to smile at Sebastian Holloway. As always when she saw him, a little fizz of happiness rose up within her, slightly pushing aside her melancholy. "Sebastian. You know you can call me just 'Grace.' I promise it won't sully your reputation to be on familiar terms with me."

"Can you be certain? I hear such *scandalous* things about you." He pushed his shaggy blond hair off his forehead, but it slid back almost immediately. Light from the window reflected off of his spectacles as he tilted his head. "You've developed an interest in mathematics and other numeric subjects?" His eyebrows raised.

She glanced down at the book in her hand. "Have I ever shown the slightest inclination for mathematics?"

"Considering that you still count on your fingers . . ." She scowled at him, but without malice. "How dare you, sirrah!"

"My most abject apologies. I'm a bookish man, unaware of social niceties."

"Here in England," she pointed out. "When it comes to the social customs of villages in the Azores during Lent, you're an expert."

He bowed. "Madam, you flatter me."

They shared sly smiles, and a shard of her unhappiness worked its way free from her mood. Being with Sebastian was always so easy, so comfortable. They didn't have the same disciplines, but that hardly mattered

when they both loved the pursuit of knowledge.

Four years ago, they'd met in this very
library. She never would have expected the
tall, fair man with a rather strapping frame
to be one of England's most devoted anthropologists — but then, she should know better than believing there was a direct correla-
tion between how someone looked and who
they truly were.

Since then, they'd become friends. A
handful of times each month, they would
attend a lecture together, or visit a museum,
or go on some other excursion. Grace
always looked forward to these outings. She
and Sebastian enjoyed each other's company, and though they didn't share a subject
of study, they both loved to observe the
world around them, often with a slightly
wry perspective, and shared their observations over cake and cups of tea at Catton's.

Over the years, she'd come to know things
about him. His love for anthropology and
the study of rituals, customs, and cultures
stemmed from his perspective as a peren-
nial outsider — a feeling with which she
could empathize.

"How did the conversation with your
father go?" she asked.

He gave her a wry grin. "Oh, it was as

delightful as expected. I stammered for fifteen minutes, he glared at me, and then we both retreated to opposite sides of the study."

"Oh, no."

Sebastian exhaled. "It's a consistent disappointment, trying to get my father to understand that his youngest son has any actual significance." He undercut this statement with another flash of ironic smile, but Grace saw the hurt beneath it.

"It's just one man's opinion," she offered.

"I know." His brow furrowed. "I know. But . . ."

"Knowing that your own parent doesn't understand you . . . I imagine it's an injury that never quite heals."

Sebastian shook his head. "Should be used to it by now."

A sympathetic ache resounded in her chest. "There's no *should* when it comes to what we feel. There aren't scientific laws when it comes to the human heart."

After a moment, he said, "My father made the charming threat that if I didn't take a place in the business I wouldn't see a farthing more than my crumb of an allowance. Pure joy it is to have such a man as my father."

"Did you tell him that you can't do any

33

true fieldwork without financial support? That you're stuck doing research by reading alone? Wouldn't that move him at all?"

Sebastian gazed at her. "John Holloway, founder and owner of Holloway Ironworks, is . . . I believe the technical term is *a closed-fisted bastard.*" He coughed. "Beg pardon about the language."

"By all means, call a bastard a bastard." She almost reached through the open bookshelf to lay her hand across his.

Almost.

Sebastian might be a fellow natural philosopher, and her friend for several years, but he was still a young man in his prime and she was a woman of marriageable age. She couldn't just go around touching eligible bachelors, not without consequences.

And . . . whenever she looked at Sebastian's hands, her belly fluttered with awareness. They were large hands, with long, blunt fingers, and more than once she'd caught herself daydreaming about what it would feel like to have his hand stroke along her arm, or down her back, or tenderly cup the back of her head . . .

Mentally, she shook herself. She wouldn't throw away four years of friendship on a few uninvited sensual thoughts. Oh, maybe when she'd first met Sebastian, she'd hoped their camaraderie might evolve into something more intimate. But he'd always been scrupulously polite and treated her strictly as a colleague and confidant.

She'd already faced rejection from the belles and beaux of Society — she didn't need to experience it again with Sebastian. So she'd carefully weeded out the seedlings of attraction, and the garden of their friendship remained tidily maintained.

"We've discussed my bastard father enough." He tilted his head. "I might be a trifle nearsighted, but I'm fairly certain I saw you talking with Mason Fredericks a few minutes ago."

Heat flooded her face. "He's back from his latest expedition."

"So I gathered." Sebastian peered through the bookshelf. "Your conversation with him looked pleasant enough to an outside observer. But then . . ." His gaze turned sympathetic. ". . . I'm not the one nursing a *tendre* for him."

"For the love of everything holy, lower your voice." She glanced around, hoping no one heard Sebastian.

"Apologies."

"Oh, Sebastian." She groaned, tipping her head forward so that it rested against the shelf. "What am I going to do?"

From somewhere in the library, a voice hissed, "Shh! People are trying to *work*."

Further mortification worked its way into her bones. God above, but she was a disaster.

But rather than gazing at her with understanding, Sebastian's expression turned opaque. She'd no idea what he was thinking or felt. Perhaps it was wrong to talk about another man with him, though it was far from the first time the topic of Mason had come up.

To Grace, he said, "Follow me." Then he strode away.

Had she pushed her friend too far?

CHAPTER 2

Uncertain where he led her, she followed Sebastian, but since his legs were much longer than hers, she had to hurry to keep up.

She passed Mr. Okafor. The librarian held a substantial book.

"Mr. Fredericks left you the first volume of the Cuvier," Mr. Okafor murmured.

So, Mason had gone. She was almost relieved so that she didn't have to wallow in her one-sided attraction anymore today. "If you'd be so kind, please hold on to it for me."

Sebastian stopped and said over his shoulder, "Lady Grace and I must discuss something in the study room — unless someone is currently using it."

After glancing with curiosity toward Grace, the librarian shook his head. "It's unoccupied until four, when Mrs. Graves has reserved it. By all means, make use of the room." It wasn't uncommon for patrons to confer with each other about sundry topics, regardless of their specific discipline.

She nodded her thanks and, before she could change her mind about what Sebastian intended to do, moved with him toward the study room.

He opened the door for her, and when she drew close to him she was struck anew — as she always was — by his unusual height.

She herself was of average stature for a woman in this part of the world, but Sebastian must have been descended from Norsemen who had long ago invaded Britain. He certainly possessed the size, fair coloring, and defined features of a Viking.

He gestured for her to enter the study room and she stepped inside.

The room contained a circular table and four chairs, with a single window that looked out into the mews, and a handsome portrait of Mr. Benezra's mother painted when she was a young bride.

Sebastian glanced at the picture. "Imagine she's heard some fairly intriguing conversations over the years."

"The world is changing rapidly," Grace said. "Who knows where we'll be in three years, let alone three decades?" She gazed at him. "What are we doing in here?"

"Didn't seem judicious to discuss your feelings about Mason Fredericks in the middle of the library. And," he added in a kind voice, "you looked on the verge of either tearing the library down to its foundation or bursting into tears."

The pressure in her chest loosened at hearing his words of understanding. She could always rely on him. "Can't I do both?"

"Surely. If you need any help with the former, I believe the library has a Pictish hammer somewhere in its collection."

She tried for a smile before giving up and dropping down into a chair. "It's hopeless. Do you know what Mason said to me at the circulation desk? First he said that he was running off to Greenland in less than two months. And then he lamented ever finding a wife who could tolerate his scientific pursuits. That such a woman was nigh impossible to find. All while I was standing right in front of him."

"Damn." Sebastian scowled. "That was ruddy thoughtless of him."

Warmth touched her at Sebastian's defense. "I suppose. But in all the years I've known him, he's never seen me as anything other than a colleague. He's always surrounded by flirting belles. And you know more than anyone that I'm decidedly *not* a belle. Nor do I want to be," she added with vehemence, "but it's hard to get someone's attention when they're encircled by sparkling fireworks and I'm a laboratory brazier, burning steadily away."

Unable to sit still any longer, she surged to her feet and began to pace the confines of the small room. Sebastian quickly stood, watching her with concern.

"I only want . . ." She shook her head, trying to make sense of her tangled feelings. "I only want him to *see me.* As I am. Not merely a fellow natural philosopher, but as a woman."

"I'm certain he knows you're a woman," Sebastian said drily.

"In an abstract sense. But no one ever held hands in a moonlit garden with an abstract sense."

Sebastian inclined his head. "Point taken. And he's no notion of your feelings for him."

"You and Jane Argyle are the only two who know." She wouldn't trust anyone but her two closest friends with the knowledge.

"Don't think I don't appreciate that." He folded his arms across his chest and leaned against the table. "He's ideal, isn't he? A man who's respected in his field as well the larger world of society. The best of both worlds."

"Never thought of it like that." Mason had always drawn her attention and admiration, from the first time she'd met him during her debut. Yes, he was handsome, but it was the *substance* of him that ensnared her. Considering it now, he did possess everything she desired but feared to reach for.

She went on, "I never told you this, but in the first months of my debut, I'd been candid with fellow debutantes and prospective suitors about my love of reptiles, my fascination with amphibians. The *looks* I'd received, the *laughter* . . ." She shook her head as if she could dispel the hurt that still resounded. Being snubbed was a terrible thing. It struck to the very heart of the need to belong. "Only Mason was kind. Only he listened and asked questions and seemed to believe that my work was worthwhile. That *I* was worthwhile."

In those months, she'd come to see Mason as the lone beacon of light in the dark cavern that was the Season.

"Oh, Grace." Sebastian's look was one of deep sympathy. "I . . . *we* here at the library, *we* think you're worthwhile."

"And I'm grateful for it, truly." She dipped her head, humbled by the kindness of her colleagues. With them, she didn't have to

41

retreat behind a shield of irony. She didn't need to pretend to disregard their opinions using a protective barrier of wit.

"But it's not the same as winning the heart of a man you admire," he added.

"I'm being foolish, aren't I?" Yet the need within her, the palpable ache to be seen and accepted and loved — that didn't feel foolish. It felt alive and so very close, as if the pain lodged just beside her heart, cutting into her with each beat, reminding her over and over that she wasn't enough. She would never be enough.

At least she had Jane. And Sebastian. Her two friends. That was something. It was more than many people had, and she ought to be grateful.

"Not foolish." Sebastian regarded her sympathetically. "It lies at the core of us, the need for love and recognition. All my years of watching people, observing them as they go about the rituals of their lives . . . it always comes back to love."

Seeking relief from the oppressiveness of her feelings, she teased, "How deeply romantic. Are you turning from anthropology to poetry?"

"What rhymes with *kinship systems*?" He raised an eyebrow.

"Flagship Tristams?"

He kissed his fingertips. "Perfection."

A moment later, they both broke into laughter. She leaned into the release, allowing the absurdity to ease pressure from the hurt at the center of her.

"Thank you," she said.

He looked baffled. "For what?"

"For listening to my self-indulgent diatribe. The next time we meet, I'll be less of a sapskull."

"Reminds me." He rifled around in his pockets before producing a crumpled piece of paper, which he held out to her. As she read it, he went on. "At a private home in Chelsea, there's a temporary exhibition of medieval woodcuts that's open to the public. I heard that some examples of early studies of reptiles were included. Come with me tomorrow?"

"I would," she said at once. "Only . . . woodcuts of lizards aren't exactly your bailiwick. Is there anything there that would interest you?"

The corners of his eyes crinkled. "The whole world interests me."

"If I was talking to anyone else, I'd say that statement was an exaggeration. However, it's *you,* so I know that you mean that with complete honesty." She smiled fondly at him, her good friend.

43

It was a wonder that he was still a bachelor. He never even spoke of lovers. Why could no woman ever see what a wonderful man he was? But, then, finding people who could support your scientific interests was a difficult task. He was also poor as a churchmouse, which, unfortunately, meant that he hadn't the financial means to court anyone.

Sebastian returned her smile, then pulled out his timepiece. "Damn. Supposed to be at McKinnon's bookstore to pick up a special order." He bowed, then asked, "I'll see you tomorrow? We'll meet at the exhibition?"

"Tomorrow at the exhibition," she said brightly. Grace shooed him toward the door. "Now go, and enjoy your new books."

"There is nothing more enjoyable than new books," he said solemnly. "Except old books."

"Truer words . . ."

With a wave, he left the reading room. She stood alone, torn between gratitude and despair. Gratitude for Sebastian's camaraderie, and despair that Mason had put her firmly in the classification *Amica asexualis*.

Nothing would ever change that. She was as fixed as a pin through a butterfly.

Seb took advantage of his long legs to walk quickly from the Benezra. Brisk afternoon air cooled his face.

He needed distance between himself and Grace, distance that would help clear his head and remind him of some Very Important Facts.

She was the daughter of an earl and could trace her ancestry back to before the Tudors.

He was the son of a man who'd made his fortune from mining and selling iron, and his grandfather had been a blacksmith with barely any literacy.

Her pin money was likely ten times the amount of the pittance that was his quarterly allowance.

In four years, not once had she looked at him with anything warmer than friendliness.

She was besotted by Mason Fredericks and *only* Mason Fredericks.

She owed Seb nothing. He couldn't feel anger or resentment that she considered him strictly a friend.

But, *damn,* none of that made it easier to

hear about her infatuation.

He neatly dodged around a liveried messenger hurrying down the street, and side-stepped around a fallen meat pie someone had dropped. Physical action came so easily and without thought. He could settle into the movement, confident that his body would perform as it needed to, even excel in the motions required. At least in that regard, he had full confidence.

Oh, and thanks to the fact that he couldn't secure money to fund field research, he knew his way around a library.

That totaled up to two areas of expertise. When it came to *talking* — more specifically, *wooing* — he devolved into a stammering blancmange.

Which was one of the reasons why he never tried to say anything remotely flirtatious with Grace. He'd never tell her that her gray-blue eyes reminded him of the sea at dusk. Or that he could spend hours contemplating the curve of her neck. Or give voice to the fact that when he saw her, he forgot anything unpleasant that had happened to him earlier in the day and it was as though the sun had broken out from behind a heavy cloudbank, brightening everything within him.

The reason — the *only* reason — why he

could talk to Grace at all was because she thought of him merely as a friend. He didn't lose his awareness of her as a woman, but so long as she valued his platonic companionship, he'd keep all thoughts of kissing his way across her collarbone to a minimum, thank you very much.

The sign for McKinnon's came into view. He breathed out, letting the last of tension slip from his body.

"Afternoon, Mr. Holloway," the bookseller called from behind a table laden with tomes of every size. "A moment, and I'll head back to fetch your order."

"At your leisure, Mr. McKinnon." Seb slipped between the bookshelves, which, along with the Benezra Library, formed the walls of his spiritual home. He had to content himself with other people's research, since having the funds to actually go out into the field — outside of England — and conduct research of his own was a distant dream.

Grace stepped into the foyer of her home, her face heating as she recalled her mortifying conversation with Mason. Then Sebastian had listened so patiently to her bemoaning that humiliating interaction. He always listened — one of the reasons why she was

47

so grateful to call him a friend.

"Oh, thank goodness you're home, my lady!"

She paused in the act of handing Katie her bonnet as Grenville, the butler, hurried forward. Grenville's mouth was tight, and creases of worry fanned out from the corners of his eyes.

Considering how he had once calmly announced at teatime that a fire had broken out in the kitchen, the butler's tense expression shot alarm through Grace.

"What is it?" she demanded.

"The earl . . . your father . . ." Grenville's gaze lifted to the top of the staircase, toward her father's bedchamber.

Grace shot up the stairs, hiking up her skirts to take them two at a time. Every stride made her heart pound harder as countless disastrous scenarios played out in her mind.

In the hallway outside her father's bedchamber, she nearly collided with a middle-aged man in dark and serious clothing. A servant carrying a covered basin was on his heels. It took her addled thoughts a moment to recall that he was Dr. Campbell, the family physician.

"Lady Grace." Dr. Campbell bowed. "I've just been attending the earl."

"Tell me what's wrong with him." She gripped the physician's sleeve, dimly noting the whiteness of her knuckles.

"I've bled him, and he's resting now."

"But what happened?"

Dr. Campbell hesitated. "I don't want to overset you. Young ladies can have delicate temperaments."

She fought down a wave of impatience. "You attended my birth, Dr. Campbell, so by now you should know I *have* no delicate temperament."

"He suffered a collapse less than an hour ago," the physician said after a pause. "After examining the earl, I suspect it was angina pectoris."

Cold sheeted through Grace. God — when her father had fallen ill, she'd been at the library, nattering on about her fascination with Mason.

"I bled him," Dr. Campbell continued, "but in order to have a full recovery, he must have rest and peace of mind." He stared at her meaningfully, as if she planned to bang a kettledrum beside her father's bed.

"Yes, I understand." She released her grip upon the physician's sleeve.

"I'll call tomorrow to check on his progress."

She gave the physician a distracted nod

before heading into her father's bedchamber. The curtains had been drawn, shutting out the last of the day's light, with the fire and a lamp casting flickering illumination on the too-still person in the bed and the figure seated beside him.

Her mother's face gleamed with tears, and as Grace moved closer, the countess half rose from her chair with a choking sob. "Oh, Grace."

"Mama." She rushed forward to embrace her mother. The countess felt so frail and delicate, her bones as breakable as a dried reed, and for the first time, Grace truly realized that both of her parents were mortal and finite. A shudder ran through Grace's body. "Why did no one fetch me from the library when it happened?"

"There wasn't time. One moment, we were having tea, talking about dining with Lord and Lady Pugh, and the next, he was on the floor, face white as paper, and his hand clutching his chest, and I . . . and I . . ."

"Shh." Grace rocked her mother, painfully aware that their roles had reversed and it was she who now offered comfort. "Dr. Campbell said he can recover with good rest."

"Easy for him to say." Her father's alarmingly thin voice came from the bed. "He's not engaged to play cards with Lord Liverpool tomorrow night."

"Papa." Grace released her mother to kneel at her father's bedside. She clasped his hand in hers, and he weakly squeezed in response. The sleeve of his shirt had been pushed up to reveal a bloodstained bandage wrapped around his arm.

He was terribly pale, his gaze faintly unfocused as he looked down at her. "Come, now, there's no need for tears."

She brushed her fingertips across her face and discovered they were wet. "Is there anything I can do?"

He was silent for a moment. "There is one thing."

"You've but to name it." She sat up straighter, relieved at being able to take action.

"What I want will help *both* of us . . ."

"Go on," she urged.

"I want you to marry."

She laughed, and then realized that he wasn't jesting. Abruptly, she let go of her father's hand. "Sir?"

"Hear him out, Grace," her mother said as she lowered herself to her chair.

Grace could only stare back and forth between her parents. Clearly, they'd spoken to each other about this. That couldn't be good.

"I worry about you, my dear," her father said softly. "Your Seasons have been . . . less than ideal."

Another sudden, startled laugh broke from Grace's lips. "Disastrous, more like."

"We knew you were not quite an Incomparable." Even in his weakened state, her father spoke with a hint of wry humor. "Still, we've held out hope that you might find a man who understood your . . . peculiarities. We've hoped, but each year the possibility has grown more and more unlikely."

Grace pressed her lips together. Having her parent articulate her failings as a Society debutante was a sharp needle piercing between her ribs. True, her parents had been tolerant of her studies, but that was not quite the same as having her work — and *her* — celebrated.

Her father went on, "My little health episode makes me think about what will happen to you when I'm gone. That time may come sooner than any of us expect."

"Let's not talk of that."

"But we must."

"I always thought . . . perhaps Charlie might take me in." She and her older brother were on amicable, if not warm, terms with each other, and his wife, Anne, was kind. Their three children were quite high-spirited, and it was commonly accepted that, wherever they were, at least one piece of china would be broken within fifteen minutes.

"Is that the life you want?" her mother asked. "Reliant on your sibling's generosity? Having no husband, no children, of your own? Worried that one day, you might not have a roof over your head?"

"I . . ." Constriction gripped her lungs. True, living as Charlie's dependent was not ideal. His home would never quite be hers, and she'd be, at best, tolerated as the eccentric maiden aunt. If her brother passed away before her, she would have to hope his children would support her into her dotage. She'd be passed around like a worn coat, just a little too good to be thrown away, but too frayed and old to be of use.

A burr of anger flared within her, that a woman could not exist in this world on her own. She would always be subject to a man's munificence, always be less than because she'd been born a female.

Yet how could she refuse her father his one wish? How would it be possible that, as he lay ill and exhausted, she could deny him this?

"Surely there's someone you've met," her father said, though his words were enervated. "Some gentleman of means that you might consider marrying."

"There's no one —" But that wasn't true. There was Mason.

Charming, handsome, intelligent Mason, who accepted her as a fellow natural philosopher. Her infatuation with him could easily grow into something much deeper, much stronger . . . And, it couldn't be denied, he was a viscount's son. Her intellectual and material comforts would be assured. He was all things perfect for her future husband.

Save one small problem. He didn't see *her* as a future wife.

"Please," her father murmured as his eyelids drooped with weariness. "Please find yourself someone to wed. For me," he added.

His eyes closed, and his breathing deepened as he drifted to sleep.

"Go on, dearest," her mother whispered. "I'll watch him for now. Have your supper and a bath." The set of her mother's jaw indicated no arguments would be permitted.

"Very well," Grace said. "But I'll be back

later so you can eat and rest." She kissed her mother's cheek before leaving the room.

In the corridor, Grace took a few steps before sinking down onto her haunches, gasping as if someone had just rammed an elbow into her stomach.

"Find yourself someone to wed. For me."

Lord above, she could not refuse her father his wish. But, of all women, how was *she* to find herself a husband when the one man she could ever think of marrying refused to think of her as anything other than a colleague?

CHAPTER 3

She was late. She was never late.

Seb tried to smooth out a wrinkle of concern as he waited outside the exhibit in Chelsea, but no matter how he attempted to distract himself by observing the interactions of pedestrians, he circled again and again to worry. Maybe she'd gotten into an accident en route. Or she might have fallen ill.

Surely, if something was awry, Grace would have sent word. He distressed himself unnecessarily. But the gray skies grew heavier with each passing minute, and as he stood on the curb, the first drops of rain spattered on his shoulders. A moment later, the storm began in earnest.

He'd no choice but to take shelter inside the exhibit. So he dashed up the steps of the town house, and, at a footman's pointed look, wiped his boots on a mat in the foyer. He showed the servant the wrinkled announcement.

"The exhibit is in the downstairs dining room and parlor," the footman said, pointing over his shoulder.

"If a young woman with dark brown hair arrives," Seb answered as he removed his hat, "I'd appreciate it if you informed her that Mr. Holloway is waiting for her within."

The footman glanced at Seb's threadbare coat and scuffed boots. "Not much of a description. Get lots of young women with dark brown hair coming through."

"She has a particularly intelligent mien."

"Oh, well, in that case." The servant rolled his eyes.

"Her servant will be reading a book," Seb said through gritted teeth.

"Right, gov."

Seb resisted the impulse to snap a retort, reminding himself that the task of patrolling rigid British social hierarchy was often consigned to those who served the elite. He would not shoot the messenger — or, in this case, the footman.

After casting a glance toward the front door, he drifted toward the dining room. The soft, murmuring tones used by gallery patrons rolled out into the corridor.

Inside the dining chamber, which had been transformed into a gallery, framed illustrations covered the walls, and small groups and individuals in fashionable clothing circled the room as they studied the multitude of images. Seb moved to study a rather intriguing picture of a creature that looked to be half fish, half bishop.

"Peculiar, isn't it?" a female voice asked from behind him.

He straightened and turned toward the woman. Her blond hair gleamed beneath the brim of her stylish bonnet, and she gazed at him coquettishly with wide green eyes. He gulped.

A minute went by. And then another. She seemed to expect him to answer.

Sweat rolled down his back. What was he supposed to say? Something flirtatious? Something droll, or perhaps scholarly?

Words filled his mouth, and yet he could give voice to none of them. It was as though he had been presented with a coffer full of words and he had to select the best ones from the pile. There were too many options, too many ways to speak and fail.

"Er . . ." He coughed into his fist. "Well . . ."

He reached the limit of his ability. No other syllables or phrases made it past his lips.

"Made a friend, Miss Susan?"

With an internal groan of despair, Seb watched as a young man wearing what was likely the latest Continental style approached. The dandy lifted a brow as he took in Seb's ragged appearance.

"Didn't know this exhibition admitted charity cases," he drawled. "How did you get in?"

Heat poured into Seb's face and his hands coiled into fists. But a gentleman didn't brawl, and while Seb wasn't of genteel birth, he understood how public fisticuffs was considered the height of boorishness. The one weapon a refined man could use was his wit.

Seb opened his mouth to say something clever and cutting.

Nothing came out.

Miss Susan giggled. "The poor thing. He hasn't been domesticized." She took her companion's offered arm. "Come, William. If we wait for him to answer, we'll be standing here until All Souls' Day."

As William and Miss Susan ambled off, trailing laughter behind them, embarrassment and anger tightened Seb's muscles. He squeezed his eyes shut and struggled to take a calming breath.

"I'm sorry, Sebastian."

His eyes opened at the sound of Grace's

voice, and she stood in front of him, her gaze soft with sympathy. In the corner of the room, her maid sat on a chair while she read.

"They were beastly," Grace said.

He inwardly groaned. "You witnessed that?" *Perfect.*

She nodded. "Never seen it in action before. Is that how it always is?"

"Not with people I know, people who I consider my friends." Christ, could he feel any more mortification? "But if they're strangers to me, or I'm in social situations, I simply . . ." He shrugged stiffly. "You know. You've seen. I turn into a maladroit oaf with the finesse of a badger."

"You have a better vocabulary than a badger."

"Except I can't access it when I'm too busy mumbling." He held up his hand. "My gracelessness is hardly worth discussing. Not when you've got that set of your mouth you have when you're unhappy."

She let out a long exhale, and her shoulders drooped. To keep from reaching for her and offering physical comfort, he pretended his feet were bolted to the ground and his arms were weighted with sandbags.

"My father fell ill yesterday." At Seb's exclamation of alarm, she continued. "He's recovering, told me this morning that I was to continue on with my usual schedule. He insisted I come out this afternoon." She shook her head as if she could not quite believe her father could be so commanding when ill.

She went on, "Tomorrow he's leaving for our country estate to rest. Because he insisted, my mother and I are staying in London. But, after this brush with mortality . . ." Her gaze slid up toward the ceiling. "He urged me to marry. Soon."

Seb straightened. "Ah."

Grace — married. A concept he never truly wanted to contemplate. He supposed he'd believed they would go on as they always did, meeting at the Benezra or taking jaunts about the city together, friends until their dotage. A husband for Grace would certainly change everything. He crushed a flare of jealousy beneath his mental bootheel. What she wanted, what she desired, these things belonged to her alone, and he couldn't let himself feel possessiveness. It wasn't fair and it wasn't right.

Still. He made sure to keep a scowl from his face. As lightly as he could manage, he asked, "Anyone fitting the bill as your potential groom?"

She glanced around to ensure that no one

was nearby. "You know who."

"Someone with the initials *M F.*"

"The same."

He made himself nod, though it was sodding difficult. "That should make both you *and* your father happy. Your naturalist would be the perfect candidate." Fredericks had the wealth Seb didn't, with the means to keep Grace secure and generously supported.

Goddamn it.

"Except the man in question doesn't consider me bride material." She exhaled. "To him, I'm a colleague, and nothing more."

Thoughts churned in Seb's mind. Despite his disgruntled mood that she was fixated on Fredericks, a familiar lift of energy came from contemplating a particularly complex topic. He welcomed it rather than think about the fact that, even if he couldn't offer for Grace's hand, she never considered him a candidate for husband.

"Forgive me," he said, "but I've a strong urge to don my scholar's cap."

"Don away." She waved her hand.

He couldn't stop himself from smiling at her. She always encouraged him whenever he dove into the anthropological waters, never chiding him for his excitement.

"Here's what I'm thinking — value's relative in many societies. When something's recognized as being precious, everyone desires it." Warming to his topic, he continued, "One could take a thing — an object, or even a person — and if a respected individual in the community treats it or them as valuable, others invariably follow suit."

She frowned, clearly perplexed. "Pull up on the reins. How does any of that apply to me and . . . the gentleman in question?"

"Sorry. I forget that not everyone is as hopelessly mired in ethnography as I am." He felt a corner of his mouth turn up in a contrite half smile. "What I mean to say is that if someone from London's elite showed you a marked preference, thus indicating your value as someone to be desired as a mate, then others, including the esteemed but myopic Mason Fredericks, will do the same."

She straightened. "Who could have that effect?"

"Some noteworthy figure," he said with a nod. "A person so admired by men and women alike that this person's opinion would be highly respected." He heard how his tone grew more animated as he delved further. "He should be known by everyone, esteemed, but *just* rebellious enough so that whatever he says or does is doubly potent. It's known that a hint of disobedience makes certain personages extremely appealing."

"The idea's sound, but . . ." She spread her hands. "A rake who consorts with demimondaines and fellow libertines isn't going to look in my direction. And where would I locate anyone like that? Sneak into a gaming hell, approach a man with a dashing coiffure and jaded eyes, and proposition him to pretend to court me?" She snorted. "Things like that don't happen."

"Er, no," Seb conceded. "Perhaps you could find someone of your acquaintance?"

"My elder brother's friends are all married, and I know few other men."

"The Duke of Rotherby," he said abruptly. "He's a very good friend of mine, and a bit of a rake. Everyone hangs on his word, too."

She widened her eyes. "I couldn't ask an actual *duke* to feign wooing me."

"Right. Not quite feasible." He chuckled ruefully. "Perhaps I should think about challenging Lady Marwood for the title of Most Outrageous Tale-Teller in London." He dragged his hands through his shaggy hair, pushing it off his forehead and dislodging his spectacles in the process. Quickly, he

64

replaced his glasses.

When Grace came back into focus, he found her staring at him, as though she'd just made an incredible discovery.

Alarm prickled the back of his neck.

She grabbed him by the wrist and, with surprising strength, pulled him into the empty corridor. He was so stunned he couldn't register the fact that this was one of the few instances where she actually touched him. Certainly it was the longest amount of time she'd ever done so.

Using that same strength, she positioned him to stand in front of her, and for the rest of his days, he'd never forget the look in her eyes as she gave him a thorough survey.

Oh, God.

Then she stepped closer, her scent of flowers and loam surrounding him, and his sense of reason winked out of existence.

Grace's heart pounded and she could barely catch her breath as she narrowed the distance between herself and Sebastian.

He held himself very still and confusion shone in his gaze. Despite their years of friendship, this was the closest they had ever been, mere inches from each other. His body radiated heat.

Definitely warm-blooded, she thought

65

through the haze of nearness. For a brief moment, she didn't exist in a morass of worry over her father, or his implored wish for her to marry. Just then, she was only aware of Sebastian, and the gleam of an idea that was utterly preposterous . . . wasn't it?

Raising up on her tiptoes, she lifted her hand, but stopped before she could touch him. "May I?"

Slowly, he nodded.

His breath puffed against her hand as she raised it to his face. Carefully, she plucked the spectacles off his nose. The metal was warm from his skin.

She slipped the glasses into his jacket pocket. Still balancing on the tips of her toes, she gently brushed his hair back. Nothing had ever felt quite so soft.

As she stroked his hair away, her fingers grazed his skin and her breath left her in a sudden gust. He, too, jolted.

It's only Sebastian, she reminded herself. *My friend.*

But with his hair off his forehead, and his spectacles gone, she finally saw his bare face. And while she'd been aware of him as a man from the beginning, now she allowed herself the freedom to truly see *him.*

His jaw was square, and he sported a faint cleft in his chin. A light blond stubble grazed his cheeks and framed his astonishingly sensual lips. His nose was beautifully proportioned, large and masculine. High cheekbones emphasized eyes of bright, crystalline blue.

He possessed a long, strapping body, with wide shoulders that suggested athleticism. With his height, his bodily mass, and his handsome — no, *striking* — features, she knew with absolute certainty that one of his ancestors had braved northern seas to claim a home and mate for himself here in England.

This was what it must feel like to encounter a rare and magnificent species. The world suddenly became much, much larger.

"It's you, Sebastian," she whispered to him. "I need *you.*"

An expression of pleasure crossed his face — his brows lifting, a smile raising the corners of his mouth — followed a second later by a look of pure panic.

"Me?" He fumbled to retrieve his spectacles. "You can't possibly mean that."

"I do." She imagined that her eyes were almost feverish as she stared up at him. "*You* are the man I need to play the part of my admirer."

"But . . . but . . . ." He backed up, putting needed distance between them. "Your world isn't my world. Never has been."

The wall met his back, and it would have struck her as ludicrous, a man well over six feet tall retreating from a woman of her diminutive stature, except she was too focused on the idea that coalesced in her mind.

He glanced toward a passing footman, but the servant was too busy being uninterested to notice.

"Not so." She advanced. "Only last week at the Rudstons' ball, I counted no fewer than three men of industry and business amongst the guests, as well as their wives and adult children. One of those men was your father."

She thought she heard him mutter, *Damn,* but wasn't entirely certain if she was imagining things.

"All right," he conceded, "you've a point. Maybe other industrialists' sons have made their entrée into Society. Not me. Never me."

"But you *could.*" She took another step toward him.

He held up his hands, and she halted in her advance.

"You've seen what happens when I'm in unfamiliar company. Feral dogs have more eloquence. Apologies — but what you're

68

asking of me can't be done."

Unexpected hurt jabbed Grace. "Can you not at least *pretend* to court me? Or . . ." A horrible thought struck her. "Am I truly so unappealing?"

"No," he said quickly. "You're quite . . . quite pleasant."

"Pleasant?" She wrinkled her nose. "Like a cup of tea?"

"Charming. Delightful." He seemed to want to say more, but his jaw tightened. Then, "*You* aren't at issue here. It's me. I can't be a Society beau. I'm not, and never will be, a rake."

A thread of desperation unraveled within her. She *had* to marry, and the one man she could imagine taking as a husband was just out of her reach.

"You aren't a rake and the darling of the *ton* now. But . . ." She caught her breath, excitement at his potential rising within her, and she whispered, "We can *make* you into one."

"Impossible."

As Sebastian tried to sidle around her, his body brushed hers and a hot jab of awareness struck her low in her belly. No — she couldn't think about that now.

"It's not —"

"Look at me." He spread his hands. "I'm

just a tongue-tied scholar in scuffed boots. The idea that anyone could mistake me for a suave man about town is ludicrous."

Grace did look at him. Her gaze moved over the length of him in a perusal she'd never permitted herself before.

She could see it, the possibility within him, that hidden beneath his rather threadbare clothing and painful shyness existed the makings of a rake. It was like standing beside one of those newfangled engines that ran on steam in the moments before it surged to life — the capability of tremendous force was a silent presence. All Sebastian lacked was the proper fuel, and then, he would be unstoppable.

But *he* didn't believe it.

There might be one way to appeal to him. Trying to keep the frantic desperation out of her voice, she said, "Think of the research possibilities."

"Oh?" He tilted his head, frowning thoughtfully.

It wasn't an outright *no.* There was hope, and she seized it with both hands.

"What do you study on those periodic wanders you go on?" Every few months, Sebastian would take a small pack and a fresh notebook and venture out into the English countryside, something he'd done since she first met him. Of particular interest to him was documenting customs and traditions that were on the verge of dying out, which happened more and more with the advancement of technology and improved roads.

She often had to repress feelings of jealousy that, as a man, he had the freedom to do something like that while she, as a woman and the daughter of an earl, could go nowhere unchaperoned.

"Rural communities' courtship rituals," he said. "The stages of wooing, how a suit is presented, the patterns of behavior between courting couples." As he spoke, animation filled his words, but then he caught himself and added in a more contained voice, "That sort of thing."

"Now you can study London high society, too." She spread her hands encouragingly. "Just imagine the book you could write. A thorough investigation into British courtship rituals of both commoners *and* nobility."

His gaze turned faraway, and she couldn't stop the tiny curl of pleasure she felt in knowing that, of all the things he valued most, the acquisition of knowledge was the most significant to him.

"An anthropological work that could be truly groundbreaking . . ." he murmured.

71

For many heartbeats, she held her breath. She was balanced on the very narrowest of ledges, with her father's wish to see her wed impelling her forward.

"I know what I'm asking of you is monumental." Hope and terror clashed within her, half fearing and half desiring his answer. "But it would mean so much to my family. To *me.*"

A pause. She died and was reborn a thousand times within that pause.

"Yes," he said.

"Yes?"

"I'll do it."

Impulsively, she flung herself at Sebastian and wrapped her arms around him. Giddy happiness swirled around her. "Thank you, thank you!"

Half a breath later, she realized something.

She was *pressed* tightly against Sebastian. Her body snug to his. And he was quite warm and quite tall and quite, quite muscular — far more brawny than she'd suspected. He also smelled delicious, like the scent of paper and wood smoke and leather mingled into one intoxicating fragrance that was heated by his skin.

They'd never stood close enough for her to catch his scent. Until now. It was like her first drink of claret, when she'd realized that she'd have to be very careful not to let the wine lead her into danger.

Oh, goodness.

Abruptly, she released him and took several steps backward. She cleared her throat, striving for some fragment of lucidity. "We can start tomorrow afternoon at my home. You know where it is? The house on the corner of Weymouth and Harley Streets."

"I'll find it." He looked perplexed. As perplexed as she felt.

"Tomorrow, then."

"Tomorrow."

She hurried away, aware of his gaze on her back. Aware of the fact that she'd just convinced Sebastian *and* herself to do something truly outrageous.

Jane Argyle paused in the middle of polishing her telescope's eyepiece and set the device on the sofa cushion beside her. Books, equipment, and half-drunk cups of tea filled the parlor of her snug Greenwich home, attesting to the fact that both Jane and her husband, Douglas, devoted the majority of their time to the study of astronomy.

Grace sat on the floor of the parlor, sorting through the stack of books Jane had requested help with categorizing. Periodically, the Argyles' personal library required herding, especially after Jane had visited booksellers' shops.

"I have serious reservations about this plan of yours, Grace." Jane's gentle tone took the sting out of her words, but Grace felt her invisible hackles rise. "Is this what your father meant by finding yourself a husband?"

"He didn't specify which methodology I should use, only that I'm to wed someone." Grace checked the spine of a book. "Johannis Hevelii, *Annus climactericus*?"

"Put that in the stack for Uranus." Jane shot Grace a quelling look when a giggle escaped Grace's lips. "Do grow up."

"Can't help it! Why name a planet Uranus if you don't want people snickering?"

Jane sighed, then smiled. "Yes, well, we haven't even gotten into discussions about galactic bulges."

Tension released from Grace's chest as she and Jane shared a cackle. She hadn't felt this sense of relief for over twenty-four hours, and the pressure of her father's health and his desperate request for her to marry was a vise constantly squeezing her.

"Of all men to play your dashing suitor," Jane said when their laughter quieted, "why

Sebastian Holloway? He's an agreeable fellow, but not quite rake material."

"Without his spectacles, and with his mane of disheveled hair off his face, he's quite . . ." Grace cleared her throat. She'd known, in a way, that he was a fine figure of a man, but she hadn't truly understood the depths of his allure until today. What a revelation that had been. Her body still resonated with the shock. Her friend had the face and form of a Corinthian.

She'd been tricked by his camouflage. But he wasn't *Chamaeleo chamaeleon,* shifting the colors of his skin to blend in with a leafy canopy. He was a spectacularly handsome man, hidden behind the facade of a reserved scholar.

"He'll make a convincing Society beau," she continued. "Just needs a little polish."

Jane raised her eyebrow. "And *you* propose to polish him. Forgive me, my dear, but your expertise is in the study of reptiles and amphibians, not London bucks."

"Not all of my expertise comes from fieldwork. Recall that you and I first met in the Benezra Library, conducting research." Grace stood and walked to a table overflowing with more texts. She picked up a volume and held it up. "Books can provide a wealth of information."

75

"True enough." Jane tucked a lock of her tightly curled black hair into her cap, a legacy from her West Indian father.

Grace examined the book in her hand. It was coming loose from its bindings, and the pages were speckled with foxing. "This one's a loss."

"No! That's Mayer's *Opera inedita*! His images of the moon are irreplaceable."

Grace smiled wryly as she set the book down. "Why invite me over to help with your books when I don't know the first thing about astronomy?"

"Douglas can't sort — he starts reading and then he's lost for the rest of the day." Jane tilted her head. "When does this monumental task with Sebastian Holloway begin?"

"Tomorrow. Which will give me enough time to go through my father's library and search out relevant works. I have a night of research ahead of me," she added with glee. An evening spent poring over books and learning new facts was truly the closest one came to Heaven, though tromping around in a field and turning over logs and rocks in search of reptiles was just as wonderful.

"Is he the man you've got your heart settled on?" Jane rose and walked to Grace.

"Sebastian?"

76

"Mason Fredericks."

"Oh . . . yes." Her pulse thudded just to think of him. "The passion in his voice when he talks about life cycles and habitat variation . . ." She sighed. "He *cares,* Jane. Truly cares about his work. Nothing could be more attractive to me. And when we discuss the benefits of conducting field research versus keeping specimens in a laboratory, I *feel* the connection between us. If I need to wed someone, he's the perfect choice for me."

She could picture their life together. Mornings spent lingering over the breakfast table, discussing the very latest in scientific developments. Afternoons would be out in the field as they observed and recorded creatures in their native environments. Then there would be fascinating suppers with like-minded friends and colleagues. And afterward, she and Mason would retire to their bed . . .

"Doesn't hurt that he's handsome, too." Her friend winked.

Heat crept into Grace's cheeks. "Females use appearance to help judge the health and viability of future offspring."

Jane pursed her lips knowingly. Of course, Grace's closest friend could recognize that she sometimes resorted to technical terminology whenever she felt flustered. And Mason certainly flustered her.

"One would have to engage in copulation with a mate first." Jane's gaze twinkled. "So? Are you thinking about copulating with Mason Fredericks?"

Grace covered her eyes with her hand. "Let's not get ahead of ourselves. First, I need to get him to notice me as more than a colleague."

"And *then* copulation."

"Let's hope so." When it came to sex — with someone other than herself — she had no actual experience. But from what she'd heard and read, it was one of the great pleasures of life. With two people in profound communion it had to be extraordinary.

Jane smirked. "If you need any additional information on that topic, I'm happy to provide my wealth of knowledge. Douglas is a very thorough lover."

"We play whist together! Don't talk about him that way." Imagining Douglas engaged in carnal pursuits was . . . disquieting.

"And he's *my* husband." Jane laughed as she tapped a finger on the tip of Grace's nose. "But I'll spare your tender sensibilities. For now." She tilted her head and looked at Grace, her gaze soft. "I only want you to get your heart's desire."

"Thank you." Warmth gently stole through Grace. How fortunate she was to count Jane as her friend. "As do I."

And it would all begin with ensuring that Sebastian was sufficiently proficient in the art of being a Society beau.

She and Sebastian had a considerable amount of work to do.

CHAPTER 4

Seb spent the evening in his rooms on Howland Street, attempting to read but failing as he jumped to his feet every five minutes to pace the creaky floorboards.

Anxiety over tomorrow shot bolts of energy through his limbs, making it impossible for him to remain still or concentrate. When his downstairs neighbor shouted, "Keep it down, Ironfoot!" he compelled himself to sit. Yet focusing on a text was hopeless, and so he stared at the weblike crack on the ceiling until St. Patrick's chimed one o'clock in the morning and he went to bed. He fell into a fitful sleep but kept jolting awake from dreams of Grace either jeering at him in disdain or weeping in dejection at his horrific botching of the job.

He had to do right by Grace. He had to become the rake she needed. For her sake, and his own. No room for failure. *No room for failure.*

That refrain chased itself in circles in his mind whenever he startled into wakefulness.

He'd had better nights.

Fortunately, his landlady forgot to heat his bath, so he managed to startle himself awake with icy water the next morning. As he bathed, he attempted to distract himself from fretful brooding by singing a taproom melody. When he finished the last refrain, his downstairs neighbor yelled, "Bravo! Now do 'A Lusty Young Smith'!"

By the time Seb reached the final *jingle bang, jingle, hi ho!* his spirits were much improved. There was something in a tune about a blacksmith and a buxom young maiden rogering each other six times in a row that cheered up a fellow.

His elevated mood came crashing down as he approached Grace's Mayfair home that afternoon. Never before had he been to the imposingly large house, and as he stood in its shadow, a cold feeling coagulated in his stomach.

God. They came from such vastly different worlds. Oh, his father had built himself a grand home with no fewer than six bedchambers in St. John's Wood, but that house was less than half a decade old whilst the London residence of the Earl of Pembroke

surely predated that by at least fifty years —
and that was only its most recent iteration.
Morbid curiosity had once made Seb look
up Grace's family's entry in *Debrett's* to
discover that the earldom originated during
the war between the Yorks and the Lancas-
ters.

Now he walked up the steps leading to
the Earl of Pembroke's sprawling yet refined
home and two words echoed in his head.

Fuck. Me.

His classmates at Eton had come from old
power and wealth, but he'd never had to
walk into their homes and pretend as though
the sight of a literal coat of arms on the door
knocker didn't shake him to his nouveau
riche core.

He raised his hand to use the door
knocker, drawing a steadying breath. The
fact that a person happened to be born to a
particular family and was the by-product of
generations of selective propagation didn't
make anyone better than anyone else. If
anything, aristocrats seemed determined to
breed away health and vitality.

If peers wanted to make themselves less
viable and more irrelevant, they were doing
a bang-up job.

The door swung open before he could
knock, revealing Grace. She smiled at him

— was there a hint of relief in her smile, as though she'd feared he wouldn't come? — and he forgot all his high-handed thoughts about the titled and elite.

"Come in, come in." She waved for him to step into the foyer. "I don't usually answer the door, but I'm trying to keep your presence here known to as few as possible, and I've only so much pin money to bribe the servants. My father left this morning and my mother's out, so other than the servants, we're on our own."

Dazed, he entered her home. The foyer was large enough to host a good-sized assembly, complete with dancing. "It's taking me considerable effort to keep from trying out the acoustics in here."

"Charlie and I used to stand at different ends of the foyer and whisper naughty words to test if the other person could hear them."

Unable to stop himself, Seb walked to the farthest point in the vestibule. "Give it a go now."

She raised her brow, then brought her cupped hands to her mouth. *"Bum."*

Her whisper resonated close enough as if he could feel her breath softly against his ear. He started as a stroke of heat licked up his spine.

What the devil?

Seb shook himself. This was merely an amusing diversion with a friend, nothing more. He could play this game without finding himself mired in unexpected desire.

"That hardly qualifies as a naughty word." He folded his arms across his chest.

"Suddenly you're Dr. Johnson," she said irritably. But she whispered into her hands again. *"Arse."*

Damn and hell. It happened again, that same caress of arousal that rose up from hearing her speak mildly profane terms. It had to be the novelty of hearing a lady of gentle birth — and his friend — utter coarse words.

Nonetheless . . . He'd have to think about this later, hearing Grace swear. *Delightful* was too mild a term for it.

As if donning an invisible coat of platonic interest, he said with easy affability, "Much better."

"Your turn," she instructed. When he was silent for a moment, she added, "Now you've grown demure. What a shame that all the books you've read have left no impression on your vocabulary."

"Trying not to shock you, dearest." He started. Damn — had he actually called her *dearest*? Out loud?

Praise God, she didn't seem to notice. She put her hands on her hips. "Try me."

He debated before raising his hands to his mouth. *"Shag."* It was a fairly tame word, but he wasn't about to give her a full lexicon of all the filthy words he knew. And he knew quite a lot.

Her cheeks reddened, which also ranked highly in his enchanting moments of the day. But, heavens help him, this little game he'd orchestrated had not gone as planned. It had started as an amusing whim between two friends and shifted into his uncomfortable awareness of her as woman.

"Think we've proved the acoustics work." Thankfully, he sounded properly sardonic and didn't growl with arousal. "Shall we get down to business?"

"Follow me." Grace ascended the stairs, and he followed.

Do not look at her arse. Don't look —

He looked at her arse.

To his dismay, it was perfectly delicious, round, and full, and his palms itched to stroke along her ripe curves. He could have been happy living out the rest of his life without knowing that Lady Grace Wyatt possessed a spectacular behind, but, thanks to his roving gaze, he'd been expelled from that innocent Eden.

Stop it, churl.

Feeling like a randy buffoon, he forced himself to look down at his feet, concentrating on the steps beneath him. It didn't quite assuage his guilt, but better that than leer at a woman he considered a friend.

On the next floor, she walked down a corridor before opening a set of double doors, revealing an exceptionally large, handsome room with parquet floors and not one but two unlit chandeliers. A few elegant chairs and small tables ringed the chamber. At one end stood a lacquered pianoforte, awaiting a pair of hands to bring it to life.

Seb slowly moved into the ballroom, his gaze drifting upward to the coved ceiling adorned with ornate but elegant plasterwork. He measured the length of the room by pacing from one end to the other. With his rather long stride of thirty-six inches, he calculated that the ballroom was nearly eighty feet long.

"We could hold an archery contest in here," he murmured.

Grace grinned. "Charlie and I used to play cricket in this room when the day was too rainy to venture outside." She pointed to an impression the size of a cricket ball that marked one of the walls. "That was him throwing too wide."

"You must have left your own souvenirs."

She grimaced as she nodded toward one of the tall windows lining one side of the chamber. "They had to replace that glass." She shook her head. "As punishment, I didn't get pudding for a week."

"A couple of wild creatures, you and Charlie," Seb noted.

"Perfect beasts, it's true. We were torments to our parents."

"And now . . . ?"

"Charlie's got his own family to torment him. And my mother and father are surprisingly tolerant of a daughter who likes to muck about with amphibians and lizards."

He shoved aside the sudden press of envy. His own parents wanted a different son, and Seb wanted a different family. No one had what they wanted, and, in a way, he'd come to peace with it. He couldn't change himself into a future giant of industry.

"They're also worried," she grumbled, "that such a daughter needs a husband."

"And you?" he asked.

"What of me?"

"Do *you* think you need a husband?" The question slipped out, yet once he'd spoken it, he craved the answer — to know what *she* wanted. In their four years of friendship, though they had shared details of their lives, they'd never fully explored their deeper desires, or shared their most secret hopes.

As if raising an unseen shield, her expression turned cynical. "I don't keep specimens. It's too cruel to confine a wild creature."

"Grace." He took a step toward her. "Tell me honestly. Do you truly want to marry?"

Fascinated, he watched the play of emotions across her face as she fought to keep her scorn in place — but the mask slipped, and her gaze turned dreamy, her mouth soft.

She let out a long breath. "I used to fantasize, when I was younger, before I was out. Not about a husband, but about a man who'd walk beside me in the field. Who would ask me about my work and genuinely *listen* rather than hear me with amused or fond forbearance. He wouldn't merely tolerate me. He'd —" She caught herself, and snorted as if she found herself ridiculous.

But she wasn't ridiculous. Not to him. And the tangible longing in her voice had reached into him and wrapped itself around his heart. True, he'd known that Mason Fredericks had long been the object of her infatuation, but Seb hadn't fully comprehended that Grace had wants and needs that went beyond her studies.

"It's just us, Grace." He spread open his hands. "You and me. I promise I won't laugh or say something cutting."

"He'd . . ." She shook her head. "I can't. I can't talk about this now."

Seb nodded. If she wanted to open herself to him, it would happen as she desired it, and when she was ready. He was humbled that she'd given him as much as she had.

She cleared her throat. "Returning to our purpose for being here . . ." She walked quickly to the pianoforte, where books were stacked atop its shiny surface. Picking up a volume, she said, "These came from my father's collection. Conduct manuals, given to him when he was a young man navigating Society and the marriage mart."

Seb headed toward her. "If he received those books as a young man, they must be rather archaic by now."

"They're about forty years old, according to the frontispieces. But," she said decisively, "proper decorum is timeless. Things can't have changed all that much."

Having reached the pianoforte, he plucked one of the books from the pile. He flipped it open and the image of a bewigged young gentleman looked back at him with an expression that could only be described as *privileged.*

"Seems logical enough," he said. "But these books might not be necessary. You've been out for some time now. Surely you've seen the behavior of rakish noblemen, so you can simply instruct me on how to act."

She pressed her lips together in a wry smile. "Never paid much attention to rakes. Perhaps because they've shown a marked lack of interest in *me.*"

Anger bubbled up hotly. "What the deuce is wrong with those nobs? It's a sure sign of societal decay when a woman like you is overlooked." He scowled, outraged on her behalf.

Another hint of pink stole into her cheeks, and he couldn't look away. In all their years of friendship, they'd never truly been alone, in private. She seemed more fully herself, less guarded. Each moment with her was a new discovery, and he awaited these unfolding revelations with bated breath. It felt as though he'd been given a new book filled with knowledge he didn't know he craved until he opened the cover.

"We're friends, Sebastian. No need for hyperbolic blandishments."

"We're both natural philosophers, Grace," he corrected gently. "Exaggeration has no place in our world."

Their gazes met. And held. It was vertiginous — in the best possible way. As though he tumbled through an endless, warm ocean. At the same time, electric awareness spread along his limbs.

Disappointment scored him as she looked away, breaking the spell. Yet the blush didn't leave her face.

"There are new developments in the sciences," she said crisply, "but Society remains a constant. Surely these books will tell us everything we need to know."

An hour later, Seb stood in the middle in the ballroom, silently thankful for all the time he spent conditioning his body. Unlike his social clumsiness, physical activity had never been an obstacle, yet today, he'd never felt so awkward. Of a certain there had to be some kind of award . . . perhaps a ribbon pinned directly to the skin of his pectoral.

"Keep your shoulders back," Grace instructed as she circled him, an open book in her hands. "Chin high. Arms held slightly away from the body with a slight bend in each."

In an attempt to replicate what she described, he stuck his chest out and lifted his chin as his arms stuck out in ungainly angles, but damn if his normally adaptable body felt as cumbersome and graceless as a

91

musk ox.

"This doesn't feel right," he said through clenched teeth.

"Of course it doesn't. Manners are supposed to run contrary to our natural impulses." She tapped her fingers against the underside of his jaw. "Lift this higher."

Little explosions of heat went off where she touched him. He shoved the unwanted reaction aside.

"If I lift my chin up any more," he muttered, "I'm going to tip onto my back and flail around like an overturned turtle."

"If you do, I'll just flip you back onto your stomach."

"Comforting to know." He struggled to hold the posture, which became even more difficult as she stood close to him, emanating her subtly floral scent.

His awareness of her grew with each moment they spent alone together. When they had met over the years at the library, or on their occasional scientific forays around London, it had been much easier. They'd been two colleagues who shared an interest in observing the world around them. But with no one else around, and his attention fixed solely on her, he became more and more responsive to her. The set of her mouth as she worked through a problem.

The way her smiles began in the corners of her eyes before her lips curved.

He didn't welcome this new attunement to her. It made things sodding complicated.

"I'm supposed to just pose here like this? Rakes simply stand around social gatherings like absurd statues?"

"There's walking, too." She glanced down at her book.

He exhaled slightly as she backed up. Which was more difficult — attempting to emulate rakishness, or ignoring the way his body flared to life whenever she was near him? "God help me."

"It says here that your pace must be elegant and measured. No, go slower," she instructed as he took a step. "And your feet need to be pointed and slightly turned with each step. Draw attention to your calves and ankles."

Seb did as she instructed, walking unsteadily as he attempted to force his body into yet more uncomfortable positions. His muscles silently protested the peculiar movement. Yet it was a relief to concentrate on an external task rather than observe the lines of her wrists.

"This can't be right."

"It isn't." She looked between him and the book, her expression intent. "Do you

93

have a walking stick? It seems to be required."

"Don't have one." A trickle of perspiration rolled down the back of his neck. He sweated less during the weekly football matches he played on Hampstead Heath.

"Just a moment." She dashed from the room.

He scowled in mingled alarm and dismay. Had he frightened her off? Perhaps he was so ridiculous she had to run away to laugh in private. Ridicule wasn't pleasant — God knew he'd experienced his share — but he'd learned how to ignore the derision of people he didn't respect.

If *she* mocked him, however, the wounds would take forever to heal.

Soft, quick footfalls sounded in the hallway, and then she appeared in the ballroom doorway, holding a yard-long tree branch that was roughly two inches wide.

Relief shot through him, followed quickly by puzzlement.

"Found this." She approached, holding the tree limb out to him.

"Did that come from the garden?" Gingerly, he took the branch from her.

"My bedroom."

He frowned down at the thick piece of wood. "Why do you have a tree branch in your bedchamber?"

"What do you suggest I use for turning over logs and rocks when I'm looking for reptiles?" She looked at him as though he had sprouted antennae. "I can't very well use my bare hands and risk injuring myself or the animal."

A very good point.

"I'm to use this as my walking stick?" He swiped it through the air, careful not to hit her with it. The branch had the same heft and size as a fencing foil. Its familiarity helped anchor him a little, reminding him that he wasn't *entirely* lost in this endeavor. Still, a bit of solid ground beneath his feet would be welcome.

"For now, it fills the role of walking stick." She gestured in invitation. "Try strolling with it. Swing it carefully but with aplomb."

"Aplomb?"

"That's what it says in the book. And remember, take your time. Be leisurely."

He exhaled in an attempt to breathe past his frustration. No one had promised him this enterprise would be easy. There was pleasure, too, in overcoming obstacles — or so he reminded himself.

Steeling himself, he began to walk. It was a challenge, maintaining an exaggeratedly upright bearing while pointing his toes and swinging the branch-cum-walking-stick, and after a few steps, his every muscle was white-hot with effort.

"What the deuce do gentlemen do if they're in a hurry?" he said through clenched teeth. "It'd take me a quarter of an hour to walk ten yards."

"Perhaps gentlemen of fashion are never in a hurry," she suggested.

"It could be an emergency. Someone could be on fire and I'm carrying a bucket of water."

She shrugged. "Bring them the bucket — elegantly."

"Christ above, this is ridiculous." Exasperation sizzled through him, and he couldn't decide which aggravated him most: the cryptic rules of polite society that seemed to flout common sense, or himself, for being unable to decipher the encoded rules.

"It is," she said with a nod. "But it's what we have to do."

He resisted the impulse to curse even more floridly. Being unable to perform for himself was an annoyance, but being unable to perform for Grace charred him with self-directed fury.

"Sebastian." She lay a hand on his arm. The feel of her was both a thrill and a balm. "Look at me."

96

He fixed his gaze with hers, and the flames of his frustration were quenched by the cool blue of her eyes. The crush of thoughts whirling in his mind calmed. He couldn't quite recall what had made him so angry, not with her touching him and her gaze holding his.

"The only person who expects you to immediately get this right is you," she said softly.

"They used to pay me to write their papers for them," he said. "Students at Eton, and then at Oxford. Hardly mattered the topic. Present me with an assignment, and I can figure out precisely what to say and how to say it. That's never in doubt. The same can be said for a physical task. Swim from one end of a lake to the other, or run a mile as quickly as possible — I can do all that."

"But *this* stymies you."

He nodded, relieved that she understood him, yet that relief guttered when she took her hand from his arm.

"You'll do this, Sebastian. I've every faith that you can meet this challenge."

The gentle conviction in her words lifted him. It was a benediction, to have her trust, when he knew she gave it so sparingly.

"How about we move on to bowing," she

suggested. "We can circle back to walking another time."

Seb straightened his shoulders as his hands curled into fists at his sides. He *could* do this. He *would* do this.

"Yes, bowing." He shook out his body, loosening it. "What do I have to do?"

Bent over her book, she read aloud. " 'A gentleman must present himself as the epitome of effortless grace and studied artlessness.' " She looked up with a frown. "How can one *study* artlessness?"

"That's what you get with a culture that loves its stratifications." He snorted. "Try, but not too hard. The more effort you expend, the less likely you are to attain your goal."

She blew at the strands of hair that had worked free from their pins to charmingly frame her face. "It's so much easier in the animal kingdom. Eat, sleep, procreate."

Heat crept up his neck to hear her say *procreate.* Again, a word that itself wasn't particularly salacious, but on her lips . . . Mentally, he gave himself a shake. *Stay focused on the task.*

"There's also avoiding becoming someone's dinner," he said. "Seems similar to life amongst human elite. Wait — I could put that in my book." He pulled a notebook from his pocket and scribbled on a blank page.

"I've seen packs of ravening matrons devour helpless debutantes like lionesses tearing into gazelles on the savannah." She shuddered. "A sight that will haunt me to my grave. And one of the reasons why, after my first Season, I've avoided balls, assemblies, and any other festive gatherings. I was easy prey."

"Hold a moment." He planted his hands on his hips as the truth behind her words sank in. "Help me understand — why you, of all people, aren't considered . . . what do they call it? *An excellent catch.* What's valued in the ranks of the elite, if not intellect? You have it, in abundance."

She coughed as her cheeks reddened. "Thank you. It's a quality not much esteemed in aristocratic females. Or English females in general."

"Needs a thorough reexamination," he muttered. A surge of anger pulsed through him. The most insidious parts of cultures were the ones so deeply ingrained that no one could question or challenge them without appearing like the veriest madman.

He marshaled his anger enough to write down more notes. *Women of intelligence not prized. Why???*

"It does," she said with a nod. "But not today. Today, we focus on bowing." She cleared her throat as she tapped the book in her hands. "It says here that to bow properly, a man must stick his leg forward, while also bending at the waist. At the same time, he removes his hat with a sweeping, polished motion. It must be smooth and elegant."

"I'm supposed to do all of those things at once?" He swallowed as he set the tree branch aside. "Can I pick two out of the three?"

Her finger moved over the open page. "It doesn't appear so. Oh! It also notes that the lower and longer the bow, the greater respect you show someone."

Good God above, send me help.

"Very well," he said, forcing cheer into his voice. "Here I go."

Seb thrust his right leg forward. As he did this, he hinged from his hips. Before he could reach for his invisible hat, his balance swung wildly out of control and he stumbled. He barely managed to swallow his profanity before straightening.

Grace's look of concern was quickly replaced by an artificial smile. "That wasn't so bad."

"You're a terrible liar."

"I am," she agreed with a sigh.

"I can master this." He spoke with far more conviction than he felt, but the stakes to this were much greater than when he'd learned how to swing a cricket bat or climb a tree.

He tried the movement again, feeling ten kinds of foolish and awkward as a wolf-hound on its hind legs. Thank God no one was watching. Or were they? Did he hear footsteps and giggling out in the hall?

Maybe the servants watched him. Maybe they didn't. He'd have to get used to an audience.

He bent forward, and pretended to doff his hat. Since he was likely going to be in rarified company, he ought to keep his bows low and respectful, so he went deep.

When he stood upright, a fillip of happiness danced through him to see admiration in Grace's eyes.

It was an addictive feeling, making her happy.

She clapped her hands together. "Much better. Although . . ." She consulted the book again as a worried look flitted across her face. "That's just for meeting people in the street. If you're going to approach a woman in a ballroom for a dance, you do the first bow, and then a ceremonial bow after."

"*Another* kind of bow?" He groaned.

"Your legs are open, and as you bend at the waist, stick your arm out to the side. Like this." She set the book down on the pianoforte and then, with a lithe economy of movement, demonstrated the bow.

As she leaned down, Seb was afforded the most spectacular glimpse down the front of her dress. Her breasts pressed in soft rises above the neckline of her sprigged muslin gown, and, feeling like the worst kind of cad, he couldn't tear his eyes from the sight.

He forced himself to look away. *Stay focused, jackass. Grace is your* friend. *She trusts you. Don't betray that.*

After mentally shaking himself, he copied her movement. To his surprise, he didn't pitch over like a drunken stevedore.

"Very good," she said as she rose back up. "You're nearly there."

He nodded, trying to suppress the pleasure that coursed along his limbs whenever she gave him even a teaspoon of praise. It dawned on him that for all the years of their friendship, they'd never actually complimented each other, as if to do so would disrupt their platonic balance. Today, they'd crossed that line, and there was no going back to their old roles.

He did and he did not want to go back.

"Is there more?" he asked.

"Perhaps we should practice how to take snuff. That's what the book says gentlemen do."

"Sorry, but no." He glanced past her, seeing the garden through the windows — and not seeing them. A hundred images coursed into his brain, and none of them were pleasant. "Tobacco serves a ceremonial and spiritual purpose for many tribes in the Americas. If I used it, it would be like stealing from them."

To his relief, she didn't look upset or irritated by his refusal. "Of course." She added with a pained expression, "Most commercial tobacco crops are tended and harvested by slaves. It's . . . repugnant."

Thank God she understood. "We'll get by without snuff."

"We will." She knotted her fingers together, and her expression turned sheepish. "I ought to mention that, in a week from today, Lord and Lady Creasy are hosting their annual garden party. It's one of the highlights of the Season. Mason will be there. And . . ." She swallowed. "You will make your debut."

It was as though someone had thrown him into a freezing lake. He couldn't catch his breath. "A week? That's not much time."

"He leaves for Greenland in less than two months, so we must work quickly." She strode to him, and when she once more placed her hand on his forearm, he felt reasonably confident that he'd never breathe again. He couldn't understand it — unlike common wisdom that said he'd grow inured to something the more he was exposed to it, he was growing *more* sensitized to her touch.

"You can do it, Sebastian." She looked up into his face, her eyes lovely and serious.

"Glad one of us believes that," he muttered.

"Our next step is a crucial one." She smiled, and his gut unclenched. "Field-work."

CHAPTER 5

With Katie in tow for the sake of propriety, Grace and Sebastian left her home and walked north to Park Square. Grace kept her hand lightly resting on Sebastian's arm as they strolled together. He felt delightfully firm beneath her gloved hand — but perhaps that could be attributed to the tension silently emanating from him.

"It's just a practice run," she assured her friend. "The stakes are very low."

"But they aren't." His voice was taut. "Even a trial of my abilities will determine the course of the next week, and whether or not this project has any chance of succeeding."

"You will," she said firmly. "Besides, hardly any hypothesis requires only one test to see whether or not it can be proven. There aren't failures in scientific methodology. Only opportunities to learn."

He made a soft exhalation through his

nose. "I've quite a lot to learn."

Was it his apprehension she felt or hers? This scheme *had* to work, and yet she was taut with concern on his behalf. She hadn't known until now how much Sebastian was eager to please — at the library, he would assist others with tasks such as fetching books from high shelves or carrying someone's stacks of tomes, but he didn't seem to extend himself overmuch.

Yet here, with this plan to become a rake, he was trying so very hard, and she ached with sympathy.

Was he fighting so fiercely to succeed for the sake of his future book — or was it for her?

It had to be for the book. If he worked this much because of *her* . . .

She banished the thought. Or she tried. A tiny voice whispered that perhaps, just perhaps, *she* was his motivation. And if that was the case, then he felt a good deal more than friendliness toward her.

He could. Did he? And did she want him to?

Lord knew, she'd revealed things about herself to him that she'd never told anyone before, not even Jane. She had not permitted herself to think about such thoughts. Yet he'd drawn confessions from her, and it had felt so natural to speak to him of the most secret chambers of her heart.

She'd had enough sense to keep from blurting of her hope for love. *That much* truth was too much. Yet perhaps he was exactly the person with whom she could be entirely vulnerable, no barriers, no protective wit. Just her and him.

She wouldn't allow herself to entertain such thoughts. They led to dangerous places, places she did not know how to navigate.

Fortunately, she didn't have time to consider that any further when they reached Park Square. The green park was ringed with stylish terraced homes in the process of being constructed along the crescent and surrounding the square. The elegant residents of Marylebone Road in their pristine and fashionable garb mixed with laborers coated with stucco, paint, and sawdust.

"I assume you have your methodology already planned," Sebastian said drily.

"That's where Katie and I are going to sit." She nodded toward a bench. "I brought a book to camouflage myself while observing as you practice your newfound skills."

Katie had already buried herself in her Lady of Dubious Quality novel and barely glanced up when her name was mentioned.

"Walk around a little," he said, "attempt to bow, that sort of thing?"

"Exactly. Even better if you approach a woman and strike up a conversation."

Other than the time in the foyer earlier today, never in the course of her friendship with Sebastian had she ever heard him say any coarse imprecation. Surely he didn't mutter *Fucking hell* under his breath just now. Surely not.

"All right."

He gave a decisive nod before stepping back. It was a shame, because there was something warm and tingly about standing near him. She'd felt it earlier in the ball-room, and she felt it now, and it wasn't entirely wanted. Over the duration of their friendship, she hadn't permitted herself responsiveness to his physical self. But there was no denying it now.

"I still don't have a walking stick," he said, "and grabbing a branch from one of these plane trees is likely considered gauche."

"Do your best. And good luck."

She walked quickly toward the bench, barely aware of the pleasant spring after-noon, or the sounds of construction, or indeed much of anything at all except nervous anticipation. It wasn't unlike direct-ing a play, and watching the performance

108

from the wings. There was nothing she could do but watch, and hope.

Their afternoon efforts had been . . . not quite what she'd anticipated. But everything had to have a beginning, and a rocky start was to be expected. Again, he *tried* so hard. She couldn't help but be touched by how earnestly he was working, and the way in which he threw himself fully into the project. For all his easygoing manner, Sebastian had a core of determination and perseverance. He didn't give up.

And if she was being honest with herself, it wasn't entirely difficult to look at him. She'd known it years ago and she most decisively knew it to be so now. True, he hadn't quite mastered the dashing air of a rake, but she hadn't been able to stop herself from observing the pull of fabric across his shoulders and legs. As if beneath his clothing, gentle and thoughtful Sebastian Holloway possessed the body of an athlete, lean and taut with muscle.

Come to think of it, in the past, he'd mentioned football and cricket matches and other physical endeavors. She'd never fully understood how such activities could reap such delightful benefits. Now she knew.

Certainly, her more primal self had taken notice. And liked what it saw.

He's your friend. Don't be rude.

Grace lowered herself onto the bench. Katie sat at the other end of the bench, her nose buried in her novel. From her reticule, Grace produced a slim treatise on the reproductive behavior of lobsters — which wasn't precisely in her area of study, but she had heard very good things about the treatise's author, a fellow female naturalist.

Despite the quality of the writing, Grace barely saw the words marching across the page. Instead, her focus honed in on Sebastian, who seemed to be preparing to enter a pugilism bout as he stood at the head of a path.

He tipped his head from side to side and swung his arms in wide arcs before shaking out his hands, and jumping up and down, landing lightly on the balls of his feet.

A passing nanny with a pram gave him wide berth, and a bewhiskered gentleman immediately turned and walked hurriedly in the opposite direction.

Sebastian appeared not to notice. But after a few moments of this, he seemed as though he had properly loosened his muscles. And then he began to walk.

He moved in the deliberate, stylized way that the guide had instructed. His feet were pointed, his shoulders back, while each movement carried a purposeful elegance. His motion verged on languid, precisely how the book had instructed. A dancing master would have been proud, had Sebastian been his student.

He executed a flawlessly elaborate bow to a trio of gentlemen, and a glow of satisfaction spread through her.

All the work they had done earlier in the afternoon came to fruition. He was doing exactly what he was supposed to do.

Except . . .

Anxiety chewed on Grace's insides, banishing her sense of ease. Everyone who espied Sebastian looked at him as though he'd recently fled from Bedlam. People skirted around him or walked to other paths so that they didn't have to encounter him.

Was something wrong with the book we used? Was our approach flawed?

Oh, God. No.

Sebastian stopped in front of a young lady, also accompanied by her maid, and proceeded to bow so low his nose nearly scraped the gravel. He was near enough to Grace that she could hear him.

"A most beauteous afternoon to you, lady fair," he said in a strange, nasal voice. "Indeed, mine eyes consider themselves blessed to look upon your countenance."

The lady's eyes went wide. She clutched her shawl tightly around herself, as if for protection. A strangled laugh escaped her maid before the servant said, "Come along, miss."

She herded her charge away like two lambs narrowly escaping the butcher's knife.

The crushed look on Sebastian's face struck deep in Grace's heart. His shoulders bowed and he shook his head slowly in what appeared to be weary resignation.

Grace leapt up from her bench intending to go to him, but before she could, a man of exceptionally striking features strode forward. The newcomer was nearly as tall as Sebastian, but the quality of his clothing was much finer. There was something vaguely familiar about him.

"What the deuce was that, Holloway?" the man demanded.

Sebastian groaned. "You saw that?"

"Most of it. Thought I was going to have to shove a stick between your teeth to keep you from biting off your own tongue."

"Here, now," Grace said hotly, coming to stand in front of the two men. She set her hands on her hips. "No need to be insulting — whoever you are."

Hot indignation pulsed along her veins. It mattered little that the man in question was

112

clearly a wealthy gentleman, or the possessor of startling good looks. He couldn't mock Sebastian.

"Rotherby," Sebastian said on an exhale, "I mean, Your Grace, may I present Lady Grace Wyatt? Grace, this is the Duke of Rotherby."

The Duke*? Oh, dear.*

No wonder he looked familiar. She'd been introduced to him years ago during her come out, and occasionally crossed his path at various social functions her parents forced her to attend.

She dipped into a curtsy. Perhaps manners could salvage the situation. "Your Grace."

"Lady Grace." The duke nodded. "I'd say it's a pleasure, but I'm rather alarmed by the state of my friend's health. We may need to call for a leech."

"No need." Looking spent, Sebastian dragged himself away to lean against a plane tree. "There's nothing wrong with my physical health. But my mental state has taken a drubbing. Especially my pride."

Both Grace and the duke moved toward Sebastian.

"I'm sure we only need more practice," she said.

"Practice doing what?" Rotherby demanded. "Terrifying the local populace? If that was your intent, you've done a brilliant job."

Sebastian gazed at her cautiously. "Should I tell him?"

"Do you trust him?" she asked.

"Is he standing right here so there's no need to speak of him in the third person?" the duke added.

Ignoring him, Sebastian said, "He's one of my oldest friends. Kept me safe from the worst bullies at Eton. He's trustworthy."

Well — she couldn't take issue with anyone who had protected young Sebastian from harassment. "I have faith in your judgment."

Concisely, Sebastian explained to Rotherby what he and Grace attempted. She fought to keep from wincing when Sebastian came to the part about her lack of cachet in Society . . . but then, the duke was part of that world, and already knew what a nonentity she was within its confines.

No wonder she liked it so much better in the field. No one judged her. No one expected her to be someone she was not, or change to fit an ideal she didn't value. There was only dispassionate Nature, who didn't give a fig about things like *ladies' accomplishments.*

"Fredericks, the naturalist?" Rotherby asked.

"The same, Your Grace," she said.

"Not a bad fellow," the duke mused. "So that . . . *display* I just witnessed . . . *that's* what you've determined a Society gentleman and rake does?"

"We found it in a book," Sebastian said.

"Was it by chance the *Domesday Book*?"

"It belonged to my father when he was making his entrée into Society," Grace replied curtly. "Given the wear on its pages, it appears that he'd made good use of it. Surely manners cannot change so much in that time."

"Forty years in London Society is a millennium. But neither of you understand that." Rotherby looked back and forth between her and Sebastian, an expression of disbelief writ plainly on his face. "It's the blind leading the bespectacled."

"We can find other books," Sebastian said, a hint of impatience in his voice. "Recent ones. Surely McKinnon's has an ample stock. All we need to do is a bit more research."

Grace nodded in agreement. "Research solves everything."

The duke pinched the bridge of his nose as he squeezed his eyes shut. "Good. God."

115

He exhaled jaggedly before lowering his hand and opening his eyes. "I'll just have to clear my schedule. That way we can get to work as soon as possible. Time's slipping away."

Grace shot Sebastian a befuddled look. "Forgive me, Your Grace, but what do you mean by 'We can get to work'?"

"It's patently obvious," Rotherby said with deliberate patience. "You both are extremely intelligent when it comes to scholarly knowledge, but utter naïfs when it comes to navigating the treacherous London social scene. You need a guide. Someone who knows every twist and turn of the labyrinth."

"*You,* Rotherby?" Sebastian's mouth opened in shock. "That's not necessary."

"It most assuredly *is* necessary. You're my friend, and like hell will I let you founder and drown." Rotherby looked at Sebastian with wry fondness, before pulling a timepiece from his waistcoat pocket. "I'm due home to meet with my men of business. But I shall see you both tomorrow at two o'clock. Bond Street, outside Walton's tobacconist shop."

He said this as a command, not a request. Not much of a surprise, given his lofty status.

116

"Certain about this, Rotherby?" Sebastian asked.

"We're asking quite a lot of you," Grace noted.

"If what I witnessed today is any indicator of your trajectory," the duke said grimly, "then it's not a matter of certainty. It's necessity."

CHAPTER 6

As Seb approached Walton's tobacconist shop on Bond Street, a small gathering of gentlemen and a couple of women had collected around a single individual standing outside. They all wore what they likely hoped were ingratiating smiles, all their attention focused on one man in particular.

Rotherby.

His friend gazed coolly over the heads of the people encircling him, but when he caught sight of Seb, his look brightened.

"Here now," Rotherby said dismissively to the crowd, "find somewhere else to be."

"Of course, Your Grace."

"Another time, Your Grace." And so forth, as the group thinned, until only Seb and Rotherby remained in front of the shop's window.

"Poor blighter." Seb shook Rotherby's hand. "If it wasn't for your blinding good looks, colossal political influence, and inestimable wealth, I might pity you."

"Complaining sounds churlish," his friend said and exhaled. "But, God, what a massive pain in the arse. Ah, Lady Grace."

The duke bowed as Grace emerged from the crowds thronging the street. Her maid trailed behind her, and Grace actually had to guide the servant down the sidewalk, since the maid walked with her nose buried in a book.

"Your Grace." She curtsied. "Sebastian." She spoke his name with a gratifying amount of warmth. He smiled in response.

"Do call me Rotherby, Lady Grace," the duke said. "It's what my friends do."

"Of course, Rotherby." She looked pleased by the lack of formality between them. Glancing sympathetically at Seb, she asked, "Are you very weary from yesterday's debacle?"

Seb snorted. "I've faced greater indignities." He shot a glance at Rotherby. "Do *not* tell her any tales about me at Eton."

"I remain silent as a ghost." Rotherby held up his hands. "But there was this one time when I'd dared Holloway to steal everyone's spoons before breakfast and he —"

"Enough." Seb clapped his hand over Rotherby's mouth. "We're here for a lesson, not to recount my youthful foibles."

"But there were so many," his friend said, his words muffled by Seb's palm.

"Because *you* and the others goaded me into them. Otherwise, I would have been a model student."

Grace's eyes sparkled as she looked back and forth between Seb and Rotherby. "We needn't have a lesson. You two are much more fascinating than a dull shopping street."

"It's something we — *I* — must do." Seb made a show of reluctantly pulling his hand away from silencing Rotherby. "How do we proceed?"

"Follow me." The duke held out his arm for Grace, and as she took it, a tiny sizzle of something hot and barbed worked its way along Seb's spine.

The deuce?

It was entirely illogical for Seb to feel anything that resembled jealousy. First of all, Rotherby's gesture had been one of politeness, devoid of any romantic intention. Secondly, and this was most important, if Grace did fancy the duke even a fraction, she could do whatever she pleased with her feelings.

Shaking his head at his own irrational emotions, Seb followed Rotherby and Grace across the street to a crowded tearoom.

Elegant gentlemen and ladies packed the establishment, filling the tables and standing wherever they could find room.

"No room at the inn," Seb said, narrowly avoiding an elbow in the stomach from one of the patrons.

Rotherby merely donned that slightly superior look he sometimes sported. No sooner did he take three steps into the shop than a tall East Indian man in pristinely tailored clothing appeared.

"Your Grace," the man said, bowing, "welcome to my shop. I am Rohit Mohan. Your table awaits."

He gestured to an empty table by the window, perfectly situated for anyone to watch the fashionable multitudes passing by. A small handwritten sign atop the table proudly declared that it was reserved for His Grace, the Duke of Rotherby, and anyone who had the temerity to try to sit there would be summarily escorted from the premises, never to be permitted entry again.

God — how different Rotherby was from Seb. How charmed his life seemed. But Seb knew the price his friend paid for such attention. Better to dwell in relative obscurity than carry the burdens of prestige and popularity.

Rotherby led them to the table, and Seb hurried forward to pull out Grace's chair. He wasn't *entirely* hopeless when it came to proper behavior.

Once they had all been seated — with Grace's maid wedged in at a nearby table — Mr. Mohan took their orders. Seb pulled a notebook and pencil from his pocket.

"Ever the good scholar," Rotherby noted wryly.

"You broker deals in Parliament without batting an eyelash," Seb answered, "but studying . . . that's *my* métier."

"He isn't the only one who came prepared." Grace produced a small, leather-covered journal from her reticule.

She and Seb shared a smile, and he tried not to notice how the curve of her lips made little curlicues of pleasure dance through him.

"What you two did yesterday." Rotherby shook his head. "Even when that book was published, it wouldn't have served your purpose. You cannot learn the proper methods for being a rake from anything written."

"Because it's a secret," Seb guessed.

"Because it comes from here." Rotherby tapped his hand on his stomach.

"Instinct," Grace said. "Like a tortoise retreats into its shell when threatened. No

one tells it what to do. It just knows."

The duke nodded. "The moment you try to quantify it, it slips away."

Seb slapped his hands on the table as frustration bubbled. "So our task's impossible."

"Not so." Rotherby held up a finger. "There's observation, too. Surprised you didn't think of that — man of the sciences that you are. And lady of the sciences," he added with an inclination of his head toward Grace.

Seb exhaled, loosening the grip of his vexation. His friend was right — there were things one learned only through nonverbal, unrecorded cues. Numerous cultures possessed rudimentary written systems, and in some cases there were societies that had no written language at all. And yet they all functioned. They all thrived.

And, if Seb didn't clamp down on his impatience, he'd fail not only himself but Grace, as well. It would be gratifying to have a book published — but *her* happiness was as stake.

"Enlighten us, Wise Old Rotherby." He picked up his pencil and held it ready.

His friend bristled. "*Old?* We're both four and thirty, for God's sake."

"But you've been walking this road for a

long, long time." Seb shook his head sadly. "And it shows."

"You rotter," Rotherby growled. "I ought to shove a teapot up your —"

"Children," Grace said with the timeless voice of a woman who must, yet again, control unruly boys. "Can we focus, please?"

All three of them looked out the window, watching the passing traffic. Here and there were servants or laborers, but for the most part, the crowd consisted of finely garbed men and women making their way leisurely up and down the sidewalks.

"We're early enough in the day that women are not looked at askance for being on Bond Street," Rotherby said.

"Because of the prostitutes," Grace said solemnly.

Mr. Mohan coughed in surprise as he approached the table. The teapot and cups on the tray he carried rattled, and he just managed to keep a grip on the bamboo handles. He managed to pour them all cups of steaming tea before retreating to someplace where, most likely, genteel young women didn't openly discuss harlots.

"How do you know about that?" Seb asked. He couldn't quite find it in himself to feel appalled. Sexuality was discussed much more frankly in countless cultures. It

didn't make sense why, in England especially, raising women to be completely
ignorant about sex was something to be
desired.

Still, his cheeks did feel a bit hot to hear
her blithely discussing prostitutes.

"Overheard Charlie," she said with a
shrug, "talking with one of his friends, back
when my brother was unmarried and something of a buck. It's quite interesting what
men discuss when they believe themselves
to be alone."

Rotherby himself looked a trifle unsettled.
"We needn't concern ourselves with the
demimondaines and sporting hotels —"

"You mean *brothels,*" Grace noted. Her
pencil moved across the page of her journal
as she repeated the word.

"Don't write that down," Rotherby exclaimed. "It's . . . er . . ."

"Not germane to the subject," Seb filled
in.

Before Grace could object, the duke
plowed on. "In any event, I would ask you
to take note of the men outside, and how
they interact with the ladies. Not the older
gentlemen who've settled into a comfortable middle age. The younger set."

"The ones with the tightest breeches,"
Grace noted. Her pencil moved in rapid

strokes. "Showing off their thighs in an evident courtship display. Very common within the animal kingdom."

"Are you *sketching*?" Seb asked. "Male *thighs*?"

She rolled her eyes. "Of course. We have to use every available avenue to record our findings." Grace held up her journal, and, true enough, she'd marked the paper with very accurate drawings of male femoral regions. She hadn't neglected the crotch areas, either.

Seb glanced down at his own pantaloons. They had been perfectly serviceable not but five minutes ago. Perhaps a trifle faded, and not quite fashionable, but they did little to highlight his own physique. He looked like a collection of tree branches swaddled in wool — a far cry from the strapping blokes outside in buckskin breeches.

"Yes," Rotherby said lowly, "a visit to my tailor is definitely on the agenda." He waved toward the men outside. "Some of these chaps are trying too hard. They're aping the Bond Street Roll and styling themselves like dandies. Pay no attention to them," he added in a high-handed tone.

"Why not?" Grace demanded.

"Observe," the duke said, flicking his finger in the direction of two men, one in a green waistcoat and the other in a pair of polished, tasseled boots.

As Seb and Grace looked on, a pretty young lady neared the pair. The men quickly pasted smirks on their faces, as if they were possessors of a secret about the woman that she herself could never know.

"Good God, their faces," Seb noted under his breath. "As if anyone couldn't see what they're doing."

"What *are* they doing?" Rotherby asked pointedly.

"It's obvious, isn't it? They're trying to inflate their own social value while simultaneously diminishing her. Sorry," he added with a deliberately condescending look to Rotherby. "Making themselves out to be grand so she feels small."

"I know what you meant," his friend snapped.

"With the intention that she will seek to raise her sense of worth by associating with them." Grace sent Rotherby a patronizing glance. She spoke to him with an exaggeratedly slow and loud voice. "They want her to feel special if they talk to her."

"I *know* what you meant, too," Rotherby grumbled. "I did go to Oxford, for God's sake. I'm not a completely overbred ninny."

Grace caught Seb's eye, and they both

suppressed their laughter. It wasn't fair to torment poor Rotherby — he *was* doing them a favor — but it was hugely entertaining to dent his ducal pride, and sharing the teasing with Grace made it even better.

"I see what you two are doing," Rotherby said with annoyance. "And it's fortunate I'm a man with a very long fuse or else I'd chase the both of you out into the street."

"I run very quickly," Seb countered.

"And having a brother makes me an expert in dodging a grumpy older man," Grace added.

"Four and thirty is *not* old! To blazes with both of you." Clearly irate, Rotherby started to rise, but when Grace lifted her hand in a placating gesture, Seb took hold of his friend's jacket cuff.

"We'll stop," Grace said at the same time Seb insisted, "Here, now, we're sorry."

Looking somewhat mollified, Rotherby sat back down. "Don't forget, I have six estates managers who report to me. Not to mention I've got Liverpool's ear, so we can stop with the *Rotherby's a Buffoon* tomfoolery."

"Look outside," Grace said, thankfully drawing attention to something other than mollifying Rotherby. "The woman just passed right by the dandies. Good lass."

The two would-be rakes appeared momentarily crushed by being ignored, but only for a moment before donning their condescending expressions once more and swaggering down the street.

"A failure in every way," Rotherby declared. "Too much affectation. Too desperate."

One of the tearoom employees set a plate of cakes and little sandwiches on the table. "With Mr. Mohan's compliments," she said. "The cakes are baked fresh daily by Catton's." She curtsied and backed away.

"Then what *do* we look for?" Grace asked, picking up a sandwich.

"All well and good to tell us what not to do," Seb agreed. He took a bite of cake. "Somebody out there has to be an example of a true and successful rake."

"There." Rotherby's gaze skimmed back to the street. "The bloke in the burgundy coat. He knows what he's doing."

Curious, Seb turned his attention to the man in question. He moved easily, without exaggerated movement, but possessing sleek agility that carried with it an animal quality. Seb couldn't quite determine what contributed to the man's air, only that it subtly advertised erotic possibility. Perhaps it was his upright but not rigid posture. Perhaps it was the minute forward tilt to his pelvis,

129

drawing attention there.

This man's smile wasn't a superior smirk. It was subtle and aware, as if he had things planned that anybody would eagerly agree to.

By the strictest societal standards, he wasn't precisely handsome. It appeared as though he'd broken his nose years ago, and his chin was slightly soft. But *he* felt utterly confident in his looks. And that translated to an allure that caught every woman's attention.

When he tipped his hat to a passing woman, she fluttered her eyelashes at him and fussed with her shawl.

They both stopped right in front of the window, and while the glass muffled the sound of their conversation, whatever the gentleman said to her was well-received.

"Damn." Seb leaned forward. "Can't hear what he's saying."

"It doesn't matter what the words are," Rotherby said. "Could be talking about biscuits or quizzing glasses. All that matters is how he's looking at her."

"Like she's the only woman in existence," Grace murmured.

Rotherby rapped his knuckles on the tabletop. "Exactly so."

A moment passed, and the man moved

on, but the lady remained for a minute, gazing after him wistfully.

"Shouldn't he have stayed?" Grace asked. "He might have made a conquest." She shuddered. "Ugh. What a dreadful word."

Seb shook his head. "As though sex is a battle with one victor and one who's been defeated."

"Some rakes will go for the quick seduction," Rotherby said dismissively. "It's a false equivalency between the number of women they bed and their value as a man. Selfishness and stupidity, the lot of it. No, a true and good rake promises that every moment with him gives pleasure. Not merely what happens in the bedchamber, but all the moments leading up to it."

Seb wrote all of this down verbatim. It was all so damned fascinating. "Sex unites mind as well as body." He'd known this to some extent, but to hear Rotherby, a man who'd had many lovers, express it thusly made it much more clear.

"The power of the imagination," Grace said with a nod. "Of course."

She and Seb shared a grin as though they had just discovered how to transform lead into gold. Nothing was better than a discovery. It was almost — but not quite — as good as sex.

Rotherby devoured a small iced cake before dusting crumbs off his hands. "Very good. You're both learning. Now it's time to put theory into practice."

CHAPTER 7

A light rain began to fall just as Seb climbed into Rotherby's carriage. He looked over his shoulder, concerned that Grace might get caught in the weather, but she was nowhere to be seen.

"Don't distress yourself." Rotherby clapped a hand on Seb's shoulder. "I saw her get into her own carriage. She got out of the rain just in time."

"Ah. Good." Seb exhaled and took the rear-facing seat, while his friend sat opposite him.

Rotherby knocked on the roof of the carriage and a moment later, they were off, heading toward Grace's home. She'd instructed Rotherby to drive straight back to the stables so he and Seb could enter her home through the back, just in case any inquisitive neighbors caught sight of a ducal carriage outside.

Silence reigned for a few minutes.

Thoughts churning like surf, Seb mulled over the lessons Rotherby had imparted back at the tearoom. The role of being a rake — of rakehood itself — seemed to come from within, from the intangible quality of masculine confidence, which was something that couldn't be taught, only lived and experienced.

Seb had gone to bed with exactly five women in the course of his thirty-four years. His last lover had been the widow of a friend. It had been a comfortable, if not especially passionate, affair. Seb and Mary had amicably ended things three months ago when she'd decided she wanted to look for a new husband — a man who could comfortably support her, since her widow's portion was a meager one. Knowing that he could not meet her financial expectations, Seb had stopped visiting her bed.

She was engaged now, to a mercer. He and Mary had crossed paths in Kensington, and nodded politely at one another. No tears. No rage or fury. No pleas to resume their affair. It was all quite . . . civil.

God. His sexual history was exceedingly tame, barely containing the makings of a Lothario. But he'd have to find manly assurance within himself . . . somehow.

"How long have you been friends with

Lady Grace?" Rotherby asked abruptly.

Seb furrowed his brow, surfacing from the depths of his thoughts. "About four years, I believe, give or take a few months."

"You don't know the date specifically?"

"Why should I?"

"I thought bookish men kept journals."

A corner of Seb's mouth turned up at the word *bookish*. That was one way of describing him. "Observations and notes of an anthropological nature. That's what I record in my journal. Chronicling my own life would make for dull reading." He peered suspiciously at his friend. "Why would you ask about the date I met Grace?"

"Women like to know these things," Rotherby said with an airy wave of his hand.

Seb nodded. He might know more about kinship structures and the societal configuration of a barter economy, but he could certainly trust Rotherby when it came to what women of British Society wanted. His friend was a favorite of women, even back in their Eton days, when young lasses from the village would sneak him notes and posies.

"I do remember that she was wearing a blue dress with a peach-colored ribbon sash," Seb mused, thinking back to the day he'd met Grace. "She was smiling over a book she was reading, and then she asked if she could borrow a pencil because she'd forgotten hers and was too shy to ask the librarian if there was one she could borrow."

"Did you give her a pencil?"

"Yes," Seb said after a moment. The day unfolded in his memory like a Jacob's ladder toy. "But it was my only one, so I tried to memorize the notes to write them down later."

"Anything else you recall about that day?" Rotherby asked.

He'd stammered at her. He remembered that. An attractive woman whom he didn't know had struck up a conversation with him, and he'd been his usual anxious self, worrying what to say and how to say it, and if she could tell how nervous he was speaking to her, with an added dose of apprehension that she might walk away or even laugh.

Yet a curious thing had happened whilst he'd fumbled for words: she'd gone on speaking in a friendly and warm voice, as if she didn't mind at all that he was tongue-tied. When she'd asked him a question about his own field of study, she'd waited patiently for him to get past his faltering, giving him smiles and nods of encouragement.

He hadn't seen judgment in her gaze, only

136

amiable curiosity to learn more about him. And within minutes, he'd forgotten all about his anxieties. He could talk to her, be himself, without fear.

"She told me about a particularly fascinating creature called a skink, which is primarily found in the southern parts of the Continent."

His friend's brow furrowed. "What the hell is a skink?"

"A variety of reptile. That's what she studies. Reptiles. Amphibians, too."

"Not something darling and cuddlesome, like . . . I don't know . . . puppies?"

Seb snorted. "I think there's enough research done in the field of puppies. Reptiles and amphibians are her area of expertise."

"Why?"

He blinked. "I . . . don't know."

Rotherby sat back, folding his arms across his chest. "So you know all this about her." He narrowed his eyes. "Do you have romantic designs on her?"

Alarm shot through Seb and he sat up straight, nearly slamming his head into the carriage's ceiling.

He sputtered in indignation. "We're friends. That's all."

"You've never talked about her."

"It wasn't relevant to the discussion." Was that truly the case? Even from the beginning, he'd prized his friendship with her, and kept it close, as if discussing it might somehow rob it of its specialness. He couldn't help repeating, "We're merely friends."

His alarm didn't quiet when Rotherby gazed at him with a look of patent disbelief.

"Men and women can be friends," Seb declared hotly, "without things becoming romantic or sexual."

"True," Rotherby said, inclining his head. "However. Lady Grace is also intelligent, amusing, and pleasing to the eye. Don't you think so?"

". . . I . . . ." God, how long was the distance between Bond Street and Grace's home?

He glanced at the door of the carriage. Jumping from a moving vehicle wasn't one of his talents, but a person could always learn a new skill. The rain fell harder, drumming on the top of the carriage, but Seb didn't worry about getting wet or muddy. He just wanted out of this bloody vehicle.

Rotherby said with a smirk, "The degree of your alarm makes me believe that you *do* consider her intelligent, amusing, and pleasing to the eye, as well."

"I might." Damn . . . was it true? He jolted with unwelcome understanding. "All I desire is keeping her categorized as a friend. In any case," he added quickly, "that's what *she* wants."

Praise be, the carriage finally slowed, and a moment later, the footman opened the door to announce, "We've arrived, Your Grace."

As Seb and Rotherby dashed across the stable yard, Grace opened the kitchen door. She waved them inside, calling above the rain, "Come in quickly before you're soaked."

Despite quickening their pace, both he and Rotherby collected enough precipitation to leave small puddles in the kitchen hallway. Seb almost offered to clean up the mess himself, but his mother always admonished him for trying to do the servants' work for them. It didn't matter that he'd grown up with a houseful of people paid to do his family's bidding — he could never acclimatize himself to having someone else do a task he could do on his own.

"The servants have been sworn to silence, with a good deal of financial inducement to ensure it." Grace waved them toward the stairs leading from the servants' area of the house into the family's living area. "We'll have tea in just a few moments. Unless you prefer something stronger. Claret? Whiskey? I think that's what gentlemen drink."

"Alcohol will cloud my judgment." Seb followed her up the staircase. He deliberately kept his head down to stare at his boots rather than repeat his mistake of looking at Grace's figure.

"In that case," Rotherby declared, "a dram of whiskey for all of us — that is, if you'll join us, Lady Grace."

"Do ladies drink whiskey in mixed company?" Seb asked.

"Perhaps they don't," Grace said, "but I will." They reached the top of the stairs, then stepped into the corridor outside the ballroom. She murmured to a footman a request for liquor and three glasses. The servant nodded and disappeared to carry out her bidding.

She moved on to the ballroom, candles lit within to hold back the rain's gloom. A cheerful fire burned in the fireplace at one end of the chamber, and a trio of chairs had been assembled close to it.

"It gets so terrifically cold in here when it's dreary outside." She stood in front of the fire, warming her hands. "But the amphibians adore this weather, so I can't complain."

"Holloway told me you study reptiles and the like," Rotherby said, also coming to the fire but putting a respectful distance between himself and Grace.

Which left Seb with a less respectful position between them. He wedged his body into the gap, conscious of how little space separated his giant feet from the hem of her dress. He was like some creature from folklore, carved of rude clay and stone, lumbering beside a wise princess.

She smiled up at him, and his heart leapt into his throat. With difficulty, he swallowed it back down.

"Yes," she said. "I'm what is now known as a herpetologist."

Rotherby started. "You study . . . *herpes*? The disease?"

"Not herpes! Herpetology — the study of reptiles and amphibians."

"They share the same root word," Seb added.

"Which means *to creep*," Grace said.

Rotherby made a face. "Slimy creatures that no one loves."

"*I* love them," Grace said with a smile. She sat down in one of the wingback chairs, and Seb and Rotherby followed suit. A servant entered the room, bearing a tray that held three glasses filled with amber liquid. She took one and Seb and Rotherby did the same. "It's true that many amphibians have moist skins. Frogs and toads secrete mucus to keep their skins wet in order for them to properly breathe."

Goddamn it, but she's lovely.

The thought leapt into Seb's mind as he watched Grace animatedly describing *mucus,* of all things.

But once the words had silently sounded in his head, he couldn't unthink them. Because she *was* lovely, and simply looking at her when she talked of the creatures she loved to study made his chest tight and his pulse kick.

Oh, hell.

This was what came of spending so much time with her. His captivation with her grew from minute to minute.

"Reptiles and amphibians are wonderful animals," she continued, her face lighting up as she spoke. "Just because they don't have fur or adorable faces, people hate them. And Linnaeus didn't help anything, either." She scowled. "He called them 'abhorrent,' said they were filthy and fierce and offensive."

"Clearly," Seb said on a growl, "Linnaeus's biases shaped what ought to be perfectly objective science."

142

"What's perfectly objective?" Grace asked. She took a sip of her drink. "Humans are flawed devices. Everything we see, think, and do is colored by individual preferences, dislikes, and fractured logic." She leaned forward, the firelight shining brilliantly in her eyes. "Anyone who claims there is such a thing as objective truth is wrong."

"My gut churns when I read Westerners' accounts of other societies." His jaw firmed with distaste. "Many of them drip with a sense of cultural and racial superiority — and they twist science to defend abhorrent ideas and practices."

"Beg pardon," Rotherby drawled, "but are we going to turn Holloway into a rake, or are we going to hold a symposium?"

Damn — Seb had almost forgotten their objective. As always, their conversation enthralled him. He didn't want it to end.

Clearly, his disappointment showed in his face because she chuckled as she looked at him fondly.

"That's all right, Sebastian," Grace said. "We'll talk at length later."

"Looking forward to it." His friends were fine men, and good men, but even fellow intellectual Rowe could never quite follow him down the winding paths of his theoretical musings. It was the same with the other scholars at the Benezra Library. Where his mind wandered, they couldn't follow.

The only person he knew who kept pace with him was . . . Grace. There was no one like her.

"If we're done with the academic portion of the afternoon," Rotherby announced, "it's time for Holloway to attempt what we saw on Bond Street. And," he added, looking pointedly at Seb, "you're going to practice on Lady Grace."

Grace didn't miss the way color fled Sebastian's cheeks. He swallowed audibly.

"Here?" he asked, his voice tight. "Now?"

"Yes to both," Rotherby said. "You've less than a week to become a rake. Time is critical."

When Sebastian opened his mouth, then shut it again without speaking, looking utterly horrified, she stood and cleared the knot of chagrin from her throat. Both Sebastian and Rotherby launched to their feet.

"It's merely flirtation with me, Sebastian. Rotherby isn't asking us to copulate on the ballroom floor."

She heard the sharpness in her voice, but, sod it, he seemed appalled by merely the notion of pretending to find her attractive.

"It's only . . ." He dragged his hand

144

through his hair. "Performing for an audience isn't my ideal situation. Easier for me to be overlooked."

Her heart softened. She'd witnessed what happened to him when he was around people he didn't know, and while it was painful to watch, it surely felt worse for him. On top of that, she understood from experience that when she feared something, merely thinking about it was almost worse than the thing itself.

"We'll take it step by step," she said. "Just a bit at a time, so you can become accustomed to having people's attention."

"And you'll need to be comfortable having everyone's eyes on you," Rotherby said, setting his hands on his hips. "We want everything you do to be seen by Society — especially Mason Fredericks."

Grace threw the duke a sharp look that said clearly, *You aren't helping.* Sebastian needed patience, not pressure.

Sebastian rubbed at his chin, appearing to mull over what both she and Rotherby had said.

"You might not believe in yourself," she said with an encouraging smile, "but *I* believe in you."

He drew in a long, ragged breath before straightening to his full height — as if drawing confidence from her words. "Let's launch this ship."

Thank you, Grace mouthed silently. A slight flush stained his cheeks, and his smile was adorably boyish. And though she'd always liked to see him smile, now she anticipated his grins as if awaiting a much-desired gift. Perhaps she could make him smile more if she told him jokes. There was also tickling . . . but she'd never heard anyone say, *"Thank you for tickling me."*

She'd have to find other ways of enticing smiles from Sebastian. Her belly fluttered at the prospect.

"Do I walk?" he asked Rotherby.

"The less you think about walking the better." The duke chopped his hand through the air. "Put it out of your mind. What I want from you is to practice *attitude.*"

"How does one do that?" she asked.

"The hell if I know," Sebastian exclaimed.

Rotherby strode to Sebastian and placed his hands on Sebastian's shoulders. "Come into the room as if you're about to walk into that library where you go. Do only that. Nothing more."

"All right." Sebastian exhaled, then stepped out of the ballroom. A moment later, he returned to the chamber, walking easily, his chin up, limbs neither too loose

146

nor too stiff.

"You didn't duck your head or shuffle your feet," she said approvingly. "It was a perfectly fine entrance."

Sebastian's expression brightened. She added to her mental tally of his smiles, which she'd happily review later. It wasn't so much that his grins made him more handsome — he was already attractive — but she palpably felt his joy, his pleasure with existence.

"*Perfectly fine* is not acceptable," the duke said, and Sebastian's face clouded. She wanted to kick Rotherby.

Little knowing she wanted to do him bodily harm, Rotherby said, "Observe me enter the room." He tugged on his beautifully fitted coat and waistcoat before striding past Sebastian into the hallway.

Sebastian stood beside Grace as they both awaited Rotherby. "I don't know what I'm watching for," he whispered to her.

"A display of dominance, perhaps?" she whispered back. "Puffed chest? His skin changing color?"

"That *would* be rather incredible. Rotherby inflating and turning bright purple."

"He could set a new fashion."

"Quiet, both of you," the duke barked

from the hallway.

Grace clamped her lips together, but she and Sebastian couldn't quite suppress their snickers.

Their laughter died when Rotherby strolled into the ballroom. It wasn't a walk so much as a sensuous prowl, his shoulders rolling with each step, his legs striding with leisurely purpose. Even the rake from Bond Street seemed clumsy by comparison.

No wonder the scandal rags were full of tales of Rotherby's amorous conquests. Grace wasn't attracted to him in the slightest, and merely watching the duke walk made her fuss with her hair and tug on the neckline of her dress.

"Ah," Sebastian said.

"That's . . . quite different." Because she hadn't been able to look away from the duke. He'd captured every ounce of her focus. "I *felt* your assurance in yourself. That's the difference, isn't it? Confidence in oneself."

"Naturally, he feels confident," Sebastian exclaimed. "He's got pots of money and the face of a Renaissance painting."

"Money doesn't signify," Rotherby said with a wave.

"But one's attractiveness *does*." Sebastian walked to the duke and poked his finger into the other man's chest. "That's indisputable. *You* are handsome. *I* am not."

Rotherby looked with disbelief between Sebastian and Grace, his expression silently communicating, *Are you hearing this, too?*

She shrugged helplessly. The mysteries of the human mind confounded her, but *Sebastian's* mind was even more complex.

"Good God, Holloway," the duke burst out. "Are there no mirrors in your home? Do you avoid looking in shop windows? Is your vision that bad?"

"My own reflection is uninteresting to me," Sebastian answered.

"Tell him," Rotherby said to Grace.

Panic skittered down her spine as Sebastian looked at her with a mixture of bafflement and expectation. She could *throttle* the duke for putting her in such an awkward position. But . . . Sebastian needed to know.

"You're —" She drew in a breath. *Here I go.* "Extremely attractive."

He frowned. "I am?"

"You are," she said as her cheeks went up in flames. "Don't you know that?"

"I don't know why I would."

The utter perplexity in his voice wrung her heart. A surge of anger moved through her, and she wished she could find his father to give the man a good shaking. John Holloway had implanted in his son such terrible doubt that no matter what Sebastian encountered later in life, regardless of who told him otherwise, he'd always believe he wasn't good enough.

"You only require a bit of barbering," the duke said. He peered closely at Sebastian. "How necessary are your spectacles?"

Sebastian brought his fingers up to rest on the wire temple of his spectacles. "Not essential. I only need them for reading, but," he added, "I wear them all the time to save myself the trouble of finding the blasted things and putting them on whenever I open a book. Lost too many pairs of spectacles that way."

"Take them off," Rotherby commanded.

" '*Please* take them off,' " Grace said with a pointed look at the duke. "I don't care if you're one of the peerage's most influential men. Rudeness is not your given right."

Sebastian coughed but did not quite hide his laughter. "About time someone deflated your balloon."

"*Please* take off your spectacles," Rotherby said grudgingly.

"Only because you asked so nicely." After a moment, Sebastian plucked them from his face. Then he gazed at her with resignation. "You see? A substantially ordinary face."

"Oh, Sebastian." Grace shook her head. She took his hand and led him to a gilt-framed mirror that would, during a ball, reflect the light of hundreds of candles. She stood him before the mirror and he beheld himself wearily. "You really cannot see it?"

"It's only me," he said.

"Dolt," Rotherby muttered.

Grace threw the duke another *This is not helpful* look before turning her attention back to Sebastian. She had to convince him, had to make him understand that he was so much more than he believed.

"You *are* handsome," she said with sincerity. "Remarkably so. With your spectacles and without them."

"You truly think so?" This was asked with genuine curiosity.

"I do. However," she added, "what's most important is your comfort. Wear the spectacles if you prefer."

Sebastian turned from the mirror. "I have a better chance of playing the rake without them, don't I, Rotherby?"

"Truthfully, yes," the duke answered.

"Then I won't wear them." Sebastian slid the glasses into his pocket, and Rotherby nodded with approval.

Gazing at Sebastian, a strange double sensation pierced Grace. He was and was not Sebastian, the friend and colleague she'd known for years. She missed him, but he was right here, with the face and form of a Viking, and she could no longer feign ignorance of him as a man. That convenient lie was unable to stand with every hour spent in his presence.

Mentally, she shook herself. Her thoughts wanted corralling, and she had to keep her focus on the goal — Mason.

"To review," Rotherby said, lifting one finger, "we know you're handsome. We know," he continued, raising another finger, "that you're intelligent. That's so, isn't it, Grace?"

She nodded. At least this she could admit without delving into perilous terrain. "Exceptionally."

Fortunately, Sebastian did not try to refute this. In the minimum, he could recognize his value when it came to his mind.

"Intelligence is considered quite attractive," the duke said.

"In men," she added wryly.

"Er, well, yes," Rotherby said. "We can discuss *that* problematic notion another time. At present, we are focusing on Holloway. He has all the attributes that are an irresistible lure to women, and to people en masse. He only has to believe that about himself." The duke turned to Sebastian and pointed at the door to the ballroom. "Come back into the chamber with the same confidence you'd present a paper to colleagues you've known for years."

Sebastian furrowed his brow. "What's the topic of the paper?"

"Does it matter?" Rotherby shot back. "Pick something."

"How about the kinship structures of the Basques people located in the Guipúzcoa province?"

"That's fine," the duke bit out.

"Or perhaps I could focus on the Vizcaya province instead —"

"Sebastian," Grace said gently. "Please. Just do it."

"Yes. Right. Fine." He flexed his hands before leaving the ballroom.

A moment later, he strode back in. His posture was upright but not stiff, his gait steady with a very slight roll. In fact, if Grace had to pick a word to describe Sebastian's walk, she'd have to say *swagger*. He *swaggered* into the ballroom, his expression full of self-assurance, and his long body beautifully displayed.

Heat rushed through her, followed immediately by cold worry.

Oh, dear.

She could *not* allow herself to develop an attraction to Sebastian. Not when he'd agreed to help her ensnare the man who perfectly matched her ideal husband.

Rotherby clapped his hands together. "Much better."

"Helps that without my spectacles," Sebastian said with a nod, "everything is a little hazy around the edges."

Good — hopefully he couldn't see the way she'd salivated at the sight of him.

"Excellent progress," the duke said. "That's how we want you entering a space from now on."

Sebastian pulled a small notebook and pencil from his coat. "Need to write all this down." His pencil moved across the page, and a crease of concentration appeared between his eyebrows.

If only she also had something to occupy her attention, something to distract her from all his handsome scholarly glory. Perhaps she could practice her pianoforte. But marching to the instrument and banging out Bach in the middle of Sebastian's rake lesson might be a trifle distracting.

"We haven't much time," Rotherby went

on once Sebastian put the notebook away, "so we'll move on to the next task. I want you to look at Grace."

Fresh panic shot through her. "Look at me?" Her voice came out in a squeak. No, no. She did *not* want him to observe her while she attempted to disguise her awareness of him. "How?"

"Permit me to demonstrate." The duke walked to her and came to a stop a close, but respectable, distance away.

He *gazed* at her. As though she was utterly fascinating. Nothing else but her mattered, his eyes told her silently.

She ought to feel dazzled . . . *Ought to.*

"Your thoughts, madam?" he asked.

"It was . . ." She considered it. ". . . moderately intriguing."

"Moderately?" Rotherby grumbled.

"Pleasant enough. I didn't feel faint, or forget that it's three more hours until supper." It was a relief, knowing that she could feel so little by way of attraction. Whatever it was she struggled with in relation to Sebastian, surely it could be mastered. It was merely a bump in the long road of their friendship. She could look at him and feel the same platonic camaraderie she'd always permitted herself.

The duke scowled, causing Sebastian to

snort. "Fine. You try it, Holloway."

Despite the assurances she'd given herself, dread jolted her. She didn't want more proof that Sebastian could affect her. "Is that necessary?"

"It is," Rotherby said. "He must practice. That's the only way for him to overcome his fear, and to gain confidence."

Blast.

She forced herself to smile encouragingly as Sebastian came forward, edging Rotherby aside.

Sebastian stood less than two feet from her. And then the world went still as he looked at her. He was motionless as he dipped his chin slightly so that he regarded her with thrilling intensity. It was as though the speed of her pulse was somehow tied to the steadiness in his gaze. The longer he looked at her, the faster her heartbeat raced.

She couldn't break from his gaze, held in place by the warmth and depth of his crystal blue eyes.

Be here with me now, he said wordlessly. *You and I exist alone together. I want to be with you and you only.*

Her fear shifted into pleasure. She fell into that pleasure without cessation, without caring if she stopped. She wanted this sensation to last forever, to be, at last, the center of someone's universe.

"How is *that,* madam?" the duke said with a hint of irritation.

"It's . . ." *Terrifying. Wonderful. Mystifying.* ". . . Nice."

Rotherby clapped his hand on Sebastian's shoulder, who seemed to surface from the depth of his focus. "*Nice* is better than nothing. Felicitations, old man. You're well on your way to becoming a rake."

"Thank you," Sebastian said, but his voice sounded far away. As though he was still in that secret, special place with Grace, occupied by him and her.

She had to walk away. Had to go to the window and look out at empty space to collect herself, because all that she knew or understood was changing.

Sebastian was her friend. But their friendship had slipped its bonds and now ran free in the open field of possibility. Yet she had no idea where it would go, and her own heart offered no guidance or restraint.

This might be a problem.

CHAPTER 8

The distance between Seb's rooms on Howland Street to Grace's Marylebone home was far enough to necessitate a carriage ride, but the day was relatively fair, so instead of the expense of a hired cab, he again decided to walk.

He needed practice maneuvering through the world without his spectacles, so he kept them in his pocket. Since he wasn't conducting any field research, when his observational powers had to be perfect, it was easy to forgo them. The mild afternoon air held a hint of future heat. A fresh breeze, untainted by smoke or the scent of the street, blew up into his face and he breathed in deeply.

Until this moment, he hadn't realized how much his spectacles acted as a barrier between him and the world. Without them, though, perception heightened — the sound of a woman on a stoop beating the dust from a rug, the warm feel of watery sunlight on his shoulders — and his thoughts loosened from his body.

He simply *was,* no longer trapped within his head. The sensation freed him, as though he could take flight over the city and see below him the pitched roofs, the smoking chimneys, the patches of green, and the shining, sludgy Thames cleaving through London.

If nothing else, this attempt to transform him into a rake had already given him a gift. He'd learned that he needed to take off his spectacles more. It opened the world to him.

And . . . he'd been able to spend more time with Grace. His whole self felt lighter, looser, just to think of her, and the way she'd looked at him yesterday. As though she'd liked what she'd seen. She had called him *handsome,* and there'd been a moment when he'd forgotten about Rotherby, forgotten about everything, and had been secluded in a private, intimate corner of the world with him and Grace as the sole occupants.

Had she . . . was it possible . . . she'd been *attracted* to him?

His body suddenly hummed with energy. If he attempted to pry a tree from the earth, it would yield easily in his hands.

"Good afternoon, sir."

He blinked, coming back to himself. A young woman holding a broom stood on the step of a milliner's shop. She smiled. He glanced behind him to see who she addressed, but no one was there.

She's smiling at me.

The familiar choking panic rose up in a rush, and his face felt burning hot. All the fears that had haunted him for most of his life swelled within him.

Did this woman judge him as he fought to speak? Would she hurry into her shop and tell her fellow milliners that she'd just encountered a big blond oaf, and would the other hatmakers rush out to point and laugh at him?

He realized the young woman stared at him, so he tried to reply. A single, strangled noise escaped him.

Heart pounding violently, Seb quickened his pace. He prayed he wouldn't hear derisive laughter pursuing him down the street.

His stomach pitched down with disappointment. Damn — he'd been doing well, or so he'd thought. But no, he'd taken two steps forward, only to take a step back.

Perverse curiosity made him look over his shoulder to see if the young woman pointed at him and cackled at his retreat. To his surprise, she had simply returned to sweeping the step. It was as if her encounter with Seb hadn't happened, as though *he* felt the impact far more than she did.

So. Perhaps a portion of his anxiety was founded on his thoughts, but not on reality. How . . . strange.

He should tell Grace. She'd want to hear of his discovery.

At the thought of her, he was brought back to yesterday afternoon in the ballroom. It hadn't been difficult to gaze at her as though she was the most captivating person he'd ever met. She *was* the most captivating person he'd ever met. Looking at her was a pleasure. He'd gladly do it every day. And night.

Careful. That way lies danger.

He shook his head, pushing away thoughts of Grace in the soft glow of a bedside candle. They were collaborators, friends. Fellow natural philosophers. And if she felt attraction to him, it was merely because he'd been implementing Rotherby's rakish strategies. A pot of water would boil with the application of heat — there was cause and effect. It was no different with him and Grace.

Attraction didn't mean desire. One's body could respond to something without the brain or the heart getting involved. It didn't mean she wanted *him.*

He needed to remember that, especially as he rounded the corner onto Weymouth Street and Grace's home loomed close.

He strolled down the mews, and crossed the stable yard before opening the kitchen door. A footman stood waiting just beyond it.

"She awaits you in the ballroom, sir." The servant took his coat and hat.

"Has the duke arrived?"

"Not yet, sir."

Seb checked his timepiece and saw that it was exactly three o'clock in the afternoon. Rotherby's punctuality was famous. It was a jest amongst his friends that one could be certain of a disaster if Rotherby was even five minutes late.

"Do you smell smoke?" Seb asked the footman. Perhaps a fire was sweeping through London as it had in 1666.

The servant inhaled. "No, sir."

It hadn't rained last night or this morning, so flooding was unlikely. And yet, for some unknown reason, Rotherby wasn't here.

Well, everyone was capable of change. Seb himself had attracted a woman's attention on his walk, so something within him had altered. Perhaps it was the same for Rotherby.

After taking his leave of the footman, Seb continued on to the ballroom. Grace's home was becoming more familiar to him, and he glanced with pleasure upon the painting in the hallway that depicted some variety of reptile sunning itself on a rock. Clearly, it had been selected by Grace.

He found her sitting in the middle of the ballroom floor. Her legs stretched out in front of her, and she leaned back, bracing herself on her hands as she stared up at the elaborately painted ceiling. She looked so charming and lively that his sodding heart lurched happily in his chest.

This was why he'd never spent more time with her, why he'd been extremely careful to keep his emotions and body on a tight rein, because he'd known in the hidden recesses of his mind that to be near Grace for greater than a few hours here and there, he would quickly slide into infatuation.

He could see it coming — and couldn't stop it.

As if drawn by an unseen force, Seb now found himself immediately stretched out beside her, his posture identical to hers.

"What are we looking at?" he whispered to her.

"In the mural, I've counted five women with bare breasts," she whispered back. "But I haven't seen a single man with an uncovered chest."

"What about that chap?" He pointed to a figure. "The bloke lurking in the corner."

"He's wearing armor that only *looks* like his naked torso, but he's as clothed as all the other men." She exhaled. "And the women's breasts look like strange frosted cakes. I don't think the artist had ever seen an actual breast before painting this," she said darkly.

"Perhaps he never worked from life," Seb suggested.

"It seems a dreadful gap in his artistic education. What a pity."

She did nothing to ease his fascination with her, damn it. "He still managed to obtain the commission to paint the mural in your family's ballroom."

"True enough. But he *ought* to know better. First — there needs to be parity. If he's got cavorting nude nymphs, he needs naked satyrs or wrestlers or some such. And then he should use actual women as models so he can get their anatomy right." She glanced down at her own chest. "Mine certainly don't look like iced cakes. Well, perhaps they're more like petit fours."

Seb couldn't help it. His gaze went straight to Grace's breasts. He had the impression of small but delightfully full shapes that could easily be covered by his hands — and then he dragged his eyes away.

Please someone rescue me from myself.

"They're, erm, quite nice."

"I think so, too," she said with a nod, then added, "I noticed, you know."

"Your, ah, breasts?"

She shook her head. "The way you entered the room." She glanced at him from the corner of her eye. "Quite different from yesterday."

"*Different* meaning *better,* I hope."

Her lips tilted into a smile. "Oh, yes."

"Very good," he said evenly, but he felt like turning cartwheels around the ballroom.

"Don't mistake me," she continued, "there wasn't a thing wrong with you before. The duke's lessons only highlighted what was already there."

One unfortunate consequence of his fair complexion meant that his cheeks turned a deep pink whenever he experienced the slightest bit of discomfiture. They also flushed whenever he felt pleasure. He didn't have to look in a glass to know that her words had turned his face a vivid pink.

He could take refuge behind the stance of a dispassionate observer, and he quickly told her of his experience on the walk over. Deliberately, he spared no detail, including his humiliating inability to speak to the milliner. He recognized his candor with Grace for what it was — an attempt to preserve the platonic distance between them.

"Ah, Sebastian," she murmured sympathetically when he'd finished recounting his mortification. "That's a pity."

His chest squeezed. "I'm sorry to fail at this. You need a rake, and I'm not certain I can be one."

"That's not what I meant." She rested her hand atop his, and his skin went taut and sensitive. "This process is uncomfortable for you, and I hate to think of you exposing yourself to pain, especially on my account."

Her words both cooled and inflamed him. "This is for both of us. It's time I learned to throw off the bonds that weigh me down. Been afraid of making a fool of myself for most of my life. I don't want to live with that fear any longer."

As he spoke, he realized he'd meant every word. It was exhausting, walking around with this paralyzing terror that he might encounter a room full of strangers or that he'd have to speak to someone he didn't know. Perhaps he might never be what some would call *normal,* but he could be a stronger, better version of himself.

A gentle smile touched her lips. "Whatever I can do to help rid you of that fear, you've only to ask."

"I will." He forced his attention back to the ceiling so he wouldn't stare covetously at her mouth.

After a moment, she said, "Why . . ."

She seemed disinclined to continue, so he prompted, "Why what?"

"Why is it that . . . you haven't married?"

He felt his eyebrows shoot up. The unexpectedness of the question had him reeling, and that *she* had asked it was even more startling. "Honestly never considered it."

"Too dedicated to your studies, like Newton or Descartes?"

"Too poor. Barely any allowance from my adoring father, and what funds I can get through grants is barely enough to keep me in mutton and secondhand books." He spoke easily, without bitterness. His requirements were simple, and he didn't mind his poverty overmuch. It was merely something to tolerate, like the weather. In his case, the winter of his coffers lasted twelve months out of the year.

"Surely *that* can't keep you from taking a wife."

"It's enough." He nudged her shoulder with his own. "For now, we'll keep working and moving forward. For all that Rotherby can be a high-handed rogue, he does make for an excellent tutor in the art of being a rake."

"The high-handed rogue accepts your gratitude," Rotherby announced from the doorway. He carried a leather portfolio beneath his arm.

Seb was at once relieved to see his friend and also resentful that the blighter interrupted his time alone with Grace.

"Oh, blast," Grace muttered under her breath. She glanced at Seb with a wince of shared embarrassment. "I think he overheard you."

"Rotherby's heard worse from me," he said easily. "Isn't that so?"

His friend paced into the room. "Most of the names the Union calls each other are not suitable for ladies' ears."

Seb held out his hand to help Grace stand, and when she took it, awareness shot through him hotly. It took an admirable amount of restraint not to curl his fingers around hers in a primal, unthinking need, but he kept his hold on her light. He got to his feet before assisting her up.

"The Union?" She lifted a brow.

"The Union of the Rakes." Seb rolled his eyes. "A dreadful name we came up with for ourselves back at Eton. More aspirational than truthful."

"Speak for yourself, Holloway," Rotherby said.

"I generally do. Tell us what's in the portfolio."

Rotherby undid the strap holding the leather case closed before removing a sheaf of paper. Without his spectacles, Seb could not quite make out the documents, but, judging by the hazy collection of dots scattered across them, they appeared to be sheets of music.

"Today, my friends," Rotherby declared, "we dance."

"That is," the duke said, eyeing Grace dubiously, "*if* we know how."

She couldn't be insulted by his implication that a woman of scholarly inclinations — namely, her — wouldn't have any aptitude when it came to social skills. And she was grateful for Rotherby's demand because it meant she didn't have to consider why she'd asked Sebastian about his plans to marry.

Thinking of her dunderheaded question, she could have cheerfully imbibed a serious but not fatal dose of laudanum so that she could fall into unconsciousness and forget the whole thing.

Except she couldn't. There was nothing to do but keep plowing ahead.

"Be at ease, Rotherby." She placed her hands on her hips. "My parents bartered with me to ensure I learned how to dance. For every session with a dancing master, I was rewarded with a piece of scientific equipment. A looking glass, a compound microscope."

"Bribes," Sebastian said with a wry smile.

"No doubt about it — I *can* be bought."

"We had a dancing master," Sebastian said. "My brothers and I. Part of my family's hope to scale the heights of British Society." He made a wry face.

"Please tell me you applied your capacious studying ability to learning how to dance," Rotherby pled.

Sebastian shrugged. "It's nigh universal — cultures incorporate music accompanied by rhythmic movement. I couldn't apply myself to examining the *kalamatianos* dance of Greece without learning British dancing."

The duke exhaled. "That's one less mountain to scale. But we're still practicing so that, when the time comes — and it *will* come — you'll be able to dance with Grace and inspire envy in all who behold you."

"A rather tall order," Grace said, unable to keep the skepticism from her voice. She knew the steps well enough, and recalled intimately the giddy pleasure she'd experienced the early weeks of her first Season when she'd danced with gentlemen eager to make her acquaintance. Dancing had made her feel light and free and untethered from the planet's gravity.

Her mistake had been speaking to the gentlemen whilst they danced together. Foolishly, she'd talked not about the weather or her delight in the splendid room, but of her studies. She'd been open in discussing how she loved to observe the tiny miracle that was a hatching tadpole, or the incredibly fine hand that the Creator had employed when fashioning a reptile's long toes. The looks on those young men's faces . . . the disgust, the dawning realization that she might be a prize as a bride, but as a woman, she was something to be endured.

She had tried to curb her tongue. She'd prattle inane things about the theater or fashion or simply nodded and smiled at whatever the gentlemen said. Yet the more the would-be suitors enjoyed her company, the more disgust she felt with herself for pretending to be someone she wasn't.

"Must we dance?" she asked the duke.

"You must. Trust me," Rotherby said with a smug smile, "with you and Holloway under my tutelage, Fredericks shall see you as much more than a colleague."

"We'll need music," Sebastian said, glancing at the pianoforte.

The duke raised his hands in a placating gesture. "Waiting downstairs in your butler's study is a music student, a young man by the name of Mr. Scarpelli, to play piano for us."

"You're very thorough." Grace tugged on the bellpull, and when a footman appeared, she requested he fetch Mr. Scarpelli. "Thinking of everything."

"Madam," Rotherby intoned, "it is a burden to be so admirable."

"Conceit has always been in abundance for Rotherby," Sebastian said, making Grace chuckle.

"Because I've earned it." But the duke spoiled his high-handedness by grinning boyishly.

A moment later, Mr. Scarpelli came into the ballroom. From his wild hair to his hastily tied neckcloth to the slightly frayed shirt cuffs peeking out from his sleeves, he was every inch a music student. He bowed before taking his seat at the pianoforte.

"Where would you like me to begin, Your Grace?" he asked.

"I assume you have a battle plan," Sebastian said. "You always do."

"We shan't bother with country dances." Rotherby waved the notion away. "Our concern is the waltz. *That* is where you and Grace will attract the most notice."

Oh, gracious. Country dances only involved the occasional joining of hands, and the maintenance of distance between partners.

And while she'd learned how to waltz, she'd never actually done it with anyone other than her dancing master, whose touch had been deliberately and rightfully professional, entirely impersonal.

It would be the same with Sebastian. Wouldn't it? His hand holding hers, his other hand on her waist and hers on his shoulder . . . there was nothing to fear. Merely a simple transaction between friends. Something to be done for an intended purpose.

Even so . . . contemplating a waltz with Sebastian felt as though moths were fluttering in her belly.

Mr. Scarpelli shook out his hands before setting them on the pianoforte keys. At the duke's nod, the musician began to play. Grace attempted to distract herself by tapping her feet in time with the air. *One* two three, *one* two three.

Sebastian breathed in deeply, then moved to approach her. But Rotherby stepped forward and placed his hand on Sebastian's chest.

"I'll demonstrate first," the duke said.

"But I already know how to do this," Sebastian protested.

"You know the *steps,* but not the art." Rotherby bowed to Grace. "Would you do me the honor?"

She raised her brows in surprise. A waltz with a duke? How unexpected. And likely the dream of many young women. Many *other* young women.

Rotherby came toward her and held out his hand. She took it, and he led her to the center of the ballroom.

They bowed and curtsied before taking their positions. The duke held her in the proper stance. They looked into each other's eyes. They really *were* quite nice eyes. Deep and richly hued like coffee. Just like yesterday, he regarded her as though he found her captivating.

174

Yet there was no leap of excitement at his touch, no thrill of contact. He was merely a person she knew, with her entirely unmoved by his closeness.

It made no sense. He was handsome, finely built, and exuded charm. But nothing within her came alive to have him escort her to the center of the ballroom. She did sense a fizz of excitement to dance again, after years of avoiding it.

She and the duke waltzed. She slipped easily into the steps, her body recalling the tilt and sway, and while she leaned into the spinning and freeing sensation, a whisper of disappointment stole through her. The movements themselves were fine, but dancing with Rotherby was like practicing with her dancing master. It wasn't particularly special or wonderful, only mildly interesting to observe.

"Guide her, Holloway," the duke said without taking his gaze from Grace. "Move with her. Create a miniature world that consists only of you two."

"I see," Sebastian said, writing in his notebook.

"He doesn't need to *seduce* me." Alarm at the prospect shot through her. Not that she found the notion unpleasant. Far from it — and that was worrisome. "This is for show only."

"Have you never been to the theater?" Rotherby asked. "The greatest performances come from actors and actresses who fully invest themselves in the role they're playing. *They* must believe they are who they pretend to be."

"Or else no one else accepts them as the ingénue or brooding hero," Sebastian said as the music and dance continued.

The duke nodded. "Holloway has to be convincing. Everyone who looks at you dancing together will see a man at the height of his masculine powers, and will inevitably turn their attention to the woman who has captivated him."

"And *I'm* that woman?" Grace couldn't quite keep the skepticism out of her voice.

"This is as much about *your* performance as it is Holloway's." Rotherby's gaze bored into her. "I want you to believe yourself to be a woman capable of ensnaring Britain's greatest rake."

Her feet slowed, and the dance stuttered to a stop. The music went silent. Her whole body tensed as her hands fell away from the duke.

"I can't make myself into the sort of woman men flock to." She blinked hard from the burn of her shame, and though it hurt to confess such a thing to Rotherby and Sebastian, they both needed to know the immensity of the task that lay before them. "I once saw a gentleman throw back his drink to shore himself up for the task of dancing with me."

The duke's jaw tightened, and Sebastian cursed softly.

"That man was an ass," Sebastian growled, taking a step toward her. "Give me his name. I've studied cultures that flay their enemies, so I'm certain I can make him suffer."

"Sounds messy," she said, absurdly touched by his bloodthirstiness on her behalf.

"I'll wear a butcher's apron to minimize the mess." Sebastian said firmly, "You don't need to alter yourself for anyone. Especially not Fredericks."

No one had ever said such a thing to her. Something stung her eyes, and she realized it was the heat of unshed tears of appreciation. "But Rotherby said —"

Sebastian drew closer. "Trust in me, Grace. Trust that when the time comes, Fredericks will be utterly captivated by you. And if he still can't get his head out of his arse, then he's not worth the effort."

"You seem to keep swearing in my presence," she said, because it was either make a jest or gratefully kiss him.

Kiss him.

Wait — what?

Rotherby stepped back, and put his hands on his hips. "Pair up, you two. I want to see you dance together."

CHAPTER 9

She was still reeling from her mind's insistent demand that she kiss Sebastian when he set his notebook down. In and of itself, putting his notebook aside was not especially remarkable. But then he shucked off his coat and draped it over a nearby chair, and Grace felt the ground beneath her shift.

God above. In his shirtsleeves, Sebastian was a vision of robust masculinity. As he moved, the lawn of his shirt pulled snug across tight, sculpted muscles. The backing of his waistcoat drew taut across his wide shoulders. When he bent down to tug at the top of his boot, she was treated to the sight of woolen trouser fabric draping his firm buttocks.

Her mouth actually watered, as if she'd lifted a silver dome covering a plate, and discovered not a drab meal of boiled carrots, but a luscious roast dripping with juices.

She clapped a hand over her mouth to stop her frenetic giggle. She couldn't compare a fellow human being to *meat.* That was beyond disrespectful.

But, Lord help her, he was gorgeous.

And she was about to waltz with him.

Confusion turned her thoughts hazy. Something was happening to her, something she couldn't understand. The pleasant affection she'd always felt in Sebastian's presence was growing hotter, making her skin tight and her head spin. It frightened her a little even as she moved toward it.

Within a moment, he stood before her. Collecting herself with the staunch reminder that this was all part of the plan to find her a suitable husband, she straightened her spine. Then he held out his hand, and she took it, before he settled his other hand on her waist.

"It's warm in here, isn't it?" he asked. His eyes gleamed and his chest rose and fell in an elevated rhythm.

"Must be," she mumbled, but the fire wasn't lit, and clouds dampened the sunlight coming in through the windows.

"Mr. Scarpelli, if you please." The duke's voice sounded leagues away.

Music started up again, jarring her thoughts.

Sebastian murmured, "Ready?"

She could only nod.

They danced. And suddenly she understood why, not so long ago, the waltz was considered a sinful, wicked dance unfit for polite assemblies. As she and Sebastian turned around the ballroom floor, she *felt* him everywhere. At the sensitive point where their hands touched, at the burning site where his hand rested on her waist, and all the other places within her. The dance was a shared pulse, his heartbeat becoming hers, their bodies synchronizing.

He was solid and hot and so very large. How had she been able to recognize this for four years and yet not know it in the receptiveness of her body?

"Don't forget to look at each other," the duke instructed. "Gaze into each other's eyes."

She tugged her attention up from the knot of his neckcloth, up higher, until his gaze secured to hers. Thoughts scattered as she spun in the blue of his eyes because the way he *looked* at her . . . as though she was adored, desired beyond reason . . . beyond sense . . .

But it was a performance, wasn't it? He was merely pretending to feel these things for her, as the role of rake and admirer demanded.

Surely he could hear the pounding of her heart, so much louder than Mr. Scarpelli's playing.

"Excellent work, both of you," Rotherby said above the music. "You've got me convinced — and I believe nothing."

The duke's voice fractured the spell surrounding them. They pulled apart, staring at each other, and she imagined her bewildered expression mirrored his.

"Do I keep playing?" Mr. Scarpelli asked.

"That's enough for now." She could not stop looking at Sebastian.

His brow furrowed. He visibly seemed to collect himself, and then, to her relief and disappointment, donned his coat.

"Now," the duke said, "there's something I've been meaning to discuss with you, Holloway. Your wardrobe."

Sebastian glanced down at himself. "What I wear is serviceable enough. I've had this waistcoat for years."

"And it deserves some rest to repay its decade of valiant service," Rotherby noted. "A rake is never dressed in clothing that's old enough to marry."

"After paying my rent, what's left goes mostly to books."

Rotherby snorted. "You must have a sizable library, then."

"It's not the size," Sebastian replied drily. "It's what I do with it. Very thick volumes."

Fire danced along her cheeks as she caught his implication. He was much more . . . ribald . . . than she'd realized. And she recognized then that Sebastian possessed a great deal of knowledge about the world's sensual side. He was a bookish man, and shy, but he was also vigorously hale. Surely, he had sexual appetites.

Surely, he had lovers.

She started at the acidic bubble of jealously rising within her. But she couldn't feel that way about him. He wasn't hers, never had been. Never would be.

"We need to outfit you, Holloway," the duke said in a matter-of-fact tone. "You can't be a rake in ill-fitting, superannuated garments."

"Perhaps it escaped your notice because you could lend money to God," Sebastian replied, "but a wardrobe is a considerable expense. One I can't take on."

"I'll supply the funds," Rotherby said.

Sebastian scowled. "Absolutely not. I won't have anyone pay for my clothing."

"Don't be an ass, Holloway," the duke said impatiently. "Get yourself some new rigging."

Shaking off her unexpected — unwelcome — possessiveness, Grace noted the volley of words between the two men. Neither seemed inclined to budge, but both were too prideful to make any concessions.

"You can always sell the clothes when this is over," she suggested. "One could buy quite a lot of books from the sale of a waistcoat alone."

Several moments passed. And then Sebastian let out a long, rough breath.

"All right," he muttered.

The duke clapped his hands together once. "A decision you won't regret. I'll take you to my personal tailor this afternoon."

"But," Sebastian continued, "consider it a loan I intend to repay."

Grace opened her lips to argue, but Rotherby shot her a quick look that advised her to remain silent.

Men were ridiculous sometimes.

"You're ridiculous," Seb grumbled.

"Common knowledge dictates that a man needs no fewer than seven waistcoats," Rotherby fired back. His reflection appeared beside Seb's in the floor-length mirror. "Wouldn't you agree, Ruis?"

A measuring tape draped around his neck, the tailor spoke around his mouthful of pins. "Indeed, Your Grace. Appearing in the same waistcoat twice in one week is gauche."

"It's excessive," Seb said. He shifted as Mr. Ruis held the measuring tape up to his back. "Calculated display to create a societal impression of wealth and prosperity — which is a fallacy because everyone knows that wealth doesn't equate with happiness."

"We aren't talking about happiness." Rotherby folded his arms over his chest. "We're trying to impress London Society, and it doesn't care about whether or not you feel any sense of personal fulfillment. It merely wants to know if you've got a carriage and a country estate. Sod happiness."

Surely volumes could be written about the inherent delusions and problematic values of the British elite.

"And in the case of capturing Mason Fredericks's attention," Rotherby continued, "you need to appear at your finest. Consider your book: you can't analyze the courting customs of the *ton* if you're excluded on the basis of your garments. If not on behalf of your work, then on Grace's behalf," he said, just as Seb was about to voice another objection.

Damn, but Rotherby didn't play fair.

"All right," Seb said, his words grudging.

185

"For her sake. And the sake of my book," he remembered to add.

"Maravilhoso," Mr. Ruis said, somehow managing to smile without swallowing a pin. He patted Seb on the shoulder. "You'll have no cause for complaint when you see what I make for you. And may I say, *senhor,* it shall be a pleasure to dress you. A man as tall and *vigoroso* such as yourself will show marvelously well in my garments. I seldom have such fine customers."

Rotherby coughed loudly into his fist while glaring at the tailor.

"With the exception of Your Grace, of course," Mr. Ruis added hastily. He busied himself with a bolt of muslin, holding it to Seb's torso.

A moment passed, while Seb observed in the mirror the activity in the tailor's shop. Men who radiated privilege and affluence strolled in and out of the elegantly appointed business, striking poses as they conversed with each other. They paid almost no attention to the shop assistants that hovered around them like hummingbirds, as if it was the height of indelicacy to acknowledge the labor involved in maintaining their appearance.

"You and Grace danced well together," Rotherby said lightly.

Too lightly.

Seb narrowed his eyes. "We both received an education in dancing. Expected that we'd perform the movements with a degree of aptitude."

"*Aptitude.* That's what you're calling it."

"What else is there?" Seb moved to accommodate Mr. Ruis as the tailor took the measure of his leg.

"I'm no man of the sciences," Rotherby said with a smirk, "but I believe in the parlance one might say you and Lady Grace wanted to take bites out of each other. Metaphorically speaking."

"*Senhor,*" Mr. Ruis said with admonition, "please do not tense your body. You must be relaxed as I get your measurements."

Seb forced himself to exhale, trying to loosen his muscles. "Whatever you believed you saw, it wasn't there."

"I thought you academic types put faith only in what you perceive," his friend noted. "The veracity of observation, and all that."

"The human machine is also a faulty one." Seb turned as the tailor adjusted his stance.

"Appeared to me like your machine was steaming." Rotherby picked up a newspaper from atop a nearby table, but it was clear by the speed in which he turned the pages that he wasn't reading a bloody syllable. "Is there anything going on between you two?"

Seb's jaw went tight. "I shall say it one last time. We. Are. Only. Friends."

He had to keep telling himself that. If he let himself believe there was a whisper of true attraction on her part, he'd be in danger. Considerable danger.

Because these past mornings, he'd awakened with his body humming in anticipation of seeing her. Because he collected impressions of the world around him with the intention of telling her about what he'd seen. Because, even now, he drifted into fantasies of her staring up at him with a hungry gaze, and her hands sliding up his chest as she lifted onto her tiptoes.

"She didn't look at you like one friend looks at another," Rotherby said, peering over the top of the newspaper.

Within the confines of his chest, Seb's heart pounded. Was it possible — she felt as he did?

"Everybody gets stars in their eyes when dancing," he said, his dismissive tone more for his own benefit than Rotherby's. "Blushing, breathing heavily — all typical for someone when they dance. I don't study physiology, but I know that much."

"Except," his friend pointed out, "she

188

didn't blush or breathe heavily when she danced with me, and I'm a ruddy, good-looking fellow."

There was truth to Rotherby's words. Grace had appeared attentive but not enraptured in her dance with Rotherby. And women *always* looked at the duke as if he was the treasure of El Dorado, the lost city of Atlantis, and the open gates of Paradise all combined into one.

But Grace was a natural philosopher. Her values operated differently from the majority of the populace. The fact that she had a *tendre* for Mason Fredericks rather than some dashing rake was proof of that.

"I'm telling you," Seb said tightly, "she doesn't think of me in that way. I am merely a means for her to reach her goal."

Rotherby rolled his eyes. "Even if you're right — which you aren't — what about your feelings for her?"

"Immaterial."

"Oh ho! That means you *do* have feelings for her." Rotherby threw the newspaper onto the floor, and an instant later, an assistant cleared it away.

"Senhor Holloway," Mr. Ruis reprimanded, but Seb couldn't help it. He had to move.

Seb paced away to busy himself with a

stack of fashion prints. He sorted through them, seeing without seeing the images of men in Paris's latest styles. What a simpler life the prints depicted, liberated of every concern except the need to be handsome. It was no wonder that the fashionable figures existed in a world almost entirely free of place or context. No one there struggled with uncomfortable, unwanted feelings.

"I may — *may* — find myself thinking of Grace as more than a friend, but I repeat, whatever I feel for her doesn't matter. She wants Mason Fredericks. I can barely afford to feed and house myself, let alone two people. And I have no expectation that she will repay my years of friendship with her affections. Nothing can or will transpire between us."

He had to keep reiterating this, as many times as it took.

"That's a damned pity." Rotherby sighed. "I'd hoped . . ."

Seb spun to face his friend. "You were late today *on purpose.*"

"Of course I was." Rotherby threw up his hands. "Wanted to give you time alone with her."

Even now, nearly two decades since they'd left Eton, Rotherby still looked out for Seb. He placed his hand on his friend's shoulder.

"It's appreciated. Truly. But your efforts to form a romantic attachment between Grace and myself are misguided. She and I will remain friends. Only friends."

"I still hold out hope," Rotherby said with a wry smile.

Seb patted Rotherby's shoulder. "This will be the first time in your charmed life that you'll be disappointed."

CHAPTER 10

Grace stared at the preserved African chameleon floating in a suspension within a thick glass jar. All its beauty, its shifting-hued skin, its life essence — all of it was gone. Now it floated in a permanent life-in-death within the upper-floor exhibition at the British Museum here in Montagu House.

She sighed.

"Why must men kill a thing in order to study it?" she said wearily.

Standing beside her, Jane made a soft noise of disgust. "Because that's what men *do.* Capture a creature and either bend it to their will or end its life. Nothing can exist independent of them, or else they fear their cocks will fall off."

A thickly whiskered gentleman standing nearby made a startled cough as he glared at Jane and Grace. When Jane merely glared right back, the man trundled off, muttering under his breath about *indecency* and *proper female behavior.*

Grace smothered a giggle behind her fist as Jane winked at her.

"Of course," Grace said once she'd collected herself, "your husband is the exception to that rule. Hasn't put *you* in a cage. Or a jar."

"Not *yet,*" Jane said. "But one never knows. Men can be so irrational and unpredictable."

Grace and Jane moved on from the case full of its reptile specimens, walking slowly through the chamber. Perhaps she and her friend ought to study the fossils rather than take in the melancholy collection of dead, stuffed, and preserved animals. She was always torn about coming to the British Museum — it held such vast repositories of knowledge, yet everything came at a price. Even the friezes from the Parthenon had been ripped from their homeland and brought to England. It hardly seemed right.

Did Sebastian ever come here? Surely he'd find exhibits of interest — but maybe he, too, thought the museum to be a highly problematic space. She ought to mention it to him this afternoon when they'd meet for their next session. A thoughtful man, Sebastian. And . . . appallingly attractive.

193

"How fares your transformative project?" Jane asked, as if reading Grace's thoughts. Hopefully, her friend couldn't read *all* of Grace's thoughts.

"We're still in process." Grace stopped in front of a case holding a number of geological specimens. The solidity of the rocks and minerals brought comfort. They reminded her that while the forces of her own life sometimes felt wildly unpredictable, the Earth would always go on. "Three more days until Lord and Lady Creasy's garden party, when Sebastian makes his debut."

Despite the comforting nature of the rock specimens, the thought of Sebastian appearing with her before Society's elite made her heart pound. They'd soon discover whether or not all their preparation was for nothing, and whether or not they had consigned Grace to permanently remaining merely a colleague to Mason — as well as consigning Sebastian to a lifetime of derision.

"Judging by the wobble in your voice," Jane said, lifting her eyebrow, "you're not precisely looking forward to tea and sandwiches *en plein air.*"

"We've asked a lot from him," Grace admitted.

"More than he can provide?"

"Difficult to ascertain at this stage.

194

But . . ." Her pulse fluttered. "He has potential." Hidden beneath his ill-fitting clothes and gentle manner, he'd the body of a mythical hero and a surprising seductive allure. Her hands still radiated warmth from where she'd touched his body during their waltz, and she'd never forget the intensity of his gaze as he'd looked at her while they danced.

Jane tilted her head. "Much as I adore the man, I'm afraid I'll have to see his metamorphosis in order to believe it."

"Not much faith." Grace gave a rueful chuckle.

"We're women of science." Jane shrugged. "Visual proof is always necessary." She turned to survey the room, and then straightened, her eyes going wide. Jane whispered, "Remember to act nonchalant."

"What? Why?" Grace eyed her friend with puzzlement. "I don't understand what you're talking about." She exhaled. "I told you already, I don't want to see the secret collection of stone phalluses."

"Good afternoon, Mr. Fredericks," Jane said.

Grace whirled around to find herself staring like a mooncalf at Mason Fredericks, who stood just a few feet away. Spots of color appeared on his cheeks as he struggled to pretend that he hadn't heard Grace bleat the word *phalluses.*

She wasn't much given to thoughts of a religious or spiritual nature, but at that moment, she prayed to any available deity to strike her down with a convenient bolt of lightning.

"Good afternoon, Mrs. Argyle," Mason replied.

Jane curtsied in response, but Grace saw in the way her friend kept her lips glued shut it was all Jane could do to keep her laughter in check.

"And, Lady Grace," Mason continued, turning to her, "it's always gratifying to see you."

"You, as well."

They stood together in silence, and Grace fought to keep from shifting from foot to foot. Strange — now that she'd determined a path to attract Mason's romantic notice, she could hardly put together a sentence that didn't include dull inanities.

"Do you enjoy visiting the museum?" Jane asked in an overly loud voice.

Mason smiled, revealing the dimple in his left cheek, and Grace's insides somersaulted. "It's impossible not to appreciate the breadth of this collection. I've been coming here since I was a lad. Much to the disappointment of my sport-loving father," he added with a wry grin.

Don't sigh like a ninny, Grace reminded herself sternly. But it was a struggle.

"However," he continued, sobering, "there's something so disheartening to see this many animals robbed of their lives for the pleasure of mankind. The world is magnificent enough without anyone trying to drive a stake through it."

Grace beamed. "That is my belief, as well."

"Is it?" He smiled again, and when his gaze met hers, she barely sensed the floor beneath her. "How wonderful. You understand me perfectly."

This was her chance. She could impress upon him that they loved the same things, and that their hearts and minds were perfectly aligned, if only he could think of her as a woman. "Yes, I —"

"Ho, Fredericks!"

Mason lifted his hand in greeting as a gentleman with gingery hair hailed him from across the room. "Aldwich! What a pleasure to see you. I meant to ask —" He took a step toward the redheaded man before hastily bowing to Grace and Jane. "Ladies, do excuse me."

And then he was gone, already halfway

across the chamber before Grace could formulate a reply.

Grace's body went leaden with disappointment. She fought to keep her head upright, and a pleasant look on her face, as if she hadn't had her heart crushed beside the display of rocks and minerals.

"Ah, hell," Jane muttered. She took Grace's hand in hers. "I'm sorry, my love."

"It's all right." Her gaze followed Mason as he and Aldwich strode from the room, talking animatedly.

"It will be different when he sees you with Mr. Holloway," Jane said, her voice encouraging. "He'll finally realize what a gem you are."

"Rather irritating that men seem to only value what other men possess," Grace muttered.

"They're simpler beings," Jane said. "They haven't the finer powers of discernment that women have. Even Mr. Fredericks is, at heart, merely a man. Douglas, too, has limits on his imagination."

"And yet," Grace said on a sigh, "we want them, anyway." Sebastian's face flashed in her mind, and her body heated to recall the way she'd felt waltzing with him. *More.* She wanted more.

Jane grinned. "*Someone* must be responsible for the continuation of the species."

"Rather noble of us to shoulder that responsibility."

" 'Twas ever thus." Jane looped her arm through Grace's. "Come. Let us seek out two things that never fall short of our expectations."

"Books and cakes?"

"Precisely."

Anticipation coursed beneath Seb's skin as he climbed the stairs to the ballroom. It took sizable effort to keep from taking the steps two at a time. And while the prospect of yet more instruction on how to become a rake didn't give energy to his limbs, the expectation of seeing Grace did.

He smiled to himself when he heard her voice float out from the ballroom. He couldn't make out her words, but Rotherby's reply was a low chuckle. Seb had witnessed the alluring effect of his friend's deep laughter on women — and a few men — but Grace had given no indication that she found Rotherby attractive. Thank God.

Difficult enough to know that Fredericks was Grace's ultimate goal. Seb didn't need to feel any resentment toward Rotherby, one of his oldest friends.

As Seb neared the ballroom, his steps

slowed. What the deuce? Numerous voices murmured within the chamber, talking softly, and beneath their conversation came the sound of clinking porcelain.

Frowning with puzzlement, Seb entered the ballroom. A table stood near the farthest window, around which sat five people enjoying tea and cakes. The three women wore aprons over serviceable, sturdy clothing, and they all wore caps covering their hair. Maids? One of the men wore the family's livery, and the other man had tucked his buckskin breeches into very worn boots. A footman and groom.

"Ah, you've arrived." Rotherby approached Seb. He looked pleased with himself, but Grace, who followed, appeared more uncertain.

"It's going to be fine," she said in a voice calculated to calm someone — which only made alarm prickle along his neck. "These are our servants who've been generously compensated for their time. We're going to go slowly."

"Go slowly with what?" Seb demanded.

"Today," Rotherby announced, "you're going to practice talking with strangers."

True fear slicked coldly down Seb's back. He swallowed, but his mouth had gone dry, making him cough.

"Steady there," Rotherby said, thumping Seb between his shoulder blades. "Soldier on and you'll triumph. Push through any fear that's holding you back. That's how you win the day."

"I thought military strategy was McCameron's bailiwick." Seb hated the tremor in his voice, and pushed against the dizziness that darkened the edges of his vision.

"This isn't battle," Grace said, sending Rotherby a sharp look. "Simply telling Sebastian to push on won't help him feel comfortable around people he doesn't know."

He thought he heard her mutter, *Men.*

It was a measure of Seb's anxiety that he barely noticed when Grace took his hand and led him away from the servants, Rotherby following. She stood directly in front of him, and held his gaze with her own.

"Let's keep you tranquil," she said in a mild voice. "Can't talk to strangers when you're already overwrought, isn't that so?"

He managed to nod.

"I've been thinking," she continued in that same, soothing tone, "about when animals are chased by predators. They burn energy as they flee for their lives. And then, when the chase is over, and they've survived, that

201

energy has been released. They can be calm."

He rasped, "Because the danger has passed and they don't need to run any longer."

She nodded. "Perhaps that fear you feel when you talk to people you don't know is akin to what animals feel when threatened by a predator. But if we can get that energy out of you, out of your body, it's possible that your mind will realize that there's no danger."

"What do you suggest?" Rotherby asked with a puzzled frown. "We get a lion from the Tower of London to chase Holloway?"

She rolled her eyes. "Don't be absurd. But running is an excellent idea." She smiled up at him, and the fretful thudding of his heart quietened. "Our garden isn't vast, but I warrant a few laps around the perimeter should do the trick."

Seb stared at her. "You propose that I'm to run around your garden like a racing hound? And that will make me calmer."

"Precisely."

Seb rubbed at his chin. "Thinking on it, I always feel tranquil after galloping up and down the football pitch. Sleep well afterward, too." As theories went, hers had considerable merit. There was only one way to put it to the test. "Which way to the garden?"

She beamed at him, and the jolt in his pulse had nothing to do with fear. "I'll show you the way. Rotherby, make sure the servants have enough to eat and drink."

Rotherby scowled, evidently displeased that he was to see to the servants' refreshments, but other than a grumble, he didn't object.

Grace guided Seb out of the ballroom and down a set of stairs that led to a salon facing the garden. She opened French doors, letting in the soft spring air, and they both stepped onto the terrace. Espaliered trees lined the brick walls surrounding a wide lawn, with hedges containing beds of sweet-scented flowers peppering the expanse in a neat pattern. At the very back of the garden was a glass house. Without his spectacles, Seb couldn't be quite certain if anyone was inside, but he hoped it was currently unoccupied.

She nodded toward a path covered with crushed shells. "Will that suit?"

"Reasonably." He tugged off his coat, and she gathered it in her arms. Grudgingly, he admitted, "Feel a bit foolish."

"You *look* fine," she murmured, her gaze on his shoulders.

The sight of her holding his coat hit him deep in his chest. It was a primal, instinctive gratification, a window into an intimacy that he hadn't realized he craved until that moment.

He shook himself. She needed him to secure Fredericks's attentions. The less he permitted himself to take pleasure in her, the better.

"Off to pretend lions are chasing me." He gave her a small salute before trotting down the steps of the terrace. His boots hit the shell-strewn path, which crunched as he took his first strides. At first, running with no purpose felt ridiculous. But after jogging several paces, his body recognized the movement, and within minutes, he'd completed one lap around the garden.

Three times he made a circuit. Three times he passed Grace watching him from the terrace. He could admit to himself that when he passed her, he made certain to lengthen his stride. It was a timeless — shameless — display of masculine prowess, as if he said to her, *Yes, Fredericks is wealthy and charming and learned, but can he do this?*

After the third lap, he stopped at the foot of the terrace steps. He set his hands on his hips as he looked up at her.

"You don't seem very winded," she said with a raised brow.

A small gloss of sweat slicked his forehead, and he dragged the side of his hand over it. "The lions have been too indulged from their life in the Tower. Regular servings of beefsteak can take the fight out of a creature."

"How are you feeling?"

"I feel . . ." He searched the jagged peaks of his anxiety — and was startled to find they'd been worn down into softer hillocks. It wasn't as though he felt no unease at the prospect of speaking to strangers, but it seemed more manageable than before. As he climbed the stairs to her, he confessed, "Rather good, in truth."

Her eyes sparkled as she handed him his coat. "The lions served their purpose, after all."

Yet as they returned to the ballroom, and he heard the servants chatting over their tea, his jaw grew tighter and tighter. Before entering the large chamber, she stopped in the hallway and motioned for him to bend closer to her.

"Occasionally," she said on a whisper, "when I get nervous, like when I have to go to a dinner and I'm certain all the other guests will be so much more sophisticated than me, I think about something that's steady and constant, something that never varies. And I realize that my breathing is always there. So I just think about taking a long, slow breath. Then another. Then another. Try it with me?"

This seemed another strange, almost silly exercise — but she'd been correct about getting the energy out of his body. Straightening, Seb closed his eyes and breathed in, then let it out in a deep exhalation. He did it two more times

Peace settled over him.

He opened his eyes to find Grace gazing at him thoughtfully "Did you learn all this from studying amphibians and reptiles?"

"It's quite amazing what one can learn from paying attention," she said with a cheeky grin.

"Ah, there you are." Rotherby strode toward them. He peered at Seb, but when he spoke, his voice was gentler. "Ready for your next task?" When Seb nodded, Rotherby said, "I'm going to break the servants into two groups so you'll have more opportunity to practice."

"Right," Seb said, but even he could hear the thread of tightness in his words.

"Sebastian," Grace murmured. "What are you afraid of?"

"That . . ." His mind ran through count-less terrible scenarios, making his muscles go taut. "I'll pass out or . . . say exactly the wrong thing."

"In all your life," she said softly, "tell me how many times that's happened to you."

"There was that time when . . ." He sorted through the catalog of his memories. He recalled innumerable instances when he'd panicked about losing consciousness or blurting something gauche, but as to actu-ally doing those things . . . "I don't know if I ever have."

She tilted her head toward one of the maids, who stood with the groom. "Let's see if it happens with these good folks."

Taking another breath, Seb approached the maid and groom. Fear climbed up his spine as he neared the two people, and they observed him with a mild curiosity, but he reminded himself to remain focused on the in and out of his breath. Edged anxiety receded, so that by the time he joined the duo, he was able to say with some measure of calm, "Did you enjoy your tea?"

"We did, sir," the maid said. "I like Cook's cress sandwiches the best. Taste like sum-mer."

For a terrifying moment, Seb's mind emptied and he could think of nothing to say in reply. But as he struggled to speak, the groom said, "Sure and the sandwiches are nice, but nothing tops Cook's plum cakes."

"And who can argue with a plum cake?" Seb said with a sage nod. "It's categorically known to be the most delicious of all cakes."

The groom and maid chuckled, and within moments, Seb and his companions were chatting easily. In fact, only when Rotherby and Grace appeared beside him did he realize that he'd lost track of the minutes. Grace nodded her thanks to the groom and the maid before she, Seb, and Rotherby retreated to one corner of the ballroom.

"That seemed to go rather well," she said, and her praise sifted through him warmly.

"The dragon I thought I'd face turned out to be only a large lizard." He glanced at her and said quickly, "But no reptilian life was slain. We had a nice conversation, instead. Although," he said as a grim thought struck him, "surely they thought I was a buffoon."

"How do you know?" Grace tilted her head as she posed this question. "Did they say to you, *My goodness, you're quite silly?*"

"Well . . . no. But perhaps you instructed them to be polite." That had to be it. Otherwise — was it possible that all this time, he'd been misconstruing what he believed people thought of him?

The idea was galvanizing.

"Before you arrived," Grace said, "Rotherby and I asked them to act as naturally and unaffectedly as possible. And I assured them that there'd be no punishment for their honesty."

"Truth is, Holloway," Rotherby added, "even a man as abundant in intelligence, influence, and charm as I can't know what's happening in someone else's mind. Surely, it's the same for you. Unless . . ." Rotherby narrowed his eyes. "You were the product of an unholy union between an ironmonger and a witch. Come to think of it, you *do* often mumble incantations under your breath whilst poring over ancient tomes."

"If I was a witch's son, don't you think I would conjure myself a less arrogant friend?" But Seb and Rotherby shared a grin.

Grace shook her head at them, yet she smiled as she spoke. "My mother's advice to me before my come out, and I was nervous about trying to converse with England's most polished diamonds, was to ask the people I talked with many questions. Wish I'd listened to her," she added, her expression briefly darkening.

God, what Seb wouldn't do to take that

pain away. It enraged him, that the world of the *ton* was so blind and stupid and hurtful.

Before he realized what he was doing, he'd taken her hand and given it an encouraging squeeze. His breath held — other than his holding her whilst they danced, he'd never before taken the initiative to touch her. Nothing had ever felt quite as good as her returning the squeeze. It made the pleasure he'd felt at successfully talking with strangers pale into the color of ash, as the point of contact between them bloomed color throughout his body.

Yet his stomach clenched in disappointment when, a moment later, she let go of his hand. For the best, in truth. He'd be unable to pay attention to anything Rotherby said if he and Grace touched.

"Nothing people love so much as to talk about themselves," Rotherby said, unaware of the tiny drama being enacted in front of him. "Keep bringing the topic back to them, they consider you the most spectacular conversationalist and a sterling example of humanity."

Wryly, Seb said, "We all know that I am, in truth, as diabolical and nefarious as one of Bonaparte's spies."

"I've something for you." Grace hurried to a small table and grabbed a folded item resting on top of it. She returned and held the item out to him. Gingerly, Seb took it, feeling soft leather against his skin. A pair of gentleman's gloves. "In case you start to fret about what to say or what someone's thinking, direct your attention to the sensation of these gloves in your hand."

As he stroked his fingers back and forth across the leather, he did, in truth, sense himself firmly anchored in the present moment rather than spin off into worry.

Marveling, he said to Grace, "These ideas of yours, they're ingenious."

Her cheeks pinkened. "I thought to myself, if I was in the grips of anxiousness, what would be the gentlest means of getting past that? Because you can't just beat the mind into submission," she added with a look at Rotherby. His friend spread his hands in acknowledgment of his failed strategy.

Soft warmth spread along Seb's limbs, spreading into his heart, which seemed to fill his chest. She worked so hard to help him overcome the obstacle of his fear.

"Are you feeling up to trying again?" Grace asked. She glanced at the three remaining people he hadn't yet spoken to. They'd risen from the tea table, and talked amongst themselves near the pianoforte.

He inhaled slowly, and let out a long exhalation. "Ready to scale the dizzying heights of social success."

With the gloves in his hand, and his breathing steady, Seb approached the trio.

It wasn't perfect. He stammered at the onset, and twice used the feel of the gloves to keep him centered on the present moment. But the mind-numbing terror waned, he asked questions, listened to the answers, and his attempts at humor weren't met with blank stares. The people themselves had fascinating stories to tell. One maid had come all the way from Northumberland to help pay for her brother's medical education in Scotland. A footman had secret ambitions to open a dress shop that catered to the rising ranks of the bourgeoisie.

Seb was actually disappointed when Rotherby and Grace came to collect him.

"It was an honor to meet you," Seb murmured to the trio, then said to the woman from Northumberland, "and be sure to have your brother write me. I know fine men at the medical university in Glasgow that he should meet."

"Thank you, sir!"

"Excellently done," Rotherby said as they ambled off.

Over her shoulder, Grace announced to

212

the gathered servants, "Thank you all for your assistance. That will be all for today." She turned back to Seb, smiling widely. "You ought to feel proud of yourself."

"Proud," he said truthfully, "and exhausted." It was as though he'd run around the garden a hundred times rather than three. Clouds filled his head and he longed for some quiet corner of the world in which he could take shelter for a few moments.

"Then we've done enough for today." Grace's words were decisive. "It's time for some respite."

CHAPTER 11

"I cannot imagine why Rotherby didn't want to join us." Grace gently pushed aside tall grasses and carefully stepped forward, testing to make certain the ground beneath her was both stable and free from any creatures who might object to being trod upon. In one arm, she carried a woolen blanket. "It's a perfectly lovely day."

Sebastian followed in the path she created, moving his big body with surprising agility. "Not much for field excursions, the duke. Rotherby's more comfortable harrumphing in Parliament or smoking a cheroot in the study." He squinted with pleasure at the afternoon sun blazing overhead, hanging in a sky of faultless blue.

The blue of Sebastian's eyes.

She nudged that thought aside, or she attempted to. But she couldn't forget how he'd gazed at her in the ballroom, warmth in his look, and humble gratitude — as though she'd given him a gift. The gift of life with less fear in it.

She'd been glad to do it, glad to be able to play some part in making him happier, more confident. He deserved that much.

"Rotherby's loss in not coming with us," Grace said, yet she was glad that the duke had opted to stay in the city rather than come out to this meadow a mile northwest of London.

These past days in the ballroom, with her and Rotherby and Sebastian, she'd enjoyed them — but the duke was *always there,* and she'd begun resenting his presence. She wanted Sebastian to herself again. A selfish wish, and one she shouldn't make, but there it was. She missed their friendship . . . even as her responsiveness to him strengthened.

It had been no hardship to watch him run. To see his athletic body put to use, and to see a healthy flush in his cheeks and the shine on his skin. Such things made a woman think things, things she'd no right to think.

"What are we looking for?" Sebastian said, and she appreciated that he kept his voice low lest he frighten any nearby animals.

"I thought we might be able to see some viviparous lizards engaging in their mating behavior."

215

"Lady Grace Wyatt!" Seb exclaimed in a shocked voice. "I never suspected you to be one of those deviants who like to watch."

She turned to wink at him. "Don't tell my parents."

They reached a spot in the field where the grasses were shorter, and a number of large stones baked beneath the sun. Grace unfolded her blanket and dropped down onto it. She patted the spot beside her. "Here's a likely spot to observe."

Sebastian hesitated for a moment, then lowered himself to the blanket. He stretched out his legs as he leaned on one elbow, the picture of masculinity in repose.

Though she and Sebastian had ridden in her carriage out to the field — with the curtains drawn, of course, to subvert possible scandal — here in the meadow, with barely a few inches between them, she grew acutely sensitive to his nearness. Katie waited with her novel in the carriage, so Grace and Sebastian were truly alone for the first time.

Grace barely heard the drone of bees or the birdsong that wafted from a stand of birch trees, too attuned to him to notice much of anything.

Fortunately, she had enough reason to notice the mottled green-and-brown lizard

216

sunning itself on one of the rocks. "There," she whispered to Sebastian, pointing to the reptile. "A female. You can tell by the dark line on her back."

Sebastian put on his spectacles, which he'd produced from his coat's inside pocket. "Having herself a fine afternoon."

"Ballrooms can be so very tedious for common lizards."

"For common anthropologists, too," he said drily.

"An *uncommon* anthropologist," she corrected with a smile. "With a trove of knowledge."

He smiled back, but when he looked at her, his gaze was thoughtful. "My knowledge of *you,* Grace, is where I fall down."

"We've known each other for years," she said in a deliberately casual tone. "Surely you know anything that's worth knowing."

"How'd you become interested in herpetology?"

"Ah." That was a topic she could discuss without worry that things might drift into more personal territory. "I didn't grow up in London, but on my family's estate in Hertfordshire. Such a wondrous place, full of wild green space and creatures of every variety. I hesitate to use such hyperbolic words as *paradise,* but in its way, it was."

217

"Sounds enchanting." There was a note of wistfulness in his voice, and she understood that their upbringings had been considerably different.

"During my birth," she continued, "there had been . . . complications. My mother lost her ability to bear children, and so Charlie became my parents' main preoccupation, being the heir."

"They neglected you?" His body tensed — he was angry on her behalf.

"More like benign inattention. Which turned into a great gift. Whenever my governess set me at liberty, I was out of the house like a rocket, tramping across our estate, exploring every part of the landscape. There was so much to see, so much to learn."

He nodded. "The world's a wondrous place."

"And exceptionally big and surprising, especially when you're a child." She smoothed a hand over her skirts pooled around her. "We had a pond not very far from the house. I went there every day. It wasn't quite beautiful, not in any way a Romantic poet might consider, but to me it was — full of so many living things. *Bufo bufo* and *Lissotriton vulgaris* and *Natrix natrix helvetica,* all going about their lives."

218

She felt a fond smile touch her lips. "There's something delightfully quiet about amphibians and reptiles. They're fragile, and shouldn't be handled much. They need to be left alone."

"Sounds like someone I know," he said with a teasing grin.

She chuckled, liking too much when he joked with her, and the way it made her belly feel full of stars.

"They also don't have fur or adorable faces. They don't show emotion the way people want them to, so they're believed to be without feelings." Her jaw tightened as indignation rose within her. "It's not true. What they feel is subtler than what humans want. They feel, only it's kept here." She pressed a hand to the center of her chest.

"Never thought of it that way," he admitted. They both looked up as the shadow of a bird of prey crossed the meadow. "I must own that I'd not given much thought to the interior lives of reptiles and amphibians. They *do* seem emotionless and indifferent."

"I can't speak for them, of course," she said quickly. "No one can, but I know it's wrong to condemn them for being different or defying our expectations." She heard the heat in her voice, but felt no fear that Sebastian might belittle her for being passionate about herpetology.

How could she feel so comfortable with him and be so aware of him at the same time? The paradox mystified her — and frightened her.

Yet she was grateful all the same when he said gravely, "A lesson everyone could stand to learn."

She steadied herself with a breath. "In any event, I studied all the creatures of the pond, barely moving so they'd be comfortable around me. One day, I went out to the pond and it had been drained to make ready for landscape improvements." Just thinking about it made her throat tight and her eyes hot. "The creatures' home — where they ate and slept and mated and had families — was gone. It was awful. And no one cared. No other humans, anyway. My mother consoled me as I sobbed, but she didn't understand. We'd destroyed their world, and all to make something *prettier.*"

"I'm so sorry, Grace." The genuineness in his gaze, in his words, reached deep within her.

"Thank you. Almost twenty years have passed since that day, but sometimes the wound is still raw." She drew in another long breath. "I never knew what happened to all the creatures that once called the pond home, but as a result of that day, I became aware of the harmful effects of humanity on the natural world. I became determined to study it so that everyone can learn its significance."

"Admirable," he said sincerely.

"It's not much," she murmured, "but it's what I can do. I'm currently working on a paper that describes the deleterious effects landscape *improvements* have on the habitat of English reptilia and amphibia."

"I consider myself an utter ass to have never asked you about this before." He chuckled ruefully.

"You're asking now, so that's something."

He looked unconvinced. "The bare minimum of effort is hardly worth commending."

"And yet so many men believe that it is." Movement caught her eye, and she whispered as she pointed, "There. Do you see it?"

Sebastian went very still as he peered in the direction she indicated. "That lizard's biting the other's tail — is it an attack?"

"Mating behavior." She gave a soft laugh, and his laughter joined hers. They watched the two lizards as the male continued to hold on to the female's body as he attempted to position himself to deposit his seed.

"Perhaps we should give them some privacy," Sebastian suggested.

"The only species that finds sex shameful is humans." She looked over at him and found herself ensnared by his gaze. It held a heat she'd never seen before, an intensity that riveted her and shrunk the size of the world to encapsulate only her and him.

Everything slowed. At the same time, her heart knocked powerfully within her chest. She glanced down at his mouth, finding it impossibly captivating, profoundly tempting. Drugging sensuality coursed through her body as her gaze traced the contours of his lips. What would he taste like? The question burned her.

All the hours together, the dancing, the physical contact, it all distilled into a hot need that stole her breath.

When she managed to tear her eyes from his mouth, she discovered that he watched her from beneath lowered lids. His nostrils flared, and he swallowed thickly.

Wordlessly, they leaned closer to each other, and closer still, until bare inches separated them. It felt inevitable, yet unexpected.

Dimly, she was aware of him removing his

spectacles. Then his hand came up to cradle her jaw. She shivered at his touch but stroked her cheek along his palm. Pure instinct moved her so that any attempts at cohesive thought scattered like dandelion seeds on the wind.

"Grace," he rumbled. "I want —"

"Yes," she gasped. She wanted, too.

Their mouths met. The brush of their lips was soft — at first. It held an acute sweetness with a hint of shyness as they discovered each other. How could his lips be so soft?

Incrementally, the kiss grew hotter. She opened for him, his heat seeping into her, and the tip of his tongue dipped between her lips. He tasted of tea and sunshine. With that first savoring, her body caught fire and she gripped the hard flesh of his shoulder to bring him closer.

He growled as the kiss grew heightened. She had read many times of men making sounds of primal need, but never heard it herself, and to hear him in its throes now shot fire and potency through her.

He adored her mouth thoroughly, boldly, as if he couldn't take her deep enough. And, heavens above, how she loved it.

For a man who conducted himself so quietly, Sebastian could *kiss*.

Great God. I'm kissing Sebastian.

Her friend. Her cohort. *Not* her suitor or her rake. That was all for show, merely a performance.

Realization came in an icy gust. Curse her, but she'd mistaken his commitment to his role for genuine desire. And she had *known* that he was playacting, but her foolish body had believed. Now she felt like the veriest ninny.

She pulled back abruptly. His eyes opened, hazed by arousal. But that merely meant he'd had a physiological response — there was no greater significance.

Mortification rushed through her. She had to find some way to correct this and put everything back to where it had been before.

"Goodness." She fabricated a laugh. "Anyone watching us would truly believe we were a courting couple. A job well-done. You're to be commended."

For a moment, he said nothing as he stared at her. A brief look of bewilderment crossed his face and . . . hurt . . . ? But no, that couldn't be. It was gone in an instant. Then he straightened and cleared his throat. Wryly, he said, "Never say that applying oneself to one's studies doesn't pay off."

"Right. Right." She was repeating herself. Desperate for something to look at besides the tempting acreage of his body or the enticement of his mouth, she pointed her gaze toward where she'd last seen the lizards.

Sebastian followed the direction of her look. They both observed as the lizards continued to circle, the male attempting to secure the female by holding her with his mouth.

The female suddenly turned and ferociously bit the male on his leg. At once, the male released her. He scurried away underneath the rock, while the female continued to bask, seemingly content now that she'd discouraged her would-be suitor.

A shame that Grace couldn't bite herself as a reminder that the attraction she felt for Sebastian was simply a ruse. She would save him, and herself, future embarrassment.

In only a handful of days, Sebastian would make his debut as a rake. He would play the part of her suitor so she could capture Mason's attention, and she had to remember that the things he said and did were in service to that role.

But, bloody hell, pretend or no, his kiss would haunt her to the end of her days.

CHAPTER 12

It was an unqualified disaster.

The garden party was but one and a half hours away, and Seb had done his level best to attempt a dashing arrangement of his neckcloth — to no avail. The more he fussed with the length of white linen, the more appalling the result, until it now hung limply around his neck like a wilted onion.

How had three days passed so quickly? Each afternoon, he'd spent hours in the ballroom of Grace's home, with Rotherby quizzing him and guiding him in everything a would-be rake needed to know and do. The lessons had, in and of themselves, been readily digested. But it hadn't been the proper way to kiss a lady's hand that haunted his waking — and dreaming — hours. Nor had he stewed over the names of London's most popular gaming hells.

No. His thoughts had circled around Grace. The way her lips pursed just before she laughed. How her eyelids lowered a fraction as she contemplated a new fact or bit of information. The trails of gold he felt whenever she lightly touched her hand to his forearm.

And that kiss . . .

He thanked any and all available deities that she'd reminded him in the sunlit field that he was her pretend suitor only, and that whatever he'd experienced as they kissed — desire, yearning, feelings that were far from platonic — all of that existed in him alone. She had her sights fixed firmly on Fredericks.

That didn't mean he stopped thinking about kissing her, or that he didn't want to do it again.

He wouldn't, of course, but he *wanted.*

In two hours, Seb would pretend to court her in front of an audience — so she might attract another man's interest.

He hadn't really thought things out when he'd decided to undertake the scheme.

Even so, none of this mattered if he couldn't sodding tie his sodding neckcloth because no sodding rake ever set foot outside without looking his sodding best. Sodding Rotherby had sodding said as much.

The calisthenics he'd done at his sporting

academy this morning had burned away his anxiety, but this neckcloth debacle brought it back to the fore. How could he feel calm and comfortable enough to play the rake if people were busy sniggering at the flopping fabric around his neck?

Seb glared down at the neckcloth. Perhaps if he concentrated hard enough, he could make the damned thing obey his will and tie itself.

Bang! Bang! His attempt at mind control broke apart at the sound of someone pounding on his front door.

"Wait a bloody moment," Seb yelled. He stalked through his rooms, muttering to himself. This was not what he needed right now, moments away from one of the most important events of his life.

He threw open the door, revealing Rotherby and a slim, beautifully dressed young man with glossy black hair. The stranger carried a mahogany case under his arm.

Rotherby's gaze drifted down to Seb's pathetic neckcloth. "Oh, dear. I see we've come too late to prevent the murder of your poor cravat." He glanced at the man standing behind him. "Can it be revived, Beale?"

"It will take some doing, Your Grace," Beale replied, "but consider what miracles

I've wrought with your wardrobe." The well-appointed man clicked his tongue as he surveyed Seb from top to bottom. "Is *that* what you're wearing?"

"These are my brand-new clothes," Seb protested. He'd put on a dark blue waistcoat and a deep brown jacket, and sported buff breeches, which tucked into his tall boots. Only a moment ago, Seb had thought himself rather fine-looking in his attire, but apparently, his opinion was rubbish.

"The garments themselves are fine," Beale said airily, "but the assemblage requires attention."

"I'm sorry — who are you?" Seb asked.

"Ah, right," Rotherby said, stepping past Seb as he breezed into the room. "Holloway, this is my valet, Beale. I had a feeling you might require a little assistance, so I enlisted his aid."

Seb nodded curtly at Beale, who barely inclined his head in response as he approached Seb.

The valet glanced around the front parlor of Seb's rooms, his gaze touching on the piles of books on every available surface, including the floor. "I take it the housekeeper has gone on strike."

"When she tidies up," Seb said flatly, "I can't find anything."

Without a word of warning, Beale reached out and grabbed a handful of Seb's hair.

"Beg pardon!" Seb cried.

"A good thing I brought my tools," the valet said. "*This* needs work. I've seen less thatching on a Buckinghamshire cottage. And *this.*" He released his hold on Seb's hair and ran a palm down Seb's cheek. "Did you shave with a trowel?"

It had, in fact, been the most attention Seb had ever paid to his toilette, but here again, he evidently had no understanding of what was required.

"Um —"

Beale held up his hand in a demand for silence. "Never mind. Strip to your small-clothes so I have a blank canvas."

Seb threw a worried glance at Rotherby, who had made himself comfortable by shoving a stack of books off the settee and taking a seat.

"Do as Beale says," his friend advised. "I find it best never to argue with him."

"Fine — but have a care with my books, old man. We can't all of us afford enormous personal libraries." Any further comment Seb might have made was silenced by Beale's impatient tugging at his clothing.

One hour and a considerable amount of work later, a dressed, shaved, and barbered

Seb stood in the middle of his parlor as the valet circled him. Beale's eyes were narrowed, and he tapped his finger against his chin, evidently in deep contemplation. From his place on the settee, Rotherby also studied Seb.

"Well?" Seb burst out after several agonizing moments.

Silence. And then Beale gave a small nod. "I am a virtuoso."

Seb regarded the valet cautiously. Was Beale being ironic, or was he sincere?

"What do you think?" Seb asked Rotherby.

"The most important thing is," his friend returned, "what do *you* think?"

"I . . . don't know." Seb looked down at himself. All the hues of his garments harmonized — at least, he believed they did, since he had little understanding of color theory. There were no frayed cuffs, no loose buttons or worn patches. That was an improvement.

When he'd refused to work at Holloway Ironworks, his father had severely reduced his allowance, which meant severe economizing. He had grown used to looking shabby — it was an indicator that he didn't have to be John Holloway's obedient son. Still, he hadn't realized just how threadbare he'd become.

As little as clothing indicated a person's integrity and the truth of their heart, pretending as though garments didn't matter was naïve. It was slightly galling.

But to play the game, one had to obey the rules, as well as wear the uniform.

"Take a look in the mirror," Rotherby said.

"I don't have one."

Rotherby shot to his feet. "You truly do not possess one? Not a pier glass or even a tiny looking glass?" When Seb shrugged, his friend let out a noise of frustration. "How the hell do you shave?"

"By touch. My hands are perfectly capable of sensing the amount of beard on my cheeks and chin. I don't need to *see* anything."

"That explains why you always look like a threadbare carpet." Rotherby waved his hand in a gesture of dismissal. "Never mind. Trust me when I say you look the epitome of a stylish rake. Wouldn't you say, Beale?"

"The image of you in that abomination of an ensemble has been burned into my mind." The valet clicked his tongue. "But, was I not scarred by that mental picture, I would consider you the most modish rake in London."

Rotherby pointedly cleared his throat.

"After Your Grace, of course," Beale

added. He stepped back, permitting Rotherby to approach.

Seb watched his friend's expression carefully. "You're certain? I look presentable?"

"More than presentable. You are an Incomparable." Rotherby kissed his own fingers. "Beale has transformed you."

Seb exhaled. He wanted, *needed,* to be everything Grace desired him to be, and he could not consider failure. He'd been a disappointment to his family — he refused to disappoint someone he truly cared about.

"But none of what I or Beale say signifies." Rotherby tapped a finger to the center of Seb's chest. "It's what's here that matters. Think of all the lessons you've learned over the past week, all the confidence you've gained."

Seb's head swirled with all the information Rotherby had imparted to him, and his body twitched in recollection of the countless drills he'd performed — walking, bowing, standing, and making conversation. Especially making conversation. His belly knotted as he thought about a party full of strangers, but as he tucked the leather gloves Grace had given him into his pocket, he ran through the horrendous situations that might unfold.

Was it possible that he'd disgorge the

contents of his stomach on the shoes of an MP? Yes. But *would* he? Unlikely.

He now possessed an arsenal of tactics to help him move through his anxiousness. Concentrate on his breathing, keep the gloves in his hand to anchor him in the present moment, ask questions, and listen to the responses.

He could do this.

"Everything we've done this week," his friend continued. "It's all stored within you. It was already there. We just gave it shape and direction."

Seb ran a hand down the front of his waistcoat. The silk whispered against his skin, grounding him to the now moment. He would not think of what would happen in half an hour, in a day or week or month.

"My carriage awaits us downstairs," Rotherby said.

Seb drew himself up and it was a measure of the excellence of his tailoring that his clothing didn't hinder his movements, rather heightening them instead. No wonder so many societies relied upon special ceremonial garments to induce in the wearer a sense of pride.

"Let's go be rakes," Seb said.

Nervousness skipped like a stone along

Grace's spine as she stood with her family in Lord and Lady Creasy's garden. She could find no calm in the potted hosta plants or in the waters of the many fountains that dotted the large green space — a sure sign of her agitation.

The viscount and viscountess were justly celebrated for their lush and sizable garden here in the heart of Mayfair, and their annual party during the Season's height was a highly anticipated event — especially because invitations were hard to come by.

Grace and her parents attended annually. She often broke away from the other guests to poke around beneath hedges and in the sunny patches along the paths, searching for reptiles. Not today. Today, she stood with a rigid back between her mother and her brother's wife, the two other women chatting easily.

She almost envied them. Neither her mother nor Anne knew what was to happen today, but Grace did, and she gazed longingly at circulated trays bearing flutes of sparkling wine. Yet she couldn't take a sip. She needed all of her wits about her.

Her gaze shot toward the top of the terrace's steps. Still no sign of Sebastian. God — when would he get here so everything could finally *begin* and she'd no longer be held in this agonizing suspense?

"What's got your stays so tight, Gracie?" her brother, Charles, asked. "Is there a heated controversy in the world of toads and frogs?"

She shot her brother an aggrieved look. It didn't matter that they were no longer children — teasing her continued to be one of his favorite pastimes.

"Ah, don't quiz her so, Charlie," their mother said with the same weary tone she'd used since her children were in leading strings.

"I haven't been to any social event this Season," Grace said tightly. "This is my first."

Charles said, "Remember how, in your come-out year, you hid in the retiring room at Lord Darvington's? I think you were in there for three hours."

"Two and a half," Grace answered. Heaven help her, if her family couldn't stop themselves from recounting her every youthful folly. "And I *had* danced for fifteen minutes before. I just found the rest of the night to be . . . uninteresting."

She didn't mention that during her dance with Lord Darvington's son, she'd caught him making a face at his friends, as if he was impossibly bored.

"You won't be ducking into any retiring room today." Charles glanced meaningfully at the steps to the terrace. "Mason Fredericks just arrived."

Heat flooded Grace's cheeks. She couldn't stop herself from looking over at Mason. Sunlight turned his light brown hair almost golden, and his eyes twinkled as he said something to Lord Creasy to make their host laugh heartily.

She tore her gaze away from him. In an airy voice, "Why should that be of interest to me?"

"Because," Charles said with a sly grin, "as soon as I said his name, your face went red as a bottle of claret."

Damn, was she as transparent as that?

"You *do* lose your composure whenever Mr. Fredericks is around, dearest," her mother said sympathetically. "And lately, you sigh when his name is mentioned."

"And you —"

Grace cut off her brother. "Yes, right, I understand your meaning." She tried to take the advice she'd given Sebastian, concentrating on her breathing. "I *may* be somewhat discomfited because he's here, but it's nothing worth publishing in the *Hawk's Eye.*"

She kept silent about the other reason her nerves were taut and her pulse throbbed in her neck. Sebastian was due at any moment. The plan was truly about to begin.

"I imagine that Lord and Lady Creasy are themselves quite agitated," Grace's mother said. "After years of inviting the Duke of Rotherby, he's finally agreed to attend. That's a considerable coup."

"I've heard that he's bringing a friend with him," Anne added. She added in a shocked whisper, "A commoner."

"Not any commoner," Grace's mother said with the triumphant air of one who has exclusive gossip. "The oldest son of the iron magnate, John Holloway."

"Wasn't Holloway at Lord Stoulton's the other week?" Charles asked.

"Yes, and he brought one of his other sons with him. No one knows much about the eldest son, but everyone knows Holloway's richer than the Royal Mint."

"Does that mean that your friend Mr. Holloway is John Holloway's son?" her mother asked.

"He is," Grace said.

"Strange, I've never seen your Mr. Holloway at any gatherings."

Her brother chuckled. "Wouldn't that be amusing if *he* was the commoner coming with the duke?"

Blast. She and Sebastian hadn't discussed

the fact that they had a preexisting relationship, so they would have to improvise when they encountered each other today.

But this concern was only one of many thoughts spinning through her head. Not only was Sebastian about to arrive, Mason circulated nearby.

The object of her desire moved easily from group to group of attendees, laughing, chatting. Everywhere he went he was met with smiles and enthusiastic bonhomie. The nearer he came to where Grace and her family stood, the faster her heart raced. Would he remember how awkward she'd been at the British Museum?

"Mr. Fredericks," her mother said when Mason was only a few feet away.

"Lady Pembroke." Mason bowed as he addressed everyone in her family. "Lord Wale, Lady Wale," he said to Charles and Anne. He turned to Grace and her belly seemed to cartwheel across the lawn.

"Lady Grace," he said brightly, clasping his hands behind his back. "Wonderful to see you away from the animal graveyard that is Montagu House."

Her heart lifted, while she struggled to keep from fidgeting beneath his gaze. As lightly as she could manage, she said, "I'd liberate the animals from the Royal Menagerie at the Tower but that might be unwise."

"They might wreak havoc amongst the populace," he said with a grave nod.

Happiness sparkled in her chest. Striving for a wry tone, she said, "It's not the populace I worry about so much as my fearing for the animals' safety."

"Quite right." He inclined his head, conceding her point. "Who thinks of the animals' well-being?"

Another fillip of pleasure moved through her. Their conversation wasn't nearly as horrendous as it had been the other day. Perhaps there was hope for her and Mason, after all.

"Where is Lord Pembroke?" Mason asked, glancing around. "He usually accompanies you to this event, and I'd looked forward to talking with him."

Yes — the very reason why she'd undertaken this enterprise in the first place. The mention of her father helped bring her careening emotions under a degree of control. "Perhaps you haven't heard, but my father is recovering in the country from an illness."

A fold of concern appeared between Mason's brows. Earnestly, he said, "My apologies if I spoke too lightly."

"No need for contrition," she assured him.

It gave her great joy to say, "We've heard from him only this morning and he's rapidly improving. He ought to be fully recovered by the middle of summer."

"Do give him my best wishes for a rapid convalescence."

The sincerity in Mason's words warmed her. "I shall. I'll write to him this very day and describe the gathering, down to each blade of grass and glass of sherry, and will be certain not to omit your good wishes."

Yet as she reveled in the smile she shared with him, feeling the first real rays of optimism, Lord Creasy stepped forward.

"Mr. Fredericks," their host said, "I have no fewer than three young ladies who are requesting the pleasure of your company. Three *marriageable* young ladies."

"Excellent," Mason said cheerfully. "As a rapidly aging bachelor, I can't miss an opportunity to meet marriageable ladies. Lady Grace, my lord and ladies." He bowed smoothly, a consummate gentleman. "Do excuse me."

The viscount led an eager-looking Mason away.

Grace's shoulders slumped and she let out a long exhale. As soon as she began to entertain hope, it was dashed apart by a handful of careless words. Was it even possible to have Mason consider her as anything other than a colleague?

"I'm sorry, dearest," her mother said in a kind and warm voice.

"It was merely an oversight on his part," Anne added. "I'm sure he thinks of you as an eligible woman."

"The rotter," Charlie muttered.

"It's fine," Grace said, holding up her hands in a silent plea for silence. "I'm truly fine. Thank you," she added sincerely. She was grateful for her family's support, truly grateful, but even their words of balm stung like vinegar.

Those glasses of sparkling wine looked *awfully* tempting right now.

She lifted her hand to signal a servant to bring her one, but an excited murmur rose up from the guests and she froze.

Someone new had arrived.

Lord and Lady Creasy hurried through the crowd, quickly making their way along the lawn and up the terrace steps to greet the arrival.

The Duke of Rotherby stood at the top of the wide stairs, wearing a polite but somewhat disinterested smile as the viscount and viscountess welcomed him.

"Well, well," Charles said quietly. "I hadn't expected him to actually show."

Anne lifted up on her tiptoes. "Someone's come out with him. The iron magnate's son. And . . . oh, my gracious."

"Yes, indeed," Grace's mother seconded.

Grace caught sight of Sebastian, who came to stand beside Rotherby.

She didn't have much experience with conducting experiments around the phenomenon of electricity. She knew almost nothing about it, other than it could be generated using special pieces of equipment, and that it was frequently bright — and used on the dead to induce spasms that resembled life. It was a potent, powerful force that the scientific community was only just beginning to understand.

But as little as she knew about electricity, she felt it now shooting through her, crackling with energy and fire as she beheld a transformed Sebastian. Never in her life had she been so astonished, so utterly robbed of logical thought. As empty as her mind had become, her body roared to life at the sight of him. She sensed every nerve, every one of her breaths and heartbeats.

He was and was not the same man. It was as though the shape and color of him had been polished to gleaming perfection, more brilliant than any diamond.

"Ahem," Charles grumbled. "Your

husband's standing right here, Anne. No need to devour the bloke with your eyes."

If Anne made any reply, Grace didn't hear it. She couldn't hear anything beyond the pound of her pulse and the rasp of her breath.

Sebastian's mop of blond hair had been cut and styled into an artfully tousled arrangement that looked as though he'd been striding along windswept moors — or rising from his lover's bed. His cleanly shaven jaws made hard angles above a pristinely tied neckcloth, drawing attention to the shape of his mouth.

She would have gladly let her gaze linger on his face, but her interest kept venturing downward, drawn by the sight of his athletic body dressed in an impeccably tailored white waistcoat, and double-breasted ink-blue coat, both of which highlighted the width of his shoulders and narrowness of his waist. His long, leanly muscled legs were encased in buff breeches, which were tucked into lustrous Hessian boots.

"*That* man is your friend?" Grace's mother whispered. "I had no idea he was a such a splendid Corinthian."

"Neither did I," Grace whispered back.

Seb was certain he was going to pass out.

Scores of eyes were all looking at *him,* assessing him, judging him. The urge to flee coursed through him, but he was too busy being light-headed and slick with sweat to move. If only he could be somewhere, anywhere, so long as it wasn't here and he could hide himself and be safe.

His hand drifted to his pocket, and unconsciously he reached for the gloves Grace had given him. The smooth leather was cool at first, but warmed beneath his touch. And as he ran his fingers over the glove, the whirling in his head began to subside. His breathing calmed.

A breath in, a breath out. Slow and steady.

"Welcome, welcome," a man's voice called jauntily. "Your Grace, an honor."

Rotherby murmured, "Lord Creasy, Lady Creasy." He inclined his head slightly. "May I introduce my friend, Mr. Sebastian Holloway."

When the elegantly dressed middle-aged couple turned their attention to Seb, it took him half a second to remember he was supposed to bow.

Bless the stars that Seb had practiced bowing over and over, because his body knew how to effortlessly execute the move without Seb having to think about the mechanics.

Wasn't he supposed to say something? Yes — he'd rehearsed what to say on the way over in Rotherby's carriage. "My sincerest gratitude for receiving me in your delightful home." He ought to speak more, shouldn't he? Oh, right. Ask questions. To Lady Creasy, he inquired, "Is this charming garden your own design?"

The lady pursed her lips in pleasure. "I worked with a very talented horticulturist, but much of the concept came from me."

"I can tell," Seb said without thinking. "Remarkable originality. Some truly unexpected touches that delight the eye." Good God, where had *that* come from? Seb didn't know his way around a compliment if he'd been presented with a compendium of them. And yet, some part of him knew what to say.

Lady Creasy giggled. *Giggled.* And fanned herself.

Seb shot a look at Lord Creasy, worried that his host would be angered by his wife flirting with a stranger. Astonishingly, Lord Creasy beamed as if he'd earned himself a spectacular favor.

"Come," Lord Creasy said with hearty bonhomie, "let us introduce you to our other guests."

As Seb and Rotherby followed their hosts

down the stairs, into the garden, Rotherby spoke under his breath. "Slight stumble at first, but first-rate recovery. Keep it up."

Given that Rotherby could be parsimonious with compliments, Seb couldn't ask for a stronger endorsement. He might truly be able to do this. *Might.*

Lord and Lady Creasy looked especially proud of themselves as they introduced Rotherby and Seb to their guests. Seb continued to hold on to the gloves, using them like a talisman that adhered him into his physical body rather than spin endlessly in his mind. Yet he needed something, an idea or image to keep in his thoughts that took him to a place where he felt happy and comfortable and perfectly at ease.

The reading tables at the Benezra was one of his favorite places in all the world. He pictured books spread before him, could smell the paper and leather, with all the time he desired to simply read. And . . . in this fantasy of the library . . . Grace sat opposite him, smiling as she wrote something in a notebook.

He felt his lips curve into a small smile, one of private pleasure meant just for him and Grace.

To his astonished pleasure, the guests he met seemed to think his smile was for them, and they returned it as though they and Seb were the only ones in on a secret jest. Incredible, but the elegant, powerful people he encountered were eager to find a reason to ingratiate themselves with him.

Guests bowed and curtsied deeply when they greeted Rotherby, yet the men shook Seb's hand vigorously and the women curtsied low enough to present views down the front of their gowns. Well.

He recalled Rotherby's lessons on confidence, and how it originated from within. The rake on Bond Street had inhabited himself so effortlessly, as though he had nothing to prove.

Removing his own stakes wasn't an easy task, but he tried to pretend that he was slightly amused by, nigh, indifferent to, the statuses of the people he met.

Seb tried to greet them all with his half smile. He'd murmur, "My pleasure," or "My honor to meet you," and then immediately ask a question about something — anything. If they were enjoying their Season, or what part of the Creasys' gardens they liked best, or even the name of the ladies' mantua maker so he might tell his mother where to have her gowns made. Perhaps he was mistaken, but it appeared that the ladies batted their eyelashes while giving him sidelong, lingering glances.

Did they . . . was it possible . . . they found him *desirable*? He smothered any sense of exultation — he couldn't be confident. Not yet.

His unease at being with strangers simmered beneath his calm, but rather than shove it aside, he mentally nodded in acknowledgment. *Yes, I see you, anxiousness.* That simple act of accepting his fear's presence somehow lessened it, and he breathed easier and easier.

He felt peaceful enough to quietly snicker as Rotherby looked bemused and then mildly annoyed that he was no longer the focus of everyone's attention.

Seb could not quite keep track of everyone he met, but the guests included an archbishop, several powerful MPs, and Prinny's closest confidants. The company was indeed rarified, and yet no one mattered to him quite so much as one person in particular. Grace was here, somewhere, but he couldn't try to look for her, lest he tip his hand too soon that they were acquainted with each other.

This would be the first time she would see him in his new clothing, wearing the persona of the rake. And his anxiousness rose up again in an edgy surge, because of

249

everyone's opinions, *hers* mattered the most.

Grace couldn't stop looking at Sebastian, watching his progress as he moved through the party. Even if her fate wasn't inexorably tied with his, *not* looking at him wasn't possible. In his new clothing, he was magnificent, yet she also sensed from him self-assurance that increased from minute to minute.

Apprehensive and curious, she glanced at Mason, standing beside a table of refreshments. Mason's brow was furrowed with curiosity as he watched Sebastian's progress through the party.

Grace's belly fluttered. This was precisely the reaction they wanted to engender in Mason.

The trembling in her belly doubled when Lord and Lady Creasy guided Rotherby and Sebastian toward her family. Was this what actresses felt moments before they stepped in front of the stage lights? As if they might combust with nervousness and excitement and fear and hope?

"Your Grace," Lord Creasy said to Rotherby, "I believe you know Lady Pembroke; her son, Lord Wale, and his wife, Lady Wale; and her daughter, Lady Grace."

The duke bowed, and one couldn't tell from his impassive civility that he and Grace and Sebastian had spent the last week in seclusion together. He was clearly an expert in navigating social waters.

"A pleasure to see you all again," he drawled. He tipped his head toward Sebastian. "This is my good friend, Mr. Sebastian Holloway."

"Honored to make your acquaintance," Sebastian said. After bowing, he effortlessly bent over Grace's mother's hand, and did the same for Anne.

His attention turned to Grace, and the world slid to a stop.

She knew in her mind, she *knew,* that the look of deep, sensuous interest in his gaze was strictly for show. Her body, however, had not received the missive. Every nerve came alive. She felt the spring breeze across her face and upper chest, and sensed the sun's warmth on her flesh — or the heat came from within her and she confused Sebastian with the sun. Easy enough to do, when staring at him dazzled her.

He narrowed the distance between them and took her hand in his. Energy sparked at his touch. She couldn't blink or breathe or move as he kissed the air above her knuckles, his gaze never leaving hers.

"Lady Grace." His voice was a seductive murmur, yet loud enough for everyone nearby to hear him. "A delight to find you here today."

"Mr. Holloway," she managed to breathe.

He didn't relinquish his hold of her hand. Not for many moments. And when he did, it was with visible reluctance, their hands slowly sliding apart.

It was a miracle that she remained standing.

"You're *him.* Grace's friend. She never said that you —" Her mother shot another look at Grace that indicated Grace had a considerable amount of explaining to do later.

"I'm honored that Lady Grace considers me a friend," Sebastian said.

"We've been friends since Eton, Holloway and I," Rotherby said, blessedly ignoring Grace's mother's reaction. "At Oxford, too."

"Is that so?" Grace's mother let out a little hum, a sure sign she was pleased by the fact that Sebastian was close friends with a duke.

"You're a newcomer to the Season?" Charles asked, an edge in his voice. "I've never seen you before."

Grace fought a frustrated, frazzled sigh. Her brother might enjoy badgering her, but for all that, he never lost his protectiveness where she was concerned.

"My circle of friends is a varied one, my lord." As Sebastian spoke, his gaze never moved from her. "Perhaps our paths haven't crossed until today, but I'm happy to remedy that."

Charles grumbled, but he subsided when Anne shot him a *Keep quiet* look.

"Lady Grace," Sebastian continued, "I look forward to deepening our friendship."

"As do I," she said, her voice breathless. *That,* at least, wasn't feigned.

There was a brief lull, and the corners of Sebastian's mouth tightened fractionally. She'd seen that happen before, when he had practiced talking with strangers. It was a sign of his discomfort. He struggled, internally.

What should she do? Panic over *his* panic clutched at her. She had to help him in some way. Perhaps she ought to take charge of the conversation. Or she could spill wine on herself and create a distraction.

Yet before she could speak or do something deliberately embarrassing, Sebastian said to her mother, "My lady, your daughter has spoken at length about your remarkable singing ability, particularly of traditional songs."

She *had*? Maybe once, ages ago, but surely

Sebastian didn't remember an offhand comment about her mother singing songs as she worked on her embroidery. It was simply part of ordinary life in her household, so she hadn't thought anything of her mother's habit.

Clearly, however, Sebastian had been paying attention.

"My singing is hardly remarkable," her mother said, but her cheeks went rosy.

He continued with an interested expression, "Which of those songs is your favorite?"

"That is a difficult question, Mr. Holloway. But I would have to say that I love to sing 'The Woods So Wild.' "

"Byrd's version or Gibbons's?" Sebastian asked. "I do love Byrd's interpretation."

Grace stared at him. They'd never discussed his interest in old English music — but today was one discovery after another.

"Why, I don't know which," her mother confessed with an amused shake of her head. "You must call and we will sing both to see which I like better."

Grace glanced back and forth between her mother and Sebastian. Though her mother did enjoy company, she almost never invited anyone for a visit, preferring to make calls rather than take them. Sebastian might be a newcomer to implementing charm, but he seemed to be a natural.

"It would be my pleasure," he said easily, as though he truly did want to pay a call. "I hope Lady Grace will join us."

Everyone looked at Grace, and every part of her flushed hotly. She'd forgotten that part of the plan was to aim attention in her direction. It was more than a little unsettling. The fact that Sebastian could move with such ease despite all the focus he drew, despite his shyness, was remarkable.

"That would be . . ." She swallowed around her self-consciousness. "I'm not much of a vocalist, but I will do my best."

"Delightful." His gaze transfixed her, and she forgot her awkwardness. She forgot almost everything except how wonderful it felt to be the center of his awareness.

"Your Grace, Mr. Holloway," Lord Creasy announced, and she briefly surfaced from the spell of his regard. "If you'll come with me, there are many more of my guests who are eager to greet you." He gestured for the two men to move on.

Rotherby inclined his head at Grace's family and turned to leave. Sebastian, however, remained — to give her one final, lingering look.

Grace felt his look from the crown of her

head to the very tips of her fingers and on to her toes. It was thrilling, and terrifying, and wonderful, and bewildering.

It's a performance, she reminded herself sternly.

But it was a remarkable performance, and her body didn't seem to care if he wasn't sincere.

"Mr. Holloway?" Lord Creasy pressed.

"Yes. Of course." Sebastian bowed before moving on.

Come back! her body cried.

Not real, she reminded her body.

I. Don't. Care, it answered.

The moment he'd gone a safe distance, her family crowded around her. Their whispering voices all joined together. Grace hardly heard them, still mired in the confusing and delightful mess of emotion and sensation Sebastian had left behind.

"Did you see that?" Anne asked.

"It really happened!" Grace's mother exclaimed.

Charles appeared perplexed. "The way he looked at our Gracie . . ."

She barely heard them, until her mother asked, "You have uttered not a single syllable that your Mr. Holloway was . . . was . . ." Her mother waved her hand in Sebastian's direction. "Like *that.*"

"Like what?" Grace asked, and she was grateful she was able to select two words from her vocabulary and affix them together to make a scrap of sense.

Her mother narrowed her eyes. "You know what I mean. He's not some scholar with his nose stuck in a book."

"He's a *rake,*" Anne said excitedly, then quelled her excitement when Charles scowled.

"It hardly seemed necessary to discuss his sartorial choices," Grace said, fighting for steadiness in her voice.

"And when you insisted he was only a friend," her mother continued, "we took you at your word."

"We *are* only friends." That, at least, wasn't untrue.

Her mother lifted an eyebrow.

"That wasn't the way one chum looks at another," her brother said.

Grace glanced over at Mason, still positioned near the refreshments table. He looked back and forth between her and Sebastian as if trying to work out a particularly intriguing theory.

When Mason's gaze caught with hers, there was a dawning comprehension in his eyes. He finally *saw* her. Not as only a fellow natural scientist, but a woman.

Her heart, already stimulated beyond reason, leapt within her.

Maybe, just maybe, this whole outlandish scheme would work.

CHAPTER 13

All the best bookshops had secrets, and McKinnon's was no exception. In addition to the sizable stock of "French" novels for anyone requesting *stimulating reading material,* the bookshop had a small room tucked away in the back that could be used for reading — or clandestine meetings.

"Your reserved books are in the storeroom," McKinnon said to Seb and Rotherby by way of greeting.

Seb nodded, and Rotherby gave his thanks before they moved through the labyrinth of shelves, past the patrons scattered throughout the shop.

"Slow down, Atalanta," Rotherby huffed behind him. "No need for a race."

Only then did Seb realize he practically ran between the bookshelves. He tried to reduce his pace, but it was ruddy difficult when his body buzzed with energy. The ride over in Rotherby's carriage had felt like a stint in a golden cage, confining him. Glancing down at his hand, he was surprised to see that he didn't actually glow with excited triumph. He remained steadfastly mortal. But he didn't feel mortal. After today's wildly efficacious debut of his rake persona, he'd become a towering titan. Oh, there had been some stumbles, but he'd managed to recover, and he'd walked hand in hand with his anxiousness so it hadn't overtaken him.

Once Rotherby caught up with Seb, he walked at a more moderate speed until he reached a corridor at the back of the shop. He turned a corner, then knocked twice on the narrow door at the end of the hallway.

"Bufonidae," he said through the door.

Rotherby rolled his eyes. "I don't know what that word means, but I've an idea, and you both need to expand your social circles."

"It's the name for the toad family," Seb said.

Before he could add that he'd expanded his social circle considerably only an hour before — and with astonishing success — Grace said through the door, "Enter."

After making certain that no one was observing them, he and Rotherby went into the room, then shut the door securely behind them.

The chamber was a small one, with room

for one table, three wobbly, mismatched chairs, and one battered wingback chair currently occupied by Grace. Her maid sat in one of the rickety chairs, nose stuck in a book, but Seb barely gave the servant a glance as he took in Grace's radiant face.

"You were *marvelous.*" She shot to her feet and wrapped her arms around him.

For a moment, he couldn't move, frozen in place by the sensation of her soft body pressed to his. It was all he could do to keep himself from burying his nose in her hair and inhaling her fragrance.

He took a more moderate breath before embracing her. Loosely. Which went against his every instinct demanding he hold her close.

"Nothing for me?" Rotherby asked wryly.

Grace peered over Seb's shoulder, but she didn't move to hug Rotherby. "A fine performance from you, as well."

To Seb's disappointment, she stepped back, releasing her hold on him. She took her seat, and Rotherby did the same. Seb's energized limbs protested the thought of sitting, so he remained on his feet. What he wanted, what he truly *desired,* was to kiss Grace. To feel his mouth against hers.

But that had been an experience he'd never have again. The thought tempered his ebullient mood.

"That was," she said, eyes bright, "the most superb display of territoriality that I have ever witnessed, and I've observed the *Coronella austriaca*. The smooth snake," she added for his and Rotherby's benefit.

At her words, Seb fought to resist expanding his chest and puffing. He wasn't used to feeling pleased with himself, and he instinctively reared back from that feeling. "It did go rather well," he permitted.

" 'Rather well'?" Rotherby snorted in disbelief. "Old man, you could hear the pantalets dropping like autumn leaves."

"An exaggeration." Seb threw a glance at Grace before fiddling with the buttons on his waistcoat. Part of him wanted her to recognize that there were some women who found him attractive, but, even so, he wasn't entirely comfortable mentioning pantalets in her presence.

"Not a bit," Grace replied vehemently. "Every woman fluttered their eyes at you and giggled as if they were just out of the schoolroom. Surely you noticed."

He coughed, unwilling to admit that he'd secretly been pleased by the female attention he'd received. "Not precisely."

Which was something of an untruth. He *had* noticed, watching himself and the party guests from a distance as if observing a particularly fascinating social behavior. He had been both the performer and the audience, inhabiting the character of Sebastian Holloway, rake, while simultaneously watching the whole thing unfold as scholar Seb Holloway. He couldn't wait to write about it.

"The response of the female guests was considerable," Grace said sunnily. "It was as though they were eager to peel away your clothing."

Seb lifted his chin, and reluctantly admitted to himself that it felt as though the top of his head brushed the ceiling. The women *had* looked at him with barely veiled sexual interest. Never before had he been the recipient of so much primal validation. It made him want to dig valleys out of solid stone with his bare hands. As though he could do anything.

"I just gave them a bit of eye contact and a husky chuckle or two," he demurred.

"Whatever techniques you employed," she said enthusiastically, "they worked. I wouldn't be surprised if you wound up with a new paramour. Or paramours."

He shifted as unease tightened his body. Discussing with Grace the possibility of taking other women to his bed was not something he relished. She seemed all too eager to hand him off to another woman. Damn it, hadn't they kissed not but a few days ago?

She might have forgotten, but he hadn't. And it rankled. Whatever validation he'd felt moments before drained away.

Smarting, he sought to change the subject. "Noticed something today. The male guests didn't dismiss me. They took my measure and seemed to determine I was more than viable. No one challenged me for dominance. It was as though they thought their best bet was to become my ally, increase their own status. One viscount actually invited me to join him at Tattersall's, and three other gentlemen invited me to someplace called the Orchid Club."

"Never heard of it," Grace said with a frown. "Perhaps it's some kind of botanical society."

"Perhaps," Seb said thoughtfully. "Don't have much use for botany in my work."

"Well," she continued with a considering look, "I'm always on the lookout for new organizations to join."

Rotherby coughed into his fist. "The Orchid Club's area of focus includes a different variety of wildlife than would interest you, Grace."

"In truth," she said airily, "my schedule is

264

honestly too full to accommodate joining any new societies."

"Other things vie for your attention at present," Seb said.

"Let us not forget the object of this whole endeavor," Rotherby interjected. When Seb and Grace both sent him mystified looks, he said with a touch of exasperation, "Fredericks."

"Of course!" Grace's expression brightened. "He seemed quite intrigued by you, Sebastian."

"More than that," Rotherby said before Seb could reply, "he looked at *you,* Grace. Seemed to consider you in a new light."

Seb's ebullient mood pitched down, as if it had willingly jumped off a cliff to drown in icy waters. Damn, his emotions kept veering wildly, and it exhausted him. Truth was, he reminded himself, he *ought* to feel jubilant that Fredericks had taken note of Grace. That was what he *ought* to feel. What he *did* feel was a surge of anger that the naturalist had noticed Grace because another man had done so. Couldn't the fool see how wondrous she was?

Grace, however, seemed delighted by the news.

"Did he?" Her fingers dug into the chair's arms as she leaned forward.

265

The energy that had hummed through Seb's body leached out, leaving him frayed and weary. He slumped into the remaining chair.

"Quite," Rotherby said decisively. "Fredericks took passing interest in Holloway at first, but when our man here lingered with you, *that* made Fredericks's ears prick up. Especially because Holloway seemed smitten."

"Thank you for that, Sebastian," she said warmly. "It was a most convincing performance."

"Happy to oblige," Seb answered with a small bow. He was glad his words didn't sound as hollow as he felt.

Something deep within him made a silent, frustrated growl. Because while he'd played the part of the rake when moving from guest to guest, speaking lines he thought a rake *should* speak, when he'd been with her, he hadn't needed to calculate the right thing to say for maximum effect. Words had sprung to his lips, words that had come from a place of authenticity.

Nothing he'd said to her had been a lie. The realization hit him hard, stealing his breath.

She thought he had been performing — but he hadn't been. Everything he'd said was real.

She does not *need to know that.*

"We've got Fredericks primed," Rotherby said, scattering Seb's thoughts. "But we'll need to do more to get him to see what a jewel Grace truly is."

"Oh, well, now," she said, seemingly discomforted by Rotherby's praise, which set off sparks of frustration in Seb, that she didn't value herself enough.

"What do you suggest?" Seb asked.

"My valet, Beale, did his own research and learned that every Friday afternoon, Fredericks goes for a ride in Rotten Row. Today is Tuesday, which gives us three days to prepare." Rotherby studied Seb. "How are you with the ribbons?"

Seb frowned. "I don't know anything about women's coiffures or bonnet trimmings. Is it relevant? Unless," he added, "you want me to dress Grace's hair. Which also seems immaterial to our objectives."

"I mean *reins,*" Rotherby said, looking on the verge of kicking his chair apart. "I'll put it plainly — can you drive a phaeton or any other sporting vehicle?"

The final droplets of Seb's exultation leaked away, and he found himself longing for the comfortable, safe world of books. "I can't afford anything like that. Been some time since I've driven, so I'm a bit rusty."

"Let's pray you'll pick it up again quickly." Rotherby jabbed a finger at him. "Come to my home tomorrow. We'll make you a dab hand before Friday."

Grace blinked. "I'm sorry — what happens on Friday?"

It was a relief to know that Seb wasn't alone in his confusion, but, then, Rotherby always did things according to his own satisfaction and without discussion, leaving everyone else to catch up.

"Wear a pretty new frock and bonnet," Rotherby said, rising to his feet, "because Holloway here is taking you for a drive."

"Oh, this is unusual," Grace's mother said as she took a seat in the drawing room.

"What is?" Grace looked up from the volume on the reproductive habits of reptilia from Asia. It was a decent enough book, and a subject worthy of study, but she'd barely read any of the printed words.

It was Friday. The day she and Sebastian were to go out driving. Though it was thoroughly planned and discussed, her anticipation and nervousness had built all week.

They'd parted company at McKinnon's as friends, yet today he'd be his other self. The

268

self she didn't quite know how to navigate.

"Whenever it's time for morning callers," her mother said, "you are conspicuously absent."

"As are you," Grace said.

"I felt like spending the afternoon in my drawing room," was the airy reply.

"Ab absurdo." Grace pretended to return to her reading, yet inside, she was aflutter. There had been little opportunity to communicate with Sebastian since they'd parted company at McKinnon's, and there was something about seeing him now that made her restless and apprehensive, as if he wasn't the Sebastian she'd known for so long.

But he wasn't the Sebastian she'd known, he was someone else. The same, and yet very, very different.

For one thing, she knew what it felt like to kiss him.

Don't think about that. It didn't happen.

Yet it *had* happened, and no amount of stern lectures to herself seemed to cure her of her fixation with his mouth.

Just read. It was what she did best. As she tried to make sense of the printed words in front of her, a footman came in with a tray bearing a card, which he brought to Grace's mother.

A small smile of triumph lit her mother's

face. "He's here."

Grace's stomach clenched. She was nearly as nervous as she'd been at the Creasys' garden party.

"Show him in," her mother told the footman.

The servant bowed before retreating. The moment he left the room, Grace's mother fluttered her hands at Grace. "Go stand by the window. The light there is exceedingly complimentary."

Grace almost snapped that she would do no such thing. But she needed to give people the impression that Sebastian's attention was welcome. Which it was, although not in the way that everyone believed.

She got to her feet and moved to the window, conscious of how the light filtered through the curtains to touch her hair and the curve of her neck. Yet her thoughts blurred — was she preparing for Sebastian's arrival for the benefit of her mother, or was she displaying herself to *truly* garner Sebastian's admiration?

She couldn't tell. And that uncertainty disconcerted her.

"Mr. Sebastian Holloway," the footman said from the doorway.

The servant stood alone for a moment, and Grace thought she saw Sebastian standing off to one side in the corridor, as though preparing himself to enter the room. And then a thrum of excitement pulsed within her as he strolled into the drawing room, wearing the same smile he'd worn at the garden party — as if he was in his favorite spot, with his favorite people. Today, he wore a burgundy coat and cream-colored waistcoat, and his boots were polished as glass. Under his arm, he carried a tall-crowned hat. He held it perfectly as he swept into a bow.

"Mr. Holloway," her mother said loftily, as if she hadn't reversed years of her usual custom to see him.

"Lady Pembroke," Sebastian murmured. He turned to Grace — a jolt of awareness shot through her when their gazes met — and bowed again. "Lady Grace."

She nodded in response, but said nothing. Her wildly beating heart seemed to have lodged itself in her windpipe, making it impossible to speak.

"My thanks for welcoming me, Lady Pembroke. I realize it's somewhat unusual for a man of my standing to be given the honor of being received in your home."

"You *are* an intimate of His Grace, the Duke of Rotherby," her mother said indulgently.

271

"In truth," Sebastian replied, striking a pose that appeared entirely effortless but also displayed his long body beautifully, "I left his company not but a quarter of an hour ago."

Her mother smiled, and Grace felt as though she was watching a play where she recognized the actors but had absolutely no idea how the plot would unfold. Was she the audience, another member of the cast? She had no idea.

"Much as I enjoyed our discussion at the Creasys' gathering," her mother said, "I'm not certain that my voice is ready for singing today." Her hand fluttered at her throat.

"I've a collection of early songs and ballads," Sebastian replied, smiling. "We could perform duets another time. Your clear soprano will be a delight to hear."

Her mother preened. "I observe that you are wearing gloves suitable for driving. Did you just come from a jaunt?"

"If Lady Grace would favor me with her company," he said breezily, "it would be my honor to have her accompany me on a drive down Rotten Row."

Even though Grace knew perfectly well that the invitation was coming, it still sent a pulse of exhilaration through her body.

Her mother glanced at her — silently

seeking Grace's answer. Ah, bless her. Not every woman had parents who would do nothing without permission.

She gave her mother a small nod.

"By all means," her mother said. "Only, you must take your maid with you."

Only that morning, Grace had given Katie a new salacious novel — purchased earlier that week at McKinnon's — which would keep her maid well occupied. "I'll go up and get my things."

She hurried out of the drawing room, conscious of two sets of eyes on her as she departed the chamber, and took the stairs to her bedroom as quickly as she could without thundering loudly on the steps. Still, excitement urged her to climb the stairs quickly.

In her bedchamber, she found Katie seated on the floor, beside the fire, already deep into the new book. Her maid guiltily climbed to her feet and tucked the volume behind her back when Grace entered.

"There'll be time enough for that in just a few minutes," Grace said, nodding at Katie's hidden hand. "We're going for a drive with Sebastian."

Katie squinted at her. "My lady? Do you mean we're heading to Hampstead Heath to look at them wriggly, scaly things?"

"I mean," Grace said, planting her hands on her hips, "that we're going to Rotten Row with Mr. Holloway. No reptiles or amphibians will be involved in the afternoon's activities." When her maid continued to stare at her in disbelief, Grace added, "My spencer and bonnet, Katie. Now."

The maid snapped out of her astonished reverie and then dove into the clothespress. She couldn't be faulted for being surprised. It wasn't as though Grace made a habit of driving with gentlemen, as if she were any other marriageable young woman.

Fifteen minutes later, Grace descended the stairs, clad in a straw bonnet and pale blue spencer that her modiste had insisted on, declaring the garment wonderfully flattering for Grace's eyes and complexion. She hoped Sebastian liked how she looked in it.

This is for Mason, *of course.*

Of course.

Katie waited in the foyer as Grace approached the drawing room, from which emanated the sound of her mother laughing. Looking into the chamber, she found her mother wiping tears of mirth from her eyes. Sebastian regarded her mother with a faint smile, but that smile widened when he caught sight of her.

"Lady Grace." One of his brows lifted, displaying his approval of her choice in spencer, and God above, did she enjoy seeing his reaction.

"Ah, there you are, darling," her mother said. "Mr. Holloway has been so very charming."

"There's nothing especially noteworthy in being charming to such a delightful person," Sebastian said easily.

Grace ought to offer him a shovel, since he seemed inclined to bestow flattery with a liberal hand. But her mother actually made a sound similar to a giggle, so it was evident that she was the only one who thought Sebastian's blandishments a trifle heavy-handed.

"Shall we?" Sebastian offered her his arm.

Of course. They *would* have to get moving if they wanted to reach Rotten Row in time to encounter Mason, so she took Sebastian's arm. She ought to be used to the unexpected solidity of his muscles, and yet awareness skittered through her when she rested her hand atop his sleeve and felt the firmness of him beneath the fabric.

"Do enjoy yourselves," her mother called after them.

They stepped outside to find what had to be the highest, shiniest two-wheeled vehicle waiting for them in the street. The pair of horses drawing the vehicle were sleek chestnut creatures who displayed all the benefits of selective breeding. Meanwhile, the groom holding the horses' bridles preened beneath the wondering attention of passing pedestrians.

"Cor," Katie muttered.

"Oh. My," Grace breathed.

"You like it?" Sebastian asked her. He lowered his voice. "It's Rotherby's curricle, on loan for the day."

"My knowledge of sporting vehicles is undeniably paltry," she admitted on an exhalation, "so I can say with certainty that I've never seen anything like it." She eyed the towering vehicle. "It looks rather challenging to pilot."

"Rotherby refreshed me on how to drive this sort of thing," Sebastian said. He glanced at Katie. "There's a seat in the back for a groom. You can take that."

"Yes, sir!" Katie said, already climbing onto the perch at the back.

Sebastian and the groom helped Grace up into the extremely high seat, before he took his place beside her. The seat wasn't particularly large, leaving her little choice but to press the side of her leg to his. Heat from his body radiated into hers, making her feel

276

feverish and doing little to soothe her roused nerves.

After Sebastian secured the reins around his left hand, the groom handed him a long whip, which he held confidently in his right hand. With a click of his tongue, he signaled the horses, and a moment later, the beautifully sprung vehicle began to move.

The next phase of their plan was underway.

CHAPTER 14

Much as Seb was acutely aware of Grace sitting so close beside him, he had to divide his attention with guiding the curricle through Marylebone traffic

"You never said anything to me about the fact that you could sing," she said, and while her words verged on accusatory, her tone was not.

"Mr. Okafor would be annoyed if I broke into song in the middle of the Benezra."

"Depends on what you sing," she replied pertly.

"Given that most of the songs I know usually involve people rutting, he might not appreciate my musical offering."

She laughed, and the sound caressed silkily down his spine. It had been too long since he'd heard her laugh, especially because they'd been so preoccupied with the serious task of transforming him into a rake. So to hear her give way to mirth now gratified him.

"Here I thought you were a chaste scholar," she teased, "not someone who roars bawdy tunes."

"Firstly, I *croon* more than *roar*," he said, pretending to be affronted.

"And secondly?"

"I'm far from chaste." The moment the words were out of his mouth, he regretted speaking them. Because it was impossible to ignore the fact that the kiss they'd shared had set him afire with hunger for her, just as it was impossible to ignore the fact that she didn't share his hunger. Not for *him,* in any case.

Was it better or worse for her to view him as devoid of sexuality? Neither option made things comfortable between them.

A brief quiet fell, and Seb concentrated on driving. He was grateful that there was so much traffic so that he could be occupied with something besides stewing over what he should or shouldn't say to her.

"I should have asked at the beginning," Grace said after a moment. "If you had a . . ." She cleared her throat, and when he glanced at her, he saw hectic color in her cheeks. "A lover. I didn't think to ask, and if I'd be stealing your company from anyone."

"There's no one," he said gruffly. He didn't want to explain his prior arrangement with the widow Mary, or how long it had been since he'd taken a woman to bed. To speak of it — with her — made him burn with a strange mortification.

"No one *at present*?"

"No. One," he gritted.

"Ah." Was it relief he heard in her voice? And why, if that was the case, did that make him feel exultant? "That was a prime display of how to charm a lady's mother, what you did at my home."

He fought the impulse to puff his chest, but, by God, he *had* done quite well with the countess. Considering how, not but a fortnight ago, he would have preferred to drag himself across a stable floor rather than talk with Grace's mother, he could acknowledge that he'd made some progress.

"It's not difficult," he said, "when it's clear that she's a good person. Her love and care for you is unmistakable. While you were up in your room, she interrogated me about the company I keep, and if my intentions toward you were nefarious."

"Oh, God." Her cheeks turned bright pink. "I'm so sorry."

"I'm not. Hers were all excellent, relevant questions. I assured her that Rotherby didn't associate with anyone of suspect character, and that my interest in you was strictly proper. Then I provided some distraction by telling her an amusing anecdote about my time at Eton. Well, it wasn't amusing at the time it happened, but years later I can find the humor in it."

He maneuvered the horses around a tipped-over wagon, silently thanking Rotherby for what had been an exhausting day of learning to drive a curricle.

"Don't leave me ignorant," Grace said avidly. "You *must* tell me."

"Rotherby and I were in the same house at Eton, but we'd no real interaction with each other. Not until he and I and three other boys received a special punishment for various misbehaviors." He fought a grin, remembering that long-ago day when his life had taken an unexpected turn.

She leaned back, regarding him with a furrowed brow. "I can hardly believe that *you* committed any transgression."

"Therein was the amusing anecdote I told your mother." His lips quirked at the youthful folly of his past self. "I was punished because . . ."

"Fighting?"

"No."

"Sneaking off to the village to meet girls?"

"I wrote angry, contradictory statements in the margins of school library books."

"What? Oh, no!" She covered her mouth with her hand.

He gave a rueful chuckle. "It's true. I felt that the authors of those books were being inaccurate and biased, particularly in their assessment of the difference between the sexes, so I contributed my own refuting statements. The headmaster and house captain both disagreed with my approach, and so I was disciplined for defacing school property."

She laughed. "How exceptionally *you,* Sebastian."

"Everyone's capable of change," he said, shaking his head, "or so I hope, but in my case, I haven't undergone that considerable a metamorphosis."

"What did the duke do to warrant *his* punishment?"

"I'll let him tell you. However," he went on, "we needn't waste time discussing me, Rotherby, or our ridiculous crimes. It's precisely the opposite of my intention."

He clicked his tongue at the overcrowded traffic surrounding Manchester Square, but couldn't resent it overmuch. The slower it took to reach Rotten Row, the more time he had with Grace.

They reached Park Lane, and continued southward, passing grand residences that fronted Hyde Park. Despite the congestion on the street and sheer number of vehicles, pedestrians' heads turned to watch Seb and Grace in the elegant curricle. For the first time, he drew notice not for who he was, but for what everyone believed he *owned*. It wasn't entirely pleasant.

He could have been anyone. A good man, a terrible man, but he was to be admired because he possessed an expensive vehicle.

How bloody strange.

She said pensively, "It's hard to remember that beneath your polish, you're still the same Sebastian — my friend."

"I'm still me," he agreed neutrally. He *was* her friend, and it wasn't right or reasonable to want more from her. *Remember that.*

"Is it . . ." she asked lowly, ". . . very uncomfortable, pretending to be someone else?"

"It's as though . . ." He struggled to put words to things he'd never fully articulated, not even to himself. "I am still me, only with a bit more . . . gloss. Like lacquer over rough wood."

She nodded slowly. "That makes sense."

They'd almost reached the entrance to Rotten Row, full of men and women on horseback or slowly riding in vehicles just as luxurious and expensive as the curricle, in calculated displays of wealth and standing.

"I hope," he said to her, "you never change to please anyone."

Her voice was almost too soft to be heard above the surrounding din. "I won't. I am who I am, and I'm happy with that."

A fraction of tension left his body. "That's good." He made the turn onto Rotten Row, joining the throng. "And now the curtain goes up on the next act of the performance."

The sights and sounds — and scents — of Rotten Row were all new to Grace. Not once in the course of her few, unimpressive Seasons had she ever ventured onto the famed path, given that there was little chance of spotting any reptiles or amphibians on the gravel and tan track. There were, however, horses in abundance. And many, many people.

Vehicles and people atop horses traveled along the path at a sedate pace, ensuring not just safety, but also the greater opportunities to see and be observed. There were expensive vehicles of every variety, including spindly phaetons driven by dashing gentlemen, and open-topped carriages holding groups of people. Men and women in smart riding clothes sat atop sleek horses, hacking up and down the track.

As a mating display, it certainly was far more extravagant than anything she'd observed within the amphibious and reptile world. But fascinating, nonetheless.

The pageantry was slightly undercut by the earthy smell of horse manure. Which seemed rather apt.

"I don't see Mason," she said under her breath as she scanned the path. "Perhaps we've missed him." While she felt a prickle of disappointment, she couldn't help but be glad for more time alone with Sebastian.

When she'd asked him to fill the role of rake and faux suitor, she'd done so with specific intentions. Mason was precisely the sort of man that she could envision as her husband. Intelligent, scientifically minded, witty. She'd been certain he was the man she wanted to marry. Yet these past weeks with Sebastian clouded her judgment and left her deeply confused.

She'd asked him to help her, because he was her friend. He'd undertaken this task for his own gain, yes, but also for the sake of their friendship. Were she to suddenly turn to him and announce, *Sorry but I'm developing feelings for you, which violates the terms of our agreement and likely isn't what you want at all* — well, she'd ruin what she and Sebastian shared. How could he trust her, especially because she didn't know her own heart?

She had to stay silent, and stay fast to her plan of attracting Mason.

"If we provide the onlookers with an overt display of flirtation," Sebastian suggested in a low voice, "it's certain that word will reach Fredericks via the usual conduits of information."

He nodded toward a trio of women in a carriage, their gazes all fastened on him and Grace. Two gentlemen on horseback also craned their necks to get a better look at both the curricle and the people riding in it.

"So odd," Grace murmured. "Being the object of people's positive attention."

He looked at her, his expression pensive and a little sad. "Was it very terrible for you, your debut?"

Rather than give in to the corrosive memory, she made herself chuckle. "Humans are far more vicious than animals."

"Goddamn them," Sebastian muttered, his anger on her behalf shamefully satisfying. "Let's make them all choke on their narrow-mindedness."

"I'd like nothing better," she said appreciatively.

He cleared his throat softly before saying in a voice loud enough to be heard by adjacent onlookers, "My thanks, Lady Grace, for favoring me by accepting my suggestion to go for a drive."

"Of course, Mr. Holloway." It felt highly artificial to speak with the intent of being overheard, but it had to be done.

Already, the women in the carriage were leaning in their direction, trying to catch every word.

"I realize," he continued, "that your time is prized, but I'm especially grateful that you chose to spend your rare leisure hours with me."

"Good afternoon, Lady Grace," a passing female rider called. "Mr. Holloway."

Grace gave the woman a nod, recognizing her as a baroness who had only curtly acknowledged her at various galas.

More greetings were lobbed at Grace and Sebastian, and she smiled and nodded at them — though that sense of unreality continued, as if she was watching everything from above. These people, who'd scorned her, suddenly found her worthwhile. Because she was with Sebastian.

How . . . unsettling. And infuriating. Why should her merit be determined by how a man viewed her?

Sebastian spoke in an undertone. "Excellent. You're the belle of Rotten Row."

"Today," she grumbled.

"We'll beat them at their own game," he said, and she appreciated that he understood her conflicting feelings. "There's a book I have about the mentality of societies, and I remember reading that in order to make something valuable, it needed to be scarce in number."

"Stands to reason that a person and their time operate in a similar capacity." When she spoke, it was loud enough to be heard by people passing near their curricle. "As it happens, I *do* have to be somewhere in an hour."

He gave her a small nod, understanding what it was she attempted to do. "You've my word that I'll have you home before then," he said gallantly. "But in the interim, let us enjoy our time together. There are so few people of substance in London. You, however, are the exception."

He sent her a look of toe-curling intensity, fraught with heat and awareness. Her body went liquid.

He's just playing a part.

But it *felt* real — especially after the talk they'd had on the way here. She'd divulged things about herself that no one before had ever desired to know. But Sebastian had. He wanted to know her better.

He *saw* her. And it felt so wondrous, as if she'd emerged from hibernation to warm herself in the sun.

"Good afternoon, Lady Grace."

She turned to give the newcomer a polite but distant greeting, yet the words fluttered away like autumn leaves when Mason approached. In his crisp riding clothes, sitting atop a glossy gray horse, she'd never seen him so dashing.

Beside her, Sebastian tensed.

"Mr. Fredericks," she said, and was pleased she sounded effortlessly polite.

"Holloway, isn't it?" Mason looked at Sebastian in the way that all males within breeding age did when meeting one another — assessing whether or not the other male was a threat, or could be dominated. "We've met a time or two at the Benezra Library."

"Fredericks," Sebastian said. The word itself was genial enough, but the stony look in Sebastian's eye told another tale.

Both men wore smiles, but the glints in their eyes — as well as the way they both sat up straighter and broadened their chests — spoke of animosity.

She bit back a laugh. How very typical

289

they were being. Even men who were scholarly and progressive couldn't seem to stop themselves from reverting to such primal behavior when competing for the attention of a viable female.

Dear God, they're vying for me. It wasn't as flattering as novels and poems seemed to think it was. No wonder she read so few novels and poems.

"Lady Grace," Mason said, "I'm glad to see you here, but Hyde Park isn't the best location for observing wildlife."

"It depends on what you define as *wildlife.* Besides, you never know what you're going to find out in the field."

"Very true." He brought his horse closer to the curricle. "Only the other day, I observed a pied flycatcher that was very far from where it's typically seen."

The name meant little to her — she guessed it was a variety of bird — but she nodded. "How surprising."

"There's nothing more exciting," he said brightly, "than discovering something out of the ordinary. Or a known entity reveals itself in a new way."

"It is one of my favorite things about the natural world," she said honestly. "We keep expecting it to behave in a certain manner —"

"Yet it doesn't," Mason said, completing her thought.

His gaze met hers, and she found herself staring into the green depths. There was understanding there. She couldn't suppress the sensation of triumph that surged through her. This was precisely what she'd hoped for.

"If you've need of company in the field," Sebastian said, his voice breaking the spell that had fallen over her and Mason, "you have but to whisper the word and I will make myself available to you."

"Thank you." She came back to herself, but she hoped her bonnet hid the blush that washed across her face when she recalled the kiss she and Sebastian had shared in the field.

Mason coughed once. "I hope to see you at the Viscount and Viscountess Marwood's ball in two nights."

She lifted her brows in surprise. He'd never mentioned socializing with her before.

"It's my intention to attend," she said.

"Do save me a dance." He flashed her a bright smile.

It seemed so easy for him, this charm, this comfort with banter, and while she instinctively warmed to it, she couldn't help but think of how hard Sebastian had worked to achieve the same effortlessness.

"I will attempt to do so," she said, "but I cannot make a promise."

Yes, that's the way. Make certain he has to work for it.

"I'll be sure to seek you out," he said, his dimple winking, "so that I get that dance."

"Provided it isn't the waltz," Sebastian said. When she pulled her gaze to him, he appeared relaxed and carefree, his body long and loose, but there was that steel in his eyes. "That's already been promised to me."

"Oh," Mason said offhandedly. "You'll be at the viscount's ball?"

"As the Duke of Rotherby's guest," Sebastian answered the way a man might draw a sword.

"How fortunate you have such distinguished friends," Mason said with hard cheerfulness, "that you might gain entrance to such exclusive galas."

"Wasn't certain about going." Sebastian shrugged. "Balls can sometimes be tedious, but I always have a good time, and," he added with a smile aimed at her, "the possibility of seeing Lady Grace is the greatest inducement, of course."

"Of course," Mason said, also sending her a smile.

It felt so peculiar to have two exceptionally handsome men smile at her as if they would do anything to gain her favor. Again she felt the strange double sensation of pleasure and annoyance.

But then, men often engendered feelings of pleasure and annoyance.

"I will see you soon, Lady Grace," Mason added. His tone was far cooler when he added, "A pleasure seeing you, Mr. Holloway."

Sebastian grunted Mason's name.

After giving Grace a small bow, Mason touched his heels to his horse and then trotted off. She was careful not to follow him with her gaze.

When she was certain Mason was out of earshot, she said to Sebastian in a gratified whisper, "You were *amazing.* It truly seemed as though you were being possessive. If anthropology doesn't prove fulfilling, you ought to consider a career on the stage."

"I'm not very skilled in that kind of performance." His words sounded oddly tight, as if he was clenching his teeth.

"Today, you were." She cleared her throat, wondering how to best approach what she had to say. "However . . . do you think . . . perhaps . . . you might behave a little less proprietarily?" When Sebastian frowned, she explained, "If Mason thinks that we're truly

293

a romantic couple, the greatest likelihood is that he'll turn his attention elsewhere."

"I'll try to strike the right balance between interested and permissive," Sebastian answered drily. He clicked at the horses, and they increased their pace.

In for a penny . . . "If I may be candid —"

"Please do."

She turned to him, and though he continued to drive, she knew she had his attention. "Jealousy isn't appreciated by women. We're not *things*. There's nothing flattering about being treated like an object."

He gave a clipped nod. "Understandable, and understood."

There was a definite chill in the atmosphere between them. Part of her wanted to say she was sorry, but then she reminded herself that speaking out on her own behalf wasn't something she needed to apologize for.

As they continued their drive, passing more people who enthusiastically greeted them, she said in a low voice, "You said nothing to me before about attending the Viscount Marwood's ball."

"This was the first I'd heard about it," he replied. He maintained his relaxed, almost languid air, though some tension remained in his voice. "Rotherby's not particularly

294

enamored of balls, but I'll convince him to go so that I can be there." He added, "We'll make sure that Fredericks gets an eyeful of you."

"Splendid." Soon, she'd see Mason again. And . . . she would behold Sebastian in his evening finery. They would dance together.

Excitement tumbled within her.

Because of Mason . . . or because of Sebastian?

She had no answer for herself.

CHAPTER 15

Seb sat in his threadbare armchair as he studied the hastily written note.

Small soiree tonight at Viscount Ombersley's. Perhaps we cross paths there? Make for a good show.

Yours, G

He tapped the paper against his lips. Since their drive on Rotten Row, two days ago, he and Grace hadn't made arrangements to be seen together in public, not until the Marwoods' ball tomorrow evening. This last-minute request posed a puzzle. He'd intended to spend the night catching up on his reading, which had been, of late, sadly neglected. An evening of solitude sounded rather welcome after the amount of socializing he'd been doing. Just him, a glass of whiskey, and several volumes about societal structures amongst nomadic peoples should be just the thing. Or he could write up his notes on his observations from the last week. That would be an excellent use of his time.

Yet . . . Grace needed him.

However . . . she'd asked him not to behave possessively, since it might deter Fredericks. Much as he knew logically that his role was to pave the way for Fredericks, it galled. Part of Seb wanted to brood and grumble and deny Grace her request for no other reason than his wounded pride. Another part of him was eager to make her happy.

Spending more time with her, however, was a challenge — because each minute made him crave more of her, more of them, together. But that wasn't what she wanted.

Goddamn it. This entire scenario was a hopeless tangle.

A forceful knock sounded on his front door.

"My God," Seb yelled, "the building better be on fire the way you're carrying on."

Pulling open the door revealed Rotherby, dressed smartly for a night out. But the man standing beside Rotherby wasn't Beale, here to scold him for his sartorial choices. Instead, Seb found himself looking at another of his oldest friends, Duncan Mc-

Cameron.

"If the building *is* on fire," McCameron said drily, shaking Seb's hand, "I'm not carrying you out."

"What if I'm overcome by the smoke?" Seb asked with a grin.

"Then I'll grab your valuables and make my exit." Seb and Rotherby both chuckled. The likelihood that McCameron, a decorated veteran and one of the most principled men they knew, would do anything unlawful was patently ludicrous. One might as well believe that Wellington himself lifted pocket watches.

"You're looking . . . different," McCameron said with typical concision. He glanced at Seb's stylish wine-colored waistcoat. "Less vagabond, more Incomparable."

"All thanks to the services of *my* valet," Rotherby threw in.

"You can't take credit for something someone else did." Seb stepped back and waved his two friends into his rooms. "Especially if that someone else is a salaried employee."

"I see you've made the place spotless for unexpected visitors," Rotherby noted as he stared at a mound of papers heaped atop what should have been a dining table.

"The noteworthy phrase you've used is

unexpected visitors." Seb quickly collected sheaves of documents and armfuls of books to clear space on a pair of chairs and his sofa.

"Save your efforts, Holloway," Rotherby said. "We're not staying long."

Seb set debris upon another pile of debris, which didn't do much to actually tidy things up and, in fact, created a precarious tower.

"Off to prowl the docks in search of fist-fights?" he asked.

To his chagrin, Rotherby walked right up to the tower of paper and books and tapped it, causing the whole structure to wobble.

"A night of gentlemanly pursuits," Rotherby said, watching the effects of his mischief.

"How delightful for you." Seb blocked Rotherby's second attempt to topple the heap of debris. Rotherby tried to dodge around him, but Seb used his body to obstruct him.

Meanwhile, Grace's note needed a response.

"How delightful for *us*," McCameron said, stepping between Rotherby and Seb. There was no way around the mass of McCameron's large frame. His athletic ability had seen him celebrated throughout his time at Eton, then made him much vaunted in his military career, and now easily pre-vented Seb and Rotherby from tormenting each other further.

"Explain." Seb looked with confusion between Rotherby and McCameron.

Rotherby strolled from the chamber and into the room where Seb slept. When Seb followed, he found his friend digging through the small wardrobe. Rotherby pulled out an ink-blue jacket and held it up for inspection.

"Yes," Rotherby murmured, "with the burgundy waistcoat this will work." He turned to Seb. "Put this on. You're coming with us."

Seb put his hands on his hips. How like Rotherby to be so high-handed about every-thing. Sardonically, he asked, "The possibil-ity that I might have other plans for the evening did not occur to you?"

"No," Rotherby said.

"As it turns out, I *do* have somewhere to be this night." He held up Grace's note. "Grace has asked me to appear at Viscount Ombersley's soiree, and —"

"You're running off to do her bidding," McCameron finished, crossing his arms over his chest.

"I'm honoring my obligation," Seb fired back. "You of all people should understand the importance of that."

Before McCameron could answer, Rotherby stepped forward, holding out the dark indigo coat. "You need not jump to oblige her every whim, Holloway. A little scarcity increases demand. Besides," he went on as Seb sputtered his objections, "in order for her plan to fully work, you cannot appear only at her side. The *ton* needs to know that you are a rake without equal, and that for a woman such as her to catch your notice, it must be a most singular occurrence. It will also make for a good addition to your paper or whatever you plan on writing."

"Therefore," McCameron continued, "you are coming with us for a night on the town."

Seb looked between Rotherby and McCameron as his thoughts spun. What Rotherby said made a kind of sense. He couldn't exist in a vacuum. "Given the nature of how verbal information networks operate within this societal structure —"

"In other words, *gossip*," Rotherby said.

"Given the nature of *gossip*," Seb plowed on as he fought to work out the reasoning, "word would inevitably circulate back to Fredericks, who would then use it as basis for his continuing escalating valuation of

Grace, thus achieving our objective."

"Exactly so." McCameron snorted quietly. "From a strategist's point of view, you and Lady Grace are employing complex tactics. You both would've been assets during the War."

"Except," Rotherby said, "Holloway would be too busy asking the enemy questions about their use of *verbal information networks* to be much good on the front lines."

"There's always need for intelligence," McCameron replied.

"Which would discount your contribution considerably, Rotherby." Seb ducked as his friend threw his jacket at him. Straightening, he said, "Not certain what to tell Grace."

Rotherby plucked the note from his hand and waved it in the air. "Tell her that you're busy tonight laying groundwork for tomorrow evening. And this is all part of your ongoing examination of the life of a rake. She'll understand."

It was an effort to nod in agreement, but Seb did so. What his friends said made sense. Yet the thought of disappointing Grace felt like the sting of hundreds of wasps. Perhaps that was precisely *why* he needed to not see her tonight. He had to remind himself that *he* was not the sought-after goal. It was Fredericks. And the more he made himself see that, the better — the safer — he would be.

Grace sat in front of her dressing table, watching Katie's hands hovering over the lopsided mass of her hair. The maid plucked a pin from between her lips and used it to secure a lock of Grace's hair into a loop, although the loop immediately unraveled and hung down Grace's neck, with the pin dangling from the very end.

"I'm either the height of fashion," Grace said with wonderment, "or I resemble the rubbish heap behind a peruke shop."

"Apologies, my lady." Katie grimaced. "It's only that . . . well . . . you see . . . you go out so *infrequently* in the evenings and . . . there hasn't been much call for me to dress your coiffure for a night out." The maid picked up the illustration from *La Belle Assemblée* Grace had provided and eyed it doubtfully. "The style's awful involved."

Grace blew a strand of hair from her face. "Perhaps it's a matter of adjusting our expectations. We were too ambitious." She turned her head slightly as she studied her crazed and tangled mane. "I think it best if we begin again. And this time, we'll set our aspirations toward something more achievable. Like this one." She turned the page in the periodical and pointed to an image of a young woman whose tresses had been shaped into a simple but pretty arrangement.

"Yes, my lady." With a defeated sigh, Katie plucked pin after pin from Grace's hair.

It didn't hurt to take extra care with her appearance — for no other reason than it gave her a measure of confidence. Not because she wanted Sebastian to look at her with admiration. The thought of watching his face light up with wonderment upon catching sight of her filled Grace's belly with squirming tadpoles.

"Will Mr. Fredericks be at the to-do this evening?" Katie asked, adding yet another pin to the heap. Gracious, had the maid used most of the hairpins in London? "That's who this is for, isn't it?"

Grace started. She hadn't discussed Mason with Katie, or the plan to win his attention. And . . . just now, she hadn't considered attracting Mason's notice. Only Sebastian's.

Oh, rot. This was an unwelcome development.

"It's all right, my lady." Her maid made a soft clucking sound. "Hard not to notice how much you fancy Mr. Fredericks, given that your cheeks turn red as strawberries if he's within fifty feet of you."

"Yes. Ah. Well." Heat spread across Grace's face and, checking her reflection, she realized she did resemble a pot of strawberry jam with eyes. How utterly dispiriting. "I suppose he might be in attendance tonight."

"Then we ought to make you look right handsome. Give Mr. Fredericks something to think about when he goes to sleep." Katie winked.

It *was* for Mason that Grace wanted to look her best. Not Sebastian. The man whose friendship she valued too much to risk ruining it.

A tap sounded at the door, and Katie went to see who it was. There was a quiet exchange with a footman before Katie returned to Grace.

"Note for you, my lady." The maid handed her a folded piece of paper that bore her name and address in a rather untidy but masculine script.

Frowning, Grace opened the missive.

Regrets, but I am engaged for the evening. No doubt you will do splendidly without me. Tomorrow?

Yrs, S

"A billet-doux from Mr. Fredericks?" Katie asked with a wink. "Hold a moment, my lady. I'm not done arranging your hair."

Yet Grace stood and drifted away from her dressing table. "There's no need to. I'm not going out tonight."

"But —"

"Please tell my mother I'll be dining in my chambers, and I won't accompany her this evening."

Katie opened her mouth to protest, but she must have seen something in Grace's expression that would not accept arguments. She bobbed a curtsy and quickly left the bedchamber.

Feet heavy, Grace moved to the fireplace and looked down at the captive flames. Disappointment weighted her like a leaden cloak. Only in the certainty of not seeing Sebastian did she realize how much she'd been looking forward to doing exactly that.

She had several worthwhile books to read, and her own thoughts about habitat encroachment to write down, and honestly, so many other things to do and contemplate that she shouldn't mind not meeting up with Sebastian tonight. She didn't need to spend more time pondering anything related to him.

But as she stared dispiritedly into the fire,

she had a terrible premonition that she'd spend the next twenty-four hours pre-occupied by Sebastian, and only Sebastian.

"This is what you do every night?" Seb asked in the carriage hours later. "Dining and billiards at Brooks's, followed by wasting extravagant amounts of money at gaming hells?"

His own evenings were, by comparison, exceedingly quiet. A solitary meal at a chophouse, then home to read.

"Not *every* night." Sitting opposite Seb, Rotherby swayed with the vehicle's movement. "Occasionally, I go to pugilism matches, or visit any number of brothels —"

"Truly?" Seb demanded.

"Not truly." McCameron, seated beside Rotherby, shooed the notion away with a wave of his hand. "Rotherby believes this line of discourse is amusing, so he persists in it."

"Never say I'm not amusing," Rotherby fired back.

"Faced with that choice," McCameron said drily, "I shall remain silent."

Seb leaned forward, bracing his forearms on his knees. "Is it true, Rotherby?"

"It isn't." Rotherby let out a sigh. "When

307

I was a younger man, yes, I did partake in such amusements. Because I had wealth and power and prestige, and back then, it pleased me to see just what such privileges I could afford. But now . . ." He glanced out the window to the passing streets, illuminated by lamps and the storefronts of shops that catered to late-night customers. "It pleases me no longer."

Seb had seen it — the way men gathered around Rotherby wherever they went, laughing too loudly at his quips, nodding like marionettes whenever Rotherby ventured an opinion, pressing him for private meetings. Exhaustion tugged at Seb to merely observe it, let alone be the focus of so much obsequiousness.

Small wonder that Rotherby seldom ventured forth in public. Yet he did so now, for Seb's sake. Gratitude expanded warmly through Seb's chest to consider the expansive limits of Rotherby's friendship.

"We needn't persist in this evening's escapade," Seb said.

Rotherby smirked. "Oh, no. I'll gladly endure a few sycophants' attempts to win my favor to ensure your status as a rake of consequence."

"Doesn't hurt that, wherever you deign to visit, pretty ladies drape themselves over you like Spanish moss," McCameron noted with a quirked eyebrow.

"That, too, is something I must tolerate." But Rotherby's grin undercut his doleful words. "There are advantages to having a place in the world."

"I'm beginning to see that," Seb said. Already in the course of the evening, he'd shaken more hands with people of consequence than in the summation of his life. At Brooks's, he'd received no fewer than seven invitations to dine with titled men. They'd looked at him with respect. For no other reason than he was seen in Rotherby's company, and because Seb worked to carry himself as though he was worthy of that respect.

He still struggled to speak a bit when talking with strangers, but when those awkward pauses fell, he'd focus on his breathing, calming himself enough to ask a question, which prompted the other person to launch into a speech — and afforded Seb time to collect himself and become immersed in the moment, rather than his own thoughts.

At the gaming hell, a queue of London's elite had stood outside the unnamed establishment's doors, and Seb had prepared himself to join their ranks waiting to get inside. But the large man attending the door had sized Seb up with a practiced mien, and permitted him, Rotherby, and McCameron immediate entrance.

Once they'd gone inside, the elegant blonde woman managing the gaming hell had extended him a line of credit that nearly made Seb choke in disbelief. *How* he was to pay for any debts he accrued was a mystery, but Rotherby had insisted that more than half the guests in the establishment failed to pay their debts.

Gambling was not a custom unique to English aristocrats — many cultures had games of chance. But Seb had never understood the appeal of wagering significant amounts of currency with the hope of increasing that amount. Judging by the glittering gems and pristine evening clothes worn by the gaming hell's patrons, no one was precisely hurting for funds.

It had occurred to him then that what everyone sought wasn't money. It was *excitement.* Something to break through the ennui that lurked behind the guests' eyes. The people at the gaming hell had their every material consideration satisfied. They wanted for nothing. And that satiety left them empty, desperately in need of something, anything, to make them feel alive.

He wanted to discuss it with Grace. Get

her thoughts on the idiosyncrasies of the British elite. Of a certain, she'd have rare and incisive insight on the topic.

Seb glanced out the window, but without his spectacles, and at this late hour, he couldn't recognize the street. "Where are we venturing now?"

"A place of pure pageant," Rotherby said. "Where the object is to ensure that you observe everyone, and that everyone observes you."

"He means the theater," McCameron added.

"Ah!" Seb straightened. Visiting the gaming hell had been intriguing but, other than the bizarre process of staking money on abstract concepts, didn't stimulate him on an intellectual level. "Excellent. I've heard there's some fine theatrical works."

"Didn't you hear me?" Rotherby rolled his eyes. "No one goes to the theater to *watch* the performances."

"How very dispiriting for the performers," Seb said.

"But good for the theater's ticket sales." McCameron flicked at his cuff, though his clothing was, as always, spotless. "Although I have heard that the audience actually remains silent for the Viscountess Marwood's *burlettas.*"

"Is that what we're seeing tonight?" Seb asked, brightening. Exciting to see a work written by a celebrated playwright, and a female one, at that. Books and treatises were quite satisfactory, but every now and again, a truly gripping tale could prove transformative.

"Alas, no," Rotherby said. "But I've a private box at the Imperial Theatre, so you're welcome to make use of it whenever you please. Though," he added with a pointed finger, "you are forbidden to keep a book in your pocket to read in case the performance is dull."

A slender volume on the marriage customs of the Outer Hebrides rested comfortably in Seb's pocket at that very moment. "I wouldn't dream of it."

The carriage came to a stop, and a footman opened the door shortly thereafter. Seb followed Rotherby and McCameron as they climbed down and joined a throng of people standing outside a large, colonnaded building. A fancifully painted sign proclaimed the building to be the Imperial Theatre.

Intriguingly, the attendees seemed drawn from every class, the high and low mingling together, silk and velvet beside coarse hopsack. Perhaps that was one of the appeals of the theater — it was a space where the class distinctions blurred. Gauging the abundance of the crowd, the actual performances had yet to begin.

Rotherby led the way, the crowd parting as he strode through the multitude. Seb and McCameron took advantage of their friend's status, moving briskly in Rotherby's wake. Heads turned in their direction, people's regard moving from the duke to the men accompanying him. But rather than returning focus to Rotherby, approving gazes lingered on Seb.

Despite the fact that Seb had been out all evening, it still unsettled him, to be amongst so many people.

"Everything all right?" McCameron murmured beside him as they breached the theater's lobby. "Looking tight in the mouth."

Naturally, a born tactician like McCameron could see the minutest detail amidst swirling chaos. Seb felt a flare of gratitude for his friend's concern.

He took a deep breath, and then another one. "Learning how to navigate new territory."

"I know this isn't comfortable for you," McCameron said.

"It isn't," Seb agreed. "It might not ever be."

313

"And that's all right." Cameron clapped his hand on Seb's shoulder. "You're managing, and that's enough."

Small wonder that Seb had formed such strong ties with the other members of the Union of the Rakes. They had an instinct for saying what he needed to hear.

"A crush, wouldn't you say, Holloway?" A prosperous gentleman of middle years appeared and nudged Seb with his elbow. Seb had no idea who the gentleman was or how he came to know Seb's name, but he beamed at Seb as though they shared a delightful secret.

For a moment, Seb couldn't think of a single word to say in response. And then his silence unnerved him. But he stroked the glove in his pocket, and his worry receded enough for him to say, "Come to the theater often?"

The gentleman chuckled. "Often enough to know that tonight's a fine night for sampling the evening's pleasures. Do stop by my box later. We're hosting a bevy of the finest female company money can secure and you're free to sample them."

Rather than answer, Seb inclined his head, and the gentleman's smile widened before he disappeared into the mass of bodies.

"What a genial way to invite me to have

sex with a prostitute," Seb muttered to Mc-Cameron. They neared the stairs that led, presumably, to the private boxes.

"You're now part of the London rakes' world." McCameron nudged him, and when Seb followed his friend's gaze, he discovered a blonde woman sending him a gaze of such blatant carnal interest, it was a wonder that Seb's garments and smallclothes didn't combust. "And there's the welcome committee."

Panic crept up his back at the prospect of speaking to the woman. But in all likelihood she wasn't looking for conversation. A handful of words would likely suffice to suggest they retire somewhere private. But he didn't know her at all. Nor did she know him. And while that might hold some appeal, it was minimal compared to sharing erotic pleasure with someone who fully understood who he was — all the parts of him — just as he would understand who she truly was.

Like Grace.

His mind recoiled from the thought. His body, however, had other ideas. *Yes,* it growled. *Shut up,* he snarled in response.

He gave the blonde woman a smile but did not head in her direction, instead continuing up the stairs to the next floor with McCameron and Rotherby.

315

They reached the landing and proceeded down the corridor. Curtains hung in the doorways of the private boxes, and finely dressed men and women lingered in the hallway and in the boxes themselves. They shone with wealth and abundance, their skin and garments lustrous.

The theater was essentially just as stratified as the world beyond its walls.

Rotherby addressed everyone by name, while Seb nodded and murmured noncommittal greetings to people who seemed to know him. Wherever he looked, he was met with smiles and admiring looks.

It was surprisingly . . . not unpleasant.

Rotherby stopped abruptly as two men stepped into his path. One was thickly muscled, a contrast to his finely tailored clothing, while his facial expression verged on insolent. The other possessed a lean, wiry frame and a pair of shrewd eyes so pale blue they were nearly white.

Happiness swept through Seb. It had been too long since all five of them were together.

"The meeting of the Union of the Rakes shall now commence," the wiry man said. "I nominate Curtis here to record the minutes."

"My writing looks like someone swallowed a bottle of ink and then vomited the con-

316

tents onto the page," Curtis replied.

"That's a kind comparison." Rotherby smirked. He stuck out his hand. "Rowe, Curtis."

"The devil with your handshakes." Curtis batted Rotherby's hand away before thumping him squarely in the chest with the side of his fist — the old greeting, created two decades ago in an Eton library.

Rowe glanced at Seb. "Judging by your rags, someone's been thumbing through the pages of *Ackerman's Repository.*"

" 'Thereby hangs a tale,' " Seb quoted.

"But you are no motley fool," Rowe said. "The Bond Street Loungers would soil themselves in envy were they to see you."

"An unfortunate — and messy — response," McCameron noted drily.

"Join us in my box," Rotherby declared. "We'll give you a complete accounting."

"What do you say, Curtis?" Rowe asked. "Can you behave like a tame bear for a few minutes?"

"Only somewhat tame," Curtis said. He waved in the direction Rotherby, McCameron, and Seb had been heading. "Lead on."

The five of them moved down the corridor, with Rotherby, as usual, in the lead. They fell into comfortable conversation, bypassing formalities, and just then, Seb felt lingering tension leave his body. These four men had been the salvation of his youth, and the backbone of his adulthood. For all that they were, on the surface, wildly dissimilar, they shared the kind of bond that only struggle could create.

His thoughts drifted ahead to the next few hours, spent in the company of the men he cared for most. While he would have enjoyed seeing Grace tonight, he was grateful Mc-Cameron and Rotherby had dragged him out this evening, or else he would have missed this opportunity. It was going to be a fine night.

A man stepped forward, blocking Seb's path.

Seb drew up short, and found himself looking at Mason Fredericks.

CHAPTER 16

Seb's mind blanked, but not from anxiousness. Instead, he was mystified. What was one supposed to say to the man one attempted to turn into a suitor for the woman that he . . . he what? Cared for? Held deep feelings in regard to? Or was it something more than what he felt for a dear friend? Something like —

"Holloway," Fredericks said with a nod.

Yes, of course, when standing in someone's presence, he should make actual conversation with them instead of being mired in his own labyrinthine thoughts.

"Evening, Fredericks." Seb mentally reached for the persona he'd been cultivating these past weeks, setting Thinking Seb on the shelf and donning the identity of Rake Sebastian. He made himself smile easily at Fredericks. "Always a wonderful time to be had at the theater."

Seb decided not to mention that the last

time he'd attended a theatrical performance had been fifteen years ago, when he and the other members of the Union of the Rakes had attended a bawdy pantomime performed in an Oxford public house. Seb did recall that throughout the entertainment his face had flamed hot as a Yule log and he'd kept his hands cupped in front of his stiffening cock.

"True," Fredericks said with an affable nod, "though my attendance at the theater isn't as frequent as I'd like. Always fielding invitations to dinners." He grimaced. "People like to have me at their tables in order to impress the other guests with the breadth of their cultivation."

"But you get a meal, gratis."

"True, yet I'm fortunate enough to know where my next meal is coming from. Not every man of science can say the same. At many events, I've seen men with bountiful coffers seem perfectly healthy one moment, yet when the possibility of funding research comes up, the same men of means are suddenly and tragically overcome with consumption and cannot stop coughing."

Seb fought a chuckle. Was Fredericks actually *likable*? Damn. "*Temporary* consumption."

"Oh, they are cured within minutes."

Fredericks paused, then said in a tone of forced nonchalance, "I haven't seen Lady Grace tonight."

Seb concentrated on the feel of his feet in his shoes. If he didn't, surely he'd snarl at Fredericks or at least scowl ferociously.

"Nor I," he answered.

"Pity." Another pause from Fredericks. "You appear to hold her in high regard."

The man of science in Seb appreciated the subtle, coded language he and Fredericks were employing — all hallmarks of highly complex societal structures. The instinct-guided man in Seb wanted to ram his fist into Fredericks's square jaw.

But Grace had warned him from appearing too possessive, too proprietary. And he couldn't ignore this prime opportunity to praise her to Fredericks.

"An extraordinary person." Seb fought to make his tone strike the balance between admiration and insouciance. Yet he couldn't stop himself from adding, "It shocks me that she's yet to find a gentleman who can fully appreciate her. Every aspect of her."

He narrowed his eyes, uncaring if he made Fredericks uncomfortable. Hell, the naturalist *should* feel uncomfortable for ignoring Grace.

"It's shocking." Fredericks's mouth turned

down in what appeared, to Seb's dismay, to be genuine regret. "And I was one of the blind fools who lacked the sagacity to value her as both a colleague and a woman."

Hell — there Fredericks went again, being decent.

"But," the naturalist continued, brightening, "I hope to remedy that. Unless," he went on, "I'm treading in territory that has already been claimed." He looked pointedly at Seb.

Yes, Seb wanted to bark, *she's mine.*

He choked down a coarse oath as understanding struck him.

Seb didn't think of Grace as his friend. Not anymore. He had . . . feelings for her. Feelings that went beyond platonic. Ever since they'd kissed, he'd been unable to banish the taste of her from his mouth, sweet and delicious.

Only this morning, he'd awakened from dreaming of her. It had been a sensual dream where he sensed her warm breath against his bare chest and shivered beneath her touch as he sank into her and they created endless pleasure together.

God fucking damn it.

This was precisely what he did not want to happen. Yet, despite his repeated warnings to himself, in spite of his intellectual understanding that he could not, should not, desire Grace — he'd gone and done it, anyway.

She wanted Fredericks. Not him. Fredericks was her goal. To subvert that and undermine her would be the height of caddishness.

"Not a bit." Seb had to give himself credit for not sounding as though he choked the words out. "I do admire her, but, at present, we're friends." That wasn't untrue.

The pleat of concern between Fredericks's brow smoothed. "Ah. Excellent." He beamed. "She's highly regarded within scientific circles, and I eagerly await learning more about her. Beyond her work with reptiles."

"And amphibians." Seb waited for Fredericks to wrinkle his nose in disgust that a woman should care about toads and frogs.

Instead, Fredericks nodded eagerly. "Such an intriguing field of study. It's still in its infancy, you know. We cannot begin to comprehend the scale of discoveries yet to be made." The naturalist laughed. "Forgive me. I'm enthusiastic about these things."

"Nothing to be ashamed about."

"Must be dull for you, to hear me ramble on about the natural realm matters. You're a . . . I believe Mr. Okafor said you study human societies."

"I'm an anthropologist, yes."

"So you've no interest in things such as flora and fauna."

Seb stared levelly at him. "You'd be surprised at what interests me. Not everything is to be judged from its appearance."

"Quite right. Not the first time I've been guilty of failing to look beneath the surface, but," Fredericks added hopefully, "I intend to remedy it. We share that, Lady Grace and I. A deep, abiding love for the world of nature."

A dark, angry miasma clung to Seb, and his limbs sizzled with the need to lash out, to break something. Because Fredericks was, in truth, a decent bloke. Though Seb and Grace were both devoted scholars, they didn't share a discipline, as she did with Fredericks. There would always be a divide between Grace and Seb, a lack of shared passion, unlike her and Fredericks.

He had plenty of money, and was beloved by both the scientific community and society circles.

The naturalist was precisely the right man for Grace. She'd seen that from the beginning.

Despite their kiss, she had never thought that about Seb. And she never would, now that Fredericks had come to his senses and recognized her magnificence.

"Coming, Holloway?" Rotherby stood at the entrance to one of the boxes, eyeing Fredericks. He sent Seb a silent look. *Need help?* That look promised to beat Fredericks into an afterthought, if Seb gave the word.

That was friendship. The willingness to thrash another man at a moment's notice.

But gratitude over Rotherby's preparedness to commit violence couldn't dispel the crackling, furious haze encircling Seb. The narrow corridor between the private boxes stifled him, and sitting through theatrical performances was absolutely impossible, not when Seb finally recognized how well and truly fucked he was.

He made himself smile, though it likely cracked at the edges.

"Another night, perhaps," he said to Rotherby. He tipped his head at Fredericks. "Enjoy your evening, and best of luck with . . . with everything."

Before Rotherby or Fredericks could respond, Seb turned on his heel and sped away. He didn't stop, plowing down the stairs and through the lobby. He emerged from the theater and waved away offers of a cab. Instead, he paced so quickly down the street he practically ran. A film of sweat coated his back, making his fine shirt cling to his skin. But he didn't care. He prayed the gymnasium he frequented was open at this late hour. It would be a fine night to perfect his pugilism skills, and, since he couldn't very well punch himself, he had a blazing need to pound his fists into something.

The night of Viscount and Viscountess Marwood's ball arrived, and despite Grace's full knowledge of its approach, she couldn't quell her nervousness.

As the family carriage rolled toward the hosts' home, the vehicle was too well-sprung to rock excessively, yet Grace's stomach churned all the same.

"Shall we turn back, dearest?" her mother asked gently. "You don't need to put yourself through anything unpleasant." She reached across the carriage to pat Grace's hands twisted together.

Grace worked carefully to untangle her fingers. "Why would I think the viscount's ball unpleasant? He and the viscountess are celebrated for their hospitality. I'm looking forward to tonight."

"It's been some time, though, hasn't it?" Her mother regarded her with sympathy.

"Since you've been to a ball. It's reasonable to be uneasy about it."

"My last few balls were . . . not especially pleasant." It wasn't entirely untrue. She'd vowed to herself after enduring one too many unwilling dance partners that she wouldn't return unless she had a very good reason.

Tonight, she *did* have a reason, and that alone would engender worry in anybody. But her apprehension had another reason for being. Namely, whether or not Sebastian would attend tonight's gala. The note he'd sent her confirmed that he would, in fact, be there. Yet after last night . . . she wasn't certain.

Her hands wove back together in a snarl. Perhaps he had outgrown her. Perhaps he'd become so successful within Society that he'd moved on to better things, more exciting and advantageous people.

In truth, she could no longer hold him to their bargain. He'd accomplished the goal they'd set out for themselves. The handful of public appearances they had made together achieved her desired aim — she'd secured Mason Fredericks's attention. Mason had even asked her to save him a dance at tonight's ball. The thought sent a shiver of anticipation through her, even as she battled with her complicated emotions where Sebastian was concerned.

"I've something that will cheer you," her mother said with a smile. "I believe Mr. Fredericks will be at Viscount Marwood's tonight."

"Will he?" Grace kept her words light, since she hadn't discussed with her mother her encounter with Mason on Rotten Row. Better to remain silent on her promise of dancing with him.

"Go on, now, sweetheart." Her mother pursed her lips in a playful smile. "Pretending to your own flesh and blood that you aren't mad for that chap."

Was she? She honestly didn't know anymore. Something had changed — ever since she and Sebastian had kissed. She could no longer pretend that she wasn't aware of him as a man. Yet if she was bold enough to tell him that perhaps they might be more than friends, he might tell her that he didn't reciprocate her feelings, and everything would be ruined. She had to direct her attention to Mason.

Perchance she merely needed to spend more time with Mason now that he regarded her as more than simply a fellow naturalist. Surely if she came to know him as a woman knows a man, all those giddy feelings that he used to inspire would return — possibly even stronger than before.

God above, she didn't know. Everything was a muddle right now, including how she felt about Mason and Sebastian. Her heart was as murky as the most stagnant bog. And while she loved bogs for the abundance of creatures they supported, when it came to her feelings, she much preferred clear water.

The carriage slowed as it joined a queue of similarly elegant vehicles outside Viscount Marwood's home on Mount Street. Men and women in their glittering finery alit and climbed the steps, where they were met by a row of servants who took coats and hats and presented the guests with flutes of sparkling wine. Music curled out onto the street, joined by the sounds of chatter and laughter.

Grace exhaled, pushing back her nerves. Visions of her previous humiliations spun through her head in their own dances. Retaining her sense of self in the face of the *ton*'s rejection had nearly been her undoing. She'd pretended that she hadn't wanted anyone's approval, but she knew the truth, that it had hurt to be scorned for the thing she loved.

The carriage finally came to a stop, and footmen helped her mother and Grace get down from the vehicle. Like the other guests, they climbed the steps and gave servants sundry garments in the foyer. When a footman offered Grace a flute of wine, she quickly grabbed it and downed the contents in two swallows.

The wine did nothing to set her at ease.

As she and her mother climbed the stairs to the ballroom, guests' gazes lit upon her like bees in search of pollen. She felt the probing touch, the search for something useful, yet instead of flitting away in pursuit of other, showier flowers, they lingered on her — the result of Sebastian's notice. It was nearly impossible not to feel some bitterness. It had taken a man valuing her to persuade these people that she was worthwhile. The unfairness of that fact stuck in her throat like a bone.

She resisted the impulse to touch her hand to her upswept hair or give in to the urge to shake out the skirts of her celadon-green silk gown. For two solid hours, she and Katie had wrestled with all the components of her ensemble for tonight. She'd told herself that appearance didn't matter, but this was a lie she couldn't believe.

"The Countess of Pembroke, and Lady Grace Wyatt," the butler announced as she and her mother entered the vaulted chamber.

The vast space was illuminated by huge crystal chandeliers, which cast their light upon scores of London's elite. Dancers dominated the parquet floor, while many more guests circled the room, greeting each other, assessing the relative significance of the other attendees, and watching for anyone who could affect their own status for good or for ill. Servants circulated with more trays of sparkling wine. Punch was served from an enormous bowl that sat atop a long table heaped with sweet and savory delicacies.

The teeming room was hot enough to delight any cold-blooded animal. Surely the beings that populated this chamber were far colder than any reptile or amphibian.

Upon her announcement, more heads turned in Grace's direction with the same speculative notice as the people she had passed on the stairs.

She scanned the many faces for Sebastian, looking for his height, his fair coloring. There were other tall men, other blond men, and she gazed at each of them, most likely with an intensity that some would consider gauche.

Heaviness settled in her belly. Sebastian

331

wasn't here.

"Lady Pembroke, Lady Grace, we're honored." Viscount Marwood approached, favoring them with a dazzling smile.

"Welcome to our, ah, unassuming home." The viscountess, a petite brunette with a charming gap between her teeth, gave her words a slight ironic inflection. Grace recalled that Lady Marwood had been born a commoner, and, judging by the hint of London in her accent, she'd never quite developed a comfortable relationship with the sparkling spectacle that was a Society ballroom. "We've invited two hundred of our *closest* friends. What are their names again, my love?"

Grace liked the viscountess immediately. "Who wouldn't be pleased to be included in such a *small,* tightly knit circle? I hope that later, we can exchange confidences and plait each other's hair."

Lady Marwood's lips twitched.

"Can I resist showing off my delightful wife?" Lord Marwood asked. "More to the point, should I?" He shook his head, as if the absurdity of the question didn't warrant an answer.

"Are you expecting —" Grace bit back her words just before Sebastian's name fell from her lips. "Expecting more guests?"

"Who can keep track of anybody in this . . . abundance?" Lady Marwood said. "Is there someone you particularly want to see?"

"No one," Grace began.

Her mother said in a sly voice, "Only a certain young naturalist recently returned to the city."

Grace managed a weak chuckle, but was it too much to ask for a rhinoceros stampede?

"That gentleman is currently engaged in conversation with Lord and Lady Blakemere." The viscount tipped his head toward a corner of the room, where Mason chatted with a blond man and a woman with vibrantly red hair.

Grace's stomach gave a slight jump, which was something of a relief. Thank goodness she wasn't entirely inured to Mason's presence.

"It's the work of a moment to gain his attention. Especially," Lord Marwood added with a grin, "if it paves the road toward tender feelings."

"You must never stifle your feelings," the viscountess said with a sage nod. "It's a sentiment that ensures a full house every night at the Imperial."

"My thanks," Grace said quickly, "but that

isn't —"

Before she could stop him, Lord Marwood strode across the ballroom. Straight toward Mason.

CHAPTER 17

Don't stare. Look anywhere else other than him. Oh, isn't that a pretty potted fern? Yes, it's a fine example of . . . Adiantum capillus-veneris, *with its clusters of bipinnate fronds.*

But it was no use. Grace's gaze kept returning to the mortifying sight of Lord Marwood talking to Mason, and nodding in her direction with an encouraging smile. God preserve her from well-intentioned people.

For his part, Mason glanced over at her with an expression that might have actually been eagerness. Might have been. Yet it was impossible to know if he was merely acting interested for the benefit of his wealthy and well-connected host, or if he genuinely desired to search out her company. Knots of apprehension formed in her muscles. Memories of past mortifications flashed in her mind — men at balls just like this one snickering at her or staring at her like she was some variety of tree fungus.

She swallowed around a wave of nausea.

"He's a fine man, Lord Marwood," Grace's mother said.

"Erp." Grace watched the whole scene between the viscount and Mason as though watching the world's most humiliating pantomime.

Her and Mason's eyes met.

She managed a small wave. *Please don't feel obligated to talk to me,* she hoped her wave communicated. Her body sparked with the need to bolt, but she gripped hard on the reins of her impulse, and instead kept her feet fastened to the floor.

Mason said something to Lord Marwood before bowing to the viscount, as well as Lord and Lady Blakemere. Then he detached from the group and headed in her direction.

"I do believe I need some refreshment," Grace's mother said. She moved on, leaving Grace alone to await Mason's arrival. Time moved with agonizing slowness as he neared.

"Lady Grace." He bowed, and she inclined her head.

"Mas— I mean, Mr. Fredericks." Her voice was remarkably steady, and she tried to take comfort in that.

He looked exceedingly well in his simple but finely tailored evening clothes, his sandy hair brushed forward, and his green eyes bright.

"I'm exceptionally glad to see you here," he said, then added in a confiding tone, "Chatting with Lord and Lady Blakemere is pleasant enough, but neither one of them have any understanding about patterns of seasonal migration."

"For humans, or for animals?"

He chuckled. "Animals, of course, but surely a lengthy treatise could be written about the migratory patterns of gently bred Englishmen."

"Certainly," she said wryly, "the plumage changes depending on whether one is In Town or, as they say, rusticating."

"Not very sturdy plumage." He plucked at his cream-colored waistcoat. "Can't keep out a brisk wind and far from waterproof."

"As a species, the English aristocrat is very poorly equipped for withstanding variances in climate and habitat." She tried not to feel too much pride that she'd managed to actually chat with him without sounding completely foolish.

They smiled at each other, and it was strange . . . her heart didn't precisely throb with pleasure from their conversation. Still, she was left with a soft glow that came only from communicating with a like-minded soul.

But her pleasure held an edge, faintly cutting, and after a moment, she said, "You've done your due diligence, so now I liberate you."

"How do you mean?" He tilted his head.

"Obliging our host. You've talked to me for a sufficient length of time, so you're free to search out other companions."

Mason's brow furrowed. "A poor opinion of your company."

"Excuse me, Mr. Fredericks," she heard herself say, "but until quite recently, you yourself seemed disinclined to engage with me in any realm outside of the scientific. My opinion of myself is as fixed and assured as ever. *Your* perception is the only thing that has altered."

Good God — where had that come from? She almost stammered an apology, taken aback by the sudden vehemence of her words. After all, Mason had only done as he was supposed to.

Yet resentment bubbled up acidly within her. Shouldn't someone take an interest in her on the basis of who she was, rather than who they believed her to be? Yet that was precisely what she had done, and couldn't help but feel some regret that she'd set her sights on someone who needed to be shown — by another man — that she was worthwhile.

The machine, however, was in motion, and she'd set out to ease her father's worry for her future. No turning back now.

"Entirely correct." Mason lowered his gaze, and a shadow passed over his face. "I must own my foolishness. There is no excuse but my ridiculous blindness. All I can do is ask for your forgiveness now, and pray that you and I might move forward as not just colleagues, but friends."

Tendrils of her indignation dissolved — though it would take more than a few contrite words to soothe the hurt caused by his disregard.

Still. "We may be friends," she said.

"Brilliant." His smile was wide and appeared sincere. "If it isn't too presumptuous, might I prevail upon you to remember your assurance from the other day that we might share a dance together."

"I'd be delighted."

How very curious. She combed through her emotions, hunting down that spinning exhilaration she usually felt whenever she was near Mason. Yet all she could muster was a gentle lift of pleasure — a far cry from the dizzying heights she expected.

What the deuce is wrong with me? I'm getting what I want.

A thrum of excitement went through the room, and while the music and conversation didn't stop, there was a brief pause as though the guests awaited something truly incredible.

"His Grace, the Duke of Rotherby. Mr. Sebastian Holloway."

She slowly turned to face the entrance to the ballroom. True to the butler's announcement, there stood the duke, who was, she supposed, absurdly handsome. But she barely spared Rotherby a glance. Instead, her gaze fixed on Sebastian as if the possibility of looking anywhere else was unbearable.

And there went her heart, pounding as though it meant to leap from her chest, while she nearly stumbled from the force of pleasure at seeing Sebastian in his stark, almost severe, evening attire. His coat was a green so dark as to be nearly black, while the rest of his ensemble was a symphony of cream and white.

I wish he'd stop doing this. Making me giddy just from looking at him.

If he felt any anxiousness from being at the ball and being amongst so many strang-

340

ers, his expression gave none of that away. She hoped he felt calm and relaxed — most especially for his own sake. She didn't want him in distress.

"A good chap, that Holloway," Mason said, clearly unaware of the direction of her thoughts. "Saw him yesterday at the Imperial Theatre and we had a fine chat."

So. That's where Sebastian had gone rather than be with her.

And why shouldn't he have a night out? He had every right to enjoy the fruits of his labors. To be a true rake.

Perhaps the fears that had held him back for so long no longer shackled him. Perhaps he could break free of them, even for a little while. A blossom of delight opened in her chest that, if he wasn't entirely liberated from his anxiety, he knew better how to navigate life with it. That was truly something to be celebrated.

Happiness in his achievement made her eyes misty. She was so glad for him, so proud that he'd made that happen for himself.

"Are you all right, Lady Grace?" Mason asked with concern.

"It's rather warm in here," she said. "It's making my eyes water a little." She quickly used her knuckle to wipe away any incipient

341

tears before they could fall.

Just then, Sebastian's gaze found hers.

She froze, torn between pleasure and apprehension. Did her face betray the cyclone of emotions within her from merely looking at him?

"How delightful," Mason said cheerfully beside her — though his voice sounded miles away to her. "He's heading in our direction."

Trepidation and hesitancy fell away the second Seb saw her. Until that very moment, he'd been uncertain about coming to the ball. Now, all the anxiety, all the doubt — they meant nothing to him to see Grace shine like a beacon of spring beneath the massive crystal chandeliers.

The low scooped neck of her pale green dress highlighted the elegance of her collarbones and the hollow of her throat. Between the bottom of her short, puffed sleeves and the top of her long white gloves, he could see delicious bands of bare skin, which had until this night been hidden by pelisses or spencers. She'd done something to her hair, too, so that it piled atop her head in the kind of fascinating curls that jumbled masculine thought. All he wanted to do was wrap those curls around his fingers and, with the lightest urging, pull her head back so he might bring his mouth to hers as he'd done before . . .

Objections rose up like flecks of foam upon the waves. He shouldn't, couldn't, think of her this way.

And yet. He did.

Rotherby said something to him but Seb couldn't hear a word, his ears full of the sound of his thudding pulse.

His body moved without thought. All he knew was that he needed to shorten the distance between them. He had to inhale her fragrance and watch the air vibrate around her from the force of her unbreakable will.

He cleaved a path through the room, barely remembering to skirt around the dancers. A few more yards, and he'd be near her.

Too late, he realized that Fredericks stood beside her. And that the other man looked warmly at Grace.

The best thing to do was stay away. After all, she'd gotten what she wanted. Fredericks seemed enchanted. Seb's presence wasn't necessary — might actually impede the progress of Grace and Fredericks's burgeoning attachment.

The hell with it.

He didn't stop or divert his path. *Not* being near her was an impossibility. All he could do was heed the wordless demands of his body.

"Lady Grace." He bowed, and his chest swelled to see a stain of pink rise in her cheeks. "Fredericks," he added, because he wasn't entirely a churl.

"Holloway, a pleasure to see you again," Fredericks said with hearty bonhomie.

"Yes," Grace added, her voice breathy. "A pleasure."

The opening bars of a waltz curled through the ballroom. Couples positioned themselves on the floor, readying for the music to truly begin.

"This dance is promised to me," Seb said. He held out his arm.

For a moment, Grace merely looked at his proffered arm, her expression alarmingly blank. God, had he put her in an uncomfortable position? Making her do anything against her will or wishes was intolerable.

"Unless," he continued, trying to give her an exit, "you are feeling fatigued or —"

"We can dance if we want to." She rested her hand on his sleeve, and though she'd done the same thing countless times before, seeing her gloved fingers atop the dark fabric of his coat sent a hot bolt of desire through him.

He guided her onto the dance floor, hardly sparing a thought or glance for Fredericks. All that mattered was Grace, shining and vivid beside him. Her gaze clung to his. They took their positions for the waltz — his right hand upon her waist, hers upon his shoulder, and their left hands clasped — and when the music began and they moved in the dance, everything melted away.

As they turned, their left hands clasped overhead, and their bodies were brought close together. They'd practiced the steps before. But this dance was new and different and seductive beyond all reason. She swayed with him, responding to his gentle guidance.

She looked up at him with an expression bordering on wonderment, as though discovering something that defied logic yet existed, anyway. He was pulled in by her tide, yielding to the gravity that drew them closer, and closer still. Her loamy, floral scent teased him, and the heat and softness of her body roused his own to acute awareness. He couldn't tell if it was night or day or winter or spring but he knew with absolute certainty that the silk of her gown had taken on the warmth of her flesh, and that same warmth flowed into him like a torrent.

There were cultures that used dance as a means of prayer or summoning magic. He understood that now, more fully than he ever had before. Because what else were he and Grace doing if not weaving a spell that bound them together and filled the ballroom with enchantment? It would not have surprised him to look up and find the coved ceiling replaced by the branches of ancient oaks.

I'll give her anything she wants.

The thought didn't frighten him. It filled him with certainty and purpose.

He couldn't recall any of the reasons why he needed to keep himself at a distance, why he couldn't adore her with his mind and his body. He couldn't remember much of anything, his thoughts hazy from having her in his arms. The kiss they'd shared seemed long ago, too long, and demand to repeat it and taste her once again roared through him.

When they'd practiced this dance, he hadn't known what it was to kiss her. Now he did, and their movement across the dance floor became tinged with erotic potential.

Her cheeks were flushed, and she moved her gaze back and forth from his eyes to his mouth, as if she, too, was brought back to

346

that sunlit field where the air had been ripe with the whirring of insects, the smell of grass, and sensual possibility.

You aren't supposed to want her, a faint voice in his mind pointed out.

But why?

He had no answer. Not when they were entangled together like this.

And then, too soon, the music ended. She blinked — he probably did, as well — and, several moments later, stepped back.

He remembered he had some kind of role or function to serve. It took him a few seconds before he recalled what he was supposed to do. He held out his arm, and she took it. His whole body protested as he walked her back to the side of the chamber, where Fredericks waited. The naturalist appeared slightly puzzled, but Seb didn't give a fuck about that. He only cared about the moment when Grace's touch disappeared.

Taut as a pianoforte string, he bowed, despite wanting to hold her tightly. He made himself smile. "It was my honor."

She stared at him, her eyes brilliant, her cheeks still pink as peonies. Then she turned and hurried away.

The corridor to the ladies' retiring room stretched before Grace as though it was miles away, but she had to reach it. Had to get to someplace secure and safe.

She felt curious looks from other guests as she walked quickly. Managing a distracted smile, she nodded at a few people she vaguely recognized before — at last! — the door to the retiring room appeared before her. She pushed it open and dashed inside.

She sank down on a low tufted stool set before a mirror. Similar arrangements of furniture ringed the room, and other ladies made use of them, patting their hair into place or checking if their cheeks were too flushed. A few women chatted, but all of them cast assessing glances in her direction.

"May I assist you, my lady?"

Grace started and stared at the maid's reflection as the servant stood behind her.

"I . . ." She didn't know what she wanted from the maid.

That wasn't true. She wanted to pour out her heart to the servant. *I have feelings for another man, someone who thinks of me only as a friend. I thought I wanted someone else, but I don't know if that's true anymore. Please help me make sense of myself.*

"No, thank you," Grace said instead.

The servant curtsied before moving on to a duo of women who entered the retiring room, both of them fussing with their gowns.

Grace gazed into the mirror, but she didn't look at herself. Instead, she stared hard at the reflection of a window, its curtains open to reveal dark panes of night. The view itself was of the mews.

None of this calmed her or helped her to make sense of the riot going on inside her mind or her body. Something had happened when she and Sebastian had danced, his arms around her, something that built upon the kiss they'd shared. He wasn't merely a friend to her, not anymore. She desired him. The realization had made her flee the dance floor.

What the deuce am I supposed to do?

One thing she couldn't do was stay in the retiring room all evening. Although the idea had merit . . .

Grace took a breath to gather her thoughts and calm her sensitized body. She rose, and, after handing the attending maid a coin, emerged from the retiring room. She took measured steps back toward the ballroom, the music growing louder and louder as she walked, and heat spilling out like its own tropical climate.

She paused at the side entrance to the ballroom. Dancers were going through the forms of a quadrille, moving in the patterns that had been ingrained in her since girlhood.

Her heart clutched. Mason and Sebastian stood together at one side of the ballroom, neither speaking, although it appeared a relatively friendly silence. Both of them looked in her direction.

Both men smiled and moved toward her. At the sight, the breath that she'd caught in the retiring room fled.

What woman wouldn't adore being the object of two very handsome men's attention? Who wouldn't swoon with delight at such a prospect?

But the reality of her situation was far more complicated and confusing than delightful.

"I trust you're feeling better," Mason said with a small bow.

"Better?"

"You . . . ran off. Looking a mite feverish, in truth." Mason tilted his head. "Some punch might revive you." He took a step toward the refreshment table.

"Or a whiskey." An inscrutable smile — the likes of which she'd never before seen him wear — curved Sebastian's lips.

Her heart set up an unsteady rhythm as she contemplated his mouth.

Does he know? How he affects me? And what do I do about Mason?

Whiskey unquestionably sounded more tempting than punch, but she said, "Neither, thank you. I'm quite recovered. A momentary giddiness from the heat of the room."

The quadrille came to an end, and the opening bars to a cotillion began. Mason turned toward her and held out his hand.

"Would you do me the honor of joining me in this dance?" He added, "If you are feeling well enough, of course."

She stared at his hand. This was precisely what she'd wanted.

Her gaze went to Sebastian, standing close by. While he retained a slight smile, his eyes were cool, and the whole of his expression was inscrutable and she couldn't tell from it if he wanted her for himself.

But they were friends only. He'd said so after they had kissed, and she feared the repercussions if she were to reveal to him that she wanted more from him than friendship.

"Delighted," she said to Mason, and placed her hand atop his. Mason's gloved hand beneath hers felt warm and steady.

She waited for her pulse to speed up or her mouth to go dry or some sign, any sign, that actually touching Mason moved her. But her body continued its normal functioning, and her feet were steady beneath her as he led her onto the dance floor.

It took the effort of an Amazon to resist looking back at Sebastian. She didn't, but she sensed his gaze on her as she took her place for the cotillion.

She faced Mason, and he smiled charmingly at her while the other dancers moved into their positions. He truly was a very fine-looking man, and the intelligence and awareness in his eyes only heightened his attractiveness. And now, finally, she and Mason were about to dance with each other — the culmination of fantasies finally made reality.

The music began in earnest, and the dance commenced.

Seb's work was done. He'd danced with Grace and now she danced with Fredericks. Deliberately, Seb avoided looking at the couple as they turned around the floor. Seeing her stare adoringly at Fredericks whilst the naturalist gazed at her with stars in his eyes wasn't something Seb relished.

Dark, primal urges demanded Seb tear Grace from Fredericks. He had to occupy himself, and find a means for distraction so that he didn't yield to his instincts.

He glanced around the room. The guests not dancing congregated in small groups, some of the same sex, some comprised of men and women. It struck him that, for all the fine clothing and jewels and glasses of expensive wine in their hands, the guests were no different from the people he'd studied in villages and rural towns. They assessed and flirted, they laughed and leaned closely to people they wanted to attract, they gave polite yet reserved smiles to those that they wanted to keep at a distance.

Perhaps they considered the other person's political and financial value, but, at bottom, most everyone hoped to find someone they could at least care for, if not love.

Seb looked at Grace and Fredericks dancing. All he thought and felt was the wish to trade places with the other man — and that wasn't what Grace wanted.

The room became hot and choking. He couldn't draw enough air into his lungs. The darkness outside the ballroom beckoned, and, making certain not to glance in Grace's direction, he headed quickly through the open French doors.

Grace's movements were rote. The cotillion was one she'd learned early in her prepara-

353

tion for coming out, so there was no question of whether or not she remembered the steps. They carried her as she turned and retreated, spun and promenaded. She and the other dancers were part of a clockwork mechanism, gears moving together.

She *felt* mechanical, too. Remote from herself, even as she smiled back at Mason. He was an accomplished dancer, evidence that he was no stranger to events such as this ball. He partnered her well, and when their hands met, he didn't grip her too tightly or touch her too limply. Everything he did was correct. Everything was just as it should be, but it was merely pleasant. Nothing more.

She chanced a quick look around the ballroom, but Sebastian was nowhere to be found. Her heart sank, but she couldn't blame him for leaving. This part of his work was done. Now he was free to do precisely what he wanted, free from the obligation of her company.

The music came to an end. She curtsied to Mason, he bowed, and then he guided her off the dance floor — toward her mother, who smiled to see her on Mason's arm.

This was what her father wanted, and what Grace had believed she wanted. But she didn't know what she wanted anymore, and the idea of making conversation at that moment felt like a crushing vise.

"Forgive me, Mr. Fredericks." She came to a stop. "I feel I must take some air."

Mason frowned in concern. "There is a balcony. I will escort you."

"No. Thank you," she added. "It's much appreciated, but I need a moment to myself."

"As you like." He inclined his head, but his tone was reluctant.

She didn't look back as she went quickly to the open doors at the farthest part of the ballroom. Outside, a handful of guests stood at the iron railing, fanning themselves and murmuring pleasantries about the evening, the ball, their host and hostess, and any of a hundred other topics she could not find the emotional wherewithal to discuss.

Was there nowhere to be alone?

The balcony was quite long, stretching the whole length of the ballroom and even a little beyond. To her relief, shadows engulfed one end and it didn't appear as though anyone occupied the space, which made it the perfect place for her to seek solitude.

She quickly slipped toward the shadows.

The darkness enfolded her like an embrace. And then a pair of strong male arms encircled her in a *real* embrace.

CHAPTER 18

Alarmed, Grace yelped and pushed at the arms surrounding her. At once, they let go. But she turned to berate their owner for his presumption.

"You're insolent, *sir*," she ground out.

"My apologies but you were on the verge of trodding on my foot and — *Grace?*"

Stunned, she asked, "Sebastian?"

She peered into the dark, and as her eyes adjusted to the dimness, she could just make out his form. He was mostly made up of shadows, yet details emerged: his fair hair pale in the night, the width of his shoulders, the shine of his eyes. And . . . he was standing very near. Warmth from his body was as close as the darkness itself. He smelled of spice and expensive wool, with the faint hint of perspiration beneath that caused her senses to prickle. It thrilled her, his scent, even as she told herself that she shouldn't feel anything from his nearness.

Shouldn't. But she did.

"Where's Fredericks?"

Sebastian's question sounded almost indifferent — but a faint edge cut through his words.

"Inside, I imagine. I needed to take refuge from him."

"Was he disrespectful to you?" The bite in his tone made it clear that if Mason *had* taken liberties, Sebastian would happily make him suffer.

"He was in all ways an exemplary gentleman," she said quickly. "Only . . . he was there and my mother was there, and I desired a moment to myself."

A pause. "I should take my leave of you."

"Don't." To her own ears, her words were a plea. Only then did she realize that she still had her hands spread on his chest.

She dropped her hands and took a step back, putting needed distance between them. A handsome man, a shadowed balcony . . . It was all too easy to fall into the realm of fantasy, but those fantasies had no room in her reality.

"The night's a success, then?" His voice sounded a trifle rough, as if he pushed words out from his throat, but that was most likely the result of being in an overheated ballroom.

"Thanks to you, a roaring success," she said with far more cheer than she felt. Because her head was hopelessly muddled, and she had no answers for any of the questions that ricocheted through her. "You needn't stay. If there's somewhere else you'd rather be . . ."

After a moment, he said, "There's a small village on the northern outskirts of London. The wanders that I go on from time to time? When I was in the middle of one, I learned about this place. Once a year, the village celebrates the springtime with customs that date back hundreds of years. As if the celebration has been trapped in amber and forever preserved. But I've never been to the place itself, not in all the years I have known of it."

"Is it soon, this festival?" It comforted her to speak to him about his work, as if they could, somehow, return to the simpler time when they were merely friends. Before she'd gone and ruined things by having feelings for him.

"Tonight, in fact. I intend to go there after the ball. To observe the festivities."

"Ah." Of course his life would continue on without her in it. She was grateful that the ball hadn't been too taxing for him. "It sounds like a wonderful adventure."

A pause. And then, "Come with me."

She went still with shock. He couldn't have said that — could he? "Go with you to the village?"

"Why not? We used to go on excursions together, before all of this." He gestured to his evening finery. "It will be like old times. Two friends having their own adventure." His smile flashed in the darkness, and a pulse of responsiveness moved through her body.

"I . . ." She ought to say no, return to the ball, and spend the rest of the evening by her mother's side. *Ought* to, but didn't *want* to. She'd played the dutiful daughter, encouraging the right man to pay her attention. She wanted something entirely for herself.

And it would be so nice, so much less complicated, if she and Sebastian could go back to their original roles as friends. Well — she could *pretend* to feel only amity toward him, instead of this thorny desire.

She asked, "How do we get there?"

His grin was brilliant — she loved seeing this unexpectedly impulsive side of him. "We'll require a carriage."

"That can be arranged." Her pulse hammered. She could hardly believe she was doing this. It felt wild and reckless and magnificent yet brought her back to those simpler times that now seemed so long ago.

"Make your excuses to depart on your own. Then wait for me at the north side of Hanover Square." He rubbed his hands together. "This will be a lark. You'll see."

His excited enthusiasm was contagious, and offered relief from the constraints of the ball, and decorum, and all things proper. She stepped away from him and without his warmth, cool night air surrounded her. Moving into the light, she chanced a look behind her, yet the shadows were so complete at that corner of the balcony that anyone passing by would never have observed her with Sebastian.

Inside, life continued as it always had. Dancers filled the floor, and guests ringed around them, chatting and saying witty or dull things. She felt herself full to bursting with her plans to go to the village, but she couldn't let anyone know. The secret belonged to her and Sebastian.

"There you are, my dear," her mother said, nearing. "I couldn't find you after your dance with Mr. Fredericks."

"I required a little air," Grace said.

From the corner of her eye, she caught movement by the French doors. She feigned interest in the ornamental plasterwork surrounding them, enabling her to see Sebastian as he reentered the ballroom.

Giddiness rose up within her on a tide of champagne bubbles.

He didn't look in her direction — a disappointment, but she understood his rationale — as he walked to the Duke of Rotherby. Sebastian murmured something to his friend, who nodded in response, before he slipped from the ballroom.

The plan was in motion.

She barely heard her mother as she talked of the gossip heard at the ball. Grace made herself nod and look attentive while time inched by. Sebastian needed a head start, since they could not be seen leaving the ball together, yet she felt each minute like the slow progress of moss growing on a stone wall.

After she'd counted a full five minutes, she made certain that her mother noticed her wincing.

"Are you well, child?" Her mother frowned worriedly.

"I must own that my head aches." She made herself look regretful. "Much as it pains me to leave, my head hurts me more. I believe I'll go home for a nice lie down."

"I'll accompany you." Her mother stroked a hand across her forehead.

"Oh, no," Grace said quickly. "I'd hate for you to miss the rest of this delightful ball."

"Take the carriage," her mother said. "Viscount Marwood said his carriages were at his guests' disposal. Go straight to bed and if your head is too sore, tell Katie to mix you a tincture of laudanum."

"I will." Grace inwardly winced in guilt at deceiving her mother, but the lure to slip off with Sebastian to have a friendly adventure was far too enticing to refuse. "Please tell Lord and Lady Marwood goodbye for me. I'll see you in the morning."

Before she could think better of it, she hurried away, though she was conscious of keeping her step light and expression slightly pained as would befit someone suffering from a headache.

The ball ceased to exist for her as she went down the stairs, its music and laughter fading with each step. When she reached the foyer, where more guests were arriving, she collected her wrap from a footman. A tremor of excitement made her hands shake as she adjusted the silk's folds around her shoulders.

"Please have my carriage brought out front." How calm she sounded.

"Yes, my lady."

Moments later, the family carriage pulled

up to the curb outside. She strode to it, hardly able to believe what she was about to do. Yet the lure Sebastian had offered was too good to resist.

"Home, my lady? And shall I wait for your mother?"

"Dennis," she said to the coachman, "do come down here for a moment."

Too well-trained to look puzzled, the driver secured the reins before clambering from his seat to stand before her. The footman had already alit from his perch behind the carriage, so both servants regarded her with professional expectancy.

"My mother will find her own way home," she said in a low voice. "What I'm asking of you now, it can never be revealed to *anyone*. Especially my parents. I promise you," she added urgently, "your silence will see you handsomely rewarded. Can I rely on you?"

No going back now.

The footman and coachman said together, "Yes, my lady."

"Very good. Take me to the north side of Hanover Square. We'll wait there until I give additional direction. We must leave now."

Wordlessly, the footman opened the door to the carriage. With her blood rushing in her ears, she climbed in. The door shut with a click.

The vehicle swayed as both servants climbed back onto their seats. There was a slight jolt, a sway forward, and then they were off.

It would be something to share with Sebastian, this trip to the village. Something that might turn the hourglass back to who and what they were before everything changed. She hoped — but a grain of doubt lodged itself in the furthest corner of her heart.

It was all Seb could do to keep from running to Hanover Square. His legs pumped beneath him at a somewhat measured speed, though the pace was far too sedate. It was barely ten o'clock on a relatively balmy spring evening, and people and carriages continued to fill the streets of Mayfair. He'd surely attract attention to himself if he ran flat out.

Yet, God above, how he wanted to race at top velocity. He wasn't entirely certain what had possessed him to suggest that Grace accompany him to the village. Only that it seemed right, and he wanted to share something with her. If she was willing to spend time with him, as a friend or something else, he was happy to oblige — but he expected nothing from her in exchange.

This was about being with her, away from the narrow world of society.

He hurried past elegant houses and town houses, many with windows blazing as they, too, hosted large gatherings for Britain's elite. He wove through crowds of party-goers in their finery, managing a nod here and there when someone tried to hail him.

That was still new, being the object of attention. He'd forgotten, and cursed his negligence. He could leave no footprint tonight. No one could know where he'd gone, or with whom. Bond Street had to be avoided, so he cut down an alley, and exhaled in relief when he could finally break into a run.

At last, he reached Hanover Square. And there, on the north side, stood Grace's carriage. His already thundering pulse became the boom of cannons. Yet he forced himself to a relatively sedate stroll as he approached the vehicle. The curtains within had been drawn.

A footman waited beside the carriage, but as Seb neared, the servant opened the door.

"Give directions to Williams." Her voice sounded breathless with exhilaration.

Seb shot a glance at the footman. "Are they — ?"

"Their silence is assured."

Seb turned to the patiently waiting footman, and relayed the route to their destination. The servant nodded, and in a low voice conveyed the directions to the coachman. With their course settled, Seb climbed into the carriage.

After smothering his envy for Fredericks, joy came tumbling out of him — anticipation of the adventure, and pleasure that this was for him and Grace.

The carriage shuddered, then rolled forward. He realized then that they were alone in a closed carriage, and sudden awareness of her filled him. The dim light from the curtained window turned her skin to soft pearl, and he could feel her breath, rising and falling, and God help him, how he wanted to kiss her. He wanted everything.

But he couldn't have everything. He could only have this time with her because there was no doubt in his mind that Fredericks would call on her soon — and then it would all fall neatly into place. He didn't fool himself into believing that their friendship could continue as it had. It would change irrevocably.

These moments with her were precious, fleeting. He would grip them tightly until they slipped from his fingers.

"This is mad, isn't it," she said and

laughed. "What we're doing?"

"Entirely."

There was a rustle of silk as she shifted. He bit back a growl, picturing her legs beneath her skirts, before she reached across the carriage, and clasped his hand. They both wore gloves, yet the feel of her was another delicious torment.

"I'm happy," she said, urgent. "I'm happy that if I'm to be mad, it's with you."

CHAPTER 19

As the carriage rolled to a stop, sounds of merriment rose above the wheels' clatter. Unlike the sedate and refined ball, the music here was uninhibited and wild. A fiddle and a drum sent notes careening into the night. Raucous laughter tumbled like acrobats.

It was impossible for Grace to know what made her stomach feel tight and fluttery — the possibilities the night held, or the fact that she'd be alone with Sebastian this evening, in a place where no one knew them. As if anything that happened here was freed from consequence.

Nothing is free from consequence.

She pushed the thought from her mind.

The footman opened the door and helped her down. Sebastian also alit, and together, they took in the spectacle.

A cloudy sky obscured the stars, but torches illuminated everything. Sand-

369

colored brick structures as well as low stone buildings formed the majority of the village, which clustered around a large grassy square. A church spire rose up beyond the high street, and ancient elms spread their branches over rooftops. It was not unlike many little settlements dotting the English countryside, with the revelry at the center of the village a timeless sight.

Women wearing crowns of flowers danced in the square, the ribbons tied to their wrists fluttering with their movements. They made complicated figures as they spun and reeled. Villagers with ribbons pinned to their clothing clapped in time to the music, while children held hands and turned in circles. Nearly every adult held a tankard, and even the men wore floral diadems. Torches illuminated everything with gold-and-red flickering light, making the scene look straight from a medieval tapestry.

A few villagers cast curious looks at Grace and Sebastian, warily eyeing the fine carriage that was so unlike the heavy drays and wagons nearby that held casks.

"Dare me to empty that," Grace said, pointing to one of the casks.

"Oho, a drinking contest?" He crossed his arms over his chest. "I'll have you know that at Oxford, I bested Rotherby every time he challenged me to a drinking battle. He either passed out or cast up his accounts whilst I was still bellowing tavern songs."

She eyed him, but her lips quirked. It felt so good to be back to their old teasing ways. "I'm not certain that's anything to boast about. *I'm exceptionally good at drunkenness.*"

"*You* were the one who begged me to dare you to drink."

She put her hands on her hips. "Dare me to do something else."

Just as he opened his mouth to speak, a barrel-chested man approached them with a hint of wariness. Sebastian held up a bottle of wine.

"Fine claret for your celebration," Sebastian said cheerfully.

The man took the bottle, cradling it carefully with his thick fingers. "Thank 'e, sir. Join us, there's a lad. And your lass is welcome, too." He strode off, holding the bottle over his head. A resounding cheer went up from the crowd.

Astonished, Grace eyed Sebastian. "You sneak! I didn't even see you holding that. Where did it come from?"

"Nicked it on my way out of the ball." He flashed her a grin. "Lord Marwood's known for his hospitality. I doubted he'd mind

371

missing one more bottle."

She shook her head. "Dancing, being a rake. Now we add larceny to your list of abilities."

He winked at her, a very wicked wink that made him into the veriest golden-haired rogue, and a surge of awareness coursed through her. She realized at that moment that scholars didn't just read, they *knew* things, naughty things.

Sebastian was a very good scholar.

Her body heated with understanding. Sebastian was in all things very thorough. She'd no doubt that, as a lover, he would shake his partner's world to its very foundations.

Oh, gracious.

Attempting to distract herself, she focused her attention on the continuing festivities. "I've never done anything like this before."

"As you said, if we're to be mad, we can be mad together." He held out his hand, and she noticed that he'd removed his gloves. "Time to join in."

Dare she? When it was so difficult to remember that they were only friends.

But the temptation was too powerful to resist. She tugged off her gloves and let them fall to the ground before weaving her fingers with his.

Palm to palm, they touched. His hand was so much larger than hers, and while it wasn't rough like a laborer's, it was strong and capable. Heat coursed through her like a river of fire.

She looked at him in the torchlight, which made golden planes of his face and cast dangerous shadows along his jaw. He looked back, his eyes gleaming.

The moment held.

They moved as one, striding toward the festivities. The drumbeat grew louder as they neared, but her own heart was loudest of all.

A young woman skipped toward them and wordlessly set a crown of flowers onto Grace's head. Fresh and floral scents enveloped Grace.

"And one for the gentleman," the young woman added as she placed a floral circlet on Sebastian. With that, she capered away.

The dance came to a close, and as the women left the green, a group of men took the field. They carried staves tied with ribbons that they spun and knocked together in time with the music. Each knock of the staves together sounded deep in Grace's chest, resonating with the profundity of an ancient rite.

She glanced toward Sebastian. He wore a

wide smile, his expression both intent and delighted, and to see him so elated by watching this timeless custom made her insides cartwheel.

I want him to always look like this. Enthralled. Happy.

When the men's dance finished, the same barrel-chested man strode into the middle of the green with his arms upraised. The music stopped and voices quieted.

"Now comes the best part o' the night," he announced. "The Lass-Lifting Race!"

A cheer went up.

"Your pardon," Sebastian said to a passing bearded man. "I've heard about this but I don't know what it is — the Lass-Lifting Race."

A grin split the man's face. "On a field just past the church, the lustiest lads race toward their lasses, then they pick 'em up, put 'em on their shoulders, and the two of 'em turn around and race back. Plenty o' mischief, both ways."

More giddiness coursed through her. This was very far from a ballroom — and she adored it. "What do the winners receive?"

"Win?" The man scratched his head. "Ain't no winners, missus. At the end, everyone gets strawberry and rhubarb pies, and the night's over."

"Looks like it might rain." Grace glanced at the cloudy sky.

"Then we just get nice an' muddy," the man said with good humor. He peered at Sebastian. "You running, my lad and lass?"

Sebastian opened his mouth as if to immediately decline. But then he glanced at her, a mischievous light in his eyes. "Shall we?"

The idea of Sebastian carrying her on his shoulders while they ran across a field in the middle of the night was . . . delightful. She felt every inch of his skin where their hands interwove. She'd feel even more of him if he carried her.

"Oh, yes," she answered.

Sebastian beamed at her and she beamed right back. They would have gone on grinning at each other like fools if the bearded man hadn't said, "Best get a move on, you two. They're taking their places on the field as we speak. Don't want to be late starting or else they throw parsnips at you."

The man ambled off.

Most of the revelers streamed out of the square and toward the church. Several dogs accompanied the procession, barking with excitement, while men carried torches to light the way.

"This truly *is* mad," Grace felt compelled

to point out to Sebastian.

"So it is," he said jauntily.

They both hurried after the villagers. She had impressions of a few shops, and more cottages, many with tidy gardens. Fences bent with time lined the dirt road that led them past the church to a vast, dark expanse. People with torches stood to one side of the field, and about a hundred yards away, more villagers with flickering torches marked the other end of the meadow.

At the closer side of the field, men ranging in age from barely into their teens to hovering close to middle age prepared themselves for the race with deep knee bends, stretches, and arm swings. Almost all of them had shucked their coats and waistcoats, and some boasted brawny, burly frames, while others were lean and pared down. Women stood with the torchbearers at the far end, and they called out encouragement to the men.

"Better ready yourself, fine sir," a villager cried to Sebastian.

To her dismay, Sebastian released her hand, but to her delight, he pulled off his coat, waistcoat, and neckcloth. The fine fabric of his shirt clung to him, and she wished there was a precedent for running the race bare-chested. Alas, it was not to be, yet she still enjoyed the sight of him in only his shirtsleeves.

He caught her ogling him, and instead of a look of warm amiability, he sent her a smile she could feel between her legs.

What she felt for him was far from friendship — but she didn't want to call an end to tonight. She wanted it to last forever, the air crackling, though she couldn't tell if it was from the incipient storm or the pull between them.

With a start, she realized he felt the attraction, too. And it all made sense now, the dance they'd shared at the ball, and the tension between them in the carriage on the way here.

He wanted her. As she wanted him. Their kiss had planted the seed, and now it flowered brightly.

Maybe it was only physical attraction, but it still ensnared her, still called to her.

"Off you go." He nodded toward the other side of the field. "And be certain to cheer for me."

"I'll shout loudest of all."

Still shaking from her revelation, she walked as briskly as she could across the field. Tall, wet grass clung to the hem of her skirts. Without Sebastian close by, the night was cooler, the dark night sky farther away.

Should she have said something to Sebastian? That she shared his desire? There seemed no right answer. She was caught in a cyclone and had no bearings.

She neared the line of women waiting with the torchbearers.

"A fancy miss come to join us," a woman in a blue dress said, but her voice was light with humor.

"Got her a fancy fellow, too," a redhead teased. "He won't beat my Charlie."

"I thought there were no winners," Grace said.

"No winners," the woman in the blue dress agreed, "but who don't love a good gloat?"

Grace took her place between the woman in blue and the redhead. "Then prepare yourself to listen to my man gloat."

Heat rushed into her cheeks. Had she just referred to Sebastian as *my man*? It had slipped from her without thought. But he wasn't her man.

She cupped her hands around her mouth. "You can do it, Sebastian! Trounce them all!"

Her heart leapt when he waved at her. Likely ladies of older times had the same jittery anticipation when waiting for their knights to take to the field.

378

"Look lively," the redhead said. "I see Sam Dawkins with his blunderbuss."

At the other end of the field, a gray-haired man hefted an ancient firearm and aimed it up and away from the field. He shouted something, then pulled the trigger. There was a flash, and a boom.

The men surged forward.

After a night of maneuvering through the treacherous waters of a society ball, he eagerly awaited the chance to use his body. Talking was difficult, physicality was easy.

"You can do it, Sebastian! Trounce them all!"

Energy surged through his body at Grace's yelled encouragement.

"Oi," a man with wide muttonchop whiskers said beside him. "Them long legs o' yours are goin' to carry you home in shame when I thrash you." He nudged Seb with his elbow.

For a moment, his anxiousness returned, clutching him tight enough to steal his breath. But he made himself attentive to physical sensations: the air, saturated with advancing rain, the smell of the meadow, the voices of the racers as they good-naturedly provoked each other.

He drawled, "How delightful that they let

children run in the race."

The man with the muttonchops scowled for a bare moment before he grinned at Seb. "That's the way of it, lad. But," he added, "it's a good thing your lass got soft silk skirts to wipe away your tears when you lose."

Any rejoinder Seb might have offered scattered when a middle-aged man appeared with a large, exceptionally old firearm. The weapon discharged with a thunderous clap. Then there was no time for thinking or analysis or anything at all except running.

He shot forward into the night. Behind him, the crowd cheered. Ahead of him, women shouted encouragement. He couldn't quite make out Grace's voice in the midst of the clamor, but knowing she was there, waiting for him, cheering for him, his body pulsed with strength and speed.

Something heavy knocked into him. He fought to keep upright as Muttonchops rammed a shoulder into his side. All the racers jostled with each other, giving shoves and sticking out legs in an attempt to trip their competition.

Seb pushed back. Gratification roared when Muttonchops sprawled in the grass, but it was short-lived as his rival shot back onto his feet and sped forward.

The gleam of the torches grew as Seb neared the other end of the field. Grace jumped up and down as she yelled, "Trounce their sorry arses, Sebastian!"

Closer, closer.

A moment later, he and the other runners reached the line of women. There wasn't time for grace or manners.

"Mount me." Seb spun around and dropped to his knees.

Grace climbed onto his shoulders, and only when he got to his feet did he realize that her crotch pressed against the back of his head and his hands held tight to her thighs. Her soft flesh pressed against his face, soaking him in her heat. Primal awareness thrummed in him.

Fuck yes.

"Let's go!" Grace cried.

Seb snapped out of his daze. Right. The race.

Gaining his balance with her weight atop him took a few strides, but soon they were hurtling back down the field. He clutched her legs to keep her secure.

"Enemy ship starboard!" Grace exclaimed.

From the corner of his eye, he saw Muttonchops draw close, a redheaded woman riding the man's shoulders. The other couple drew close. Then Grace let out a yelp as the redhead reached over to jostle Grace. Seb gritted his teeth as he battled to keep upright, but he gasped out a chuckle as Grace shoved the redhead. With his balance upset, Muttonchops stumbled, yet he kept his feet.

Torches loomed ahead. Seb pushed himself, running hard and holding tightly to Grace. She bounced with each stride he took, but she didn't seem to mind the discomfort — she seemed too focused on yelling taunts to the other racers.

"Did a goat teach you how to run?" she shouted to a couple they passed. "I'll fetch you some leading strings after we beat you to the finish line."

He grinned like a madman. Who knew the clever herpetologist was also a fierce competitor?

Still, carrying her on his shoulders at a full run wasn't the easiest task, and it was with relief that he spotted the finish line ahead. Not too far now. His lungs and legs burned, but he wouldn't consider the pain. Not until later.

With a final burst of speed, he and Grace crossed the finish line. Shouts and claps and joyful chaos surrounded them.

Winded, Seb sank to his knees and Grace clambered off. He immediately missed the feel of her thighs around his face.

"Who won?" she demanded, her expression fierce. "Did we win?"

He felt his lips curve into a smile. Once roused, her competitive spirit was mighty. "Doesn't matter," he panted. "Not really. All that . . . matters . . . is running . . . the race."

Her brow smoothed, and she smiled in response — filling his exhausted body with new life. "Wise Sebastian."

A girl carrying a basket appeared and thrust an object into his palm. He peered at it as he staggered to his feet.

"The strawberry rhubarb pie." Grace laughed.

He held the pastry up to her. "Your spoils, my lady."

She took a bite, then licked up the flakes that clung to her lips. His groin tightened.

There was a deep rumble of thunder, and then the clouds opened up. Rain poured down, soaking everything. People ran in every direction, screaming with shock and delight.

Without thought, Sebastian grabbed Grace's hand while also scooping up his discarded clothing, then broke into a run toward a wooden structure. A barn.

And then he was inside, hearing the sound

of wood sliding into place. She'd closed the door. The barn smelled of fresh hay, but not of animals, and he couldn't hear anything shifting in the stalls. It was almost entirely dark, save for bits of light working through the slats.

He and Grace stood inches apart. Raindrops glittered on her face and neck, and adorned the smooth flesh of her chest that rose and fell. Beads of water clung to her lips, and he wanted nothing more than to lick up those droplets. The race had heated his blood, but having her so close, seeing the hunger in her gaze, he was overwhelmed with the desire he'd tried so furiously to suppress.

There was an answering heat in her eyes. Heat that he craved and feared all at once.

She swayed toward him. "Sebastian." Her voice was a siren's, husky and rich, and she stepped closer to stroke her hands up his chest. Despite his wet clothing, her touch was fire.

"Grace."

They spoke together. "Kiss me." "Can I taste you?" As she lifted up on her toes, wrapping her arms around his shoulders, he pulled her close, feeling the pliant, soft heat of her against his hardness. He loved the sensation of her pressed to him, this woman

384

he'd wanted for so long finally in his embrace. *Thank God.*

And then he thought nothing at all as their mouths met.

tumble...

CHAPTER 20

This kiss had none of their previous effort's
tentative, sweet exploration. It was hot and
explosive. From the moment their lips met,
they devoured each other with fiery demand. Their tongues lapped together, stroking, seeking to bring them closer, and closer
still.

She was in a frenzy, whipped to madness
by her need for him. He seemed lost in
desire, too, the way he kissed and touched
her with scorching possession.

One of his hands cupped the back of her
head, the other skimmed down to cup her
arse and bring her snug to him. Through
her wet clothing she felt the thick ridge of
his arousal. Shamelessly, she arched into
him so he pressed into the curve of her
belly. A rumble sounded from deep in his
chest.

Intoxicating pleasure rose within her at
that sound, that she should take this

learned, thoughtful man and drive him into a fever of need — for her.

Together, they moved, barely breaking the kiss to chart steps toward a pile of sweet-scented hay. In silent agreement, they lay down. He stretched out beside her, bracing himself on his elbow as he gazed down at her. The way he looked at her . . . as though she was the sum of all things that mattered . . . it was far more intoxicating than any wine.

Her breath came in hard, fast gulps. "Take off your shirt."

Though his gaze was afire, a corner of his mouth turned up in a smile. "Pleased to oblige." He sat up just enough to whisk the garment off.

"Oh."

She couldn't formulate more astute words. Sebastian's bare torso defied all her imaginings. He was lean and sculpted, from the definition of his pectorals to the ridges of his flat abdomen. Lovely golden hair curled on his chest and trailed down him, where a line of hair vanished beneath the waistband of his breeches. She didn't miss the thick shape straining against the front of those breeches, but she managed to tug her gaze up to admire the carved musculature of his arms, and then venture higher to see him watching her carefully.

"You're beautiful, Sebastian." She stroked her hand up his bare flesh — it twitched beneath her palm — to curve against his jaw. Stubble grazed her skin magnificently.

He exhaled and a shy smile touched his lips. "I'm glad you think so. Because I think you're the loveliest person I've ever known."

They kissed, a long, slow, voluptuous kiss that unfolded in velvet waves. Her breasts became tight and heavy, and heat gathered between her legs. His large hand covered her breast and glided back and forth over her stiff nipple. Sensation careened through her and she couldn't stop her moan.

Pulling back slightly, he asked in a gentle voice, "Have you done this before?"

"Not with another person, no." It didn't feel strange or shameful to admit this, not to him.

"On your own?" His own breathing was jagged.

"Don't you?"

The column of his throat worked as he swallowed. "Oh, yes."

"I should like to see that." The thought of Sebastian's hand gripping his own cock, stroking himself to release as he grimaced with pleasure . . . her skin tingled and she slid deeper into the waters of desire.

"My God, Grace." He growled his approval. Then, "You aren't afraid? Of sex?"

"I do read quite a bit, you know."

He chuckled lowly. "Never underestimate the abilities of a scholar." He lowered his head and kissed her so thoroughly, all rational thought dissolved. He continued to palm and caress her breasts, making her writhe with pleasure.

She stroked him, too, discovering all the beautiful parts of him, learning his feel. He was satiny and tight, while the hair on his chest tickled/scratched her palm, and when she circled his nipple, she was rewarded with his sensual hiss.

The prickle of hay touched her skin as he gathered up her skirts. His hand was hot against her stocking-clad leg, and then she gasped as he found the bare flesh of her thigh.

"Yes?" he murmured.

"Do not stop." A seductress's voice had replaced her own, lower and more breathless than she'd ever heard it before.

Higher climbed his hand, and then he dipped into the opening of her drawers. She cried out as he delved between her folds and pleasure rocked her.

"Christ," he rumbled. "You're so wet."

"I —" But she had no words. Not when

he stroked her, up and down and in gorgeous circles at her entrance. His thumb found the nub of her clitoris, and she arched up with a moan as he lavished attention where she needed it most.

She reached out to palm his hard cock through the fabric of his breeches. He made a dark animal sound as his hips pushed into her touch. But it wasn't enough. She wanted his naked flesh, and fumbled with the buttons securing his fall. He helped, tearing at the fastenings until the flap opened. Without hesitation, she wrapped her hand around his cock and the noise he made would delight her until the end of her days.

The feel of his penis was . . . exquisite. Thick and rigid and hot. She ran her hand up and down, testing the textures of silk and stiffness.

Grace managed to emerge from her pleasured haze enough to breathe, "Show me. Show me how you like to be touched."

He wrapped his hand around hers in a grip that was far tighter than she would have used if left to her own devices. It was almost punishing, but the cords in his neck stood out as he groaned with pleasure. The round head of his cock stood proud of the foreskin, and a droplet of slickness emerged to coat her fingers.

"Like this," he gritted, guiding her along his shaft. "Firm at the head, and all the way down. Yes. *Yes.*" He released his grip on her hand and she took over, stroking him.

She'd never felt so powerful. Even as he continued to caress her, sending glittering sparks throughout her body, she savored the measure of her sovereignty. He lavished her with sensation as she bestowed pleasure to him.

"Enough," he rasped and laid a restraining palm over her hand.

"You don't like it?"

"Like it too much. But there's something I want." He nuzzled along her neck before lightly biting her throat. "I want to taste you. Will you let me?" His gaze flicked downward — he didn't mean tasting her mouth.

She'd read about it, of course. The Lady of Dubious Quality had a remarkable way of describing what it was like when someone licked a woman's quim, and the thought of it had inspired Grace many times as she'd touched herself. To experience it for herself . . .

"Please," she said in a husky whisper.

"I want to hear you say it."

She shivered from his rough demand. This delightful, commanding Sebastian stoked her arousal higher. "I want you to taste me. Between my legs."

God, if she could only capture the sound he made and listen to it every day for the rest of her life. It was the primal sound of a highly aroused man. Not any man. *Sebastian.*

He pressed scorching kisses along her throat, then lower, just above the neckline of her gown. She released her hold on his cock as he continued to move down her body. And then he knelt between her legs, gently easing up her skirts before tugging off her drawers. She watched the focused desire on his face as he beheld her bared quim, and his hunger made her own need blaze.

Before she could plead with him to please, please put his mouth on her, he lowered down and gave her folds one long, slow lick. She cried out. And when he sucked on her sensitive flesh, she cried out again.

He consumed her. There was no other way of describing it. He feasted on her with a single-mindedness that robbed her of the ability to do anything but lie back and let herself be pleasured. Nothing had ever felt so wondrous — or so she believed until he slid his finger into her passage and she had to clamp her hand over her mouth to stifle her scream of ecstasy.

She'd wanted him, wanted this, forever. And to have him now worshipping her body — as though she was everything to him — filled her with a wild and uncontrolled joy.

His tongue lapped at her and circled her clitoris, while he stroked in and out of her with his finger. Deep within her, he found and caressed a swollen spot.

"Sebastian. Yes. Oh, God. I —"

She broke into thousands, millions of fragments. It wracked her sharply. But he didn't stop, and no sooner had she collected herself than another orgasm shattered her. And another. Was it possible to die from pleasure? If so, she didn't care, so long as he kept making her feel this way.

She'd experienced release before at her own hands. Yet it was as if she'd never known what it was to feel ecstasy because what he gave her was so much better, both ruthless and giving. It was as though he would do anything to give her pleasure.

Eons or seconds later, he lay beside her, his expression gratified as well as hungry.

"I'd read about that," she said, her words lightly slurred. "But it's so much better than I could have imagined."

She tasted herself on his lips when he kissed her.

"I'd like to fuck you now." A stain of color spread across his face, as though he shocked himself with his own profane language. His voice was taut, and even though she'd just had a number of orgasms, desire slammed back into her to hear him speak such earthy words. "I'll be careful. I'll keep you safe."

"Yes."

He moved to lie between her thighs. She opened eagerly for him, and her breath caught when he gripped one of her legs, hitching it high.

His cock rubbed between her folds before he fit the head at her entrance. His gaze found hers. Then he thrust, filling her.

She gasped. At the same time, he gave a deep, carnal growl.

He was inside her, and her heart was as full as her body, completely suffused by him. Yet, for all her joy, a small whimper escaped her.

"Hurting?" His brow creased.

"A little . . ." He moved to pull out, but she wrapped her free leg tighter around him. "Stay. Stay inside me. Just . . . give me some time."

He pressed his lips together and nodded. Clearly, waiting cost him, but he did so. He held still as she breathed through the pain and her body relaxed to accommodate him, gradual waves of loosening until the hurt lessened, bit by bit. Then it was gone, and all she felt was pleasure.

She pressed up, taking him deeper.

"Grace . . ." His groan was pained.

She canted her hips, working herself on him. With each movement, pleasure burst through her and behind her eyes.

"Oh, hell, yes," he hissed.

She went slowly at first but could not stop herself from moving faster and faster still. It wasn't enough. She needed more. More of him.

"Fuck me, Sebastian." She cupped her hand over the bare curve of his arse as she spoke words that she'd only read but always wanted to say. "Fuck me the way you've wanted to."

"God —" He could only rasp out one syllable before he began to thrust. Hard, powerful strokes that made her jolt.

Lord above, but she loved it. He was rough and forceful, giving his entire self to this marvelously earthy act. He was over her, and she was beneath him, spread wide for his enjoyment.

And then he moved, twisting so that he lay on his back and she straddled him. She braced her hands on his chest as she looked down into his face, gone rigid with ecstasy.

"Your turn," he rumbled. His hands gripped her hips with almost bruising force. "Fuck me the way *you've* wanted to."

His coarse directive was her undoing. She rode him, stroking up and down on his cock, losing herself to a frenzy that claimed every inch of her. Her head tipped forward as she leaned into sensation. Opening her eyes, she saw him lick his thumb and reach down between their slick bodies. He thrust up into her just as he circled her clitoris with his finger.

She clamped her teeth together to keep from crying out as another climax split her apart. It went on and on, until, at last, she sprawled atop him.

They spun once more, until she was back beneath him. He plunged into her, a handful of heavy, solid thrusts, each one accompanied by his pleasured grunt, before he pulled out and groaned his release, droplets spattering on her belly.

He lowered himself beside her. There were no sounds other than Grace's and Sebastian's own slowing breaths. The village was quiet — everyone had found their own beds. Maybe some of the villagers were doing just what she and Sebastian had done. If so, bless them. Everyone should have that kind of fathomless pleasure.

The rain had stopped, with an immense, velvet quiet following.

Sebastian's arm wrapped around her waist, and he rested his lips against the crown of her head. She felt protected. Adored. Tenderness swept through her.

"Grace," he said, his breath warm on her. "You don't have to worry."

"I know," she murmured. He'd been careful, as he said he would be, ensuring he didn't get her with child.

He exhaled with what sounded like relief. "Good. I'm glad. I won't ask more from you. You and I . . . we're friends, and I don't want to rob you of your dreams."

She frowned in confusion, unable to make sense of what he said. Her mind snagged on the word *friends*. "My dreams?"

"Of Fredericks," he said quietly. "He's who you want. And you and I can go on as we have, put this behind us. It was a onetime madness. An error in judgment, never to be repeated."

Dismay nearly choked her. Was it true — he thought making love with her had been a *mistake*?

God, she'd been so idiotic. He'd *said* that their adventure was like the old days of their friendship, and, absurdly, she had let her ungovernable emotions rule her. When he'd

397

touched her, when he'd been inside her, she hadn't felt friendliness toward him. She'd felt . . . she wasn't certain what to call her wildly careening emotions, but they overwhelmed her, muddled her thoughts. They *had,* until he'd brought her back to solid ground.

Clearly, she'd been alone in her overwrought emotions.

Never would she have anyone — Sebastian in particular — feel for her a sense of obligation but not love. That was the worst kind of trap and presaged a lifetime of misery.

"Glad we're in agreement," she made herself say, though she hurt as if she spoke in knives not words. "We'll chalk it up to curiosity."

"Nothing more." He was quiet for a moment. "So . . . friends?"

"Friends," she said.

As she lay in his arms, she squeezed her eyes shut against the confusion and pain that threatened to obliterate all the ecstasy she'd just experienced.

CHAPTER 21

Grace sat opposite Seb for the carriage ride
back to the city. She didn't cram herself into
a corner, trying to gain as much distance
between them as possible, but she never met
his gaze, and whenever their knees bumped
from the sway of the vehicle, she quickly
moved them aside. As if they hadn't just
engaged in the most intimate, carnal act two
people could. As if he hadn't held her in his
arms, treasuring how their heartbeats
aligned as they quieted in the aftermath.

He clenched his hands into fists as they
rested beside him. Several times, he opened
his mouth, but then shut it again. What
could he say to her?

Though it had devastated him, he'd made
certain that she knew he expected nothing
from her. She'd no obligation to him. They'd
given in to their attraction, and while it had
altered the very terrain of Seb's world like
an earthquake, he had made certain that if

she had set her heart on someone else, Seb wouldn't stand in her path. To ask for anything more was a violation of their friendship, and he respected her too much to demand something she didn't want to give.

With that, she'd withdrawn from him, as though, after receiving permission to walk away, she did just that.

The spring night cooled with each passing minute, but it was nothing compared to the chill within the carriage. The iciness clenched around him, squeezing air from his lungs.

How long was this damned ride back to town?

He peered behind the carriage window curtain to see the streets of Camden Town streaming past. He knocked on the roof of the carriage, and the vehicle slowed.

"Why are we stopping?" This was the first Grace had spoken since she'd agreed that they were to remain friends.

"I'll walk from here." He put his hand on the door, eager to be anywhere else but with her and the reminder that she wanted someone else.

She leaned forward. "It's miles back to Howland Street."

When had he told her where he resided?

But her words were still tight and distant.

"A mile and a half, truly," he said, forcing himself to sound jovial. "Not far."

"I see." She sat back, and while the physical space between them wasn't much altered, the expanse seemed to stretch into infinity.

He'd half hoped she might protest and insist that they continue to ride together. If not all the way to Howland Street, then perhaps until they reached Mayfair. But that wasn't to be. And he shouldn't feel disappointed that she'd agreed to his decision to walk.

The carriage stopped. With relief, Seb opened the door before the footman could, and stepped down from the vehicle. The residential streets of Camden Town were empty, befitting his mood. After the crush of people at the Viscount Marwood's ball, and the village festivities, nothing suited him better than solitude. He was too raw and tender for other people, other voices.

Though that could change — if she said she wanted him to stay with her.

He turned to Grace, one hand on the door. She remained in the shadows, wordless, her hands clasped together in her lap.

What was there to say? "Thank you," seemed too paltry, and she likely didn't want to hear him add, "for the most incredible experience of my entire life."

"Good night," he said.

"Good night," she answered, as if they were still friends who met at the Benezra Library and the occasional trip to a lecture or exhibit. Exactly what he'd offered, and she'd agreed to his terms.

Chilled to his marrow, he shut the door behind him and began to walk. The carriage wheels clattered over the road as it drove on, passing him. He didn't slow to watch it disappear down the street, going south, back to life as it had been.

But it couldn't return to normalcy. Such a feat was impossible. He would never look at her again without recalling the feel of her mouth against his, or the sweet, spicy taste of her, or the way her gaze filled with desire and wonder and something that came close to adoration when she had been beneath him.

He walked with long, brisk strides past the dark spread of Regent's Park, and along streets of refined new homes. After the tense confines of the carriage, it felt good to move and breathe the chill night air. He passed a few wagons trundling along, and a quartet of soldiers staggering as they sang a regimental tune. The men had their arms slung around each other's necks while they leaned together, offering support. Likely, they'd been in battle together, survived Bonaparte, seen the best and worst of humanity together.

A stab of longing pierced Seb. Not for war — his father had flatly refused to buy a commission for him, and had declared that he'd cut off every cent if Seb enlisted — but for the company and camaraderie of his friends.

He looked up in surprise as he found himself standing outside Rotherby's imposing Mayfair home. All the windows were dark. Save one.

He'd been to Rotherby House many times over the years, yet never at this hour. Before he could talk himself out of it, he opened the iron gate, walked to the door, and knocked brusquely.

A minute later, a sleepy-looking footman opened the door.

"His Grace is in his study," the servant said and yawned into his gloved hand.

So. He was expected.

"I know the way." Seb slipped the footman a coin for his trouble and, picking up a lit candle, moved into the massive spread that was Rotherby House.

It had been designed and constructed with

the intent to intimidate visitors and impress upon them the master's vast, almost unchecked power. Naturally, Rotherby himself had not built such a structure, and had often expressed his dislike of the place. But Seb believed there was a part of his friend that secretly needed the distance it gave him from others, cocooning him in heavy sandstone.

The door to the study stood ajar, and Seb rapped lightly. "It's Holloway."

"Enter, you wily bastard."

"Since when have I become a wily bastard?" He stepped into the room. Bookshelves lined one wall, and a massive mahogany desk was positioned near a bank of velvet-draped windows. Rotherby stood beside the low-burning fireplace, his coat and waistcoat gone, a glass of something in his hand. "If that's whiskey, I want it."

"You've become a wily bastard since both you and Grace disappeared from Marwood's ball, and me none the wiser about where you might have gone. You only said that you were leaving." Rotherby pointed to a walnut table, atop which crystal decanters were arrayed. "Help yourself to whatever's there."

As Seb poured himself a liberal amount of whiskey, he could hear Rotherby using a poker to rouse the fire.

"You're welcome, incidentally," Rotherby said drily.

Seb turned and raised his glass. "Thank you for the drink."

"Not the whiskey. I'm talking about Lady Pembroke — Grace's mother." Rotherby sprawled in a chair near the fire. "I invited her, and the Earl and Countess of Ashford, to dine with me after Marwood's ball. Kept her occupied for a good two hours while you and Grace did . . ." He waved his hand. "Whatever you did."

"My thanks." Seb had barely considered her mother, but thank God someone had taken such things into consideration. He hadn't been thinking logically at all, not when it came to her. All his reason and lucidity and carefully constructed scaffolds of scientific understanding — it all fell apart whenever he was near her.

He ambled to the other chair near the fire and lowered himself into it before taking a long swallow of whiskey. It burned his throat and cut through the haze of thought and sensation that continued to cling to him.

Belatedly, he realized that his skin still smelled faintly of her. She clung to him, the feel and flavor of her, and the gorgeous flush that rose to her cheeks when she came. All he wanted was to see that blush again as she tightened around him.

Goddamn it.

He threw back the rest of his drink and set the glass down hard on the floor.

"Son of a bitch," Rotherby said. "You slept with her. Denial is impossible," he went on when Seb didn't respond. "You've got the look of a man who's calculating the next time he can get beneath a lady's skirts."

Seb could do nothing but drop his head into his hands. His whole body felt like rusted metal. "I'm in a bad way."

"An understatement." The chair beneath Rotherby creaked as he leaned forward. "On the morrow, you'll go to her family and make an offer."

"What?" Seb straightened. "An offer of *marriage*?"

"No, an offer to buy five acres of pasture-land. Of course, an offer of marriage." Rotherby's drink spilled as he stood. "My God, Holloway. You can't just tup an earl's daughter without there being consequences. I thought you two might have snuck off to the library for some illicit reading, or whatever it is that scholars do. I didn't think you'd plow her."

It felt like so much more than *plowing.* "We were careful." Seb swallowed. An icy cascade pulsed through him.

"Whether or not there's a babe is irrelevant. She's a damned unmarried *lady.*"

Seb tipped his head back to stare at the shadows flickering on the ceiling. "But she said nothing about marriage. Not before, and certainly not after."

"Unfortunately, it doesn't matter what the woman in question wants." Rotherby paced over to Seb and stared down with an expression that was both angry and sympathetic. "Women don't have an easy go of it. It falls to us" — he knocked his knuckles into Seb's chest — "to protect them. Even when the woman outranks us, we're still men, and that makes us more significant in the eyes of the world. A damned shame, and unfair, but that's the way of it."

God above, they'd been too mad with desire to think logically. He felt like the veriest bumbler.

"Don't you want to marry her?" Rotherby asked softly.

"Of course I do," Seb answered automatically. And then, "Christ. I *do.*" He shot to his feet.

Become Grace's husband . . .

The moment the thought entered his mind, all the jangling pieces of himself fell into place. He was both deeply calm and

407

wildly excited. To wake beside her every morning and hold her in his arms every night, each day to hear her fascinating thoughts, to share her joys, and to help her weather sorrows . . .

That was *exactly* what he wanted. All this time, the hours and days he spent with Grace were simply for the pleasure of her company. Because every part of him came alive whenever he was with her. Because he craved nothing more than her happiness.

Yet . . .

"If I went to her father," he said, pacing, "asked for her hand, and he accepted, but she didn't want to marry me, wouldn't she feel trapped? She wants Fredericks, after all."

Anguish sat heavily on his shoulders, because she hadn't corrected Seb when he'd said she continue to seek Fredericks. She'd been eager to put their lovemaking behind them and progress toward her goal.

Rotherby crossed his arms over his chest. "Damn."

"Precisely." Seb raked his hands through his hair. "I like her too much to force her into something she doesn't desire. I won't do it, Rotherby."

His friend looked at him for a long moment, the expression on his face faintly wondering.

"What's it like?" Rotherby asked lowly. "To feel that way about someone? Knowing that they want nothing from you? It's so . . ." He shook his head. ". . . impossible."

The bleakness in Rotherby's eyes was a vise around Seb's chest. He'd known that his friend was a man much in demand, a person that other people sought because they believed he could do something for them. But at that moment, Seb finally saw how impossibly isolating that could be, and how lonely Rotherby truly was.

Seb began to speak, but Rotherby cut through the air with his hand. "Never mind. Don't answer that. Bloody foolish question." He cleared his throat. "I suppose then that the next step is to go to Grace and offer to make her your wife. If she agrees, then you'll have my felicitations. And if she doesn't . . ."

"If she doesn't . . ." Something wintry and cutting lanced Seb, and he rubbed the spot over his heart. It was as though he performed a vivisection on himself. "Another one of my wanders might be on the horizon. Maybe I'll hie off to the Outer Hebrides to nurse my injured heart."

"You wouldn't be the first heartbroken man to run to an island." Rotherby walked to Seb and placed his hand on Seb's shoulder. "I hope she says yes, my friend."

Seb tried for a smile, but the attempt was a dismal failure. "As do I."

Despite the fact that she'd gone to her bed weary beyond imagining, Grace barely slept. Whenever she managed to doze, she dreamt of ballrooms and torchlit fields and hay-strewn barns, and no matter where she found herself she kept feeling as though there was *something* she ought to do or say, but she'd no idea what.

And everywhere in those dream spaces, she heard Sebastian telling her to fuck him, followed immediately by his assurance that he only considered her a friend, and she ought to run to Mason. It was as mystifying when asleep as it had been when she was awake, and it made her head throb with frustrated confusion.

When she finally woke, her eyes felt like balls of woolen yarn and her body ached with unalloyed weariness. Judging by the light creeping around the curtains, it was much earlier than she had hoped it would be. But falling back to sleep was impossible, her dreams too tormenting, and so she sat up groggily and rang for Katie.

Grace's toilette was minimal — enduring Katie's hands on her made her already frayed nerves stretch even tighter. And part of Grace still wanted to cling to the lingering sensation of Sebastian's touch, even if the pleasure and happiness she'd experienced from it merely reinforced her foolishness.

"Your mother's had her breakfast and is in the parlor," Katie informed her.

Grace had no appetite, but she'd gladly sit for hours at the breakfast table if it meant she didn't have to pretend for her mother that everything was perfectly fine.

She crept down the stairs, trying to make her sluggish body as light as possible. But reaching the breakfast room meant she'd have to walk past the parlor. From the hallway, she heard the crackle of the fire and the papery sound of pages being turned.

She tiptoed past the parlor — or she tried. She'd taken two steps past the door when her mother called out, "Grace?"

"Yes, Mama." She closed her eyes and sighed quietly, but there was no help for it.

Pasting on a smile, she entered the parlor. Her mother sat on a divan, an open book spread on her lap. Grace pressed a kiss to her upturned cheek, and her mother peered at her with concern.

"You're looking pallid, dear. Does your head still pain you?"

It's not my head that hurts, it's my heart. "A little," Grace said instead.

"Then sit, my girl." Her mother waved toward a nearby chair. "I'll ring for beef tea."

"Perhaps later." The thought of food, even something as innocuous as beef tea, made Grace's stomach roil.

Her mother clucked. "As you like, but I do insist that you at least have some barley water."

Before Grace could answer, Grenville, the butler, appeared in the doorway with a tray bearing a calling card. "My lady," he intoned as he held the tray out to her mother.

"It's too early for callers." Her mother picked up the card and used her lorgnette to read it. A smile spread across her face. "But in his case, we'll make an exception."

Grenville bowed and retreated.

"In whose case?" Grace asked, her head truly starting to throb.

"Mr. Fredericks," her mother answered with a pleased smile.

Oh, God. Grace's stomach plummeted. She did *not* want to see Mason today. She still hurt from Sebastian's insistence that they were to remain friends, and to attempt coherent conversation with Mason — when she herself had no understanding of what she felt for anyone — seemed an impossibility.

"This headache is quite severe," she said weakly. "Perhaps I should go back to bed." She rose.

"Mr. Mason Fredericks," Grenville announced as Mason strode into the parlor.

In the bright light of day, Mason appeared just as handsome as ever, and he greeted Grace's mother with a respectful bow. "Lady Pembroke. Thank you for agreeing to see me at this somewhat unfashionable hour."

"You are always wanted in my home, Mr. Fredericks," her mother said warmly. She sent Grace a look of indulgence, as if she believed she was doing her daughter a favor by welcoming Mason.

"I trust you are feeling better today, Lady Grace," Mason said with concern.

She didn't have to feign her wince of discomfort. "In truth, I was —"

"Just about to read to me," her mother said, holding up her book. "But we can set that aside for the pleasure of your company, Mr. Fredericks."

Saints preserve me from mothers who think

they're being helpful, Grace thought, attempting to smile.

Mason bowed again. "You are very kind, my lady. I shall confess that I am here with a specific agenda."

"Oh?" her mother asked.

"My lady, and Lady Grace, might I invite you to join me this morning for a visit to a friend's botanic garden? It's an exceptional collection of plants seldom found within Britain. He opens it once a month to a few esteemed individuals."

"And you are one such esteemed individual?" Grace murmured.

A flush crept into Mason's cheeks. "His words, not mine. In any event," he added, "while I know your field focuses on amphibians and reptiles, I thought you might find Mr. Campbell's garden a worthwhile object of study. He has a *Spondias mombin,* which is seldom cultivated outside of Brazil."

In spite of her discomfort, Grace's interest was piqued. Wild plum was one of the favorite foods of *Iguana iguana,* and to have the opportunity to examine the plant would be extraordinary. But she couldn't accept Mason's offer. Not today.

He seemed to sense her hesitancy, so he quickly said, "I hoped, Lady Pembroke, that you'd accompany us. It's quite a lovely place, regardless of whether one dabbles in the sciences."

"How absolutely charming," her mother exclaimed. She turned her attention to Grace. "We would be delighted to see the garden. Isn't that so, Grace? I'm sure a bit of fresh air would be endlessly beneficial."

Pinned between her mother's pointed look and Mason's eager regard, there seemed no choice in the matter, not without causing Mason discomfort and embarrassment.

"I must grab my bonnet and spencer." Grace feigned a smile. "Shan't be a moment."

She left the parlor quickly. As she climbed the stairs, she couldn't help but think that the plan with Sebastian to secure Mason's attentions had worked — and she had no idea how that made her feel.

Edginess chased Seb all the way to Mayfair. He'd dressed with extra care that morning, trying on all his waistcoats and jackets in an effort to look like someone Grace would want to marry. Surely the valet Beale would be horrified to see the mountain of garments Seb had thrown onto the floor as he'd tried every permutation of clothing. But Seb didn't care about the fate of his clothes. He'd wear a flour sack if it meant securing her hand as his wife.

My wife. Despite the long, cool shadows thrown by Mayfair's enormous homes, warmth flowed through him at the thought of those two words. Grace as his partner. His companion. A lifetime together of learning and discovery and passion. It sounded . . . Perfect.

All she had to do was say yes.

He didn't want to think about her saying no. If he did . . . he'd likely crawl beneath a night soil collection wagon and never come out.

But he'd spent the rest of last night and into the early morning planning out precisely what he was going to say. He was no poet, but he hoped that his words professing his adoration and his intent to spend the rest of his life making her happy would be enough. They had to be enough.

He turned onto her street, his heart pounding with each step. Halfway down the block, he noticed the Pembroke family carriage waiting outside their home. If Grace was about to leave on some errand or outing, he ought to hurry to catch her before she departed.

Yet he slammed to a stop when he saw Fredericks emerge from her home, Grace's mother on one arm, and Grace on the other. Fredericks was dressed smartly, and he wore an equally smart smile as he handed the countess into the waiting carriage. Then he helped Grace into the vehicle, gazing at her with respectful admiration. The brim of Grace's bonnet hid her face, but Seb could well imagine the happy smile she must be wearing — she had what she wanted.

Fredericks climbed into the carriage, and a moment later, the vehicle drove off.

Seb occasionally practiced pugilism, but the invisible fist that now rammed him in his gut struck far harder than any of the other men at the boxing academy. He fought to keep from doubling over and gasping aloud.

Somehow, he managed to stay upright. But as he turned around to head home, he knew with certainty that if life was a pugilism match, he'd just been knocked flat on his back.

CHAPTER 22

"We'll have a fine day for it," Mason said as they drove toward the garden.

At his words, Grace snapped back to attention. "It will be lovely."

"Mr. Fredericks," her mother said brightly, "is it true that you dined with Wellington himself?"

"I did, my lady," Mason said. "He invited myself and several men from the Royal Society to his home for a very lively discussion."

"And what was he like, the duke?"

"Well, he . . ."

Grace's thoughts drifted away again as her mother and Mason chatted.

She'd spent most of the carriage ride to Campbell's garden swathed in restless contemplation. She *ought* to pay more notice to Mason as he engaged her and her mother in conversation, but how could she, when she kept revisiting that village barn,

418

kept seeing the scorching passion on Sebastian's face as he pleasured her, kept hearing his refrain again and again. *"It was a onetime madness. An error in judgment."*

At least this jaunt to the private garden might distract her for a while. Yet she couldn't quite bring herself to join the conversation.

When the carriage stopped outside a tall iron gate on George Street, and Mason climbed down from the vehicle to wait for her, she forced herself to look animated and pleased. This *was* an exceptional opportunity to see plants she might never have the chance to observe. She ought to pay attention and bring herself into the present moment.

Once she and her mother had gotten down from the carriage, Mason approached the iron gate. A servant in livery waited on the other side.

"Fredericks," Mason said to the man. He shot an excited look at Grace. "And two guests."

The servant consulted a sheet of paper before penciling a check mark next to what Grace presumed was Mason's name. With the paper stowed in his pocket, the servant opened the gate. "Welcome, Mr. Fredericks. Ladies."

Mason held out his arms for Grace and her mother, and they both took them. She felt the solid bunch of his arm's muscle beneath layers of fabric — yet to touch him only made her think of how thrilling it was to touch Sebastian, how his body had felt against and inside hers.

"You are invited to sketch or look at anything you see here," the servant continued. "However, you may not touch anything without one of the gardeners in attendance. Picking any plant is also forbidden. Do you accept these directives?"

"We do," Grace said after glancing at her mother and Mason.

"Then please, enjoy yourselves." The servant waved them into the walled garden.

They walked down a path of crushed shells, passing plantings that were enclosed by low metal fences. The garden itself was less than half an acre, but even that size in the middle of urban London was remarkable. There were tall trees as well as a wide number of bushes and plants, some of which were in full flower. Small groups of people as well as a handful of lone individuals wandered up and down the paths. Many of them carried sketchbooks and positioned themselves near plants as they drew.

Birdsong trilled over the garden, and the

sun had peeked out just enough to filter through the tree branches, casting pale purple shadows onto the ground. The air carried a fresh, green scent, and the walls dampened much of the sounds of traffic.

"Beautiful," Grace said sincerely.

"I thought you'd like it." Shy pride filled Mason's voice. "Shall I take you to see the *Spondias mombin*?"

The ostensible reason for being here. "Please do."

"Go on ahead, children." Her mother released her hold on Mason's arm. "I'm keen on speaking with the gardener over there about how to tend roses. I do have the worst luck with my roses, you know."

Roses? Her mother didn't give a fig for that flower.

Grace shot her mother a wry look. *I know what you're doing.*

Her mother's glance spoke volumes. *So?*

A moment later, Grace and Mason were alone.

They strolled toward the eastern side of the garden. She tried to bring herself to the present moment by observing the abundant plants around them — most of which she could not identify, signaling that they were species that did not originate in England — but all she could see was the look of tension

421

on Sebastian's face, and heard his words telling her that he was all too willing to forget their lovemaking so she might continue her pursuit of Mason.

She squeezed her eyes shut in a vain attempt to silence her mind. But it was no use. Her brain, which she'd always believed was a beneficial and blessed organ, couldn't stop tormenting her.

"Here we are," Mason said, coming to a stop. He nodded toward a tree that stood about ten feet tall — it wasn't very mature — and had long, glossy leaves. "Remarkable, isn't it?"

"Quite." She let go of Mason's arm and rose up on her tiptoes to study the small yellowish oval fruit. "How fascinating it might be to see this growing in the wild, and observe the creatures that feed upon it."

"So it would."

The edginess in Mason's voice dragged her attention away from the *Spondias mombin*. "You seem distressed, Mr. Fredericks."

"Not a bit." He flashed her a nervous smile. "You and I have not known each other for very long. That is," he hastily corrected, "we've known each other in a professional capacity. My own foolishness kept me shrouded in a fog, rendering me unable to recognize that there was so much more to you."

She couldn't help it. She was too new at hearing herself complimented and a flush of pleasure rushed into her cheeks.

"Had I more time," he continued, "I would spend a proper amount courting you. Wooing you. But, alas, I do not."

"Oh, yes, you're leaving on another knowledge-gathering excursion."

"In four weeks," he said. "There's an expedition headed to Greenland. The purpose is to study Arctic species." He swallowed. "Would you care to join me on that expedition — as my wife?"

"Oh." No words or thoughts sprang into being. She felt as though she'd been dropped from a great height, and could only struggle to breathe. Her mind latched on to the only thing she could fully comprehend. "Are there many species of amphibians and reptiles there? I don't wish to be without employment, in Greenland." The Arctic wasn't an especially hospitable environment to animals that relied on outside sources of heat.

"That's what you can find out on the expedition."

"Ah." She could not find her balance, and

the ground beneath her feet seemed made of shifting sand.

"As I said," he went on quickly, "it would have been my greatest joy to give you a leisurely courtship, one filled with shared smiles and long letters. But, sadly," he went on apologetically, "that isn't to be. The ship leaves from London's docks in twenty-eight days, and so I must ask for your hand in a less than ideal manner."

She peered at him. "Are you looking for a research partner, or a bride?"

"A bride," he answered earnestly. "You do possess a singular ability and understanding of natural philosophy, but . . ." His cheeks reddened. "I'm very fond of you."

"Fond." Not quite the declaration of love she'd dreamt of.

"Affectionate. Which, I believe, will easily mature into a deeper emotion. And I hope," he added with a hint of bashfulness, "that you might someday feel such emotion for me. Can you?"

"This is . . ." Astonishing. Staggering. How could she answer? Her whole life would utterly change.

Mason, offering her marriage. The opportunity to study in the field. Granted, Greenland wasn't a place she'd ever desired visiting, but chances to go abroad in a scientific capacity didn't come around often. Here, she was being offered the prospect to do just that.

Here was everything she'd wanted, what she had *believed* she wanted, and yet she could summon no happiness. There was no pleasure in this moment, no sense of triumph.

Dimly, she thought, *I should tell Sebastian.* He'd like knowing that they'd achieved their goal, and she wanted to share it with him.

As she struggled to find words, Mason held up a hand. "You needn't decide at this moment. Take some time. Discuss it with your family."

"All right." As her mind whirled, she felt herself nod. "I'll think about it."

Thankfully, Mason bid her and her mother farewell once the carriage stopped outside their home. The return journey had been a fraught one, between her own uncertainty and Mason's anxiety over her answer. If her mother had noticed, she kept up a pretense of cheerful talkativeness, remarking on the abundance of unusual plants that had filled the garden and her intention to speak with her gardener about obtaining a few exotic breeds for their country estate.

Yet, every now and then during her

mother's monologue, Grace felt her parent's perceptive gaze on her, assessing, investigating.

No doubt, Mother would want a thorough debriefing once she and Grace were in private. But what could Grace tell her — that the man she'd thought she'd wanted had offered her marriage, whilst the man she cared for and made love to didn't want her.

It was with considerable relief that, as she and her mother stepped into the foyer to hand their bonnets to a waiting maid, a footman handed Grace a folded note.

Meet me at five o'clock in the reading room at the Benezra.

— S.H.

Her heart stuttered as she read the note, and she couldn't stop her mind from running through scenarios — most of them terrible and resulting in pain.

She could pretend she didn't get his note. But that was horrendous, to contemplate deliberately ignoring Sebastian's request.

Yet as she stood in the foyer with his note in her hand, understanding struck her with so much strength she lost her breath.

She'd told herself that Mason was the man

who would suit her best, who would check all the boxes of what she wanted in a husband. But she had been so focused on this, she hadn't seen the truth — the truth about Sebastian.

He was kind. He possessed generosity and boundless intelligence and curiosity about the world around him — everything that had made him such an excellent friend. She kept returning to him over and over again because he was a genuinely good man, and he valued her for herself.

The tall clock that stood in the foyer proclaimed it to be quarter to five in the afternoon. She'd just enough time to reach the library.

"Going to the Benezra." She pressed a kiss to her mother's cheek and hurried out before her mother could try to detain her.

After giving the coachman instructions, she climbed into the carriage and attempted to distract herself on the ride to the library by cataloging the species of toads common to Great Britain. Unfortunately, there wasn't an abundance of different species within the British Isles, which left her with entirely too much time to fret and stew.

The carriage pulled up outside the library, and she tried to draw comfort and strength from its familiar exterior.

She climbed the stairs and greeted Mr. Pagett as he opened the doors for her. Instead of going first to the reference desk, she veered off toward the reading room.

Grace paused outside the small chamber. The glass inset in the door revealed Sebastian within, caroming back and forth, his eyebrows low in thought.

Elation lightened her step, but dread also coalesced in her stomach. How was it possible to feel both happiness and worry when looking at someone? Yet she did.

After taking a breath, she rapped smartly on the door and entered.

Sebastian halted in midpace. The set of his mouth was tight, his jaw clenched. But his hair was mussed, as if he'd been dragging his hands through it. That couldn't bode well.

He waved to a chair, but she shook her head. They stared at each other, words drying up like a creek bed at the height of summer.

"Thank you for meeting me," he said after many long moments.

"I'll always make time for you." She bit back a groan — perhaps Sebastian didn't want to hear her speak of any attachment to him. Especially since they'd been intimate with each other.

This strained reserve between them didn't feel right, either. Not when he'd held her so tenderly, or made love to her with such raw passion. The things he'd made her feel . . . the words they'd said . . .

"Fredericks is a good man," Sebastian said. "He cares for you."

She blinked, momentarily stunned by the idea that Sebastian somehow knew of Mason's proposal. But that couldn't be possible. "He *is* good."

"Circumstances have changed between you and me." The way he spoke, its excessive formality, scraped along her nerves. "Last night, I acted from impulse without considering the repercussions."

A wave of cold sheeted through her at his phrasing. "There were two of us in that barn."

He nodded stiffly. "So there were. Neither of us were thinking very clearly, and —" He shook his head. "I'll be plain."

"Yes, do."

"I'm not a gentleman by birth, and it will be judged a mésalliance, but . . ." He cleared his throat. "I will marry you. If that's what you desire."

She stared at him. She hadn't permitted herself to think what it might be like to receive an offer of marriage from anyone,

429

and here she'd received two in one day.

Though she'd never spent much time fantasizing about someone asking her for her hand — she'd actually have to have a suitor for that to happen — this was *not* how she'd hoped Sebastian might propose to her.

"Mason asked me to marry him," she blurted.

Sebastian stilled, then said, "Today."

"And he wants me to accompany him on an expedition to Greenland."

Her gaze locked on Sebastian's face in an attempt to read him. He appeared stunned, his mouth slightly open. A flash of something that might have been sorrow appeared — but it was gone in an instant. In the time between heartbeats, his expression smoothed over.

"But that's wonderful," he said, smiling. "I congratulate you. You've achieved your objective — the plan has been a success."

A shard of cold pierced her, and immediately after, she was entombed in ice. So. This was how it was to be. It was almost surgical, the severing of the bonds between her and Sebastian. Yet the pain wasn't contained and clinical. It filled everything.

"It has been." She forced her mouth to form a smile, when all she wanted to do was drop to her knees and sob brokenly.

So easily. Sebastian let her go so easily. As if he was relieved she hadn't forced him into matrimony. That he'd escaped a terrible fate of being her husband.

"When does the expedition leave?" he asked.

"In twenty-eight days," she said with remarkable evenness despite the fact that she'd been eviscerated.

His mouth tightened, yet he answered calmly, "Barely a month from now." He brought his hand up, as if to adjust his spectacles, before he seemed to realize that he didn't wear them. "I imagine you'll be quite busy between now and then."

Her mouth opened to tell him that she hadn't accepted Mason's proposal. Yet it didn't matter. Sebastian had said nothing of regret, no hint that he might feel sadness that she'd soon depart, or that there was a very real likelihood that, if they ever did see each other again, it would be in the distant future, when she might be married to someone else.

"You've performed your role of admirer admirably." Her lips felt numb. Everything had gone numb. Which perhaps was better than actually feeling the pain caused by his easy acceptance of losing her to Mason. So, like an actress speaking her lines, she said, "Thank you for that. I imagine you'll have much to write about for your book, as well."

He bowed, but said nothing.

"I should go." She glanced toward the door, wanting to tear it off its hinges and go running out, howling, through the streets of London.

"Yes, of course."

She hesitated. Was this to be it, then? She managed to restrain herself from throwing her arms around him. Instead, she stuck out her hand. "Again, my thanks."

After a slight hesitation — as if he didn't ever want to touch her again — he took her hand. But it wasn't a warm enfolding of his fingers around hers. Instead, he shook her hand as if they were polite colleagues.

She bit back a cry of despair. Even their friendship had died.

"I —" His lips pressed together. "My felic-itations."

She nodded, then slid her grip from his. Not trusting herself to speak without dis-solving into angry, confused tears, she spun on her heel, pulled the door open, and walked quickly out.

Chapter 23

"The trouble with moodily gazing into the fire," Seb said as he stared at the flames burning in Rotherby's study fireplace, "is how very appealing it seems to simply chuck myself in there."

"Here, now," his friend chided from behind his desk. "Since when are you given to melodramatic pronouncements?"

"Since Grace cheerfully announced that Fredericks had proposed." That wasn't entirely true. Grace hadn't been quite *cheerful.* Yet over and over all he could hear was the way in which she'd countered his own offer of marriage with the stunning announcement.

It hadn't quite been a complete surprise. Only logical that the naturalist would see her as an ideal spouse, the sort that her family would readily accept as the man who should be her husband. Grace and Fredericks *would* be perfect for each other. Grace loved natural philosophy. She was kind and intelligent and had a radiance that never failed to rob Seb of breath. Fredericks was . . . reasonably attractive. Marginally intelligent. Well, Fredericks possessed enough intelligence to finally recognize Grace's magnificence, so he wasn't all bad.

Nevertheless . . .

"Bloody hell," Seb muttered. He picked up the fire poker and gave the burning logs several stabs. "Didn't think the knave would work so sodding fast. A proposal. Less than twenty-four hours after dancing his first goddamned dance with her."

"Leaving for an expedition to Greenland can urge a man to action."

"He ought to take an expedition to Hades. Study the flora and fauna. Maybe he'll be devoured by a hellhound."

It wasn't fair to hate Fredericks — but that didn't stop Seb from happily imagining the naturalist being eternally eviscerated by a denizen of Hell.

A rap sounded at the door to the study, and a moment later, McCameron strolled into the chamber. He peered at Seb.

"God above," McCameron exclaimed, "you look like the bottom of the Thames, only less cheerful. What happened?"

"Lady Grace is going to marry Fredericks," Rotherby said before Seb could answer.

But hearing it spoken of so plainly felt like being flayed alive. Seb pushed away from his place by the fire and went to the window. Dusk had deepened into night, and carriages rattled past on their way to the evening's entertainments. The occasional linkboy escorted pedestrians and sedan chairs. Everyone was going about their lives with no consideration for Seb's agony. The bastards.

McCameron clicked his tongue. "Come out tonight, Holloway. Rotherby and I will take you to the Eagle chophouse and we can get roaring drunk."

"I've no desire to go out." The window's glass chilled Seb's palm. Perhaps its deadening cold might take away his blazing fury and sadness.

"But you're London's darling rake," McCameron said.

"Sod that." He pivoted to face his two friends, who both looked at him with concern. "I don't want to be a rake any longer." Even for the sake of science, becoming Society's latest object of admiration had been a worthless crown to wear.

Rotherby spread his hands. "What *do* you want?"

435

"Grace!" Seb didn't realize he'd shouted until he saw Rotherby and McCameron step backward. With an attempt at controlling his voice, he went on. "I want Grace. But she's got Fredericks now. The man she desired all this time." Saying the words made it all the more real, more concrete.

"Don't see why that ought to upset you so." McCameron crossed his arms over his chest as he frowned.

"Because, you dolt," Seb snarled, "I love her."

Rotherby cursed softly and McCameron looked dumbfounded.

It took Seb a moment to understand what he'd just said, and what it meant.

Holy God. I love *her.*

This was more than attraction, deeper than friendship, stronger than affection. He wanted only her happiness. Her troubles were his. To see her smile with genuine pleasure had become the greatest gift he could ever receive. He wanted to stand beside her as she conquered the world. Because she *would* conquer the world — of that he had no doubt.

Somewhere in the past few weeks, he'd given her his heart.

But she was to undertake her journey through life with someone else. She might bear that other man's children. They'd make discoveries that would enrich the sciences for centuries. She'd grow old with him and anticipate sharing eternity with him.

With Fredericks, not Seb. Fury and misery filled his body, his mind. It was as though his blood had been replaced by knives, and each beat of his heart pulsed cutting blades through him.

Seb had worked so very hard to win Grace her prize, little thinking of the cost to himself, or the fact that he'd guided her straight into Fredericks's arms.

"Tell her." Rotherby took a step toward him. "If you love her, you must tell her."

Seb exhaled raggedly. "That would make me ten kinds of bastard, to ruin her happiness with my own selfish desires. I will not undermine her."

"Damn," Rotherby grumbled.

"My apologies, old man." McCameron gave Seb's shoulder a gentle shake. "It's a hard place to be in, to love someone who doesn't love you back."

Seb shared a quick glance with Rotherby. Neither of them had ever truly addressed McCameron's heartbreak, as if not speaking to him about it somehow protected their friend from feeling its pain. But clearly, they'd been wrong, because the wound sounded as fresh as ever in McCameron's voice.

"You don't want to go out," Rotherby said, "which is fine. Only tell us what it is you *do* want. There's surely something that will help you through this. How about writing up that book, the one about becoming a rake?"

Internally, Seb recoiled. "The last god-damn thing I want to do is dwell on this disaster. No, I think it's time."

"Time for what?" Rotherby asked.

"To go on one of my wanders." Now that he'd proposed it, the idea made sense. He already pictured himself shielded behind his role as disinterested observer, studying the people and traditions of far-flung villages. "Surely losing myself in England's most remote places will take my mind from losing Grace."

"Will it?" McCameron asked, his voice gentle.

Seb offered his friends a weary smile. "What choice do I have?"

The night sky stretched over Hampstead Heath like the profundity of dreams, and Grace tried to lose herself in its endless black-and-indigo reaches. Unlike Jane, who stood nearby, adjusting her telescope as

Douglas held a lantern for illumination, Grace couldn't name any of the stars, which she rather liked. It kept them beautiful and mysterious. Unreachable.

"For a woman who has fielded an offer of marriage from the man she's adored for *years,*" Jane said, "there's a good deal of pensive silence coming from your quadrant."

"I'd have thought you would be capering around Hampstead Heath like a lamb," Douglas added.

"There's a distinct lack of capering," Jane agreed.

"It's disturbing," Douglas said.

"Quite so," Jane said. "*Disturbing* is just the word I'm thinking of. Perhaps even *distressing.*"

"Oh, that's a good one. *Distressing.* I like it."

Hearing the easy camaraderie and warmth between the Argyles normally soothed Grace. Tonight, however, she wanted to kick over their telescope and shout for them to both shut their mouths.

She didn't do either, but her hands formed into fists at her sides as she breathed and prayed for calm. Yet she hadn't felt calm since . . . . she honestly couldn't remember. The past few weeks had been a tempest.

Having Sebastian offer his hand but then eagerly rescind that offer when hearing about Mason's proposal certainly didn't soothe her mind or heart.

Nothing seemed right anymore. Nothing was certain.

The grasses rustled as Jane approached. She set a hand on Grace's arm. "Love," her friend murmured. "Your unhappiness is palpable. But I can't fathom it. Mr. Fredericks wants to marry you. Isn't that what you wanted?"

"I thought . . ." Grace swallowed past the hard knot in her throat. "I thought that's what I wanted. But now . . ." She shook her head as she struggled through the quagmire of her emotions. They were a swamp, sucking her down into their depths, drowning her.

She said, "When I think about life without Sebastian, I want to curl into a ball and sob brokenly. I want to hear his thoughts on the preservation of cultures and species. I want to watch that endearingly silly smile bloom on his face when he thinks he's being too enthusiastic about things. To not have any of that . . ." Her chest ached.

"You've talked quite a bit about Mr. Holloway," Jane said gently. "But hardly said anything about Mr. Fredericks."

"Oh, God." Grace felt the blood drain from her face, leaving her more chilled than the cool night. "Thinking about him, I feel fondness. Nothing more. I . . ." She pressed her hand to her mouth. "I cannot marry him. Because . . ."

She blinked furiously. "My heart belongs to Sebastian. It always has." Yet she'd been too foolish, too shortsighted, to understand that. By spending so much time with him these past weeks, she'd come to appreciate him even more. Her feelings for him had deepened and matured into something richer. "I wanted Mason, but it's Sebastian I *need.*"

The realization made the sky overhead tilt, as if the cosmos itself spun out of control. She staggered, trying to keep her feet.

Now that she'd said it aloud, she understood it entirely. How whenever she was near Sebastian she felt her entire being lifted up, and how she spent every moment apart from him waiting, hoping, to see him again. She'd adored seeing him develop his confidence these past weeks, and it seemed as though, by learning how to manage his fear of strangers and new situations, he was more comfortable — which gladdened her.

"I love him," she said suddenly.

Jane enfolded her in a tight hug. "Ah, my

darling, I'm so glad to hear you say that. Because, you know, I've long suspected that you and Mr. Holloway were perfectly suited for each other."

"You never said anything to me!"

"Or me," Douglas added. "And you tell me everything."

"Well, I *thought* it," Jane said briskly.

"But it doesn't matter," Grace said, unable to keep the misery from her voice. "He doesn't love me. If he did, he would have said so when I told him about Mason's proposal."

"That's precisely why he *didn't,*" Douglas said, raising his lamp for emphasis. "If he does care for you, he would step aside if he thought he was an impediment to your happiness. Just as he did."

Grace looked back and forth between the Argyles. "Do you think so?"

"Douglas is a very sensible man," Jane answered. "He married me, after all."

"Tell Mr. Holloway how you feel," Douglas continued. "He needs to hear it from you."

"He might reject me again." The words were acidic in Grace's mouth.

"He won't," Jane said.

"But he *might.*"

Jane pointed to a glimmering light overhead. "That is the planet Mars. It might one day break free from its orbit and hurtle into the Earth. It *might,* but it likely will not. And if, by some chance, it does crash into our planet, do you want to face eternity without ever having told Mr. Holloway that you love him?"

Grace exhaled. "Why must emotions be so ruddy confusing?"

"Because they adhere to no scientific principle," Jane said with a sage nod. She placed her hands on Grace's shoulders. "Promise me that on the morrow, you'll confess your feelings to Mr. Holloway."

Could she? Risk him turning away from her, perhaps forever? That pain would haunt her for the rest of her days.

If she didn't, she would be safer. But she wouldn't have him.

"I will." As soon as Grace spoke, a strange calm settled over her. This was right. This would work out. It had to.

Jane beamed, a jubilant expression shared by Douglas. "Wonderful. Now, will you help me find Arcturus?"

"Better that than look for Uranus," Grace said, barely able to suppress a giggle.

Jane leveled a stare at her. "How long have you been waiting to say that?"

"All night," Grace admitted.

"God help Mr. Holloway," Jane said.

CHAPTER 24

Sleep proved next to impossible knowing what tomorrow would bring. Grace considered and then discarded the idea of writing out what she planned to say. Firstly, because she didn't want to sound too rehearsed. Secondly, because she was reasonably certain she'd forget everything and wind up babbling nonsense at Sebastian.

It was with some relief that she greeted the dawn's light peeking around her bedchamber curtains. She summoned a yawning Katie to dress for the day.

The breakfast room was mercifully empty due to the earliness of the hour. But that also meant that breakfast itself was in the process of being prepared, so tea and cold meat and cheese was brought up from the kitchen to tide Grace over. She hadn't any appetite, yet made herself nibble on her food as a sign of appreciation for the kitchen staff's efforts.

After attempting to read for a few hours, Grace summoned the carriage and directed the driver to take her and Katie to Howland Street.

Once they arrived, Grace realized that an unmarried young lady couldn't very well go up to a bachelor's lodgings. Even someone as unfashionable as she knew that.

"Please send the footman up, and ask him to bring Mr. Holloway down."

"Yes, my lady."

Never had five minutes seemed so very long as she waited. Her heart plummeted as the footman returned — alone.

"Beg pardon, my lady," he said apologetically. "I knocked and knocked, but no one answered. The landlady weren't around, neither, so I've no idea where the bloke, I mean, Mr. Holloway might be."

"The Duke of Rotherby's." Yes, that made sense. They were good friends, Sebastian and the duke, and at the least, the nobleman might have an idea where she might find Sebastian.

"I heard His Grace was leaving for the country this morn," the footman said with a contrite grimace.

"Blast."

The servant cleared his throat. "Forgive my boldness, my lady, but if you're looking

446

for Mr. Holloway, the library seems a likely place. He's always there."

"Of course!" She felt rather foolish now, not having considered the Benezra. "We must go there right away."

Traffic was unusually thick, but in due time, she found herself walking up the steps of the Benezra Library. She'd been here only yesterday — it seemed ten lifetimes ago — but it wasn't unusual for her to return to the library six out of seven days.

After nodding a greeting to Mr. Pagett as he opened the door, she walked briskly to the circulation desk.

"Good morning, my lady," Mr. Okafor said in a cheerful but quiet voice.

"Good morning, Mr. Okafor." She swallowed as rising apprehension threatened to choke her. "Perchance, is Mr. Holloway here?"

"He was," the librarian answered.

"*Was?* But is no longer?"

"I'm afraid not. He came in just as we opened and returned a number of volumes."

Unease skittered along her limbs. "Is that so?"

"He's off on one of his wanders, but when I asked as to when he might return to London, he had no idea. Are you . . . are you well, my lady?"

"I'm . . ." She braced her hands on the circulation desk as exhaustion caught up with her. Followed immediately by leaden disappointment. No, *disappointment* was too mild a word. It didn't capture the bottomless sorrow that crumbled the earth beneath her feet, making her stagger.

He *knew.* Sebastian knew very well that, if she accepted Mason's proposal, she'd leave England in twenty-eight days. By setting off on his wander, Sebastian had ensured that he wouldn't be around for her departure.

He'd congratulated her on attaining Mason's affections. That's precisely what she'd wanted, precisely what she'd achieved, and to Sebastian, that meant that their involvement was no longer necessary.

At best, she was merely a friend to him. He couldn't love her and also leave.

She'd never given Sebastian any reason to believe that it was *he* she cared for. All she'd talked of, all she'd focused on, was Mason. And of course Sebastian believed she had feelings only for Mason, and none for himself. Not with how she'd endlessly prattled on about someone else.

For a woman who prides herself on her intelligence, you're so very, very stupid.

"Do you need some air?"

Her vision swimming, she gazed up at Mr. Okafor.

"Air. Yes. I —" She lurched toward the door, pursued by her own foolishness.

Rotherby glanced between the chaotic, muddy yard full of bulky and dilapidated coaches, his own handsomely sprung and elegantly appointed carriage, and Seb.

"Certain about this?" Rotherby asked above the din. "I can drive you wherever you wish. No need to bother with the discomfort of an anonymous mail coach."

Seb gave his friend a rueful half smile. "To begin with, I don't know where it is I'm heading. I plan on picking a vehicle at random and seeing where it takes me. It's my custom."

"I know that, but it's just as easily done with my coachman. I can have him pick a destination at will."

Seb pushed up his spectacles. There was no need to forgo them now. "In truth, I need the anonymity of a mail coach. To be amongst strangers with no idea who I am."

"As it pleases you." Rotherby looked as though he wanted to press the matter further, but he visibly bit back his words. The silence that fell wasn't silent at all, filled as it was with shouts, horses' neighs, and the clatter of wheels.

Rotherby's footman handed Seb his battered pack, which he shouldered. It contained none of his rakish clothing. Seb had filled the rucksack in the predawn hours, stuffing it with his old garments and four anthropology books — everything from his previous life, when he'd dwelt in complacent ignorance, knowing nothing of his feelings for Grace.

Too late now. He might wear the clothes of Old Seb, but he wasn't that man any longer. He knew now what it was to love, and to lose that love.

On the way to the coaching yard, he'd momentarily considered stopping at Grace's home to say his final goodbye. Rotherby had even permitted him to direct the coachman to drive past Weymouth and Harley Streets. But in the end, he hadn't the fortitude to see her face. He would have done something appalling, like beg her to abandon Fredericks and marry him. There were many reasons why this would have been a terrible idea, so when the carriage had slowed, he'd banged on the roof to signal not to stop. They'd driven on, to the coaching yard, where the next stage of Seb's life was to begin.

"Sorry, old man," Rotherby said gruffly.

"Didn't want things to turn out this way."

"Likewise." Seb faced his friend. "My thanks for . . . for everything."

"We surely made a rake out of you." The corner of Rotherby's mouth turned up. "Quite a damned fine rake."

"A hell of an experience." He knew with certainty that writing a book, which would contain his observations on the structures and systems of the aristocratic elite, would involve an objectivity he'd never be able to achieve. Every line he penned would be about Grace, and that wound was far too fresh. It might never heal.

"Do you want news about her?" Rotherby asked.

"That way lies madness." He might not be able to cauterize the injury, but he had to try. Otherwise, the rest of his existence would be an exercise in simply enduring rather than living.

Rotherby nodded. "I can't feign that I know what you're experiencing, but I hate that you're hurting. That cursed woman," he growled.

"No anger or blame." Seb held up his hand. "Not for her. Not for anyone. Even Fredericks. I've learned that the human heart's a willful beast, and it can't be expected to obey or follow commands."

"I'd horsewhip Fredericks in front of the Royal Society, but then, you're a better man than me."

"You'll receive no argument from me on that point."

Rotherby scowled good-naturedly.

Seb would be sorry to leave all of the other members of the Union of the Rakes behind, but it had been Rotherby who'd helped to guide him on this journey, even with his friend's time so precious. And for twenty years, Rotherby had been his supporter, his staunch ally. That was something Seb prized above any first edition of a book.

Naturally, he couldn't show or speak of this. Men simply understood each other.

Ah, the hell with it. When had adhering to codes of masculine conduct benefited any-one?

He wrapped an arm around a startled Rotherby's shoulders and pulled him close in an embrace. "I'll miss you."

For a moment, Rotherby was rigid. Then, slowly, he raised his hands and patted Seb's back. It wasn't quite an unfettered display of affection, but it would take more than one hug to undo a lifetime of conditioning.

Still — it was encouraging when a passing man snorted in disapproval and Rotherby didn't shove Seb away.

A coachman shouted, "Coach to Cramlington, Bedlington, and Morpeth leaving in five minutes. Get your arse aboard or cry in my dust."

Seb released his hold on Rotherby. "Northumberland seems a good and distant destination."

"Good journey, my friend. Hope you find some peace."

Seb's throat grew tight and thick. He gave Rotherby a nod, then strode hurriedly to join the queue shoving its way onto the coach. The jostling and noise, tremendous as it was, did not quite obscure his haze of pain.

He'd never sleep well again, knowing that Grace slept in Fredericks's arms. He would unfairly compare everyone he met to her, and would find everyone else lacking. There was every likelihood that he'd never attain the peace Rotherby had wished him.

Even so, he had to try.

CHAPTER 25

"Thank you for agreeing to meet me."

Mason managed a small, taut smile. He looked over at the specimen cases, with their rows of dead and preserved animals. "Am I to draw meaning from the location? You are no enthusiast of the British Museum, as I recall."

Grace couldn't achieve any sense of pleasure that he'd recalled what she'd said during their encounter from weeks ago. Everything within her was as lifeless and immobile as the creatures in the cases.

"Montagu House is a public place," she said. "We can talk here without concern for propriety." And Katie, immersed in yet another licentious novel, stood nearby.

He sighed. "I've a good idea what it is you mean to tell me. And it's unnecessary. Your expression is quite articulate."

"I'm sorry," she said, hurting for him. "It wasn't my intention to send false signals."

He shook his head. "It was my interpretation. There's no fault to be found." Narrowing his eyes, he said, "Is it Holloway?"

"That's irrelevant," she said, her voice brusque.

"You're right. Forgive me."

His wounded expression couldn't help but touch her. As gently as she could, she said, "We're just not meant to be husband and wife. I . . ." Her chest burned, but she had no choice but to continue. "I do not love you, and to accept your proposal would be a terrible thing to do. To both of us."

"Ah." He pressed his lips together. "That is . . . not what I desired hearing. Not what anyone desires to hear."

"If I could take your hurt away, I would." She meant this sincerely. Never did she want to inflict damage on anyone. But she had, and she'd need to live with the consequences.

"Your candor is appreciated," he said sadly. "And helpful."

Damn, she wished she could feel something for him. He was a good man, and one she'd wounded. "You'll need to find another herpetologist for your expedition to Greenland."

"So I will." His brow furrowed, and he turned his hat around and around in his

455

hands, as if he was deep in thought. Finally, he said, "Come on the expedition, anyway."

She drew herself up, certain she'd misheard him. "Pardon?"

"We still require an expert on reptiles and amphibians. I don't see why that cannot be you." As he spoke, his voice became more energized, more eager. "You can bring a companion, that way everything is respectable. What do you think? Will you join me?"

"I . . ." She blinked, stunned. "It's not quite accepted or normal, what you're suggesting. An unmarried woman voyaging to a distant shore to pursue her scientific studies . . ."

"Precisely the reason why I believe you'd be the right person for the expedition. You've gone through your life without any worry what other people think about you. That's commendable."

"Not precisely." She'd been hurt by society before, when she'd first come out, and she'd courted his good opinion, with ruinous consequences. In her journey, she'd hurt Sebastian and Mason. And herself.

"If you're concerned," Mason said, "that I am inviting you out of a sense of politeness, or that I hope I might win your affections despite your . . ." He coughed. "Despite your rejection, let me assure you that I'm guided only by my belief that you're precisely the person this expedition requires. You'd be an asset."

Her thoughts were a jumble. How to make sense of what he offered? It was an outlandish notion and yet . . . she needed to get away from England. Away from the place where she'd made such a horrendous mistake. There would be no chance of running into Sebastian, slim as that possibility was.

True, Greenland wasn't where she had ever pictured herself. The Arctic was not teeming with reptiles and amphibians.

But to go there meant getting away, occupying herself with something that wasn't her own grave miscalculation.

"I need to consider it," she said.

"Naturally. I imagine your parents will need to be consulted, as well."

She looked over at the case that held a variety of diminutive, stuffed *Rodentia.* What fragile creatures they were, these little animals with fur and tiny hands and delicate bones. They fed the majority of predators. Their lives were brief.

The world needed them. Without the voles and wood mice and other such beings, there'd be no hawks or badgers or foxes.

Everything was a great cycle, life and death intertwined for eternity. Somewhere in the middle of all this, she existed, and she tried to take comfort in that, in making herself very small. Small enough that she could curl up and simply disappear.

"Greenland?" Disbelieving, her mother stared at her across the tea table in the parlor. "That is rather far, is it not? And cold."

"A warm coat and stout boots could remedy that," Grace said gently.

"Why do you want to go, dearest? You've had a perfectly splendid few weeks. Mr. Fredericks *has* been quite attentive. And Mr. Holloway."

Simply hearing Sebastian's name made Grace's stomach knot with regret and sadness. "They were merely being kind."

She swallowed, too, any words telling her mother that Mason had proposed. Since she'd no intention of marrying him, introducing the possibility to her mother — and especially her father — was pointless and would only cause confusion and hurt.

"I'll write to Papa and tell him . . . I'll tell him that it's my intention to remain a spinster. I hope he isn't angry with me," she added gloomily.

"My love," her mother said, leaning forward to cover Grace's hand with her own.

"He would rather see you unmarried than bound to someone who does not make you happy."

Grace desperately wanted to believe that. Tears stung her eyes. "But . . . his wishes for my security?"

"We'll make certain that after your father and I pass, Charles will take good care of you. However," her mother added worriedly, "haring off to Greenland is not quite what either Edmund or I had in mind when considering your future."

"I need to leave England for a while," Grace said, her voice bleak. "Forgive me, but I can't say more. Just know that it's something I must do. I have . . . so much to learn."

All of this was true. She *did* need the chance to learn. Everything that had happened these past weeks was proof enough that she needed growth. She had been horribly myopic about her own feelings, and she had been terribly unkind to both Sebastian and Mason. Her determination and single-mindedness in pursuing her objective meant she hadn't taken notice of anyone around her. She hadn't even asked herself what it was that *she* truly wanted.

At the very least, Sebastian had grown more comfortable in social settings and with strangers. He seemed, if not happy to be amidst unknown people, then a little less wretched. That was *something.*

Maturation was a hell of a thing, painful as it was. If only she could shed literal skin as she transitioned from one self to the other. Surely that had to hurt less.

"I *will* have a companion," she added. "I'll face trials, but I can endure them."

"But will you be happy?" her mother asked.

Tears swam in Grace's eyes, but rather than brush them away, she let them trace cool paths down her cheeks.

"No," she said. "Happiness is something I've ensured I can't have. Yet this expedition will give me purpose, and that is something I need most desperately right now."

"Oh, my dearest." Her mother sighed. She set her cup down and rose to circle the tea table. As she had when Grace was but a small girl, crying over the loss of the pond on the family estate, she placed her palm atop her head and kissed her forehead. "When you're ready to speak of what troubles you, know that your father and I are here. Until then, if you truly wish to go to Greenland —"

She did not. But she had to go *somewhere.*

"I do."

"— then neither he nor I will stand in your way."

Coming to her feet, Grace embraced her mother. She was a fortunate woman, to have parents such as she did. To have the benefits and privileges of wealth and rank. In so many ways, she was blessed by Providence. She had to remember all this, had to hold to that light, because her soul could not lift itself up from the shadows in which she'd mired herself.

"Grantham!" the coachman shouted. "Stopping for the night at Grantham!"

The coach lurched to a halt. Passengers groaned as they stepped down into the inn's yard, stretching their cramped muscles after the day's long journey. A twilight sky hovered over the muddy quadrangle, and light from the inn's taproom illuminated the passengers' haggard faces.

Seb was the last to disembark, and as he unfolded his body to climb out, he stifled his own groan as his limbs protested hours of confined, jostling inactivity.

There'd been a time, not long ago, when he'd gladly accepted these pains as an essential evil he had to endure before the pleasures of a wander. Tonight, however, he

461

wanted only ale, food, and an oblivious sleep.

He shook out his arms and legs, moved his head from side to side, and then, when his aches lessened, he moved stiffly into the inn. He didn't glance at the name. It didn't matter where he was — they'd stopped at a similar place yesterday at . . . Bedford? Peterborough? One town and inn was as good as another.

"Oi, watch it," someone growled behind him.

"Pardon." He hadn't realized he'd come to a stop, and he stepped to the side to permit a ruddy-cheeked man entrance to the inn.

Shock reverberated in waves — he wasn't paying attention to his surroundings. He'd barely seen the landscape as it rolled by mile after mile. He hadn't asked questions about the local area's customs. He'd done nothing.

Except yearn for Grace. That hadn't stopped.

He saw her smile in the sunshine, and her eyes in the glint upon rivers. He heard her laugh in the wind, and in the depths of his body he still felt the wonder of holding her in his arms.

God, but he was a disaster.

Shaking his head, he approached the innkeeper, a Black woman with her hair wrapped in cheerful printed silk. "A room for the night, please."

"I've one room left, in the attic." She eyed his height. "It'll be a squeeze. You'd be right under the roof, and the bed's not so big."

"So long as it has a mattress and relatively clean linen," he said, "it will suit." He dug into his pocket and pulled out a handful of coins, which he dropped into her waiting hand.

She smiled. "We have a fine taproom where you can take your supper, sir. I'll have your key brought to you whilst you dine."

"Have you a private room where I might eat?" He wanted silence and solitude, and the cheerful din of the taproom did not suit.

"I'm afraid not, sir. The local chicken farmers meet there once a month and tonight's their night. I could bring your food up to your room, but there's not much space there to dine comfortably."

"The taproom will serve." With a nod, he moved on to the inn's crowded common area.

Heavy tables that were scarred from use but spotlessly clean filled the space, and at them sat passengers from the coach as well as other travelers and locals. Servers who looked to be the right age to be the innkeeper's children hurried between the tables, bringing bowls, plates, and tankards. The smell of ale and stew filled the air.

Seb exhaled tiredly. There were no empty tables, only a free seat here and there. He'd no choice but to sit with someone.

A pale elderly chap from the coach sat alone as he spooned stew into his mouth and read from a small volume.

Seb approached. "Might I join you?"

The man glanced up at him before returning his gaze to his book. "Suit yourself."

"Many thanks."

Seb had hardly taken his seat before an adolescent girl with light brown skin and serious gray eyes approached. "What will you have, sir?"

"An ale."

"To eat?" she asked.

"Anything." He honestly didn't care. At this point, he only wanted to fuel the clockwork of his body. Food now only tasted of dust, anyway.

The girl eyed him with puzzlement, but after a moment, she shrugged and went off to fetch him his meal and a drink.

"You ain't going to talk, I hope," Seb's tablemate grumbled. "I don't want no nattering."

"I've no intention of engaging you in a dialogue."

"Good. Just leave me to my book."

Seb peered at the little volume in his hands. *A Treatise on the Benefits of Effective Drainage.* Yes, he could see how that topic might preclude all conversation.

Seb dug from his pack one of his own books, this one on the marriage customs observed in the cultures ringing the Mediterranean. He snorted softly. Most likely, the old man with the tome on drainage would find Seb's choice of reading matter impossibly dull. Therein lay the mystery of taste.

This wasn't the first time he'd read this particular book, but he found it so engaging, the subject matter so endlessly fascinating, that he could read it a dozen times and find something new within it.

Yet when he turned to the opening chapter, he saw only lines of type that meant nothing. The letters swam before his eyes before arranging themselves into a sentence: *she loves someone else.*

He snapped the book shut.

Hellfire. Could he find tranquility anywhere? Or was that a dim and hopeless cause?

The girl approached with a bowl full of

something rich and savory. She set it down in front of Seb along with a tankard and a key, and he pressed a coin into her palm. She curtsied before moving on to another table.

The stew smelled delightful, yet when he took a bite, he tasted nothing.

Still, he knew logically that if he didn't eat, he'd grow weak and ill, so he made himself finish his meal. The ale washed everything down but had no effect on dulling the continuous pain that split him from the top of his head to the soles of his boots. Once his bowl and tankard were empty, he pushed up from the table.

"Good night," Seb said to the man across from him.

A grunt was his only response.

He wove through the taproom and plodded up the steep stairs. Close on his heels was a giggling couple, who, mercifully, found their room on the first floor. Seb continued up and up, until he reached a narrow door at the very top of the stairs. He unlocked the door before stepping inside.

"Fuck." Stars exploded behind his eyes as his head connected with the sloping ceiling. He'd forgotten the innkeeper's warning.

In the darkness, he fumbled around until

he found a lamp, which he lit. The glow flared brighter, and he saw that the room was as described: hardly more than a closet, with a bed that he could already tell wouldn't contain him. His feet, and some of his calves, would hang off the end.

It hardly mattered. In a daze, he pulled off all the garments covering his upper body. He poured water from a pitcher into a basin and hurriedly washed. With that task completed, he tugged off his boots, and doused the lamp before collapsing onto the bed.

Tired as he was, sleep would not come. The phantom shape of Grace curled against him, warm and soft, while her breath fanned over his torso.

He wrenched himself onto his back, draping his arm over his eyes.

How far will I have to go to outrun her?

The answer came, cold and brutal.

There's no distance great enough. She will always be with you.

CHAPTER 26

Even at this early hour, the docks teemed with activity and noise. Stevedores loaded cargo onto waiting ships, crews made their vessels ready for sail, while passengers stood prepared to embark. An air of anticipation and urgency hovered over the docks themselves and floated on the surface of the slick gray water. Everyone was in a fever of anticipation, eager to leave.

Grace tried to cling to this sense of excitement, struggling to grasp it like a salamander. But it squirmed away, leaving her with an echoing emptiness.

"You needn't stay until the ship departs," she said to the group of people who waited with her. "The crew has our baggage aboard. There's naught to do."

"We'll wait," her father announced. He'd recovered sufficiently to come back to London, and had insisted that he accompany Grace to the docks. She was relieved

468

to see that his cheeks were pink with health and he appeared to have more vigor than he had in years.

The others, consisting of her mother, her brother, his wife, and Jane and Douglas all nodded in agreement. For once, Katie did not have her nose in a book, since Grace's hired companion, Mrs. Poulton, had taken it upon herself to lecture Katie on the proper way to serve her mistress whilst at sea. Poor Katie — but Mrs. Poulton had come highly recommended, having worked as a companion for ladies traveling abroad for over a decade.

Grace felt no obligation to feign happiness for Katie and Mrs. Poulton. They would see her nearly every hour of every day for a minimum of six months, and it would be impossible to pretend she was happy for that span of time. Jane and Douglas knew of her heartbreak over Sebastian. But her family worried for her, and for their sake, she needed to behave as though she truly wanted to trek to Greenland.

Mason was already aboard, standing on deck as he supervised the loading of his gear. Relations between them had been cordial and professional. Mercifully, he had not attempted another marriage proposal. Perhaps she and Mason might become true friends, after all.

"To be without you for so long." Grace's mother dabbed at her eyes. "I don't know how to endure it."

"That Fredericks better keep you safe," Charles muttered. "Or I'll sail to Greenland myself and wallop him."

Despite Grace's sadness, a soft feeling spread through her at her family's concern. "I made good use of these past weeks. Learned how to shoot a gun and construct a shelter. I can build a fire, too, in the most adverse conditions. So there's nothing to fear."

"What if you don't want to come home?" her mother asked plaintively.

"I'll return." She couldn't exile herself from England forever.

"You'd better," Jane said with a scowl. "The library will be so dreadfully dull without you." She stepped close and pulled Grace in for a hug before whispering in Grace's ear, "Should I say anything to Mr. Holloway, if I see him? About your true feelings?"

Heat prickled Grace's eyes. "That would only make everyone miserable," she whispered back. "I appreciate the thought, however."

"Darling friend." Jane kissed Grace's

470

cheek. She moved back and wiped at her eyes.

"Everyone aboard!" a sailor yelled from the ship.

Here it was. The last moments on England's shore. She drew in a breath as she straightened her spine and fastened a smile into place.

"Time to go," she said with considerably more excitement than she felt.

Grace's mother burst into sobs.

As Katie and Mrs. Poulton walked up the gangplank, Grace embraced and kissed each member of her family. She let her mother hold her for a long time, patting her back as the countess wept.

When the last hug had been given, and many promises to write as often as she could were made, she took a step back from her family and friends. Their dear faces all looked back at her. Never had she felt more like a fraud.

Well. She was a different woman now. She saw now that she'd been careless with too many — Sebastian, Mason, herself. Never again would she barrel ahead, determined to have what she wanted, without thought for the consequences or who she might hurt along the way. Her maturity had been hard-won. But she wore it now like a reptile's

471

tough scales.

"I love you all," she said, trying to give each syllable the sincerity she felt. Fearing that she might begin to weep loudly like her mother, she hurried up the gangplank.

She exhaled when she stepped onto the deck.

"Welcome aboard," Mason said. He gestured to the barrel-chested man beside him. "This is Captain Collins."

"My lady." The captain bowed. "We'll have good sailing this time of year."

"You've my thanks and my trust," she said.

Captain Collins touched his fingers to the brim of his hat. He moved on to speak to another sailor, presumably the next in command, although Grace's understanding of the hierarchy of a ship was minimal. By the end of this voyage, she'd likely be much more familiar with the running and structure of a sailing vessel.

Mason peered at her. "We're not yet departed. If you have any second thoughts —"

"I don't." Which was true.

"I must take your word for it." He gave a small smile. "Expeditions are marvelous things. You'll learn less about the land and fauna you're studying, and more about yourself."

"Looking forward to it." Again, she spoke the truth. "Might I . . . be alone for a bit? This is my first time away from home and I need a few moments to myself."

"Understandable." He bowed and walked away.

As the sailors went about their tasks to get the voyage underway, Grace went to the railing. Her family and the Argyles waved to her from the dock. She waved back, and blew them each a kiss.

It did not take long for the gangplank to be raised, and the anchor followed suit. In a matter of minutes, the ship pulled away from the dock. The deck pitched slightly beneath her, but she adjusted her stance to move easily with the motion of the ship. Despite her deadened emotions, a tiny spark of anticipation flared to life within her. She was truly going on an expedition. Granted, the conditions were not ideal — they were, in fact, terrible — but she'd find some way to make the best of it.

She was a natural philosopher. She would do her duty to her discipline, to the rare privilege of representing her gender in the field.

And try her best to live with the heartbreak she'd caused.

■ ■ ■ ■

It didn't matter how much time he'd spent away from London, and from Grace. She was with him, in his thoughts and echoing in his body.

Still, he made himself slog through the countryside until the date of her departure for Greenland loomed. When he was reasonably certain that their paths wouldn't cross, he took a mail coach back to the city.

On the day of his return to London, he did not go directly home. The thought of trudging up his stairs to reach his empty rooms was a bleak one and made his stomach pitch. Instead of walking or taking a cab back to Howland Street, he hired a hack to bring him to Rotherby's Mayfair house. There was every possibility that his friend was still in the country, but on the chance that Rotherby was, in fact, at home, Seb hoped to share a glass of whiskey and sit in companionable silence beside the fire as he tried not to picture Grace's ship sailing down the Thames.

At his knock, the butler opened the front door and looked at him for almost a full minute, as if trying to place him.

Only then did Seb realize how much his

appearance had altered.

"It's Holloway," he supplied.

"Ah, yes, Mr. Holloway. His Grace returned only yesterday, so your timing is fortuitous. He was searching for you. Rather urgently."

Seb frowned. "Do you know why?"

"He did not confide the reason to me, but you will find him dressing in his bedchamber. Do go up."

Another realization — it was far earlier in the day than Seb had figured. The mail coach had arrived shortly after dawn, but he'd been too exhausted to pay attention to the lightening sky.

After handing his now quite shabby pack to the butler, Seb mounted the stairs leading up to Rotherby's bedroom.

The door stood ajar, and Beale's voice carried out into the hallway, "The buff breeches with a brown waistcoat? *Really*, Your Grace?"

Despite his weariness, Seb couldn't help but chuckle. Some things had not changed.

He rapped on the door. "Shelter for a weary traveler?"

"Holloway?" There came the sound of heavy footfalls approaching and then Rotherby wrenched the door open the rest of the way. He was halfway garbed, his shirt untucked and his neckcloth hanging loosely.

Rotherby gaped at Seb. "The hell? Have you been living in a hermitage? You surely look like it."

Seb opened his mouth to speak, but Rotherby held up his hand.

"No," Rotherby said. "Wait. Before you utter a syllable, listen." He grasped Seb's shoulders. "I've been looking for you for *ages*. Since I found out."

Disquiet tightened Seb's muscles. "Found out what?"

"Lady Grace. She —"

"What about her?" Seb demanded.

"That's what I'm trying to tell you, buffoon! She's going on the expedition to Greenland — but not as Fredericks's wife."

The floor shuddered beneath Seb's feet. "I don't understand."

"She's bringing a companion with her. Don't you see? *She didn't marry Fredericks.* They're going on this expedition as colleagues only. I heard it from Beale who heard it from —" Rotherby waved his hand. "Doesn't matter. But I wanted you to know. She's unmarried. And her ship departs from the London docks this morning."

Seb's exhaustion disappeared. Energy shot through his body and woke his perplexed mind.

Grace hadn't married Fredericks. She'd refused the naturalist's proposal.

Seb saw in an instant what he had to do. It was a massive gamble, and one that might cause him unimaginable pain, but if he didn't try, he'd regret his inaction for the rest of his miserable life.

"I need a horse," he said.

"Done," Rotherby replied immediately.

"Already summoned someone," Beale said, his hand on the bellpull. He eyed Seb. "Given the circumstances, Mr. Holloway, I will refrain from making any comment on the condition of your . . . person."

Seb dragged a hand over his jaw, feeling the rasp of his whiskers. *Damn.* There wasn't time to shave, much as he wanted to look his best. Hell, he probably appeared at his absolute *worst* but there was no helping it.

Rotherby's staff moved quickly. In five minutes, Seb found himself in the stables, slinging himself up into the saddle on a sleek chestnut gelding.

"Do you know the way?" Rotherby asked as Seb took hold of the reins.

"I'll find it. I'll find her." The horse danced beneath Seb, impatient as its rider to move.

"Godspeed." Rotherby slapped his hand on the gelding's flank.

477

The animal surged into motion.

Never had Seb sped through London at such speed. The city rocketed past him in a blur as he urged the horse to go faster, and faster still. His heart pounded in time with his mount's hooves, and sweat slicked his back as he leaned low over the horse's neck. Angry shouts from drivers and pedestrians trailed in his wake. He didn't give a sodding damn. He could run down Prinny himself and not care. All that mattered was reaching the docks in time.

Please, God, let there be time.

Soon the hulking warehouses of Wapping surrounded him. He guided the horse around massive stacks of crates, and wove between drays loaded with cargo. The sharp tang of river water announced that he was almost at his destination. Closer. Closer.

Have to reach her.

A moment later, he was on the docks themselves. But which ship was hers? He slowed the panting horse to a walk.

"Mr. Holloway?"

He swung the horse around to find Mrs. Argyle and her husband looking up at him with astonishment.

"Where is she?" Seb clipped.

Mrs. Argyle pointed toward a ship that — hellfire — was sailing away, some two hundred yards from the wharf.

His heart seized. Too late.

No.

He swung down from the horse and threw the reins to a mystified Douglas Argyle.

Seb's gaze moved quickly along the water. A rowboat could never outpace a tall-masted ship, but he had to reach the vessel somehow.

There. Yes.

Seb charged toward a trim pleasure yacht that was at that very moment preparing to push away from the dock. A quintet of well-dressed men and women lounged on the deck while the crew operated the boat.

"Hold!" Seb shouted. There was no time to think or analyze. He could only act.

Everyone aboard the yacht stared at him. They gasped as he leapt from the dock onto the deck of the boat. The impact jarred him, yet he managed to stay on his feet.

"See here —" someone began.

"The woman I love is on that ship," Seb snapped. He pointed to the vessel growing smaller as it sailed farther away. "I'll pay you whatever you want. Just *go after her.*"

Everyone exchanged glances. Then one of the well-dressed ladies said in a commanding voice, "You heard him, Captain. We must catch that ship."

"Yes, ma'am," a man in the rugged garb of a sailor said with a nod. "All right, lads," he bellowed to his crew, "let's give chase."

The fine ladies and men on the yacht cheered. Seb barely heard them. He strode to the prow of the yacht as the small vessel pushed away from the dock. His heart was a cannon booming in his chest as he willed the yacht to go faster.

God, he might not catch her.

He cupped his hands around his mouth. "Grace!"

Grace stood at the rail, watching the shore slide past. She'd seldom been on the Thames, and tried to take an interest in seeing this part of London from the water. There were warehouses and other large buildings, some in states of dramatic disrepair as they crowded close to the banks. Smaller vessels skimmed by the ship, yet she paid them little heed as the reality of her situation delved deep. She was truly leaving England and any possibility of seeing Sebastian again.

"Grace!"

Ah, damn, she wanted to see him so much she was hearing things. She shook her head, trying to banish the illusion of his voice.

"Grace! Damn it, Grace! Down here!"

She looked, then looked again.

Impossible.

"Sebastian?"

He stood at the nose of a boat, waving his arms overhead as the smaller vessel drew up alongside her ship. Surely she had to be imagining things — but would her imagination conjure an image of him so very changed? For one thing, she had never once pictured him with a beard, but now he had somewhat wild whiskers, and his garments looked as though they belonged to a man who weighed a stone more than Sebastian.

Somehow, some way, he was here now. This was no fantasy.

"I must tell you something!" Sebastian shouted to her.

"What the devil is he doing?" Mason demanded, appearing beside her with Captain Collins.

"Please, Captain," Grace said, gripping his sleeve, "dock the ship."

Captain Collins shook his head. "Impossible, my lady. We are underway."

"You can't be serious, Lady Grace," Mason protested.

Desperation clutched at her. "We must get him aboard." She gazed at the assembled sailors who'd gathered to see the spectacle. "Can anyone help? *Please.*"

Murmurs rose up from the sailors. They shifted from foot to foot, clearly torn.

"Throw that man a line," Captain Collins barked.

"Aye, Cap'n!" Two of the crew hurried to the side of the ship and tossed a rope to Sebastian as he stood on the smaller vessel.

For a moment, he stared at the rope as if in disbelief that he might attempt something as utterly mad as scrambling from one moving vessel to another. The people in his boat clapped him on his back in encouragement.

He straightened his shoulders, gripped the rope tightly, and climbed.

Grace clutched the railing as she watched him, her breath seizing in her throat. His feet left the deck of the boat as he ascended, hand over hand, using his legs to help propel him upward. Sweat shone on his forehead and he bared his teeth from the effort. His limbs shook, and his spectacles fell into the churning water. But he didn't stop.

Passengers and sailors cheered him on.

"That's it, gov!"

"Nearly there!"

"The man is insane," Mason said in a disbelieving mutter. "But determined."

She could not speak, her gaze fastened on

the sight of Sebastian getting closer and closer.

"Hang on, lad," a sailor called to Sebastian. "We'll haul you up."

Several members of the crew took hold of the rope and pulled. Finally, Sebastian was high enough to grab hold of the railing and clamber onto the deck.

She ran to him as he bent over, hands on his knees, gasping for air. He'd turned an alarming shade of red.

But he was here. On the ship.

"My God, Sebastian." She reached for him, but he held up a hand.

"Why . . . didn't you . . ." he panted.

"Why didn't I what?"

"Marry . . . him . . . ?" His gazed turned to Mason, who wore a stunned expression, then went back to her. "Become . . . Fredericks's . . . wife?"

Tears gathered hotly in her eyes. She pushed words out past the constriction in her chest. "Because," she said, her throat raw, "I love *you.*"

Hope lit his eyes. "You . . . do?"

"I do." She pressed her fingers to her lips. "I love you, Sebastian."

"Thank . . . God." He straightened. His face was radiant, even with his impressive beard. "I love you, Grace. So much."

"So much that he boarded my ship like a damned pirate," Captain Collins muttered.

She didn't pay heed to the captain, or Mason, or the sailors or passengers or the people on the other vessel. She cared about one person, and one person only.

He surged toward her just as she rushed to him. A moment later, he was in her arms as he held her close. They clung to each other, and only then did she let the tears fall, coursing down her face without cessation.

"You're here," she couldn't stop murmuring over and over. "You're truly here."

"I am, love." He tipped her face up. "If you want me, I'm yours forever."

Joy flooded her, but she could not stop herself from asking, "Can you forgive me?"

He frowned. "For what?"

"For being foolish. For not saying what I truly felt, and . . . for everything. I'm not being very articulate right now, but give me a few moments, and I shall have much to say." It could not encompass all that she felt, no words could, yet she had to try. "But I was so wrong for keeping silent when I should have spoken out."

A regretful smile touched his mouth. "We both are guilty of that crime. So I must beg your forgiveness, as well."

"Kiss her!" a sailor yelled.

"Kiss him!" the women on the smaller vessel called up.

Her gaze held Sebastian's, and she saw reflected in his eyes the infinite love she felt for him. She was giddy with it, holding tightly to him to keep from wheeling off into the sky.

He lowered his head as she lifted onto her toes. Their lips found each other, and then the world did fall away as she knew only his taste and feel and a deep sense of homecoming.

Finally, he lifted his head just enough to murmur, "Come with me."

"Where?"

"Anywhere you want to go." Emotion thickened his words. "Just be with me, Grace."

If his arms had not been encircling her, she would have shattered into fragments of pure joy. "Yes. Oh, yes. Only . . ." She glanced at Mason, who still looked rather stunned by this turn of events. "I'm leaving you without a herpetologist."

"Oh." Mason blinked. "Right."

She disengaged from Sebastian and spoke quickly. "This ship docks next in Reykjavik. I correspond with a herpetologist there. Mr. Mikkael Leifsson. When you dock, find him.

He might join your expedition."

Mason nodded. "I will." He glanced between her and Sebastian. "It's been him all along, hasn't it?"

"I'm so very sorry," she said.

He ducked his head. "Can't say this doesn't hurt — yet I'm glad. For both of you."

"You're a true gentleman, Fredericks." Sebastian held out his hand.

"And you're a son of a bitch, Holloway," Mason replied, shaking Sebastian's hand, "but I don't hold grudges."

"Fair enough," Sebastian said.

"Beg pardon, my lady, and . . . Mister whoever you are," Captain Collins interrupted. "But if you want off this ship, the time to do it is now."

CHAPTER 27

It was no small job to lower Grace, her maid, her companion, and all their luggage onto the yacht, as well as Seb himself, but he'd gladly accept the effort if it meant that he and Grace could be alone. Together. *Finally.*

He hardly noted how his whole body protested the extreme effort he'd put it through — especially after nearly a month of poor eating — because he could only circle again and again to the fact that Grace loved him.

So he practically soared down to the yacht as it sailed beside the large ship. Once his feet touched the deck, he was met by many handshakes and slaps on the back from the passengers and crew.

"To the dock?" the captain asked him.

Seb looked at Grace, her face bright with excitement and adoration, and his heart jumped. *She loves me.*

What that meant, what followed, he'd no idea. But of a certain he damned well wanted to find out.

"To the dock," he answered.

The ropes connecting the yacht and the ship were undone. Seb and Grace waved farewell to Fredericks, who stood at the railing and shook his head as if still attempting to understand what had just transpired. Then Fredericks waved back, which gave Seb some measure of peace.

In a way, Seb owed him a great debt. If it hadn't been for Grace's initial infatuation with Fredericks, Seb would never have been given the chance to know her better, and never would have known what it was to love her.

He kept his arm securely around her waist as the yacht's captain guided his vessel back to the dock. Not touching her was impossible. He wanted to have the feel of her every moment of every day.

It took far too long for the yacht to return to its berth. The moment it did, Seb leapt to the shore and helped Grace onto the dock. Sailors assisted Grace's maid and companion so that they, too, reached dry land.

"Holy Mother." Mrs. Argyle was breathless as she and her husband rushed forward.

"In all my days, I'll never see a spectacle like that again."

"It *was* rather dashing," Grace said, her cheeks turning pink as she glanced at Seb. "You were a true Viking." She nestled closer to Seb, and his weary body sprang to life at the press of her soft curves.

Grace's companion made a *tsk,* her face tight with disapproval. Clearly, she was less enamored of grand romantic gestures than her mistress.

Seb dug into his pockets and produced most of the remainder of his money. He pressed the coins into the companion's hand. "Thank you for all of your efforts. Your services are no longer required."

"I will send you the balance of your wages on the morrow," Grace said.

The companion wore a pinched expression, but she nodded, grabbed her valise, and walked away without a backward glance.

"Katie," Grace continued, turning to her maid. "How do you fancy a day of leisure?" She dipped a hand into her reticule and held up a half crown.

The maid's face lit up. "Oh! I can go to McKinnon's for new books and then eat myself sick at Catton's."

"Don't return home until late in the day,"

489

Seb said.

"I'll walk the length of London and back." Katie plucked the coin from Grace's hand and also hurried off.

That left only Grace, Seb, and Mr. and Mrs. Argyle. Normally, Seb enjoyed the Argyles' company, but, good God, did he want some privacy with Grace.

His expression must have said as much, because Mr. Argyle looked to his wife with humor. "My love, perhaps you and I ought to return to our flat. I've a distinct feeling that our presence is not required."

Grace's face turned more pink, but she didn't contradict him. Praised be.

"Yes. Yes!" Mrs. Argyle embraced Grace and then did the same to Seb. "So glad she picked you," she whispered in his ear.

"Me, too," he whispered back, and, following an impulse, kissed Mrs. Argyle's cheek.

"Here, you've your own lady for that," Mr. Argyle exclaimed jovially. "I'll see mine home."

Moments later, Seb and Grace were finally on their own. She gazed up at him through her lashes.

"My family believes me to be on the ship bound for Greenland," she murmured.

"Which means we aren't expected any-where."

His entire body caught fire. "Have the whole day to ourselves."

"Whatever shall we do with the time?" Her voice went low and husky.

Seb fought to keep from groaning aloud. Fortunately, he still had a penny, so he tossed the coin to a nearby boy. "Watch our things. We'll be back . . . later . . . for them."

"Aye, sir," the boy piped.

Seb reached down and clasped Grace's hand in his. The press of her palm to his ar-rowed sensation through him, and he drew in a deep breath. "I believe I spotted an inn not fifty yards from here."

Heat flared in her eyes. "Hurry."

It took no time at all to reach the inn, though each step seemed longer than a football pitch. As far as accommodations went, the inn was short on charm, but it appeared clean and well maintained, and so long as it had a bedchamber, that was all that signified.

"Room for the newlyweds?" the innkeeper asked as Seb and Grace crossed the thresh-old.

"Please," Grace said.

It didn't escape Seb's notice that she didn't correct the innkeeper's assumption.

"Send up a bath, as well."

The older man handed Seb a key. "Got a room upstairs on the left. Most everyone's out for the day so . . ." He waggled his brows. "Can be as loud as ye like."

"Appreciate the suggestion." Seb couldn't find it in himself to feel any embarrassment. He only wanted Grace. For this day and every day after.

Together, they climbed the creaking stairs. His hand shook as he tried to fit the key into the lock. God, but he was eager. After taking a steadying breath, he finally managed to unlock the door, and opened it.

They were inside a heartbeat later, locking up behind them. The details of the room barely registered — a simple bed, a nightstand, shuttered windows letting in soft light — before he could wait no longer, and pressed his body to hers against the closed door. Their mouths found each other, hot and demanding, open with desire. He stroked his hands everywhere — along the curve of her cheek, down her neck, over her breasts, cupping her waist — and she did the same to him. Only when she caressed him did he realize how dormant he'd been, because every part of him roared to life at her touch.

Yet . . .

She stepped back. "Please," she gasped, when he reached for her. "I must apologize first."

"For what?"

"For being such a sodding idiot," she said with a shake of her head. "I complained that Mason didn't see me, but *I* didn't see *you*. I was stubborn and selfish, and it took far too long for me to realize how much I undervalued you. My wise, funny, generous Sebastian."

She wiped at the tears that traced down her cheeks. "Here I was, angry with your father for failing to appreciate you, and I went and did the same thing. I hope," she continued, "you might forgive me someday. Lord knows I don't merit forgiveness."

He exhaled, and gave a little nod. He couldn't pretend that she hadn't hurt him — she deserved the full truth.

"It's not complete absolution," she said with a tremulous smile, "but I'm willing to work for it. Willing to work for *you.*"

"I was . . ." He cleared his throat. "I ought to have said something to you, about how I felt. I didn't want you to think that I was your friend because I wanted something from you. Truth is, I was happy to be with you, however I could. And I never dared hope that you could love me." His jaw tensed as he tried to hold back his own tears, but there was no harm in showing his emotions. So when a few drops fell from his eyes, he didn't try to hide them.

"I do, Sebastian." She went to him and looped her arms around his neck, then kissed his wet cheeks. "I do love you. And it's my intention to spend the rest of my life doing exactly that. If you'll let me."

"My lady," he said gravely, curving his hands around her waist, "not only will I *let* you, I plan to spend the rest of my life loving you in return."

He lowered his head to kiss her just as she raised up to meet his lips with her own. Sweetness gave way to heat within moments, their mouths opening to take great, greedy drafts of each other. His hips thrust against hers, and he growled when she widened her stance to bring him closer.

"I can't wait for you any longer," she whispered between kisses. "Take me to bed. Now."

There was a knock at the door, making Seb snarl. "Got your bath," the innkeeper said, his words muffled.

Yes. Seb very much needed that bath. He unlocked then opened the door, and the innkeeper trundled in, bearing a wooden tub. A lad and a girl carried buckets of steaming water, which they poured into the tub. The girl pulled a bar of soap from her apron pocket and left it on the tub's edge. She also set a towel on the washstand.

"Be back later to pick everything up," the innkeeper said with a wink. He shooed the lad and girl out of the room before taking his own leave.

When the innkeeper had gone, Seb locked the door once more and turned to Grace. "Hope you can wait five minutes more. Three weeks of wandering leave a man less than sparkling."

"By all means. But first." She turned her back to him, and said over her shoulder, "The hooks. I want to be naked so that, once you've had your bath, there's no more dallying."

Never had his hands trembled as much as they did then. But he mastered himself enough to undo the fastenings. The gown slid from her body as she stepped out from it. He could have gladly spent the next five years admiring her in her underclothes, but she made quick work of them, including her shift and stockings. A moment later, she stood before him, naked.

"Damnation, but you're so beautiful," he rasped. She was all things soft and silken, the fulfillment of his dreams. He stroked his fingertips over the bow of her collarbone, and was rewarded by her sharp inhalation and closed eyes.

Yet she didn't shut her eyes for long. "Let me see you, too," she said throatily.

Never had he stripped so quickly. In seconds, he was nude.

Her gaze went straight to his upright cock, which jerked as if she'd actually touched him. A look of fierce hunger crossed her face, but her expression softened as she took in the rest of him.

"You haven't been taking care of yourself," she lamented as she touched the shape of his ribs, all too prominent in his thin body. "You should love yourself, as I love you."

"Say it again." His pulse hammered, and pleasure erupted through him at her words.

She closed the distance between them. Nothing had ever felt so good as her naked body against his, her lushness tight to his spare form. He ringed his arms around her.

"I love you, Sebastian."

He went still, absorbing that simple but so complex phrase. A few words that contained the entirety of his happiness.

"I love you, Grace. I'll spend my whole life showing you how much I love you." He brought his lips to hers. "Let me show you."

"Yes."

It took titanic effort to break the kiss so he could bathe. But when he sank into the water, she stood behind him and took hold of the soap. "Permit me," she murmured.

He held himself still as she dipped the soap into the water, then she used it to stroke down his arms and across his chest. His skin was delectably sensitive beneath her touch, and he groaned aloud as her hands moved over his body. She kneaded his sore muscles and caressed him with just enough pressure to make him growl. When she leaned down to wash his groin and thighs, her breasts pressed into his back.

"Jesus God, Grace," he said roughly. But when he tried to wrap his arms around her, she pulled away and held up an admonishing finger.

"Not yet," she said pertly. "You aren't fully clean. There are some parts of you that need more attention."

"I guarantee you, there's nothing that — *Fuck.*"

He could say no more as she reached down to take his erection in her hand. His head tilted back and he gripped the sides of the tub as she pumped her fist up and down his aching cock. Ecstasy shot through him, blinding him to everything but the feel of her pleasuring him.

"Stop, stop," he panted when his climax loomed. "When I come, I want to come in you."

"I can deny you nothing," she said breathlessly.

"Wait for me on the bed."

"So commanding," she said saucily. Then, her cheeks turning pink, she said, "I like it." She hurried to perch on the edge of the bed.

He stepped from the bath and toweled off. Then he climbed onto the bed and edged toward the headboard, where he leaned back, his legs stretched out before him. He opened his arms, and Grace went immediately to him. She straddled him, her hands holding tightly to his shoulders. They both groaned at the feel of his cock against her slickness.

In this position, they could look into each other's eyes, and their gazes locked together as he shifted enough to position the tip of his cock at her entrance. He went motionless, demanding patience of himself, as he stared into the depths of her eyes. Love gazed back at him, boundless love.

The last time he and Grace had had sex, it had been in a darkened barn, almost entirely clothed. But now, they were naked in every way, fully present, nothing furtive or illicit. This was their moment, completely theirs, unabashed and unashamed.

He gripped her hips. Then, with one sure motion, plunged up into her.

"Ah, God." He groaned. Her heat surrounded him, clasping him deep inside her as he sank all the way in.

"Sebastian," she breathed.

Don't move, he told himself. *Never move. Make this last forever.*

Yet she had other plans. Her hips rose and fell, thrusting against him. Sensation, brighter than all the stars, shot through his body. She moved again, and again, and despite his wish for an eternity of stillness inside her, he could not stop himself from driving in and out, chasing ecstasy with her.

She ground into him as she seemed to lose herself to the demands of her body. He watched the loveliness of her face as her mouth opened and a flush spread over her skin and then —

She came, her body tensing around him. And unlike the last time they'd done this, she freed herself to cry out fully. The sound was gorgeous, throaty and abandoned. Nothing on this Earth held the beauty of her noise of total surrender to pleasure.

Yet he wanted more. More for her. For him. So he worked his hand between them to stroke her clitoris. She went taut as another climax hit her.

"This is what I want," he rumbled. "Only this. My cock in you as you come."

"I —" Whatever she intended to say was lost as yet one more orgasm shook her. It went on and on, until she tipped her head so that their foreheads touched and her breath was warm over his face.

His whole body shuddered, demanding release.

"Come," she gasped. "Come in me, Sebastian."

The last filament of his restraint snapped. He thrust hard, making her cry out, and then release exploded. He growled her name as he was caught in the tempest of pleasure, letting its storm course through him without cessation.

He couldn't stop moving his hips, even after he'd spent the last droplets of his seed. But then his body surrendered, and he and Grace sank down to lie upon the bed. They wrapped themselves together tightly as vines.

Surely, he'd never known such happiness. This was the upper extent of its limit.

"Marry me," she whispered.

He was wrong. Because *now,* he reached the pinnacle of bliss.

But he must have fallen silent, stunned

500

into muteness by joy, because a moment later she asked, "Sebastian? Say something. You're worrying me."

"Nothing to fear, love." He kissed her, long and deep. "The answer is yes. From the moment I first saw you at the library with your head bent over a book and a smile on your face, my answer has always been *yes*."

EPILOGUE:
THREE MONTHS LATER

"Let me see the list again." Grace reached across the table for the notebook and Sebastian placed it immediately in her hand. She scanned the names, nodding with satisfaction.

Everyone on the list was the top in their field. They were the best natural philosophers with areas of expertise in flora, fauna, geography, geology, and, since Sebastian was himself on the list, anthropology. Jane and Douglas would represent the study of astronomy.

More than half of their upcoming expedition to South America would include female natural philosophers. Sebastian and Grace had been approached by the Dowager Countess of Farris, searching them out to head the field division of her new foundation. It was Lady Farris's intention that her foundation would serve as a kind of watchdog, to report on damage done by England's fervor for empire and expansion.

The countess had provided funds for Grace and Sebastian to lead their own expedition, and was quite encouraging of the fact that many women would be part of the group. In addition to supplying funding from her own coffers, Lady Farris had quietly located a number of wealthy women to contribute more capital.

The expedition's intention was to report on indigenous cultures, as well as to make recommendations on the preservation of the habitats and creatures it encountered.

"I believe that's everyone," Sebastian murmured. He kept his voice low out of consideration for the other patrons of the Benezra Library, which had just recently added the volumes she and Sebastian had published about their findings about declining traditions and habitations. Only last week, they had been invited to speak at three private gatherings of those with an interest in the sciences.

Sebastian said, "You've done your work well."

"*We* have." She smiled at her husband, seated across from her. "It's always been something we've shared."

"There's something I'd like to show you in the stacks." He removed his spectacles and tucked them into his coat pocket.

"Mr. Holloway," she said crisply. "Do put your spectacles back on."

"Why, Mrs. Holloway?" Yet even as he asked this, he replaced his glasses.

"Because, my beloved husband, I adore you when you don't wear them, and I love you even more when you do."

The smile he gave her could melt a glacier. But she had enough presence of mind to ask him, "Is your intention to show me a new monograph on the breeding habits of Southern European amphibians?"

"You'll see." He rose and extended a hand to her. When she got to her feet, she wove her fingers with his — somehow, she still felt that crackle of excitement whenever they touched — and together they walked past the circulation desk.

"Good afternoon, Mrs. Holloway, Mr. Holloway," Mr. Okafor whispered as they went by.

She waved in greeting, but clearly, Sebastian was on a mission because he didn't slow his steps. Not until they reached the stacks, standing in the section that held works on engineering. He stopped, and she did the same.

Glancing around, she tried to make sense as to why her husband would believe there

504

was something of interest to her in this particular area of the library.

When she looked up to ask precisely that, her question was abruptly cut short by his kiss. His hand cradled her jaw, and his lips were tender and urgent against hers. At once, she sank into the kiss, her body always craving him.

A flicker of sense roused her to break the kiss long enough to murmur, "A fine place to seduce your willing wife."

"It's where we met," he said, his eyes gleaming. "Where I lent you a pencil and then my life truly began."

Her whole self went supple. There was no one like him, and she counted herself the most fortunate woman in the known world to have such a man as her husband.

"My love," she said, sliding her arms around his neck, "with you beside me, I cannot wait for what's next."

ABOUT THE AUTHOR

Eva Leigh is a romance author who has always loved the Regency era. She writes novels chock-full of smart women and sexy men. She enjoys baking, spending too much time on the Internet, and listening to music from the '80s. Eva and her husband live in Central California.